PRAISE FOR J'NELL CIESIELSKI

"An epic, Bond-style tale set during the first World War, *The Brilliance of Stars* grips the reader from the first page. With mesmeric settings, nonstop action, and witty dialogue, Ciesielski crafts a thrilling love story of powerful equals working tirelessly to save the world from darkness."

—ERIKA ROBUCK, NATIONAL BESTSELLING AUTHOR OF *SISTERS OF NIGHT AND FOG*

"Action! Romance! Spies! Secrets! *The Brilliance of Stars* has it all. This electrifying read from J'nell Ciesielski comes to life with historical details and sparkling descriptions that will leave the reader begging for book two!"

—AMY E. REICHERT, AUTHOR OF *ONCE UPON A DECEMBER*

"Excuse me while I go read *The Brilliance of Stars* by J'nell Ciesielski a second time. The intrigue of master assassins, a secret society, a cat-and-mouse game, all while the world is teeming with tension from the Russian Revolution and the First World War. Not to mention, while Jack and Ivy are falling in love. Who knew a grenade pin could be so romantic? This thrilling historical novel has it all, and I look forward to more 'Jack and Ivy.'"

—JENNI L. WALSH, AUTHOR OF *BECOMING BONNIE* AND *THE CALL OF THE WRENS*

"[*The Ice Swan*] is well written, with superb similes and metaphors. Highly recommended."

—HISTORICAL NOVEL SOCIETY

"Ciesielski delivers an intense love story set during World War I. Fans of historical romance should snap this up."

—*PUBLISHERS WEEKLY* FOR *THE ICE SWAN*

"A Scottish lord and an American socialite discover love during World War I in this gorgeous historical romance from Ciesielski . . . The undercurrent of mystery and Ciesielski's unflinching approach to the harsh realities of wartime only enhance the love story. Readers are sure to be impressed."

—*PUBLISHERS WEEKLY*, STARRED REVIEW, FOR *BEAUTY AMONG RUINS*

THE
BRILLIANCE
OF STARS

ALSO BY J'NELL CIESIELSKI

THE JACK AND IVY NOVELS
The Brilliance of Stars
To Free the Stars (coming August 2023)

STAND-ALONE NOVELS
The Ice Swan
Beauty Among Ruins
The Socialite
Among the Poppies
The Songbird and the Spy

THE BRILLIANCE OF STARS

A Jack and Ivy Novel

J'NELL CIESIELSKI

THOMAS NELSON
Since 1798

The Brilliance of Stars

Published in Nashville, Tennessee, by Thomas Nelson. Thomas Nelson is a registered trademark of HarperCollins Christian Publishing, Inc.

Map created by Matthew Covington

Interior design by Phoebe Wetherbee

Song lyrics are from "All that I ask of you is love" by Edgar Selden and Herbert Ingraham. New York: Shapiro Music Publisher, 1910. Audio. Public Domain.

Closing quotation is from Alan Seeger's "I Have a Rendezvous with Death." *The North American Review* 204, no. 731 (1916): 594. http://www.jstor.org/stable/25108954. Public Domain.

Thomas Nelson titles may be purchased in bulk for educational, business, fundraising, or sales promotional use. For information, please email SpecialMarkets@ThomasNelson.com.

Library of Congress Cataloging-in-Publication Data

Names: Ciesielski, J'nell, author.
Title: The brilliance of stars : a Jack and Ivy novel / J'nell Ciesielski.
Description: Nashville, Tennessee : Thomas Nelson, [2022] | Series: The Jack and Ivy novels ; 1 |
   Summary: "Adventure, romance, and espionage combine to form an epic tale in Ciesielski's latest novel set amid the chaos of the Great War"-- Provided by publisher.
Identifiers: LCCN 2022014539 (print) | LCCN 2022014540 (ebook) | ISBN 9780785248453 (paperback) |
   ISBN 9780785248460 (epub) | ISBN 9780785248477
Subjects: LCGFT: Romance fiction. | Novels.
Classification: LCC PS3603.I33 B75 2022 (print) | LCC PS3603.I33 (ebook) | DDC 813/.6--dc23
LC record available at https://lccn.loc.gov/2022014539
LC ebook record available at https://lccn.loc.gov/2022014540

Printed in the United States of America

22 23 24 25 26 LSC 5 4 3 2 1

To Bryan, the real Buck Winter of my stories

If That's How It's Going to Be . . .

· EUROPE 1917 ·

Ural Mountains

FINLAND

Baltic Sea

Petrograd

ESTONIA

LIVONIA

Dobryzov
Castle

Trans-Siberian
Railway

Moscow

LITHUANIA

RUSSIA

POLAND

UKRAINE

Carpathian M\ts

AUSTRIA-
HUNGARY

Bran
Castle

Poenari
Castle

CRIMEAN
PEN.

Swallow's
Nest Castle

ROMANIA

Black Sea

SERBIA

RUSSIA

Lake
Baikal

BULGARIA

ALBANIA

Ural M\ts

Irkutsk

GREECE

Petrograd

Moscow

PROLOGUE

SHE KISSED JACK HARD ON THE MOUTH, THEN AIMED HER BERETTA OVER his shoulder and fired a round of shots down the medieval corridor of Dobryzov Castle. The men in black toppled, bright crimson blossoming across their chests, staining the embroidered red dragon like fire heaving from its venomous jaws.

Jack tossed aside his spent gun with its silencer and flipped aside the edge of his stolen evening jacket to pull out his pistol. He cut quite the dashing figure in all his deadly finery. "Under ordinary circumstances I would never object, but is this the appropriate time for romance, love?"

They dove around a corner as terrified party guests stampeded through the corridor, crushing one another in their haste to flee the chaos.

"A horde of guards is intent on killing us. What time could be more appropriate?"

Jack peered around the corner. "Twelve guards, actually." He took aim and fired. *Bam! Bam!* "Make that ten."

"Apologies I wasn't specific enough." Hiking up the hem of her *sarafan*—also stolen, sadly—Ivy pulled a fresh clip of bullets from her garter and slid it into her gun. Blood trickled into her palm from the knife cut on her arm. She wiped it on her skirt and transferred the gun to her clean hand. "Are you certain you got both?"

"Are you doubting my skills?" His side-eye was more accusation than question.

"No, but if we're going to die, I'd like to know we took down as many of them as we could. I'd rather not have 'Failure' written on my tombstone."

"People in our line of work don't get tombstones. We get a tarp weighed down with stones at the bottom of a river." He fired another round. The sound of bodies thumping on the stone floor followed. More guards came running with a fresh hail of bullets.

Ivy ducked as bits of ancient stone pinged off her *kokoshnik*. Probably the only time she would get to wear a crown, even if it was fake, and it had to be when someone was shooting at her. "If you're trying to sour the moment of spontaneous romance, you've succeeded."

"I'll make it up to you later, love. Go!" Racing along the wall, they pushed through a side door and down a steep set of stairs, landing in the kitchen.

Dozens of eyes lifted from chopping vegetables and stirring pots to stare at the intruders. Had they not heard the mayhem erupting upstairs? Darting around the long worktable and enormous black stove, Ivy shoved through the back door with Jack on her heels.

Bam!

A bullet struck the doorframe inches from her face. A guard rushed across the service courtyard and raised his rifle with a bayonet gleaming beneath its long muzzle and aimed straight at her.

Ivy raised her pistol and squeezed the trigger. Nothing. She squeezed again. Nothing. Why did these things always jam at the worst possible moment? Whipping off her gold-sequined *kokoshnik*, she flung it like a discus. It struck the guard square in the face. He stumbled. Rushing forward, she grabbed his rifle and whacked it against his head. He crumpled.

Jack grabbed her hand and pulled her across the square as guards spilled from the kitchen door. Jutting cobblestones wobbled beneath their feet as they raced around the corner to the front courtyard where noblemen and dignitaries in black-tie formal wear and ladies dripping in jewels flooded down Dobryzov Castle's ancient steps. Screams of panic bounced off the stone walls as they pushed and trampled each other in desperation. Smoke billowed from the doors behind them.

Like ants abandoning their disturbed mound, armed guards swarmed the stairs. The bright red flash of a dragon encircling a crown was emblazoned on their chests, the only color against the backdrop of choking smoke.

"There they are!" One of the guards shoved through the crowd of terrified nobility. His comrades quickly formed a spearhead behind him, cutting through the throng of bodies with rifles raised to fire.

Ivy clung to Jack's hand. This was not going according to plan. Then again, what did? Her gun was still jammed and she was out of crowns to throw. Before she could rip off a shoe to chuck, an automobile horn blasted through the discord.

Aoogah! Aoogah!

People leaped out of the way as the Gräf and Stift Double Phaeton skidded to a stop next to Ivy and Jack. The driver rolled down his window and leaned out with a devil-take-all grin on his boyish face. "Need a lift?"

Ivy scrambled into the back seat. "Philip, I could kiss you."

Jack flung himself in next to her and slammed the door. "So could I."

Philip jerked the auto into motion, blasting the horn as people jumped out of the way. "I'd rather neither of you did if it's all the same."

The back window shattered. Jack threw himself on top of Ivy as shards of glass sprayed over their heads. Another bullet whizzed by, this one cracking off the side mirror. Levering up on one elbow, Jack pointed his pistol out the broken back window and fired. Ivy didn't have to look to know he'd hit his target.

"Where is the other auto?" Ivy eyed the hole in the back of the seat where the first bullet had lodged into a tuft of cotton. Directly behind Philip.

"Already gone with the others tucked safe inside." Philip didn't slow as they sped under the iron-spiked gate and spiraled down the drive that wound itself around the lone mountain. "You two took your time getting out."

"So sorry to keep you waiting." Jack grimaced as he touched a bleeding spot on his forehead where a piece of glass had grazed him.

After tying a torn strip of her gown around her bleeding arm, Ivy sat up and moved closer. "Here. Let me look at that—"

Crack! The front windshield crackled from flying bullets.

Philip jerked the wheel. "Keep your heads down! We've got company."

Ivy peeked over the back seat. A black auto loaded with three enemy guards roared behind them. "Where's the trigger to set off the dynamite in the autos?"

Philip tossed it to her as he careened down the winding drive of the mountain. "Don't press it until I tell you to."

"If I don't do it now, they'll be joining us for tea in the back seat."

"We're not out of range. Wait for it . . . Wait . . . Now!"

Ivy pressed the button.

An explosion shattered the earth behind them. She turned back to see the ground cave in a mighty roar, swallowing the tailing auto whole. Heat blasted her face as flames consumed the gray sky.

Dobryzov Castle, crumbling crown of the mountain, sat ringed in fire.

Jack curled his hand over hers. "I adore the way your eyes light up in the midst of danger."

Smiling, she laced her fingers through his as they watched the world burn behind them.

"Are you sure you killed him?" she asked as they left the mountain and raced toward the rendezvous point.

Jack lifted their joined hands to his lips and pressed a kiss to her knuckles. "Right in the eye. And if the bullet didn't take him, the fire will. Straight to the pit he crawled from."

"Good."

She would look back on that day a hundred times, a thousand times, and wonder what might have happened if it had all gone differently. A thousand times she would throw her head back and scream defiance to the night sky that this wasn't how it was supposed to be. Yet the Fates would gather in their malevolent cluster of stars and clutch her by the throat as they laughed, "This is how it is."

A hundred times she would run her hands over the battles stitched across her skin. A tally of every war waged against those Fates. A thousand times, again and again, she would defy them to change that one moment Death was summoned to their aid.

In time she would learn: Death answers no summons but its own.

PART I

ONE

"I THINK WE'RE SAFE FOR NOW." IVY OLWEN WIPED DROPS OF RAIN FROM her slouchy hat and leaned against the brick wall of an old warehouse to catch her breath. The stone's cold wetness seeped through the patched jacket that hung loosely on her sixteen-year-old frame. Though she secretly pined for a more well-rounded figure, remaining shapeless while surviving on the streets had its benefits. "We'll rest here a bit. Wait for the sun to come up."

Philip wheezed next to her and stuck his neck out like a scrawny goose. One year her junior, he had also escaped the build of an emerging adult. "We never shoulda come here. What's so bad about where we were?"

"It's the slums. We sleep beside mold and make friends with rats. No one bats an eye if two more street urchins like us turn up dead in the gutter. Here on this side of town, we got a chance to change that. Didn't you see those lovely horse-drawn carriages and park benches when we crossed Pennsylvania Avenue? Not one bum sleeping on them."

"I was too busy bailing water out of my shoes." He held up a foot and water trickled from a hole in the heel of his shoe.

Pushing a lock of cropped hair from her eyes, Ivy peered around the corner to see if the copper had followed them. Canal Street stretched through the gray drizzle like a wide river shimmering under the splashing raindrops. Not a soul to be seen in the predawn light, including their pursuer. Second-guessing herself wasn't a habit, but she should've waited for a sunny day to start hawking their papers in a new territory.

Runts, castoffs, orphans, and newsies were common enough in the eastern part of the city, but the western half kept its streets clean and respectable, which was precisely why she had chosen it as her and Philip's new turf. Rich people needed newspapers, too, and she intended to fill her coin bag with their shiny bits of silver.

Unfortunately, the policeman they ran into didn't agree with her. He wanted to keep his beat clean of scamps, but they'd managed to slip from his grasp and disappear into the shadows.

Philip sneezed and hunkered his bony shoulders farther into his coat until nothing but his grimy ears stuck above the frayed collar. His sandy-colored curls hung limp, which only enlarged the agitation in his eyes. "People pay just as much for the paper on the Hill as they do here in Georgetown."

"But the Hill people don't tip like folks here." She jiggled the small bag of coins tied around her waist for emphasis. It clinked with the heavenly promise of food for a few days—maybe a week if they stretched it. Her stomach pulled at the thought of being full. "Once we have enough, we'll move over to Millionaires' Row and live in high style. I bet they tip for newspapers in solid gold."

"Why didn't we go to Millionaires' Row then, instead of coming here in the rain to get run over by a train?" He pointed to the Old Dominion Railway trundling a few yards away.

"Looking like this?" Ivy pointed at the threadbare lapels of her oversize jacket. "We'd be carted off straightaway and put in a workhouse. We need to look respectable first, and that takes money. Money we'll get in this part of town."

The first thing she would purchase for them was a hot meal and a warm bed, both sensations nearly scrubbed from memory. Then a change of clothes that didn't crawl with lice and wasn't covered in patches. A lady's set of clothes. She tugged at the shorn hair curling behind her ear. Perhaps a few ribbons for when it was safe to grow it out. No need to disguise herself as a boy once they had money.

A shadow fell over them. The copper. "There you are, you little beggars. Don't you know you should've stayed on your side of town?"

Ivy puffed up to her full size, which wasn't much, and glared, despite the policeman being twice her size. "We have a right to be here same as anyone."

He towered over them, seeming swollen in size with his greatcoat and wide hat dripping with rain. He grabbed the bundle of newspapers she had carefully wrapped in an old fisherman's coat to keep them dry and flung them into a nearby puddle.

"No!" Ivy shot forward to save her livelihood, but the policeman blocked her.

The dirty water gobbled across the pages, bleeding the black ink into smears.

"It's a waste of time and resources teaching the riffraff to read. You don't need letter learning to do the jobs you're best suited for— like mucking out the streets."

"We're trying to earn an honest wage and you've ruined it."

Fury flashed across the man's face. "You need a lesson in manners!" He shoved her backward into a puddle of runoff sludge. The bag of coins spilled its treasure across the slick ground. Grinning, he reached a gloved hand toward the shiny coins. "Lookee what we got here."

"Those are ours!" Philip charged forward with skinny arms swinging.

The policeman swatted him away with his baton. "You got something else to say, thieving runt? Assaulting an officer is considered a felony." Pocketing the coins, he drew a whistle from his uniform pocket and blew. *Tweet! Tweet!* "We'll see what the judge has to say. A stint in the workhouse will set you straight."

Ivy grabbed Philip's arm. "Run!"

Forgetting the papers and coins, Ivy and Philip bolted, blurring past warehouses and train boxes as the Potomac River stretched black and glistening to their right in the pearly gray light. The policeman's boots smacked against the wet pavement behind them.

Rounding a tavern, they ducked behind a pile of crates as their pursuer ran by. When his footfalls and whistle faded, they doubled back the way they'd come and paused beside the Aqueduct Bridge that stretched across the great river to Virginia.

"Policemen are much faster on this side of town," Ivy gasped, trying to catch her breath as the rain thinned to a silver mist.

"The rotter. We're not here to steal nothing, and now we've gone and lost what coin we did have."

"We'll find another way to make it." But how, she didn't know. Two months of scrimping and saving, paper hawking, standing on street corners in the pouring rain, being chased away when an older newsie decided to make their territory his—all lost. The hunger in her belly knotted to fear. They would manage. Just as they had at the orphanage where they'd met, only to be kicked out a few short years later. Living on the streets these past six years had taught them how to survive, and above all, they were survivors. Each other was all they had.

Ivy peered over the side of the bridge. Old stone steps led to the base of the structure. Beneath the archway was a dry enough spot to plan their next move. "Let's go under here and get out of the rain. We'll rest while the sun decides if it's going to show today."

She began navigating the slippery stairs from the top of the bridge's abutment to the path wandering beside the river and toward shelter, then stopped at the bottom. Voices echoed from ahead. "Someone's already here."

"Most likely a drifter or two trying to keep dry, same as us."

"No, I don't think so." Ivy's pulse kicked up as her ears strained to make out the words. "It's not English."

Philip rolled his eyes. "If you haven't noticed by now, Pols, Czechs, Hungarians, Irish, Italians, and all other kinds of immigrants are in this city hoping to find a better life than the one they left behind. Come on, maybe they'll have a few matzah balls they can spare."

The words switched to English, though the voice was heavily accented. "No one saw you leave?"

"No one. I'm here alone." An American.

"How do we believe the word of a man willing to betray his own people?"

"Guess that's the risk you have to take."

Before she could stop him, Philip shot into a tangle of bushes and dandelion weeds growing near the mouth of the arch.

Ivy dove in after him. "Are you mad? This is dangerous. We have to leave. Now." She grabbed his arm.

He shrugged her off. "And miss the most exciting thing we've ever heard? Leave if you want. I'm staying." He grinned, knowing she would never leave him. Tar and feather the josser.

Dangerous as it was, she couldn't deny her own curiosity was piqued. Like standing on a roof in the middle of a thunderstorm waiting to see how close the lightning would strike without getting zapped. She peeled back one of the branches and peered through the leaves. Two men stood under the arched tunnel. A smattering of light from streetlamps near both entryways trickled into the gloom.

"What information can you offer me?" the man with the accent demanded.

"Anything you need. Names of congressmen disgruntled by what laws are put into legislation. Representatives looking for a leadership that will listen to their concerns instead of hushing them. Lobbyists sympathetic to Russian dealings." The American dropped his voice, but not enough to be muffled against the echoing bricks. "There are many here who long to see the dictatorship of the Romanovs fall, and more than a few are willing to fund a revolution if your people should one day rise against their injustices."

"Russia has been a slave too long. Her people starving and beaten while the tsar and his ilk swill themselves on caviar and palaces. Russia's power belongs in the hands of new leadership. With a leader who will bring great change, not only to our country but to the world. For those who are worthy. To achieve this, I am scouring the earth for those brave enough to join our ranks, those who will remain silent yet vigilant until the time comes to rise up. The worthy have been found in Russia, Europe, and Asia. Now I come to the shores of America and ask if she will rouse from her star-spangled slumber when the hour strikes." With a hand that stood out stark white against the surrounding gloom, the foreigner reached out and grasped the American's shoulder. "Are you ready for the next step, *druk*?"

"I am ready, as I know others are."

"*Zamechatel'nyy*, for the next step is not enough. Ever onward we seek."

"Don't you know it's rude to eavesdrop?" a strange male voice whispered over Ivy's shoulder.

She screamed. A hand clamped over her mouth. She bit down hard on a finger.

"Ow!"

Philip flew at the man with fists pummeling. "Let go!"

The attacker dropped his hand from Ivy's mouth to block Philip's punches. Fast as a blink, he grabbed Philip's wrists and pinned him facedown on the ground. Ivy scrambled to her feet and launched herself on the man's back, locking her arm around his throat and squeezing tight.

"Get off!" He wheezed for air as the muscles in his neck constricted.

Voices shouted from the tunnel.

"You said you came alone!" The foreign man sounded panicked at the commotion.

"Those are your men!" the American yelled.

"*Nyet!* You lie to trap me."

Bam! A gunshot. Pounding feet reverberated from the tunnel as one of the men fled in the opposite direction.

The man beneath Ivy rolled, throwing her off his back, and jumped to his feet in one swift motion. A gun flashed at his belt. He planted a boot on Philip's thin chest, then grabbed Ivy and locked his arm around her.

"Eavesdroppers *and* scrappers. Here I thought it was going to be an easy morning." The attacker's heavy breath blew across the top of Ivy's head. Immobilized with her back against his chest, she couldn't make out his features.

"Let us go." Ivy twisted against his hold, but it was a vise grip trapping her arms at her sides.

"Not until we determine what the two of you are about."

Philip wheezed from where he lay prostrate under the man's boot. "N-none of your b-business."

"I'm making it my business. Tell me the truth now or things will go a lot worse for you, that I promise." His tone was easy as a summer breeze, but the open threat rang like steel.

Philip wheezed again as he dug his fingers into the boot's leather sole.

Arms pinned, Ivy did what little damage she could by beating her fists into the attacker's thighs. "Let him up. You're hurting him."

"He should've thought of that before he took a swing at me. I'm likely to have a blinker come morning."

"Serves you right." She kicked, but he shifted and her foot struck air.

"I wasn't the one prying where I wasn't welcome."

A figure stormed from the tunnel and materialized into a man of towering height, red hair, and a black scowl. Blood ran down his arm from a hole in his jacket. "What are these urchins doing here?"

"I don't know, sir. They won't stop assaulting me long enough to find out." Ivy beat her fist again. Her attacker didn't shift fast enough and earned a punch on the leg. His fingers dug into her shoulder, numbing her arm. "Particularly this one."

"Bloody got me shot. Russians?" He spat the accusation as if it were as admirable as the muck beneath his boot.

Ivy didn't take kindly to the implication. Nor the loss of feeling in her arm. "We're not Russian."

The redheaded man yanked a handkerchief from his pocket and wound it around his bleeding upper arm. "Then who sent you?"

"No one. We sell newspapers."

"Newspapers. Anything for a headline." Disgust rolled down his long nose and jackknifed from his sneering lip. With his uninjured arm, he reached into his jacket pocket and pulled out a gun. "Take them to the river."

Ice flooded Ivy's veins, the spikes of fear chilling her all over. She'd seen guns before, had witnessed numerous acts of violence from drunken brawls to roving gangs with broken beer bottles, brass knuckles, and knives. The streets provided a tough education with a live-or-die creed, but never had she found herself within point-blank range of a muzzle. Mist softly collected around the black barrel, blurring its cold edges. The hand holding it didn't shake once. A fact not in the least bit reassuring.

"Sir, they're only boys." Was that a clip of concern from her attacker as he removed his boot from Philip's chest?

The redheaded man didn't flinch, not so much as a shudder of his finger over the trigger. "Gutter rats who would sell their souls to the highest bidder for a scrap of food. In this case, a story about Russian spies. No witnesses, you know that."

"Washington will want to see them."

The redheaded man hesitated, but his eyes were unrelenting. He was merely calculating the cold facts stacked one against another. His frigid assessment was cut short when a third man jogged through the tunnel to meet them.

Panting, he bent over and grasped his knees. "Couldn't catch him. Turned the corner at Water Street and disappeared into the mist." His gaze flicked to Ivy and Philip before shifting to the gun in the other man's hand. The black mustache perfectly curled over his lip twitched. "What's all this?"

"Spies."

Desperation clawed through the ice freezing Ivy's muscles. "We're not spies, and if you let us go, we swear never to breathe a word of this."

"That much I will guarantee." Training the gun a second longer on her, the redheaded man sighed as his eyes sharpened to decision. He shoved the weapon back in his jacket. "Take them to Washington. He can shoot them when he's done."

TWO

Jumped by two kids. Bruised ribs. A failed mission. This was not how Jack Vale had anticipated his day going.

The assignment was straightforward. Make contact with the Russian, allow him to think Jefferson was there to turn traitor and join the zealot's cause of anarchy, then root out the true leader and snuff him out. Simple. Tasks any Talon agent could do in his sleep.

Jack held back a grunt of pain as he shifted position against the broken bookcase. He wouldn't be getting sleep anytime soon. Not until this little interrogation was finished. If it were up to him, they would've sent the kids scurrying with an earful of threats never to say a word about what they'd seen under the bridge. No need to pull out his trusty Colt M1911, more affectionately known as Undertaker, to finish them off. He knew the look of terror and hunger scratched across their dirty faces, and pity overcame any need to silence them. He'd worn that look himself not so long ago when he'd prowled the streets like a stray dog.

The kids now sat in the middle of this drafty attic at Talon headquarters tied to chairs with hoods over their heads. It wasn't how he would have handled the unusual situation, but then again, Talon had its secrets to keep, and two homeless little mice could prove as much a downfall as Russian spies.

The smaller boy's erratic breathing ticked the passing minutes. "What are they going to do with us?" His voice creaked in the still air.

The taller boy, the fearless one who had bitten Jack and then tried to choke him, twisted against the ropes binding his scrawny wrists. The skin was rubbed raw. "I don't know."

Jack slid his gaze to Washington, Talon's leader, who sat silently in a chair opposite the hostages. The man was bald with a pointed nose and, despite his average build, had a presence that filled the silent spaces of the chamber with authority. Dressed in crisp white and gray, he was cut into angles with no rounding to soften his person.

Washington gave an infinitesimal shake of his bare head. The kids thought they were alone, and he wanted to keep it that way. For now.

"What kind of men stow black hoods in the back of an auto?" the smaller one continued.

"The same kind who keep guns in their pockets and have no qualms about kidnapping people, obviously." Harshness sharpened the edge of the other one's tone.

"Do you think that redheaded man will make us target practice for this Washington? I read about men like them—what meets in back alleys and carries guns."

"Since the orphanage didn't teach us to read past our first learners, forgive me if I doubt your sudden interest in stories, much less their depiction of criminals."

Interest glimmered in Washington's sharp eyes. One of his favorite tactics was simply to sit and listen in obscurity while questions were answered and information offered without him needing to say a word. It was certainly proving successful in this case.

"Wasn't our fault they decided to swap secrets under the same bridge we needed for shelter." The smaller boy snorted with indignation. Muffled by the hood, he sounded more like a snuffling baby pig. "Do you think they're going to kill us?"

Washington crossed his legs. "Oh, I don't think that will be necessary."

The boys jumped, tottering in their chairs. The taller one found the nerve to speak first. "Wh-who are you? What do you want with us?"

"The more important matter is who you are. Oh, for the sake of civility, can we not remove these hoods? Get them off. Hop to it."

Jack stepped forward and ripped the hoods from their heads, then moved back behind them. His role was to remain unseen until needed. Another effective tool for interrogation, because the hostage would never know where he came from or when.

Their heads twisted around as they took in the dusty chamber. They couldn't see much with their shoulders lashed to the chairs. Uneven shelves nailed to unadorned walls. Warped floorboards gray with age. A ceiling that gave way to rafters stained from dripping water.

Jack saw the moment their worst fear settled in. No obvious way out.

"Tea?" Washington indicated the silver tea set with three cups and a plate of cookies on a squat table before them—completely at odds with the squalid surroundings. "Allow me to pour."

Acting as if nothing were amiss in this hostage situation, he poured a generous amount of the fragrant brew for the boys before filling his own cup and adding a generous splash of milk to each. He stirred his with a silver spoon and took a polite sip.

"Ah. We might start with names. I'm Washington."

The older one's hands twisted against his ropes. "The one who wants to shoot us."

Washington's dark eyebrows, thick in defiance against the scarcity up top, lifted a fraction but without the slightest hint of surprise. "Do I? Well, we'll return to that prompting momentarily. Might I ask who you are?"

The younger one jerked forward, straining against his bindings as his earlier fear disappeared beneath a thunder of bravado. Another trick Jack knew from the streets. Knowing how to bluff had served him well as a Talon agent. "Ask all you want, but we ain't giving you nothing."

"Robust spirit, as you said, Jack." Washington's sharp gaze cut over the children's shoulders. "You've already met, but allow me to make proper introductions. This is Agent Jack Vale."

Jack's cue to move from the shadows. The kids' eyes snapped to him. Blinding gray light pouring in from the tall window at the far end of the attic washed their faces in ash.

"Yes, sir. That one jumped first, quick as can be." His gaze moved from the smaller one with keen brown eyes and settled on the gutsy one. Gray-green eyes stared back at him in defiance. "This one here nearly choked me to death."

"Did he indeed." Washington regarded them with a statement rather than a question. Admiration glimmered in his eyes. "I've tried a number of times to get my hands around Jack's throat, but he's too slippery for me. However did you manage it?"

"He attacked us first."

Jack smothered a grin. He was starting to like this kid's spirit. He stepped over to the wall and leaned against it as if all the time in the world were resting on his side. "Quietly subduing an ambush is not the same as attacking. If I recall correctly, you were the first to strike when you bit my finger."

"You shouldn't have snuck up behind us."

"You and your brother shouldn't have been there in the first place."

"We're not siblings, not by blood anyway. How were we to know it was a gathering place for criminals? All we wanted was a place to stay dry until the rain passed."

The defiance slipped from the boy's glare and in its place crawled the underbelly of fear common to someone forced to take shelter where he could. Someone who didn't have a warm house to go to or warm food to fill his belly. It was someone Jack used to be before Talon took him in. They'd taken his hardships and rough edges and refined them to a knife's tip with purpose. He worked every day to prove he was worthy of their efforts.

The boy threw his plea to Washington, who sat silently calculating the entire exchange. "Please believe us. We had no intentions beyond the inconvenience of the weather. We'll go on our way and not say a word."

Footsteps sounded on stairs and a few seconds later Jefferson stepped up through the hole in the floor that served as the entry and exit for the attic space. His scowl had grown in fierceness since the bridge, which was understandable considering the swatch of bandages padding his left shoulder. He prowled around to stand in front of the hostages.

"Shoot them now and be done with it. They heard too much."

The boys gasped in unison.

Washington's fingers hovered over the cookie plate. "Not every problem is solved with a bullet, Jefferson." He selected a cookie and took a bite before placing the remaining piece on the cup's saucer.

"The deal was nearly done! Now I've got a hole in my arm because of these slum interlopers."

Jefferson looked to Jack for agreement, but Jack merely crossed his arms and shifted uncomfortably from his position against the cracked wall. He'd learned long ago not to interfere on the rare occasion when his instructors locked horns. Jefferson might be his mentor, but Washington was too clever for anyone to run circles around him.

"It was a clean shot. Nothing you haven't experienced before. As for the Russian, we'll catch him soon enough like all the rest." After popping the remaining piece of cookie into his mouth, Washington chewed and swallowed before lifting the cup to his lips. His sharpened gaze cut over the rim to the hostages. "Neither of you backed down from a fight. You've managed to keep cool heads since being held in this less-than-pleasant place, and you've both been searching for an escape route since the moment the hoods were taken from your heads. All actions to your credit. With a little work, you might prove competent."

So Washington recognized their potential, but for Jack it went deeper than appreciation. He felt a strange kinship, like looking back through a portal of time and seeing himself. What he once was and what he might become.

"Competent in what?" The older boy may have had a defiant spirit, but this younger one carried a crate ton of pluck beyond what his scrawny appearance suggested.

Washington sipped his tea as if he hadn't just trumpeted the utmost note of temptation to a young boy. He set his cup on its saucer. "You might as well know that you have not stumbled upon a nest of criminals or traitors but rather an elite agency."

"Sir!" Jefferson's face flared red. "I must protest—"

Washington waved him away. "Your protest is noted. As I was saying, we are an elite, independent agency sworn to—"

"Sir! These beggars have no right to—"

"Jefferson."

"—understand the graveness of the situation into which they've heedlessly thrown themselves. Furthermore—"

"Jefferson."

"Please, sir. Allow me to finish."

"Jefferson, you're bleeding."

"What?" Jefferson's attention dropped to the blood splotching his bandage. "Oh. Excuse me." Muttering about secrets and danger and guns, he retreated through the hole in the floor to the stairs below. The floorboards vibrated until his stomps slowly faded away.

"Bit of a dramatist, Jefferson is, but he's a brilliant fencer and the only man I know who can render a man unconscious using only his thumb. You have not touched your tea. Oh yes." Washington motioned to Jack. "Untie them."

Jack took the knife from his belt and made quick work of the ropes. The taller boy sprang from his chair and glared back at him. Jack merely saluted him with his blade before sheathing it once more and settling back against the wall. Loose and unthreatening was the best way to calm a skittery cat. The boy backed slowly away, then quickly skirted around Washington and made for the window.

All hope of escape, evident in his expression, was immediately dashed when he looked out the glass. Jack knew the dizzying view well enough. They were four stories up in a tower with the Potomac River flowing several blocks away. To the east was the hub of Dupont Circle, upon which carriages and autos rounded before turning off one of the many spokes, including the one stretching far below the window. The ritziest neighborhood in the city, but still a prison of no escape.

"As I was saying"—Washington reclined in his chair without the least concern of his two charges making a break for it—"the agency upon which you have thrust yourselves is a beacon of light poised to roust out the bitter darkness seeping through the earth's cracks. Yet for our work to find success, our light must be cloaked in shadow."

The younger boy, who had only moved to sit warily on the edge of his chair, scratched at a dirty spot on his neck. "Are you the police?"

"While police forces are essential to keeping civilization on the straight and narrow path as provided by the law, we walk an alternative path. A narrow path intended for good but not necessarily a straight one. There. Is your curiosity piqued?"

Jack's attention shifted to the boy by the window, and he caught his gaze in the glass. Two cautious eyes in a pale rain-washed face with something else about the boy that Jack couldn't quite put his finger on. Jack probed beyond the drops of mist collecting on the grimy pane as he sought to slip into the privacy of a detachment the boy was determined to keep. There was a savage fragility in the boy, like that of an animal torn from its den and thrown into a cage for observation, begging to be set free.

Clutching the edges of his frayed lapels, the boy broke the connection and turned around to Washington as the latter finished another sip of tea. "What will you do with us now?"

"That depends on your choice. There are only two ways out of this room. One through that window there. A straight drop four stories to hard concrete. Jack can oblige you if you're nervous about taking the first step. The other is through that door." With perfect calm, Washington nodded to the hole in the floor behind the chairs.

Interest undoubtedly piqued, the boy in the chair swiveled around to gape at the hole. "Where does it lead?"

"Perhaps to the firing squad. Or a dragon's lair. Or perhaps just downstairs to a grand old building with burning fireplaces, unlike this drafty attic." Washington drained his teacup before placing it on the saucer, then stood, walked over to the hole, and descended the stairs. He waved a hand over his shining head. "Come find out."

A silent argument of twitching eyebrows and head shakes erupted between the boys and ended in six seconds flat when the smaller boy threw up his hands in exasperation and sprinted after Washington.

"Not so eager to join him?" Jack shoved his hands deep in his pockets.

The taller boy didn't move. His stare turned assessing. The sharpness of it was softened only by an unusually thick fringe of lashes. "Will you throw me out the window if I don't?"

"You're safe on that account. The latch is broken. I haven't been able to toss anyone out in months." Hiding his grin, Jack shrugged off the wall and started for the stairs.

"How do I know this isn't some sort of a trap?"

"You don't, but if we were going to kill you, you'd be six feet under by now, not standing at a window learning our exact location. Learn to trust a little."

"I've been given little opportunity for that."

He paused on the steps and looked back. The boy's chin was thrust out in a defiant tilt to meet the world as it came to him, but vulnerability lurked in the corners of his eyes. He had known trust once, but it had been snatched from him like a well-loved dog suddenly shoved out into the cold and made to fend for itself. No one deserved to be abandoned like that, to have trust stripped away so that they could no longer accept goodness in the world when they stumbled upon it. Jack had been condemned to such callousness once, but he wouldn't allow another to succumb to it. Not if there was something he could do about it.

"Then trust *me*."

Appearing as nervous as a rabbit fearing a trap about to spring, the boy followed Jack down the rickety stairs to a deserted corridor flanked by closed doors with unpolished knobs. A single gas lamp flickered from a peg on the cracked wall. Washington's gleaming bald head disappeared around a far corner. The smaller boy hovered at the corner, waiting for his friend and Jack to catch up.

"How long have you been trying to work this side of town?" Jack asked as they rounded the corner to another hallway. The names Adams, Hancock, Madison, and Rutledge were written on stained cards and pinned to each door in a row of them.

The boy swatted at a low-hanging cobweb. "Do we stand out that much?"

"Around here, yes. I know every newsie on the west side. Best way to get information."

Somewhere between being accused as a spy and having his hands untied, the smaller boy with the keen eyes regained his nerve and attempted to keep stride with Jack.

"We mostly work the Hill, but *someone* doesn't think it's good enough anymore." He shot a look over his shoulder to his friend.

His friend snorted. "I don't want to sleep on a cold floor under a leaky roof and keep scrounging for food every day. Life has to be better than that."

"Not for the likes of us. We have to fight for every inch if we hope to see tomorrow." Midsentence, the smaller boy had forgotten his friend and turned his interest back on Jack. "I've never seen anybody move like you did at the bridge. Where'd you learn to fight like that?"

Jack shrugged as they descended to another floor. This corridor was adorned with paintings of severe Talon men in wigs from over a century ago. The scent of lemon beeswax lingered around the gilded frames.

"I've picked up a few tricks out of necessity." Not to mention the hours spent training every day with the other agents.

"Can you teach me? I've never seen someone throw a punch like that. Not even at the wharf."

"Sure, kid. We all need to know how to stay a few steps ahead."

"My name's Philip."

"Just Philip?"

Philip shrugged. "The orphanage never gave me a last name to go with it. That's"—his friend jabbed him in the shoulder—"Ive. That Jefferson would've killed us for sure if you hadn't spoken up. Don't you think he would've killed us if Jack hadn't come to the rescue, uh, Ive?"

Ive nodded reluctantly. "He might have. We are grateful."

"Despite what you witnessed earlier, Jefferson's a good man," Jack said. "They all are."

"Who exactly are 'they'?"

Jack stopped and turned to look back at Ive. Hands still in his pockets, his mouth curved at the corners. "People who had something different in mind for me. Maybe for you too."

J'NELL CIESIELSKI

The corridor opened to a wide landing with a grand staircase leading down to a great hall with reddish wood walls that glowed like warm cherries on a brazier. Everything gleamed, from the gaping fireplaces at each end to the golden chandeliers dripping with candles. A king could live here with no desire to step beyond the wonders of his own rooms. High on one wall was a black flag with a golden bird whose massive wings were outstretched and claws sprawled open for a kill. Terrifyingly majestic.

"An eagle. The symbol of our great nation." Washington's voice boomed from where he stood in the center of the magnificent hall. "Do you know how close we came to having a turkey instead? If a few of our founding fathers were allowed their choice. Or a dove for that matter. Absurd."

Ive shrank into his oversize coat as if trying to disappear. "No, sir. I didn't know."

"Hmm." Washington assessed him thoroughly with his sharp brown eyes. At last his gaze cut back to the flag. "Majestic creature, the eagle. Strong, defiant, powerful. Protectors. Can you call a turkey majestic, what with that flabby thing wobbling all about?" He flapped his hand under his chin.

Ive's shoulders lowered from their hunched embarrassment. "No, sir. I can't."

"Indeed not." The man's eyes cut to Philip then back to Ive. "I see they didn't opt for the window."

Jack offered a nonchalant shrug. "Guess that proves they're daring."

"'Daring,' you say. Daring to leave the political riches of the Hill to descend on this part of town. Has selling newspapers drawn your boredom, and now you seek a new thrill of fulfillment? Stealing brooches from old ladies? Silver-capped canes from unsuspecting gentlemen? Pennies from the fountain?"

"No, sir!" Ive flared with indignation. "We're not thieves. We

28

were trying to earn a few coins selling newspapers in a new neighbor-hood. That's all."

Washington didn't relent. He used his imposing presence to bear down on the boy like one of those newfangled trollies running on electricity. "Where are these newspapers?"

"Trampled in a puddle."

"Ah, I see. A lack of evidence. Not to mention a fool's hope in selling papers on a soggy morning. Are you a fool?"

"No, sir."

"A liar then."

"I do not lie."

Washington bent to the boy's eye level, his unflinching stare probing him, searching for cracks. He seemed to find none. "Good." Straightening, he cupped a hand to his mouth and bellowed. "Dolly!"

Philip jumped behind Jack, who merely stood there grinning, content with his place in this overwhelming room. After a few more bellows loud enough to bring down the rafters, a tall, angular woman with graying black hair marched around the corner.

"That's quite enough of that! There is no call for shrieking like an uncouth backwoodsman, Washington." Dressed in a gown of dusty purple that ruffled at her throat and hem, Dolly squared her-self directly in front of Ive and Philip. "New visitors, I see. Quite the impression you're making." She speared a look at Washington, who feigned interest in the ceiling. "A hot meal is what the two of you need."

On cue, the boys' stomachs rumbled. When had they last eaten a full meal? By the looks of them, not recently.

Ive's eyes cut to the main door and the outside world mere steps away. The hopeful flash of escape he'd had at the attic window returned as he placed a hand on Philip's shoulder. Long tapered fin-gers with delicate bones. That uncertainty that Jack couldn't quite figure out niggled once more at the back of his mind.

"That's very kind of you—" Ive said.

"Upstairs, I gave you two choices," Washington said. "The window or the door. I give you two more choices now. The door to dreariness where you'll dodge puddle after puddle with no newspapers to sell and become drenched to the bone after you find an abandoned doorway to shelter in. Or a hot meal and a safe place to lay your heads for the night where you may wake on the morrow to find a new world waiting for you. One beyond the ordinary." His gaze cut through Ive's forming protests and daggered her greatest fear. "Upon my word of honor, you will be unharmed no matter which you choose."

Ive opened his mouth with another slew of reservations but was cut short by loud rumblings from his belly.

"You'll catch your deaths of cold if you walk all those blocks back to the Hill in soggy clothes," Jack said to ease the war of uncertainty and survival battling across Ive's face. For added measure he threw in, "Trust me."

Ive glanced at Philip's pleading face and conceded defeat with a nod.

"Excellent choice. It's the one I would have made. All right, Dolly. Hot food, a bath, dry clothes, and a warm bed for the night for these boys." Tucking his hands behind his back, Washington spun on his heel and walked away. "If they steal anything, make sure it's the silver. I detest the set we have."

Dolly looked between Ive and Philip, her thin lips pursed in consideration. "Right. A warm bath and dry clothes first before they wrinkle themselves into colds. Jack, you take that one"—she pushed Philip toward him before taking Ive's arm—"and I'll see to this one."

Jack glanced back as Dolly propelled Ive in the opposite direction. Ive was having none of it, and the sudden realization of what now seemed so obvious—what he had been trying to put his finger on— hit Jack full force.

Laughing out loud, he turned and guided Philip to the men's wing.

THREE

Ivy shouldn't have been surprised that they thought her a boy, not when she kept her hair shorn and wore shapeless clothing. Girls ended up in one profession on the streets, and *that* she would never become. However, there were a few differences bound to be noticed if she was forced into the gentlemen's bath.

As the boys turned left, Dolly steered Ivy to the right toward a separate set of stairs carved of wood and covered in red carpet. Ivy balked from the woman's grip while clutching her coat closed. "No, thank you. I-I don't need a bath."

"No offense intended, child, but you are in great need of a good scrubbing."

Ivy dug her heels in, bunching the carpet underfoot. "Then let me go alone. Don't make me go in there with the other"—she swallowed her panic—"boys."

Dolly stopped midstair and dropped Ivy's arm. Taking the spectacles that dangled from a thin chain around her neck, she perched them on the tip of her nose. "My dear, Washington may believe you a boy, but I've told that man more than once he needs to have his eyes examined." She dropped her spectacles and smiled, continuing up the stairs. "This way to the *ladies'* area, please."

Relaxing her death grip on the tattered edges of her coat, Ivy climbed the tall stairs to the third floor and followed the gentle swishing of Dolly's out-of-fashion train down a white-trimmed hallway with windows and pretty paintings of the countryside. One day she'd like to see such places herself, far away from dirty cobblestones and unwashed buildings. Places where mountains climbed to the heavens and oceans crashed like thunder on sandy shores. Wide green fields where she could stretch out her arms and run with no one telling her to slow down. Places where adventure waited.

A door swung open. A girl who looked to be Ivy's age with red hair and a pale narrow face stepped out, then stopped and leaned against the doorframe like a cat. Nimble and ready to pounce.

"Ah, Beatrix. Meet the new girl," Dolly said.

Ivy stepped forward and extended her hand. "Ivy Olwen. A pleasure."

Beatrix assessed her from head to toe with a cool flick of her lashes. "The pleasure is entirely yours, I'm sure." Evaluation complete, she slinked back into her room and slammed the door.

Dolly cleared her throat. "At Talon we all have our peculiarities. Some more than others. This way." She gestured Ivy into the last room at the end of the hallway. A neat space with two narrow beds, two nightstands, two wardrobes, two oil lamps, and one single window dressed in lace curtains that overlooked a back garden.

A memory wiggled on the edge of Ivy's mind. A woman sitting by a window like this one and braiding a young girl's hair. Ivy could still feel her mother's gentle fingers combing through her locks as she sang a silly song they'd made up together. The song ended and the memory drifted away. *Come back, Mama,* she wanted to cry, but in nine years her tears had yet to conjure the woman who had loved her so.

"This will be your room for the night." Dolly ran a finger over one of the scroll-legged nightstands. Impeccably clean. Ivy had the distinct feeling that if dust were present it was too terrified to reveal itself in Dolly's presence. "You will find some clothes in the wardrobe.

Hopefully they will fit. Beatrix is the only other young woman in residence and the two of you will share a washroom."

"The only young woman in the secret agency, you mean."

Dolly's thin lips flattened into a sparse line. She stared hard for a long, excruciating minute before relenting. "I see." And so she did, but clearly she did not approve. When she spoke again, her words were carefully measured. "Talon is a special place filled with superior opportunities for learning. We only take a small number who show true potential for a unique . . . teaching experience."

"Mr. Washington seems to think Philip and I show potential of some kind, but he's wrong." Ivy hovered her hand over the clean bedspread, afraid of spoiling it with her filthy hands. "He'll discover we're rather ordinary—or at least, he would if we stayed."

"You won't stay to understand what he means?"

Ivy shook her head. "We'll leave first thing in the morning so as not to trouble you any further."

"You should know that Washington never does anything without reason."

He could reason all he liked. It didn't mean she and Philip belonged in a place that hunted criminals and threatened to throw people from windows. Then again, where did they belong?

"Thank you, Miss Dolly."

"Dolly. Though I deeply appreciate civil manners, there are rules here and no one rises above them. No formal titles of any kind."

"Yes, ma'am." Ivy quickly added the rule to her new list of dos and don'ts for this odd place.

Softness creased the corners of Dolly's eyes. "You weren't always on the streets, were you, my dear? I can always tell." In a blink, the softness disappeared and she snapped back to her no-nonsense manner. "The water closet is across the hall. You've one hour to bathe and dress, then I expect to see you in the kitchen. The smell of corn chowder and biscuits will serve as your guide."

Hours later, long after the pearly light of day had descended into darkness, Ivy lay in the strange bed smelling clean and patting her full belly. The sheets were soft against her skin. Unlike the canvas and burlap sacks she'd managed to smuggle into the abandoned warehouse she and Philip claimed as their current address. How was he getting along in their new surroundings? He had been served three bowls of soup and an entire pan of biscuits before Jack had to carry him off to bed in the boys' wing. To her knowledge, he hadn't woken since.

Unfortunately, the same could not be said of Ivy. Perhaps it was her skin wanting to linger in the luxury of the soft sheets or her survival instincts having difficulty settling into the unfamiliar surroundings, but sleep refused to claim her. Throwing back the covers, she grabbed a woolen blanket from the foot of her bed and wrapped it around her nightgown, careful to allow the tiny pink bow to peep out at the top. It felt strange to be in girl clothes again, and oh, how she'd missed them. Maybe she could let her hair grow out again. She ran a hand through the short strands and frowned. No. Short hair and trousers were safer for the life she was living. For tonight, though, she would enjoy her tiny pink bow.

After padding down the dark hallway, she crossed the landing that overlooked the cherry room and the draped flag on the opposite wall. Caught in the dimmed light from the gaslit sconces, threads of gold shimmered in the eagle's wings. Sighing at the wonder, she continued her midnight exploration to the men's wing.

She crept silently past the doors with the names Calhoun, Fielding, Franklin, Hamilton written in scrawled black ink on white cards tucked into brass plates. Near the end of the hall, she spied the door marked Vale. She softly knocked.

The only answer was snoring. She opened the door and poked her head inside. Two double beds filled the room, only one of which was occupied.

She tiptoed in and gently shook Philip's shoulder. "Philip."

He groaned before his eyelids dragged open. "Ives? What are you doing here?"

"I wanted to make sure you were all right." She glanced around the room, which was lit only by faint moonlight shining through the half-shut curtains. A few personal items for grooming and post-cards depicting beaches occupied the space near Jack's bed. A bed that appeared unused this night.

"Well, I haven't been murdered in my sleep, so I guess I'm doing just ducky." Philip pulled the blanket to his shoulder and rolled to his side.

"I can't sleep. This place is too strange."

"Every place we sleep is strange. Tunnels, abandoned ware-houses, broken railroad cars. This is the first bed I've slept on in years, and I'm going to enjoy every minute of it. So should you."

"We don't belong here. We need to leave at first light."

He rolled back to face her with his bleary eyes. "Me and you have never had a chance to belong anywhere. We're two misfits trying to stay alive—that's been our only purpose. This place can give us something. I don't know what, but it's more than we've had in a long time." He yawned. "Don't you think?"

Her words stuck in her throat as his eyelids drifted closed. Her own thoughts could wait until morning. She brushed the sandy curls from his forehead, then tiptoed out of the room and gently closed the door behind her.

As she crossed the landing over the great hall once more, a cool draft skittered across her toes. She followed the intruding air to a back corner where an arched door stood partially open. She tugged the handle, and it made the barest of groans before she swung it wide to reveal a series of outdoor stairs leading up to the roof. The stone steps were cold and damp beneath her bare feet as she inhaled deeply the smells of wet pavement, raked earth, and clean walking spaces.

All familiar scents at their essence, but here they were laced with something undefinable. Must be the money making the air richer.

When she reached the rooftop, she could see all of DC spread out at her feet like a blanket with tiny twinkles of midnight candles flickering among its folds as the dark waters of the Potomac River slipped silently along its edge. Contentment settled through her. If she lived at this strange address, she would spend most of her time in this spot. No wonder birds soared so high to see the wonders below them.

"Great view, isn't it?" Ivy jumped as Jack leaned out from the shadows where he was sitting against a slanted portion of the green roof. Wearing no jacket, he had untucked his rumpled shirt and his feet were bare.

She inched away from him. He was kind enough earlier with his easy smile and the way he helped Philip, but he was still a stranger, and life on the street had taught her never to be too trusting. Especially with a man who'd been ready to toss her out a window if given the order.

"I've never been up this high. The city looks so grand from here." Of all the places in this big city, she and Philip had ended up right where she'd wanted them to be.

Millionaires' Row was always whispered about like a fairy-tale land inhabited by kings and queens of society, but nothing compared to seeing it with her own disbelieving eyes. Glittering like rubies and diamonds of brick and stone with dozens of windows, the homes were settled atop lush green lawns and surrounded by scrolling iron fences like singular crowns on an endless throne. Bright green leaves spotted with glossy raindrops unfurled from trim tree limbs in search of spring's arrival. Back on the Hill, everything remained encased in winter's gray and brown. This place mesmerized her with its extravagance, but these streets could turn vicious on intruders without warning. She clutched her blanket tighter, as if her unworthiness could be caught on the expensive air.

"That's Virginia over there." Jack pointed across the river before swinging his arm in the opposite direction. "And just beyond the Capitol Building there is Maryland."

Ivy peered into the darkness. Those states seemed as far away as the moon. "I've never been out of DC, but I'd like to visit those places one day. I want to see the whole world."

"Virginia is nice if you like the country. That's where I'm from—or was, until nine years ago."

Curiosity whittled away at her fear. She sat down a couple feet away from him and tucked her blanket in close as an early spring chill crept across her toes. By the river she had failed to get a good look at him, fighting for her life as it were. He appeared to be only a few years older than her with the hardened lines of manhood about him. Tall with dark brown, almost reddish hair, he moved loosely in the manner of a confident man while a crimp in his left ear marked him as a fighter. As the ear remained intact, she assumed he was the victor. Ivy had seen more than enough street brawls to spot a loser, but this Jack fellow had the air of anything but failure.

"Why did you leave?" she asked. "I think living in the country would be so much better than growing up in the city. All that greenery and fresh air."

"My parents dropped me off at an old aunt's house on their way to make it big in New York—the vaudeville scene. Apparently a double act was preferable to a trio. I was six. Three years later the aunt passed—which she blamed me for with her dying breath—and left me nothing, so I had to choose between living in the woods or finding excitement in the city. I chose the city."

"You struck out on your own at only nine years old?" He'd been a year younger than her when she and Philip were kicked out of the orphanage. Perhaps he wasn't quite the stranger she'd taken him for. "How long have you been here at Talon?"

"Since I was twelve." He lifted one knee up and perched his arm across the top while stretching out his other leg. His bare toes were ghostly pale against the darkness. "I miss the quiet of the country sometimes. That's why I come up here. Gives me a wide view of the open sky. Makes you believe anything is possible on a night like this."

The drizzling clouds had rolled back to reveal a soft black sky with thousands of stars twinkling from their high perches.

"I've never seen so many stars," she said.

"I tried counting them once. Only got to three hundred and eleven before I sneezed and had to start all over."

Ivy laughed, the simple sound forgotten to her ears, like an old attic door opening after years of being shut. "I've never tried. There are always too many buildings blocking them where I'm from. Not that I have time for stargazing. Too busy searching for food." Her smile faded as another old door creaked open in her mind. Dust and sorrow drifted out. "It wasn't always like that."

"Your parents gone too?"

She nodded. "I was seven. We owned a small hat shop on Fourth Street. My dad made the most beautiful hats. He was going to make me one with a green ribbon for my birthday that year, but then both of my parents got sick with the fever—my baby brother too." She picked at the edge of her blanket as the grief rolled over her. Her dad, smelling of leather and cotton. Her mom, humming in the kitchen. A family stolen from her.

"Afterward, I was sent to the orphanage for a while. I met Philip, who had been abandoned there as a baby, and we became each other's family. Then the orphanage turned us out to make room for younger kids. Said ten was old enough to make do for ourselves. It's been the two of us ever since. Watching each other's backs, laughing through the good days when we managed to find a crust of bread, and keeping each other's chins up through the bad times when we had no place to sleep."

"It's good you had each other. Not everyone is so fortunate."

"You seem to do well enough. The people here respect you." The streets were a brutal instructor that had taught her to recognize the unsavory sort at twenty paces. Try as she might, she could not peg Jack as a louse. Not after he'd pleaded for her and Philip's lives by that cold river.

"Ah, well. The luck of the orphan. A parent's rejection forces you to find acceptance elsewhere." He flashed a bright smile that faded as quickly as it came. "Or build a new family, like you and Philip."

It was true. Philip was her family and she was his, and that kind of bond never broke. Yet she couldn't block out the gloom tinging Jack's experience with his parents and aunt.

Jack yawned, not bothering to cover it. "That boy sure can sleep. I don't think a Sousa march could wake him."

"He needs all the rest he can get. Especially after today." She twinged with guilt at having disturbed his slumber to ease her own conscience.

"You do too."

Warmth spread over her insides. Besides Philip, no one had looked out for her in a long time. "I'll get by."

"You don't have to, at least not tonight. Talon is the safest place you can be."

Safe. When was the last time she'd felt that? Not since she was wrapped in the last mortal embrace of her dying parents. She doubted she would ever experience such security and belonging again, but earlier when Philip's stomach had rumbled like a freight train while he stood shivering in the middle of that great hall, she'd felt she had no choice but to accept Talon's hospitality. Part of her was relieved after glimpsing the main front door. Yes, it had offered escape but also grayness to the world beyond. A world of the ordinary. Yet nothing within these walls could be mistaken for conventional. Perhaps it was worthwhile to defy the odds of unexceptional if only for one night.

He turned to look at her, his gaze drifting to the pink bow on her nightgown then back to her face. "You should've told me you were a girl."

Ivy's hand automatically drifted to her shorn hair. She missed being able to brush the strawberry-blonde locks and twirl them around her finger. "Would it have made a difference?"

He shook his head, an easy smile sloping across his face.

She waited for that inner voice of warning, the one that cautioned her from trusting strangers, the one that had kept her alive all these years, but it seemed content in Jack's quiet ease. "Why did you stop Jefferson today?"

"I prefer we keep the innocent out of our business, and your willingness to jump on my back and choke me to save your friend isn't a kind of bravery to discard so quickly."

"Bravery must be highly prized in your agency."

"One of many traits we honor here."

"Here." She rolled the word around like a marble. "Where exactly is 'here'? What is this Talon exactly?"

Jack pillowed his hands behind his head and relaxed against the roof as his gaze drifted up to the night sky. "A place to reach for the stars."

FOUR

Ivy jolted awake in the strange bed. Four walls, a warm blanket, and sunlight peeking through lace curtains. This wasn't the usual abandoned warehouse she slept in. Then it all came rushing back. The rain and soggy newspapers, the men under the bridge, her and Philip's hands tied at tea. Jack counting stars. She was at Talon where life had taken an unexpected turn. For better or worse was yet to be seen.

Tossing aside the bedcovers, Ivy quickly threw on her freshly cleaned street clothes and hurried to the kitchen where the cook offered her a leftover biscuit slathered with jam. Gobbling it down and licking the last few crumbs from her fingers, she went in search of Philip. They needed to leave soon if they hoped to make it back to the Hill by nightfall to pick up the following day's newspapers. If they arrived too late, the other newsies would have scooped them all up, and she and Philip wouldn't have a chance to make coin. She couldn't let that happen.

Sunlight filtered through the dozens of windows to burrow into the rich woods and dance across the colorful paintings. The house was a maze of hallways and rooms of varying sizes. Some were small and cozy with oversize chairs and more books than she could count; others were large and filled with oddities from stuffed owls to sets of full-body metal armor. A museum enticing her curiosity around every corner. Ivy didn't dare give in to the temptation of touching. What if she broke something? Jefferson might make good on his threat to shoot her.

She crept cautiously through a formal room dressed in white and gold with chandeliers hanging delicately from the painted ceiling. A ballroom from another era if she had to guess. Two men stepped through a door at the far end of the room. They glanced at her and kept walking. Afraid they might boot her to the door as the would-be spy who foiled the Russian's capture, she quickly slipped into the next room.

"Philip?" Her voice was muffled among dozens of bookcases and their leather-bound tomes. Those that could not fit on the shelves were stacked in haphazard towers on whatever horizontal surface could be found nearby. Worn rugs slumbered on the dark wood floor while thick cushions on deep-seated chairs beckoned her to while away the hours in their comfort.

"Confound it all! I told that woman to leave my Socrates alone." Washington popped out from between two rows of bookshelves, his bald head shining among the dull brown covers. "Ah! Do you know where my Socrates has gone to?"

Ivy peeked over her shoulder. As far as she could tell, he was talking to her about this missing Socrates. Whoever he was, Washington was highly agitated at his disappearance. "No, sir."

"I left him next to *The Imperial Take on China's Ecosystem* yesterday and now he's wandered off. Just like the man."

"Perhaps he's gone to the kitchen? It's nearly time for luncheon."

Washington's keen brown eyes stared at her for a full minute, probing once more into the cracks she might reveal. Or perhaps he was hoping Socrates might appear behind her.

"Lunch. Already?" He blinked once, then thrust a book into her hands and disappeared down another aisle. "Find me the chapter on zoning infrastructure for the Navy Yard. What ordinances exist for submarines?"

"Submarines? In DC?"

"Certainly," he called as if it were the most natural thing in the world to witness a submarine floating up the Potomac.

Ivy frowned at the book in her hands. So innocent in appearance yet terrifying for a semiliterate girl. She flipped open the first few pages and mustiness assaulted her nose before she dragged her finger down the list of contents. "Zo-ning infra-str. Sub-sub-sub . . ."

"Speak up when you find it!" Washington's voice hurtled over the stacks.

Letters had never been a problem for her. Some of her fondest memories were of reading bedtime stories with her parents. Her mother was patient in helping her sound out the big words, while her father performed different voices for each of the characters. Then they died and the orphanage put little emphasis on furthering her education beyond basic mathematics for tallying a grocery receipt or following a recipe book. Useful skills for a female, they'd claimed. She'd taken to rescuing crumpled newspapers from the rubbish bin and reading by moonlight once everyone else had gone to sleep, simply to experience a world outside the grimy windows.

Her finger hovered over an *m* word, but it looked nothing like the sound in her head. "In-fra-struck-sure." She looked up and found Washington watching her again. Mortified, she handed him the open book. "I'm not sure if this is the one you need, sir."

He took the book without looking at it. "This one is on building codes in New Hampshire. Quail must have the one I need."

"A quail has your book?"

"A colleague of mine who runs the finest law firm in the capital city. He holds most of my legal books in his townhouse over on Q Street—along with the ones I'd rather Dolly not know I still have after she banned them. What, I ask you, is so salacious about the history of underpants? They are a map to cultural and political relevance." He snapped the book closed and tossed it on a chair, then whirled back into the mountain of stacks. "I need someone to sort all these dictionaries. The last person in here mixed the English with the Russian, and the Sudanese with the Finnish. If I'm reading ancient Persian, I need to translate my *akumā* from my *abavāmā*. You can help me."

Ivy peered around the corner of a bulging shelf, catching sight of his gray jacket as he strode to the next aisle. "Sir, as much as I would like to help, I really cannot—"

"It's easy." He appeared from nowhere and dropped an armload of books at her feet. Dust flew up. "Just put them in alphabetical order. See the letters stamped there on the spine? Any in Cyrillic, hiragana, or *abjad*, set aside and we can pilfer through them later."

She stared at the pile of foreign books he expected her to decipher somehow and shook her head. "Later? No, me and Philip need to be on our way."

"Somewhere you need to be?"

"If we don't get back to the Hill, our job—"

"Ah, yes. This newspaper business where you barely scrape two coins together in the eternal struggle of the gray masses for mediocre existence." His dark eyes glanced up from a leather-bound tome. "I'll pay whatever you miss from your job. Double. My books need sorting and most of the boys around here are too sausage-fingered to do them justice. Do we have a deal?"

Struggle. Gray. Mediocre. Each word a brick slung at her soul and sinking it further into the mire as it fought for freedom, for light beyond the grimness—a light poised to scrub out the darkness. Was that not what he had called this mysterious Talon?

A longing to find that light flickered through her soul. A match ready to strike and set fire to wood shavings. Yet she was hesitant of snuffing out the flames but also of allowing them to catch and scorch beyond her control. She had not a clue of the difference between Persian and Russian, but she could figure it out on promise of payment while she decided whether or not to let the match burn. At least she and Philip could pay for food at the end of the week.

"I'll have to talk to Philip first."

Washington waved off her worry. Ink stained his fingers. "Jack is teaching him boxing in the garden. No use bothering them when they've got the gloves on. It's good Philip came. Jack needs a sparring partner. You box?"

"Me? Not unless you think nose punching is boxing."

"Hmm." He paused midstride, his gaze ever assessing until at last he tallied a conclusion. What that conclusion was remained to be explained. "We shall see. Indeed, we shall." He walked to the open door and stuck his head out. "Dolly! We need sandwiches and lemonade. Dolly!"

"I hear you," Dolly hissed with annoyance from somewhere down the hallway. "No use shouting the walls down."

"I wasn't shouting. Shouting is *when I do this!*" He stomped out the door as their voices tangled in argument.

Ivy knelt between the mountains of books and ran her finger over the gold lettering on the top cover as her mind quickly sorted through a system. Organization came easily to her; a way of combing through disorder to construct peace and harmony for one's personal satisfaction. Her father had always tasked her with sorting the ribbons and buckles in his hat workshop. She remembered the silky strands sliding through her childish fingers in a rainbow of colors for her to tame. Before her, the stacks of books awaited her next move, her plan to bring them order. The browns, blacks, and reds didn't exactly make a rainbow, but she would provide them harmony all the same.

Sunlight crept around the room creating a halo of tranquility that seemed to hush the very hands of time as she got to work sorting, restacking, adjusting, and stacking again. More than once the pages fell open to reveal a gibberish of foreign letters or symbols, some with drawings and others with maps. How wonderful it must be to be able to read all of these—to have such vast knowledge at one's fingertips. Could one person's head hold all of it?

"There you are." She startled and looked up to see Jack leaning against the doorframe, his arms crossed and dark hair sweeping over his forehead. If she allowed her thoughts to linger, she might admit to thinking him rather handsome. "Buried in the books."

It was true. She'd buried herself so far in she hadn't realized the sun now shone on the opposite wall, and dozens of candles had been lit to accommodate the growing shadows. Six symmetrical and alphabetical stacks of books surrounded her as testament to the loss of time.

"Guess I got caught up in what I was doing." She shifted her position on the floor, and pins and needles prickled down her legs. How long had she been sitting like that? "Where's Philip?"

"Throwing an axe at a tree stump out back."

"Isn't that dangerous?"

"Hamilton is with him." Shrugging off the doorframe, he nudged a few books out of the way and plopped down next to her, turning the book in her lap so he could read it. "*The Odyssey*. The adventure tale to beat all others. Washington has twenty different translations in this library, including the original Greek. A museum in Cairo has been trying to buy it from him for years."

"My father read it to me once. I remember a sea voyage, sirens, and something about pigs." She touched the pages, wishing she could conjure his voice once more.

"If you like adventure stories and fantastical creatures, I've got just the book for you. Wait here." He jumped up and disappeared down one of the aisles, then returned a moment later clutching a large book. He sat and flopped open the pages, then positioned the book half on her lap and half on his, bumping his knee into hers as the heavy book settled on her lap. "This one's about folklore from all over the world. Selkies from Scotland, Valkyrie from Norway, vampires from Transylvania." He flipped more pages. "This is the one I find most fascinating. It's crawling in Eastern European myth."

Ivy leaned closer. Drawn in shades of charcoal were snarling humanlike creatures with their faces tilted toward a full moon. "Nightwalkers."

"Exactly. See right here?" He pointed to a word on the page. "*Ekimmu*. It means 'one who is snatched away.' This account from Sumer is one of the oldest known records of vampires. The spirit was improperly buried and returns vengeful, and over here"—he pointed at another word—"it says they take life from the living. Their victims have no choice in turning into the undead."

"That sounds awful. Not having a choice in becoming a monster."

"All they can do is hope something—or someone—comes along to cure them. Otherwise, it's eternal misery or a stake to the heart."

The illustrations were beautiful and terrifying and tumbled her young mind into unexplored possibilities of a great world far beyond her reach. "I'm glad these are only fairy stories written to entertain children. No one truly believes in undead creatures. In the old days, perhaps, but this is the twentieth century. We've advanced beyond wearing garlic around our necks for protection."

"Stories have to come from somewhere. Who's to say these myths haven't mixed with a little truth? Who's to say some people don't still wear garlic around their necks or carry a toothpick-size stake?"

A smile played at her lips. "Is this your way of confessing that you carry a toothpick stake?"

"No." He ruffled the page edges. Scratches and cuts marred his knuckles. He leaned toward her and nudged her shoulder. "But if I did, would you still sit next to me?"

Her heart lurched strangely and warmth filled her chest.

"Maybe if you promise not to poke me with it." She'd spent all day in the library enjoying the peaceful quiet as the hours slipped by, but Jack's presence tethered her to a kindred spirit eager to share the excitement of a world bursting with color and life. A tether she rather enjoyed.

"I would only brandish said toothpick in defense of your honor, my lady."

"Then yes. I'll sit next to you, kind sir."

"Good." Dimples bracketed his mouth in a display of pure charm. Color and life indeed.

A shadow fell across the pages. "Why are you two in here looking at books?" Philip circled around in front of them, his eyes bright, though not from literary excitement. The outdoors and exercise had pinked his thin cheeks, and sweat dotted his sand-colored hairline.

"Come on, Jack. You promised to show me that grappling move before supper. Besides, Ives likes to be alone sometimes. She's always saying people can be exhausting."

Not in this case. "I don't mind the company."

Jack glanced at her, the dimples around his mouth deepening, then back to Philip. "I'll show you tomorrow."

Tomorrow. They may not be here tomorrow. The contentment she had felt fizzled with the harsh necessity of reality. Ivy closed the book and pushed it off their laps. The enjoyment had to come to an end sometime. "Philip, we need to talk."

Philip rolled his eyes. "I know exactly what you're going to say, because you've got that look that says you're about to pop a bubble. That we don't belong here and we need to return to the Hill. It's dangerous here and we're in over our heads." He reached out a hand and pulled her to her feet, then eased them away from Jack and lowered his voice. "Don't you see? Things are happening here—exciting things—things we can be part of instead of living in the gutter and hawking newspapers for the rest of our lives. Stop worrying so much, cluck-cluck, and take a chance."

She made a face. "I hate it when you call me that."

"If you didn't act like a worried little chicken all the time, I wouldn't." He gripped her shoulders and held her gaze. A seriousness unaccustomed to lingering in his expression now creased his face. "You want something different in life. I know you do. This is it. This is our chance."

His words struck a match and simmered into a blazing brightness. She dropped her voice to match his. "Are you certain they aren't setting us up as target practice?"

"If that was Talon's intention, we already would've painted a big red *X* on both of you." Jack had stood and was watching them, not showing the least bit of shame for eavesdropping. Rather hypocritical considering he'd accused them of such not twenty-four hours before.

If he was going to be up front, then so was she. "Will you tell us precisely what Talon is? The earthlier bits beyond the stars, that is."

A smile ghosted Jack's face at the reference to their conversation the previous night. "You saw for yourself what we do—yesterday under that bridge. We strive to keep the balance of good outweighing the bad."

"But how did Talon form? How many of you are there? Where do you—"

"Do you always ask so many questions?"

Philip rolled his eyes. "Yes, but beware. She's only getting started."

Why was she the only one concerned about the gravity of this proposition? "When I'm trying to decide my future and whether or not to join a secret organization, yes, I believe asking a number of questions is more than appropriate."

"All of which will be answered in due time. For now, you have a test set before you."

Caution snagged her. "What kind of test?"

"Whether or not you can stomach the meatloaf for dinner. It's the least prized meal on our menu. If you can shovel it in and keep it down, we'll know you're ready for the real work ahead." His grin fully formed.

The grip of caution loosened. He made it too easy. She even found herself returning his smile. If meatloaf was the key, she would eat it with aplomb. She glanced longingly at the books surrounding her and the adventurous worlds they offered. The answers and knowledge within their pages.

Jack plucked her sleeve. "We can come back after supper and find the story of the Ice Queen. It's said she builds an icy castle every year on the surface of a lake, but it melts away when the warm days come. Every year she has to rebuild with sharper icicles."

With that promise, Ivy allowed herself to be swept to the dining room filled with savory scents. Tomorrow would be soon enough to worry about what came next, but before the world could pluck her back into its grim reality, she had a story to read.

FIVE

MAY 1914

JACK HEARD THE SHOUTING BEFORE HE ROUNDED THE CORNER. BEFORE
he saw anything, he knew the cause. Slipping past one filthy wet alley
to another, he followed the clangs and grunts that could only come
from a street brawl. He ducked around an overflowing dumpster to
find Philip squaring off with two boys around Jack's age dressed in
rough clothes, scuffed shoes, and bowler hats. A row of trash cans was
tipped over behind him.

"Told you if we ever saw you 'round here again, we'd break both
your legs," sneered one of the boys in a faded red shirt.

Fat drops of rainwater leftover from the storm slithered down
the drainpipes and pooled at their feet. The pungent scents of wet
cement, rotting garbage, and mildew hunkered low in the air.

Shorter than his bullies, Philip inched back across the slick
cobblestones. The wall of a building hemmed him in. "If I'm
crippled, you'll be seeing a lot more of me on account of me being
unable to walk away. Kinda defeats the purpose." His eyes darted
around. The only escape was back down the alley, and the goons
were blocking it.

"You always had more hot air than brains," jeered the other boy with frayed trouser cuffs. "Any brains you do got we're gonna beat out of you."

"Seeing as the numbers are odd, you fellas mind if I join in? Just to even things up." Jack strolled out from behind the dumpster and stood loose-hipped with his hands in his pockets.

"What are you doing here?" Philip peered between the bullies at Jack.

"Looking for trouble apparently."

"Scram. This don't concern you none. 'Less you want to lose a few teeth." Red shirt pulled a ring of brass knuckles from his pocket and slipped it over his fingers. He flexed them menacingly at Jack. "Beat it."

Grinning, Jack rocked back and forth on his heels. Amateurs. "I'll take my chances."

"You asked for it." Growling with warning—had these runts never been in a fight before?—the boy rushed him, brass knuckles aiming straight for Jack's teeth.

At the last second, Jack twisted and the fist sailed straight past him. He stepped back in and punched the boy in the stomach. His bowler hat landed in the gutter. The other boy came charging, but Philip caught his jacket and yanked. The boy jerked back swinging and knocked Philip in the jaw. Philip stumbled, tripped over his own feet, and fell. Blood trickled from his lip.

"Get up!" Jack ducked as his own attacker threw a wild punch. "Spit it out and bare your teeth. Don't go down without a fight."

With half a laugh, Philip swiped his cut lip against his sleeve. "You might want to pay attention to your own fight." He sprang to his feet and boxed his opponent's ears.

Jack ducked and dodged, allowing his assailant a good fifteen seconds to swing and make a general fool of himself before ending the fun with a solid right hook that split the boy's lip. He spun and hit the ground spitting out blood. A tooth clattered across the cobblestones and plopped into a puddle.

Philip gave an impressed whistle. "Say! That was some move. You'll need to teach me sometime."

"As long as you show me how to box an ear like that." Jack nodded to the boy clutching his ear from Philip's blow.

"You boys have enough good sense to get out of here now?" He picked up the hat and smacked it against the brick wall to uncrimp the brim. Then he tossed it onto the boy's back where he still hunched on the ground. "Or do I need to loosen a few more teeth first?"

After spitting again, the boy wiped his bleeding mouth on his sleeve and stood. He jammed his hat atop his head and scowled. "Stay off our street."

Jack nodded and tucked his hands back in his pockets. "I'll be sure to do that. Take your friend with you. He doesn't look so well."

The friend was doubled over with blood dribbling from his broken nose. Philip stood over him, hands curled into fists and triumph smirking across his face. With a few more threats and insults, the bullies stumbled out of the alley, leaving only splotches of blood in their wake.

Philip whooped. "Did you see that? Those two have had it out for me for years after me and Ives stole their newspaper corner. We always managed to dodge them, but they were waiting for me today. Bet they didn't expect to have their lunch served to them on a fist."

"Your footwork is sloppy."

Philip snorted. "That's all you have to say? After a good brawl and victory in our favor, all you can comment on is my feet?"

"A month of sparring and you still move like a cinder block. We'll work on that during training tomorrow."

"Come on! I know you like a good scrap. Don't tell me you didn't enjoy it." Philip threw a mock fist at him.

Jack ducked, unable to stop the smile flickering to the edge of his mouth. "All right. I enjoyed it. Happy?"

Philip whooped again.

"If it was fisticuffs you were after on this drizzly afternoon, why come all the way back to the Hill? We could have sparred at Talon or gone to the Steel Ring."

"Don't get your dander up. I wasn't looking for a fight this time. Why did you follow me?"

"You ran off without a word looking like you didn't want anyone to follow, which gave me no choice." Jack glanced down at his shoe and frowned at the new scuff mark thanks to that lumbering hooligan. "I just polished these yesterday. For that you owe me an explanation."

In answer, Philip picked up a satchel that was bunched up behind the dumpster, then climbed up the sagging fire escape. At the top of the third story, he ducked through a broken window and disappeared. Jack hurried after him and emerged into what was once the city's bread factory. Gray light drooped through holes in the roof while fat raindrops slithered down the fallen ceiling beams and plopped onto the warped floorboards.

Philip was scurrying across the large space dotted with moldy worktables, the scent of yeast still clinging to them. He stopped to kneel in the far corner and pried a loose brick from the wall, then began stuffing the hidden contents into his satchel.

Jack inched closer for a better look. Wadded newspapers were covered in burlap sacks for a makeshift sleeping pallet. A small frying pan that looked like it had fallen off a wagon and been trampled hung on a nail in the wall next to an equally dented cup. A few postcards had been carefully stacked at the baseboard—Ivy's if he had to guess based on the selection. One featured a fashionably dressed lady and another a drawing of a cherub-cheeked family picnicking in front of a white house complete with smoking chimney and porch swing.

A yearning, long buried deep inside him, or so he'd thought, flickered to life. Jack had held dreams once of just such a home and family smiling around him. With his lot in life, he'd confined such dreams to simply that—imaginings never to be gained. But it seemed Ivy still held hope for much the same. The longing flickered brighter. Knowing someone else wished for a similar dream was enough to make him feel not quite so alone.

"You lived here," he said quietly.

"Home sweet home." Philip tied the satchel and stood. His face was smooth with indifference, locking behind it a weight of meaning. "Or was. I only came back to collect a few things. Ivy didn't want to leave behind the ribbon her father gave her, and me"—he hitched the satchel onto his shoulder—"well, just a few personal items is all."

Despite the look of indifference, Jack heard and recognized the tightness in Philip's voice. The strain of appearing carefree, all while tempering a loneliness that never seemed to end and was forever overlooked. Jack knew what it meant to hold on to one thing with all his might simply because it was the only thing in life he could control. One thing that still belonged to him after life had dealt its cruel hand—a hand just as brutal as the one dealt to Philip.

Jack tugged off his cap and scratched a hand through his hair. "I came to the city with little more than a photograph I'd torn from a magazine of the Gulf Shores beaches and a comb I won at the fairgrounds when I was six. Had nothing to eat, but I wouldn't have parted with those treasures for a king's feast."

"Still have them?"

"The photograph, yes. The comb got a bullet lodged in it when I was shot while jumping off a train in the Alps. My would-be assassin tried to shoot me from behind and hit my back trouser pocket instead. My hair hasn't looked right since."

Philip gaped at him. "What were you doing in the Alps to get shot at? Chasing down anarchist mountain goats?"

More like Italian narcotics dealers. "Something like that." With a final scratch through his hair, Jack plopped the cap back on his head. "You all done here, or do you need help digging out anything else before we head back to Talon?"

A sad wistfulness washed over Philip's face as he looked around the space. "I hated this place for so long. Cold in the winter, always wet, and smells like food gone bad." Hitching his satchel, he walked across the floor. "Part of me might miss—" The floor caved beneath him.

Jack lurched toward Philip, who clung to a floorboard held in place by a single nail.

The wood groaned as the nail slipped out.

Philip's feet dangled over a two-story drop.

"I've got you!" Jack grabbed Philip's arms and yanked him up.

Philip collapsed on the floor, dazed and breathing hard. "I've w-walked . . . across these fl-floors . . . hundreds of times. They've n-never . . . done that before."

"Gets the blood pounding even more than a good ol'-fashioned alley scuffle."

Grinning, Philip pressed a hand to his chest. "You can say that again."

Laughing, Jack clapped him on the shoulder and stood. "Come on. Let's get out of here."

"Back to Talon?"

"No, the Steel Ring. I think we've earned the right to watch other men get bloody noses." Jack held out his hand.

Philip grasped it and bounced to his feet. "I couldn't agree more, brother."

The Washington Times

JUNE 28, 1914

SERB STUDENT ASSASSINATES ARCHDUKE AND HIS DUCHESS

Fired several shots, all of which lodged in vital parts, and Francis Ferdinand of Austria and Sophie Chotek, his Morganatic wife, were found to have been killed instantly.

SIX

July 1914

"How awful." Ivy closed the newspaper with its terrible headline.

GREAT BRITAIN DECLARES WAR ON GERMANY

"Men sent off to kill each other all because of an assassinated Austrian archduke."

"That new gas combination of sulfur dichloride with ethylene is being sent straight to the front and will do the work of a thousand bullets," Franklin muttered matter-of-factly. The chemistry and physics instructor raised two beakers of bubbling liquid to the light shining through the classroom's window. "Or it will, once it's stabilized in the organic compound of sulfur mustard. It causes nasty blisters on the skin and in the lungs. The enemy will be vanquished in no time."

"I doubt that brings much comfort should the enemies use it first," Ivy said, watching the man's movements.

"What?" Franklin's head popped up from behind the beakers, his wild gray hair scrambling every which way except to cover the bald spot on the very top of his head. "Oh yes, terribly tragic. Now back to our lesson. Tell me which of these will achieve combustion faster

THE BRILLIANCE OF STARS

when I add the sodium nitrate. The barium thiocyanate or sodium hypophosphite?"

"Sodium hypophosphite in a solution of water." Philip, the other half of the class, sat at his desk twirling a pencil. After showing a disturbing talent for explosive compounds, he'd shot to lead position as teacher's pet.

They'd spent four months under Talon's roof and had grown accustomed to the intermingling of chemistry and death on a Monday morning. Four months of biology, grammar, mathematics, languages—at which Ivy was surprisingly adept—etiquette, dancing, and fighting. Studies they had failed to procure in childhood now taught in lightning round. Education before enlightenment, Washington had told them. Enlightenment being answers about Talon.

Ivy cupped her chin in one hand as she leaned forward on the black tabletop, unable to reconcile the birds chirping outside with the newspaper drawing of troops preparing for battle. "Surely it could have been prevented. Did the archduke and his wife not have men protecting them? Someone to give a cry of warning before that madman took aim?"

"I've been working on early warning systems myself." Franklin squinted between the two glass jars, his small eyes magnified behind the smudged spectacles sliding down his nose. "A type of radio transmission through high frequencies on airwaves."

"Those poor children. What will they do now with no mother or father?" Hopefully they'd find a better life than she had when her family was taken.

"Back to the demonstration at hand. If I simply pour a few granules of sodium nitrate into the beaker of sodium hypophosphite like so—"

Ivy jerked from her dismal reverie to the crisis at hand. "No, Franklin! Remember the last time—"

Bang! The explosion cracked the air, rattling the windows. Black smoke billowed around the classroom.

Ivy shot off her stool and made her way through the smoke to the prone figure on the floor. "Franklin. Are you all right?" No blood. No severed limbs. She coughed and wiped her eyes before dropping her cheek to his chest. She couldn't hear his heartbeat over the thumping of her own.

With a mighty wheeze, Franklin jerked upright, knocking Ivy sideways in the process. The ends of his gray hair sizzled black. As if in a daze, he looked around and seemed surprised to find himself on the floor covered in powder and shards of glass. Again. He blinked owlishly behind his half-moon spectacles at Ivy. "You are correct. The compound is explosive."

"Let me help you up." Shaking the ringing from her ears, she slipped an arm around their instructor's ample waistline as Philip joined her and helped haul the man to standing. Several buttons from his waistcoat were missing. Perhaps that accounted for the correlating dents in the wall. Seeing the instructor well balanced on his pudgy feet, she hurried to open a window. The glass had been refitted only last month from an experiment gone wrong. Washington was threatening to forgo glass altogether and use less costly tarps to cover the windows since Franklin's experiments had blown out nearly every pane on the second floor during one demonstration or another.

Philip swept glass shards into a pile with his shoe. "Was it supposed to do that?"

"Heavens, no." Franklin tutted. "It was supposed to have fire."

Thank goodness for small miracles.

Taking out a gold pocket watch, Franklin examined the time. "That's enough for today. We'll continue tomorrow with the components of metal and their melting points. Don't wear wool. Smells like the dickens when it burns."

Leaving the classroom, Philip paused on the third-story landing as Ivy passed him and continued down the stairs. "Where are you going? We're supposed to meet Jack on the roof."

The roof had become their meeting spot. The inside halls of Talon could feel suffocatingly grand with the polished floors and centuries of past members staring down from their paintings at passersby. Open air welcomed them on the roof, and there were no instructors doling out chemical equations or barking about deportment skills. There they could jest and relax, just the three of them.

"Go ahead. I need to duck into the library first. Washington received a new astronomy book from his friend Albert Einstein in Zurich, and it might provide proof for a new constellation Jack and I found." Or at least they liked to think so. They'd met nearly every night for stargazing as he patiently pointed out each cluster and string of galactic light, further enthralling her with the myths that pinned them to the dark heavens.

Entering the library, she found the intended book stacked on a wobbly tower of botanical pamphlets and world religion texts. She hurried to stash her schoolbooks in her room, then climbed the stairs to the roof.

"What about Jefferson and Washington?" Philip stood near the ledge, pacing back and forth. Somehow the probability of falling four stories to his death never cautioned him. "Or any of the other instructors for that matter. Except Franklin; he's too old."

"Their services are better used for Talon's purposes. Whether that's in France or Germany or right here in the States." Jack glanced up as the door swung shut behind Ivy. A smile split his face. "Did you get it?"

"Right here." Ivy couldn't hold back her own smile as she held out the book that still smelled of fresh leather and ink.

He took it, his fingers brushing against hers. In that moment all thoughts of stars, leather, and ink fled from consciousness as her focus tapered to the touch of Jack's skin against hers and the flutter of pleasure it evoked. She'd felt it before when he sat next to her at dinner or asked how her right hook was coming along—a rush of delight at his nearness that made her wonder if he felt it too.

". . . purposes Washington has yet to explain to us." Philip continued a line of conversation that Ivy had missed thanks to Jack's touch scattering her concentration all about the place. "If he sees potential in us, why keep us out in the cold all these months? Is it another test to see how long before we crack?"

Sunlight glinted off Jack's head as he tilted the book to better read its title, and his dark brown hair cast a reddish glow, like polished mahogany. "I'm sure they've seen more than their fair share of men cracking under pressure in the Spanish-American War. Jefferson fought beside Teddy Roosevelt himself at Kettle Hill."

"But war!" Philip jumped down from the ledge and slapped his knee. "A chance to earn glory and a name for ourselves, and there's one booming right across the Atlantic. We could get out of these endless classrooms and sleep under the wide-open sky with real work to do. I'll prove myself on the battlefield fighting off the Hun while Washington twiddles his thumbs about allowing us to join the agency." He fairly glowed with typical boyish enthusiasm for danger.

Ivy didn't share half of his enthusiasm, nor did she mind squashing it. "You slept under the wide-open sky on the streets for years and didn't like it. What makes you think a uniform is going to change that?"

"Because only men wear uniforms."

"Which you're not." He'd sprouted like a weed over the past few months. The baby flesh had given way to more solidified bone structure, but muscle remained elusive to his slim frame. She teased him that the mop of sandy curls atop his head weighed him down more than any amount of muscle could.

"Which I'll be in two years. Jack's already of age. He can put in a good word for me."

Jack slid down the white stone wall to sit, then leaned his head back and stretched out his long legs, balancing the book across his knees. "If you want to lie about your age just to get shot at, you're on your own."

"Don't tell me getting shot has you concerned. You carry a pistol everywhere you go, like every other person in this building—except me and Ives. I bet even Dolly lugs one in her crocheted mittens."

Jack evaded the jab with expert ease. "I only shoot when necessary."

"But you'd fight if America joins the war, right?"

"I'd do the right thing if it came to it, but it wouldn't please me to go out looking for trouble for the sake of glory." Jack flipped the pages open to the table of contents.

"What about for Talon? Surely with a war on the agency's work-load has increased. Keeping the good outweighing the bad and all that."

"War or not, our services are always needed. Evil never ceases its pursuit of the upper hand."

Philip frowned at the general lack of support for his less-than-thought-out plan. "What about you, Ivy? Would you stay here and write us letters every day, or would you put on a Red Cross uniform to help the boys in need?"

"I suppose someone needs to be there to wrap those fat heads of yours." Ivy walked to the rail. Try as she might, she couldn't bear the thought of them leaving without her. Philip was her only family, and now Jack filled a part of her she hadn't known was missing, a piece she had never considered before, yet one he seemed perfectly fitted to. "The other nurses might be fooled into taking pity on you, but a scolding is what you would need for putting yourselves in harm's way."

"Always the mother hen." Philip came to stand next to her and bumped her shoulder. "Come on, cluck-cluck. You know we couldn't do without you."

She bumped him back. "You know I detest it when you call me that."

"Precisely why I do it, cluck-cluck."

Shrugging him off, she aimed a swat, but he ducked out of reach with a laugh. "Stand still, gosling."

"I hate that name."

"Precisely why I use it, gosling. Now stand still."

"And get my ears boxed? I think not. You have a lethal backhand, cluck-cluck, and I won't put myself in the line of fire again if I can help it." Still laughing, he leaped to the door and out of striking distance. "I'm taking my presence where it's more appreciated and out of danger. Like the kitchen."

"If they're smart, they won't appreciate it at all," Jack said.

Attempting another scowl, Philip turned and left, taking the burst of energy with him. Quiet filled the air with only a soft stir of birdsong to break the stillness. With the tranquility came a return of her earlier thoughts of belonging.

She pushed against a loose chip in the rail with her thumb. "What do you think will happen?"

"Cook will probably chase him out with her soup ladle before he gets to the cookie tin."

"With us, I mean. Our purpose with Talon. We've been through four months of geography, deportment, and history but have not a single guess about Washington's intentions for us or how long he'll allow us to remain."

"You remain because you decided to." Behind her, Jack grunted as he stood, then joined her at the rail. "Training the mind is not for the faint of heart. It takes dedication and discipline. What did you think when you witnessed possible treason under that bridge with the Russian?"

"That we shouldn't be there. Disbelief that such traitorous deals are actually made. Anger at the betrayal."

"And when Jefferson wanted to shoot you for everything you'd witnessed?"

Ivy curled her hands over the rail, the stone worn smooth from years of snow, rain, and wind. All these years on her own she thought the harsh elements had worn her down, but that morning under the bridge had sparked something new and untested within her.

"I've never been so scared in all my life. Not even when my family died. That was a different kind of fear, mixed with sadness and grief. This time . . . I was outraged at a stranger taking it upon himself to decide the outcome of my life, as if I were nothing more than a pest to be destroyed. I never want to feel so helpless again."

"If Jefferson had turned out to be a spy plotting the downfall of millions of innocent citizens, could you have pulled the trigger on him?"

Would she have? Could she have taken a life? Not an innocent one, but a life all the same. "I don't like people who think they can get away with harming others to their advantage."

"Which is why you jumped on my back and choked me when I went after Philip. I had the advantage, the height, the training, and yet you didn't hesitate to do what was right." Jack slowly turned her to face him. His thumbs gently rubbed the corners of her shoulders, sending delightful sensations skittering down her arms. "What you did was incredibly brave."

At the time, she hadn't thought beyond instinct. "I didn't feel brave."

"Maybe not, but it's not about how we feel. You didn't let being scared paralyze you when someone you cared about needed help, and that's what matters. Bravery is about standing up and going forward in spite of fear."

A smile tugged at her lips. "That sounds like a quote from Washington."

"The man does like his platitudes, and in this case I've learned he's right. One of my many lessons since coming to Talon." Dropping his hands from her shoulders, he leaned against the rail, gazing over the rooftops. "You'll learn soon enough. I promise."

Would she? Washington claimed to see potential, but each morning she woke up feeling like a fraud. A much more educated fraud these days, but a driftless intruder all the same. "I stayed because I want something different in life."

He stared at her for a long moment as if calculating and weighing his words. He had the bluest eyes she'd ever seen. A rich blue colored with honesty. "You were never meant for the ordinary, Ivy Olwen."

His declaration cracked her heart, the one she had sealed off to keep anyone from growing too firmly attached. Philip had weaseled his way in, but even with him she held part of herself back for fear of losing him. The heartbreak would be too much to endure again. Now here Jack was chipping further into her resolve, challenging her to set aside the fear of loss and allow him closer.

It was a challenge she was not yet ready to meet, but she could offer him one thing.

Her doubts had eased away and into the void crept her own truth. The conviction quaked through her, gathering and building strength until she could deny it no longer. "I would have pulled the trigger. To protect those I love."

His hand brushed hers, the briefest touch, but the contact was like a match striking her skin. "As would I."

They stood quietly, resisting the proclivity to fill their companionable silence with meaningless chatter. The sun slipped below the horizon of trees, blazing their leaves to orange glory in a final salute to the day.

After a lovely supper of roast beef, green beans, biscuits, and cherry pie, Ivy shuffled her full belly to her room with a promise to meet Jack on the roof in an hour to look for the stars in their new book. She pushed open her door and nearly stepped on an envelope that had been slipped under the crack. After leaning over to pick it up, she turned over the cream envelope and stared at the wax seal stamped with an eagle. Her stomach flipped. Talon's eagle. With shaking hands, she broke the somber seal and pulled out a single slip of paper. Bold strokes in thick black ink were written in Latin. Not her favorite language, but one she could decipher without too much stumbling.

Seek and ye shall find. Find and ye shall protect.

Talon's motto. Her stomach somersaulted as she read the note below.

At midnight follow the lights.

SEVEN

At precisely midnight, Ivy's door creaked open loud enough to wake the entire house. She paused to listen. No, the culprit would most likely be her hammering heart. She stepped out into the corridor. A single candle burned at the end of the hall. *Follow the lights.* Follow the lights to what? A picnic? Her death? As far as she knew, only Washington conversed in Latin. He also wasn't known for practical jokes.

When she reached the first candle, she saw a trail of light leading to the bottom of the stairs. The steps creaked beneath her feet as the flames guiding her danced in and out of the darkness. She crossed the entry hall, the golden eagle watching her in silence, his all-seeing eyes privy to the secrets of the night. Each step seemed to double her heartbeat as the silence settled around her, drawing her further into its mystery until at last she stood in a neglected hallway staring at a blank wall of stone.

"Where to now?" she asked the single candle. It answered with a flicker that shadowed the gray stones. Why lead her to a dead end? She picked up the candle and passed it in front of the surrounding walls, hoping to see a door she'd missed. Nothing. It had to be a prank. A setup to make her squirm. But who would—Philip. That little wretch. He was probably laughing at her from wherever he was hiding. When she got her hands on him . . .

She bent over to set down the candle—it would prove useless in beating that boy over the head—and the light caught a screeching eagle no bigger than a quarter carved into the wall of rock. The Talon eagle. Ivy ran her fingers over it. Odd place to put the agency's seal. She pressed it. A lock clicked. Rock scraped against rock and a portion of the wall eased away from her.

Dozens of candles lit a path to a narrow, spiraling staircase sinking toward darkness below.

This was not Philip. These intricacies defied his prank abilities—and his patience.

She looked back down the hallway then again to the stairs beyond the secret door. She'd come too far to go back now. As she stepped through the wall, the air thickened with damp mustiness. The stone steps were worn as she descended farther into the ground, circling lower and lower, as if she were in a medieval castle approaching a dungeon.

What if this *was* a dungeon? Her foot faltered, her heart lurching to her throat. No. Would-be villains didn't quote Latin and lead a fiery trail to darkened cells. That only happened in swashbuckling novels. Talon didn't boast a single swashbuckler in residence.

At last she reached the bottom where a thick wooden door awaited. A scrap of aged parchment was nailed dead center with another message in Latin.

Pass through this door and all will be as before.
To go forward, one must step back
and take a leap of faith.
Seek and ye shall find destiny.

Scratched onto the bottom corner of the paper was a tiny star.

Ivy touched the dried black ink. Jack. She could enter the door and return to what was. Life as an orphan, a nameless street rat selling newspapers to survive. She wanted more than that purposeless existence. She wanted adventure, possibility, and the chance to leave a mark on the world showing that she had chosen to *live*.

Her thumb brushed the star. Jack had promised her the truth, and this was it. He'd known all along what her answer would be.

To go forward, one must step back and take a leap of faith.

She stepped back until her heels bumped into the bottom stair. Nothing. There must be another clue. Grabbing the nearest candle, she held it out to each of the walls, across the floor, and over the steps.

There, right next to her heel, was the Talon symbol carved into the stone step. She pressed it with her thumb. The last three steps slid back to reveal a black hole in the floor.

"Jump!" came a voice from the darkness.

Ivy balked. "Are you mad? I can't see a thing."

"To discover destiny, one must take a leap of faith."

Destiny—or insanity. Which was it to be? Ivy took a deep breath, then sat and positioned herself on the edge of the hole. Looked like it was to be both. Hopefully she would survive long enough to enjoy it.

Before she could convince herself otherwise, she pushed and swung her legs, launching her body into the unknown.

She hit a soft lump.

"Oof."

The hole closed overhead, sealing her in darkness. Then a light flickered in the corner, followed by others in quick succession until she was surrounded by candles in a small rectangular space with walls of stone. Draped in the dimness between two pillars along the farthest wall was the black-and-gold flag of Talon.

Washington appeared in the center of the chamber wearing his best black cardigan and bow tie. Candlelight bounced off his bald head. "I see you got my note."

"Told you she'd jump." Grinning, Jack approached from the shadows and stood next to him. He'd changed from his sparring clothes into spiffed-up dark trousers, a button-down shirt, and a tie. Arms crossed and legs braced apart, he stood as the epitome of a man who'd just won a large bet that had been up for debate not moments before.

Ivy shifted her gaze between the two men, undecided on whether or not she liked the odds. Particularly with the ring of candles. "This isn't the precursor to a ritualistic sacrifice, is it?"

Jack rolled his eyes. "You read too many novels."

"Surprisingly, that's exactly what led me here." Time spent in the library never went to waste. "What did the other door lead to?"

"The garden fountain." Despite the dim candlelight, the shrewdness in Washington's eyes was clear and focused entirely on one thing. Her.

"From now on, there will be no going back, only forward. But first, you must pass through these pillars." He raised one hand to the left and the other to the right, indicating the columns behind him. "One of Principle and one of Liberty. Pillars upon which Talon was created and by which you will serve for the safeguarding of all mankind."

With that cryptic message raising the hairs on the back of her neck, he swept aside the Talon flag and motioned her through the space between the two granite pillars upholding the stones of Talon.

This was it. More than the mysterious note in her room or the trail of candles through the halls; more than conjugating and deciphering Latin or jumping into a magically appearing black hole in the floor.

This was the moment to forever decide her fate. A decision never to be revoked.

A bundle of excitement and nerves thrummed through her as her old life of complacency and scraping to get by faded away, and a new day of possibilities dawned before her.

Her eyes sought Jack's, his reassuring gaze grounding her. *"Carpe diem."*

At his answering grin, she stepped through the pillars, running one hand over Liberty, the other over Principle, and entered the unknown of her new world.

Which looked nothing like the dazzling possibilities she might have imagined as light flooded all around her.

If in the upstairs of Talon lingered the gentleman of old-world charm, belowground manifested the sleek upstart of modern sophistication. The space was cavernous with smooth, white-washed stone walls that curved into an arched ceiling. Electric lights buzzed overhead while dozens of lamps, sparkling with Edison bulbs, perched on a row of orderly metal desks. Telegraph machines stood neatly behind them like soldiers awaiting orders from the one telephone with a rather extraordinary handset that could be pressed to the ear and curved to the mouth simultaneously.

Maps of all shapes and countries added splashes of color to the otherwise monochrome setup. Tiny flags of varying designs and colors pinpointed cities and landmarks and were connected by cobwebs of slender white thread. The remaining space was given to racks of guns, swords, and every other imaginable weapon. A world as foreign to Ivy as the moon.

Washington walked ahead of her and slowly turned with arms out wide. "Welcome to Talon, Miss Olwen."

Ivy blinked at the enormity of it all. Perhaps she *had* been reading too many novels. "This is . . ."

"Overwhelmingly modern. I agree; but we must accommodate the changing of times if we are to remain in top working order. Our first headquarters was under a public house in Alexandria, then a sprawling estate donated by the Lee family just outside of Leesburg, but it was razed during the Civil War, and finally Talon relocated to DC—cramped among the cement and the tourists." He frowned as if longing for the wood panels and towering stacks of dusty books from his library. "Personal preferences aside, Talon must always move forward and stay ahead of the times. Our missions would never succeed if we advanced into the fray armed with muskets and sabers, though if you find yourself in a pinch, we have an excellent selection of cavalry swords in the front sitting room upstairs."

"I was going to say marvelous. Under all those stately floorboards and chandelier-lit rooms is an entire arsenal. All these months of what I thought was training upstairs . . . I barely scratched the surface of what exists down here."

"Did you think we would give you the key to the front door on the first day without testing your mettle upstairs first? Talon is neither a collection of odd personalities nor merely an arsenal." He settled on the corner of a desk. "Our history is deep and rich. It is part of your history now, too, and there is no better way to determine where we are going than to understand where we came from.

"In the wake of our glorious Revolutionary War—during which France came to America's aid—bloody uprisings swept the streets of Paris. France called upon America to return the favor of aid, but the United States said no, apologizing that we were too busy setting up our own fragile nation to spare the manpower. President Washington, however, could not leave the good French people to struggle when so many had fought for his own country. He could not refuse to help when it was the right thing to do. But how could he extend aid when his own government tied his hands?

"The solution came from Benjamin Tallmadge, George Washington's spymaster, who encouraged Washington to set up a paramilitary group that operated outside of the uniformed rank and file and without the government's knowledge. Thus, Talon was born. The United States Army must play by the government's rules, but Talon's course is set by our own discretion. When a country's government fails to send their army or extend aid to the defenseless, that is when we step in. Whatever is required to ensure that good outweighs evil.

"Diplomacy is bogged down in red tape and political jockeying. We are the knife that cuts through all of that."

Jefferson stepped from a shadowy doorway, followed by Franklin and a few other instructors. The latter two wore smiles of welcome. Jefferson seemed unable to decide between grudgingly acknowledging her and booting her out.

"Talon's sole mission," Washington continued, "is to protect innocent life and preserve peace against evil. We go anywhere in the world to root out malevolence and destroy it. We live and die by the motto: 'Seek and ye shall find. Find and ye shall protect.'"

Ivy's brain whirled to catalog the flood of information. Revolutions and covert missions filed next to the slots allotted to fighting and dance lessons. A secret association like the mysterious Masons or the historical Society of the Cincinnati. It was like opening a book to a magical world and stepping into its pages.

"Talon has been running for nearly two hundred years?"

"One hundred and thirty-one, to be exact, despite being disbanded after bringing aid to the French Revolution," Washington said. "George Washington imagined Talon as a one-time-use agency, but Tallmadge was clever enough to foresee the need for our skills beyond that and kept us running. He also made several smart investments and funneled them into a discreet account for our weaponry and travel funds, an account we still use today. With the gathering financial interest over the decades from those investments, we have managed to expand and outfit our operation with the newest technology, weapons, and training facilities available. The money also enables us to live quite independently on Massachusetts Avenue among the swells."

Hamilton, the youngest of the instructors, moved into view.

"Talon's mission and legacy have been passed down through the years as each new generation is trained to take on the mantle of responsibility, but only after they excel in crucial education." He rubbed the tip of his immaculately curled mustache. He was so fond of it that he slept with a silk mask so as not to disturb the style, or so she'd heard. "Aptitude must be proven. Only then will the candidate be asked to join Talon."

All these weeks and months—not merely the meatloaf—had been a test unto itself.

"And if aptitude is not proven?" Ivy asked.

Patting his mustache, Hamilton pulled out a desk chair and straddled it. The lightbulb above his head gleamed against his perfectly oiled curls. "You would not be here otherwise."

The admission of approval swirled golden and warm in her chest along with a sense of worthiness too long denied her grasp. Yet before she could tuck it away, hesitation wriggled its cold fingers of doubt. Of its own accord, her gaze slid to Jack, who smiled encouragingly.

"You said Talon's purpose is to ensure that good always prevails and victory is achieved no matter the cost or avenue, but should the cost not also be taken into account? How much damage is too much to continue justifying the end result?"

"In order to be the light, we must at times adopt the cloak of darkness," Washington said. "We become what we need to be, balanced by our pillars of Principle and Liberty, to champion the oppressed. Our darkness, when required, is neither wholly good nor wholly bad. It simply is. It is what it must be, and we do not stop until the mission is complete."

"But are there never causes or pursuits that go too far, that you question the rightness of?"

He clasped his hands behind his back and moved closer to her until the toes of his boots touched hers, forcing her to tilt her head back to look up at him. "My dear, you possess an inquisitive mind.

Talon's purpose is sacred, and we will defend it to the death. We go as far as required to ensure peace. Do you understand?"

She glanced at the guns behind him. Their message clearer than any broad-stroke explanation given. Perhaps next time she should weigh her doubts silently. "I believe I understand. I merely asked out of curiosity."

"Curiosity killed the cat," Jefferson muttered.

Washington's intense stare didn't waver from her upturned face, seeking and divining and confirming what he sought. "Questions should only be asked if you are prepared for the full truth. Now it is time for the oath. Are you ready?"

"H-here?" Her insides quivered like the plucked string of a violin, vibrating through her body until every nerve jittered.

He raised a single dark eyebrow, breaking the severe smoothness of his forehead. "Would you prefer we dimmed the lights and burned incense while chanting in Latin for a more atmospheric touch? Franklin can find you a black robe if that will help ease you into the spirit of solemnity."

Her whole life had crawled by in a series of grief and misfortune, existing outside of any circles of inclusion, until the day she came to Talon. Then the days had perked with meaning, and now the seconds raced her toward purpose. "No, thank you. I'd rather see precisely what I'm stepping into. No smoke and mirrors needed."

"I don't mind a bit of pageantry now and then, but the whole skull-and-bones formality and druidic robes are truly beyond the pale," Washington said as he accepted the offered book from Franklin and held it out to Ivy.

A reverent hush passed over the silent witnesses of stones and weapons surrounding them. How many ceremonies such as this had they stood testament to? How many spoken vows slipped between their cracks alongside the decades' worth of mortar? Until this moment she hadn't realized how much she wanted to add her own declaration to the construction of something greater than herself. To leave behind a legacy of hope and perseverance. Of protecting those too weak to help themselves.

Ivy moved to place her hand on the book and paused. It was old with the gilded lettering nearly rubbed off, but enough still showed to read *The Adventures of Peregrine Pickle*.

"It was all they had to swear on at the first oath taking. Straight from General Washington's private library," Washington whispered. Clearing his throat, he raised his voice to a stately level. "Repeat after me."

Ivy placed her hand on the book. "I, Ivy Olwen, being of sound mind and stern constitution, do solemnly swear to uphold the values and objectives of Talon. To protect life and preserve peace against threats foreign and domestic to the best of my ability and with the sacrifice of my life if called upon. So help me God."

Washington beamed. "Welcome to Talon, Agent Olwen."

Applause erupted, thundering off the rounded ceiling as Talon agents, nearly twelve in all, poured in from the hidden recesses to congratulate her.

"Well done," Beatrix said as she waltzed past, her red hair coiled in a perfect chignon. "I've been the only female agent here for some time. Hope they weren't trying to even the numbers by bringing in just any tattered skirt."

Ivy smiled stiffly. "Beatrix. Always a pleasure."

"Ivy!" Philip's arms encircled her from behind, and he swung her off her feet. "We made the team!" Laughing, he released her. With the amount of pride radiating from his face, he'd grown ten feet tall since she'd last seen him.

Ivy tried to catch her breath, but the excitement beating in her chest like eagle wings made it difficult. "When were you sworn in?"

"Tonight, same as you. Imagine if I'd let you pull us away from that bridge. We'd never know this was here."

Ivy twisted her head around to take in the room and the secrets it held. Secrets she would now be entrusted with. "I'm amazed, to say the least. All this history . . . All this service done in secret."

"Shame about that. People should know who's protecting them. Still, I can't wait to start on the real training. All that upstairs book-work is fine for an education, but have you seen what they teach down here?"

"I can wager a guess."

He grabbed her arm and yanked her toward the racks of weapons. Smugness emanated from his brown eyes as if he owned every last one of them. "Sharpshooting, map reading, covert occupation, sabotage, explosives. Speaking of which, how did you pass the test? You don't know how to dismantle a bomb."

Ivy dared to touch one of the smaller guns that looked sizable enough for a lady's handbag. The enormity of what she'd just given her life to and what she might be called upon to do someday settled deep, knitting into her marrow. "What test? And what bomb?"

"The test before they dropped you down here. I had to disassemble a bomb before the fuse blew."

Ivy's fingers slipped, knocking the gun from its rack. She caught it before it clattered to the floor. "You were nearly blown up?"

"To be fair, the fuse wasn't attached to anything on the other side of the wall. You were perfectly safe." Jack sauntered over and propped an elbow atop a stack of crates labeled 'Cartridges.' "Nothing like working under pressure to focus the mind. And you set a new Talon record."

"Thankfully I wasn't threatened by fake explosives," Ivy said. "I merely had to work out a riddle in Latin."

"Oh, 'merely.' So says teacher's pet." Philip made a face at her and circled around the weapons rack, picking up a gun here and touching a grenade there.

Jack took the grenade from him and plonked it back among its deadly friends. "The tests are individually designed to each recruit's strength. No two are the same."

"What was yours?"

"I had to shoot a moving target at fifty paces in the dark while being shot at." Jack made it sound like an everyday occurrence, like he wasn't the least bit bothered by it. "Earned me the sniper position."

Grenades, snipers, and secret wars. A whole new world had cracked open on her once-empty horizon—a world of eclectic spies and assassins she now belonged to. Ivy moved to an adjacent bookcase and scanned the rows of books. *The Art of War. Geo-Political Maps of Eastern Europe. Blades and Bullets: A Model for Self-Defense.* Unsurprisingly, she'd found none of these in the upstairs library.

Jack joined her at the bookcase. "I knew you'd find your way here eventually."

"Books are forever calling to me. Seems I'll be switching from fairy tales and Dickens to"—she picked up a hefty tome and read the spine—"*Anarchist Occults Through History.* That's a page-turner if I've ever heard one."

He leaned closer, his shoulder brushing hers. She caught the scent of soap and clean cotton. "I meant to the underground of Talon. You have something I've never seen in anyone."

Pride tinged his voice, stirring a flutter in her stomach. The desire to press her shoulder to his, to believe that perhaps he meant more than—

"Enough with the books." Philip came up behind Jack and threw a punch at his ribs.

Jack blocked it at the last second and stepped into a defensive stance as Philip threw another. "The first lesson will be teaching you how to jab."

"Any fault in my lack of skills is due to you. You're the one who's been coaching me in boxing."

Ducking a wild blow, Jack swerved and landed a light fist to Philip's stomach. "I went easy on you, kid. Time for the hard lessons now."

"About time, old man." Philip laughed and went at him again.

Washington walked by and clapped to cease the growing rivalry. "You'll have plenty of time to learn proper fisticuffs, along with the improper ones that often prove more effective. For now, it's time to rest. Training begins at dawn."

Once Washington was out of earshot, Philip whispered to Jack, "I'll grab my things and meet you out back."

Jack nodded. "The ring opens in ten minutes, and if we're late we'll be standing in the back. Again."

"Standing in the back of where?" They were up to no good, and Ivy wasn't about to be left out. Those two had grown thick as thieves, chasing after excitement that usually involved explosives and daring to see how far they could tempt death. It was a shared brotherhood she had no desire to join. Most of the time.

"Never you mind, cluck-cluck." Grinning, Philip pinched her on the cheek. "Go to bed like a good girl."

"Either tell me now or I'll find out on my own, and I doubt you'll like how I go about it."

The boys exchanged a look. Jack crumbled first. "The Steel Ring."

"The boxing hall?"

"Shh!" Jack put his hand over her mouth and hustled her behind the stack of crates. He loomed over her in the tight space, though not uncomfortably so. "It's supposed to be off-limits to everyone except the instructors on training nights."

"Then why are you going?"

"Because it's where the best fights are. And before you ask or demand, no ladies allowed."

Philip snickered. "At least not the respectable kind."

Jack sent him a quelling look before turning back to Ivy with the barest amount of apology in his eyes. "Another time we'll take you. Promise."

They scurried away, the imps, laughing and jockeying one another as their night of fun and adventure began without her. Resisting the urge to sneak out after them and teach them a lesson on the error of leaving behind a fellow agent, Ivy started to leave through one of the various doorways with the rule-following agents. She spotted Washington gathering a load of books under his arm.

Joining him, Ivy handed him the last one. *Battle Strategy: The Culminated Years of Alexander the Great.* "Has that Russian been caught yet?"

"No, but a recruit of his was. A Georgetown man sympathetic to a Russian revolution." Washington paused a heartbeat before adding the book to his load. "After the failed attempt with Jefferson, the Russian has been moving around DC in hopes of finding other traitors to his cause."

"What happened to the Georgetown man?"

"He was questioned and executed. Now get to bed. You have weapons assembly at zero eight hundred hours, and Hamilton makes you run laps if you're late."

New York Herald

SEPTEMBER 1916

TANKS TURN THE TIDE ON THE SOMME

Little ground has been gained on either side since the offense began in July. Introduction of new metal machinery strikes fear in Hun hearts.

EIGHT

October 1916

ARROWS FLEW PAST HER LIKE A SWARM OF BEES ON THE ATTACK. IVY DOVE forward and rolled across gravel, narrowly missing the arrow intended for her skull. In one smooth motion she rose to bent knee, then nocked her own arrow, aimed for her target while drawing back the taut string, and let it fly.

The arrow struck a tree trunk dead center.

"You call that shooting to kill?" Laughter reached her from behind the tree.

"Quit hiding and I'll show you how accurate it is." Ivy nocked another arrow, its fletch of feathers soft against her cheek as she pulled back the string.

Nothing moved. Not the air, not a leaf, not her target.

"What good is boasting about accuracy when you've yet to hit me?" Smug devil. An arrowhead to his Achilles' heel would knock that arrogance straight out of him.

"Just waiting for the opportune moment."

"Opportune moment? What does that look like? You want me to come out with raised hands and lie flat on the ground? That's the only way you'll nick me."

A blur shot out from behind the tree. Ivy's arrow flew at him. It sailed through the branches of the bush he dove behind.

"Good try. You grazed my elbow. I might have to get this shirt patched now."

Shifting her weight from her crouched position behind a rock, Ivy tucked a loose strand of hair behind her ear. A braid would've been easier than the wrapped bun, but she'd had the hanging plait used against her one too many times. A good tug on her hair was one of the best ways to physically cripple a woman.

"It's an ugly shirt anyway."

"So says the lady in khaki—the most unattractive color in the spectrum."

Her black training outfit had suffered a series of burn holes recently when she hadn't ducked in time for an explosion. She'd been forced to wear the khaki in its place. Normally she'd be mortified to wear such drabness, but she could hardly suffer that indignity if she were dead. "Not if it helps me blend in."

"Are you so sure it does?" *Thunk.* A knife lanced the ground inches from her toes. "Khaki shoes would've been a better choice."

Ivy's ears tracked the movement of his voice as it inched eastward. Closer. Reaching around to the back of her belt, she unlatched a small smoke grenade. She grinned. "Oh no. That's called distraction."

She pulled the pin and launched the grenade. *Bang!* Gray smoke billowed, gobbling the trees, bushes, ground, and air in its ferocious appetite.

Peeking around the rock, Ivy narrowed her eyes against the thickness and waited.

There. A slight cough. The smoke never failed, although this one . . . She inhaled. Why on earth did it smell like vanilla? Why would—*thunk!*

A body slammed into her. She flew backward and landed on her shoulder. Pain crashed down her arm, but she barely had a second to acknowledge it before he swooped onto her, silver knife shining.

She thrust her bow at him and the knife hacked into the wood. She flung both aside, then drove her foot into his stomach and launched him over her head.

Quick as she was rolling to her feet, he was quicker.

"And yet you were the one distracted." Jack grinned. A new blade appeared in his hand, weaving between the swirls of gray smoke. "I suggested the vanilla to Franklin. I knew you'd be too busy thinking about the smell instead of observing your surroundings. Looks like I was right."

Ivy despised the smell of vanilla. Too thick and sweet, it gobbed up her throat like a stuck marshmallow. Snorting out the offensive odor, she slid her trusty blade from its holster and twirled it between her fingers. Scars from old nicks marred the skin between her index finger and thumb. "You talk too much."

"Then let's get on with it, shall we?"

"My pleasure." She struck like lightning. Jack didn't hesitate or hold back as he pummeled her with a series of blows, slashes, and thrusts that drove her back. Using his forward momentum, she sidestepped him and hammered her knife at his neck. He spun and blocked it with one arm.

She whipped the smaller blade from her belt and pressed its sharp tip to his elbow.

"Oh, look. The hole from my arrow." She sliced the blade down, ripping the sleeve all the way to the pale underside of his wrist. Blue veins bulged against the skin. "Not sure that's repairable."

"'Bout as repairable as a broken nose, I imagine." He swung his elbow forward, aiming for her nose.

She ducked, and the hit glanced off her ear. Good thing she'd decided against earbobs for the day. "Didn't you teach me not to inform my opponent of my next move?"

Breathing hard, they circled each other.

"Ah, so you do listen."

"Sometimes, but don't let that encourage your ego."

"Well, if you listened all the time, you'd know I also instructed you not to lose focus for the amateur sake of needing to brag." Jack lunged and hooked his leg around hers and yanked.

The knives flew from her grasp as she hit the ground facedown.

Before she could move Jack jumped on her back and pinned her arms, then lowered his mouth to her ear. "You also wouldn't be losing now."

"Who says I'm losing?" She flung her head back to collide with his nose. Howling in pain, Jack rolled off and Ivy jumped to her feet, panting heavily. A cramp scurried up her side. "Aw. It's not broken, is it? I didn't hear a crunch, but it looks like it hurts."

"Is this payback for me breaking your finger last year?"

Ivy held up her left hand and flexed her pinkie. "It still won't straighten fully."

"Good." Despite his watering eyes and pulsing red nose, he goaded her with a smirk.

Ivy rushed him, swerving at the last moment to get behind him. She latched her arms under his armpits and swung her legs off the ground to loop around his body and throw him onto his back. His feet snaked around her neck and jerked her forward. She landed hard on his chest, driving the air from his lungs.

He flipped them over so her back pressed into the rough ground and pinned her arms and legs with his own.

"Yield." Sweat dotted his forehead and dampened the locks of dark hair hanging over his eyes. "Or have you yet to learn that humbling act since I've been away on assignment?"

She struggled uselessly against his grip. "You don't fight fair."

"Nothing about fighting is fair. It's ugly and dirty and you do whatever it takes to win. One person walks away from a fight.

Make sure it's you." Using his shoulder, he knocked the hair from his eyes, then stared hard into her face. The intense steel blue cut straight through the banter and into her soul.

He'd never looked at her like that. A captor of ferocity and unbending will. "I will always have the physical advantage over you. Use what *you* have."

She was helpless in his grip and iron stare. The aches and pains from training shuddered through her exhausted body, each crying out for relief. Tears welled in her eyes as she twisted to look at the hand clamped tight over her wrist.

"Ow, Jack. You're hurting me."

Horror flooded his face, driving the steel from his eyes. "I'm sorry, Ivy. I didn't mean to." He released his grip on her wrists and leaned back.

She jabbed her finger into the left indention of his neck, jamming into the pressure point. Yelping in pain, he smacked her hand away and forced the full brunt of his weight on top of her.

"Now who's fighting dirty?"

She laughed, but it came out as more of a cough. "Whatever . . . it takes . . . to win," she gasped.

"Oh, is that how it's going to be?" He smiled and adjusted the tiniest bit of his weight off her.

Air trickled into her lungs. "I learned from the best."

Something else flickered in his eyes then. Another look she'd never seen before. The shade of blue deepened, reminding her of the night sky before the stars appeared. Mesmerizing and easy to drown in.

"You haven't learned everything yet." His soft exhale washed over her face, seeped through her skin to sink into her blood, warming it to unfamiliar degrees. Her pulse picked up, and when his gaze drifted to her lips, her heart nearly skipped right out of her chest.

Light flooded them. Ivy blinked as the sudden brightness blinded her momentarily. She slowly focused in on the training room. The smoke peeled back to reveal damp brick walls with water trickling between the cracks from Rock Creek overhead, fake trees and bushes, papier-mâché rocks, and gravel hauled in from a nearby building site.

"Lighten the footwork." Tall and immaculate in his training clothes of black trousers and a white linen shirt, Jefferson strode into the massive chamber with his remarks of improvement. Which he leveled at Ivy without fail. "Next time lead with your right."

Jack sprang to his feet. "She's getting better. I hardly trip over her anymore." He sent a wink her direction. "Unlike the first year of training."

Ivy took a minute longer to recover, whether from the throbbing in her shoulder or the look he'd given her, she couldn't decide. "I've had to slow down so you can keep up."

"She'll need to perform a lot better if she's to be sent on missions abroad. You can't rely on textbook maneuvers in the field with a real enemy," Jefferson muttered.

She took Jack's offered hand and stood. He quickly let go to tighten the suspenders over his shoulders that had loosened during the fight, acting for all the world as if their moment before never passed. Perhaps it hadn't. The running, jumping, and brawling combined with a spiked heart rate from nearly being impaled by an arrow may have twisted her brain to hallucinate the way he'd looked at her. The way a man looked at a woman. Or so she'd read in novels.

She sneaked a peek at him. Utterly relaxed with his complete attention on the death grip Jefferson was explaining. The hallucination didn't seem to affect Jack one bit. Why should it? They were friends. Good friends who laughed together, raced streetcars down Pennsylvania Avenue, kept each other's secrets, and counted the stars together after a long day of pistol target practice. Jack had even renamed a tendril of constellations the Ivy Vine, which he claimed appeared only on her birthday.

A tiny flare of anticipation sparked in her stomach and curled the edges of her mouth. Would he remember to look for it tonight? At present he seemed completely absorbed in an elbow jab demonstration. The flare sputtered. Most assuredly too many novels.

"According to the reports from our agent in France, the fight has taken to the skies," Jefferson said as he examined the arrow stuck in the fake tree. "Last week a French pilot opened fire on Hun aircraft with a machine gun."

"A machine gun on a plane?" Jack picked up Ivy's bow and pried his knife from it. Splinters of wood crumbled at his feet. It was the second bow she'd maimed this month.

"A logical move when a pistol or rifle proves useless up there. A machine gun doesn't require the same accuracy."

Ivy plucked her knives from the ground and slid them back into their leather sheaths strapped to her belt. "Until the Germans start shooting back."

Jefferson's coppery eyebrows lifted as he nodded in agreement. "Precisely. For the time being, aerial assault is not our mode of operation. We have more pressing matters. Washington has called a meeting."

They deposited the destroyed arrows, hacked bow, and unused grenades on the weapons table near the door, then stepped from the chamber and followed the wide corridor past the firing range, explosives lab—where Franklin sequestered himself for hours on end—a few smaller sparring rooms, and a communications hub with dozens of blinking lights, telephones, and transmitters that buzzed at all hours. A left turn and they arrived at the assembly room where a few other agents had already gathered.

It was easily the brightest room in their underground vault with lights that flooded every inch of the white plastered walls and crisp maps that bore the marks of battles past. Harpers Ferry, Waterloo, Trafalgar, Shipka Pass. Significant scars branded into Talon's history.

"This better be good." Philip dropped onto the chair next to Ivy's along the back row. Black powder smudged his cheek and forehead. Must be ammunitions day. "I was about to test a new grenade launcher. Hamilton thinks we can file it down a few inches to better fit into a haversack. Fewer parts for assembly. I told him it's the grenade casing we need to focus on. Lighter weight material would project it a longer distance."

"Beneficial." Ivy nodded as the last few stragglers found seats. The room was full of the ripe scent of warm bodies and exertion. Rarely were they all called in together, and rarer still did it portend good news.

"Not enough to tempt him." Philip scrubbed a hand over his face, smearing the black streaks. The baby softness of his bones had hardened into the determined lines of burgeoning manhood. The gangly gosling was now fit and trim, tall and slender with quick brown eyes and hair that looked like sand darkened under the water. His only lament was the lack of blond whiskers. Tiny patches refused to grow into anything substantially manly. Which she took every opportunity to mercilessly tease him about. "I'll have to build it myself and prove it to him."

Jack dropped into the chair on the other side of Ivy as he rolled up the tattered remains of his shirtsleeve. "I tried that once, thinking I could make Reaper shoot around corners. All I managed was a black eye."

"That's because you're better at shooting that old rifle of yours. Leave the mechanics to me."

"Reaper is hardly old. He's a classic M1903 Springfield."

"There have been weapon advancements. In fact, I've been thinking of launching small propelled grenades from a device that can sit on your shoulder. I'd call it the Stovepipe."

Ivy snorted. "One day the two of you are going to blow everyone up."

Jack and Philip grinned at each other. "At least we won't die bored."

"Quiet down!" Washington strode into the room followed by the other instructors who settled themselves behind a battered table at the front. Claiming the center, he didn't sit but braced his knuckles on the wood. "As of this morning, the United States is under threat."

The chamber crackled as voices clashed over one another. Jefferson rapped his knuckles on the table to refocus attention.

"As I was saying," Washington continued. "President Wilson is determined to keep us from entering the conflict that is currently engulfing Europe. However, there is a threat attempting to force our hand. A great bear in Russia is rumbling for war."

"Wilson's a coward," Philip muttered. "We should go on the defense before they have a chance to attack."

"War with Russia?" Jack spoke up. Heads swiveled his direction. "Sir, are they not fighting against the Germans? They pose no threat to us or those we would claim as allies should we enter the war."

"It is not Russia as a whole that concerns us, but a single man threatening to undo the balance of power and tip the chaos of war to his own favor. Our agent in St. Petersburg has been able to—"

"It's Petrograd," Jefferson said.

"What is?"

"The city. They renamed it Petrograd two years ago to refrain from sounding too German."

Washington's thin lips pinched in disapproval. He never appreciated changing the facts of words to suit common approval. History did not pander to popular opinion. "Our in-country agent has smuggled out several photographs concerning our latest target. Franklin, if you please."

Closest to the light switch, Franklin flicked the button and the room flooded dark. A grainy image flickered on the wall behind the table as the mounted projector warmed up. It was the oldest picture box in the country, well used long before the machines featured in picture houses for common audiences. Then again, Talon was accustomed to having every advancement before the general population could dream of such a contraption.

"This is the symbol of Balaur Tsar, Russia's newest and most dangerous arms dealer." A sepia photograph came into focus revealing a dark flag with a dragon coiled around a crown. "No images of the man himself have been captured at this time, but this calling card is left wherever he strikes."

"How many such calling cards have been left, sir?" Jack asked.

"Three dozen, last reported."

A frenzied murmur rolled around the room. Nearly forty strikes. How many innocents had been lost in the madness?

Washington raised his hand for silence before continuing. "For the past two years he has been quietly gathering raw materials, forging them into weapons, and selling the weapons on the black market. Three months ago he started selling them to army representatives in hush-hush deals that were then processed through legal channels and handed out to soldiers on the front lines. French, German, Russian, criminal, or warlord. The man has no conscience. Profit is the only side of this war he's on, and he doesn't play by the rules."

Philip leaned over. "Lucky for us, Talon doesn't either."

"Unlucky for Balaur Tsar," Ivy whispered back.

"Illusive as smoke, Balaur makes rare appearances and is never in the same place twice, which makes him nearly impossible to track." Washington smoothed the front of his red cardigan. "Each new batch of weapons is tested on an unsuspecting village, which serves to further his infamy and ruthlessness. Next slide." A *click* and a map with Xs all over Russia became visible. "Locations of massacred villages where the various weapons have been tested before going to prospective buyers." A terrible sickness roiled in Ivy's belly as she stared at the black Xs. Entire villages of men, women, and innocent children wiped clean from existence, their bones left to rot beneath piles of rubble.

"Is he testing the weapons by himself?" Philip asked. With a mind made for detonations, he was fascinated by the methods of other enthusiasts. Insane or not.

"He is the mastermind," Washington said, "but he has a group of dedicated followers, many of whom serve as his protection guards. Many of these followers had no interest in joining the army or the revolution and instead turned to more nefarious doings. There is a great deal of money to be made in illegal weapons dealing, particularly with a war on."

Jefferson stood, casting his formidable shadow across the projected map. "In two days a team will be deployed to join our agent, code name Victory, who has been in the country for six years now. The villain must be taken down at all costs before any more weapons are sold. Calhoune"—his gaze roamed over the agents, pausing on Jack. Jack leaned forward, but Jefferson's search moved on—"and Fielding. See me afterward for your new assignment."

Two rows ahead, Calhoune and Fielding ribbed each other in excitement. The lights flickered on and agents rushed to congratulate the pair as they beamed with pleasure. It had been a while since an assassination was ordered, and it was no less than an honor to be assigned.

Meeting adjourned, Ivy, Philip, and Jack joined the group of well-wishers around Calhoune and Fielding.

"Congratulations." Ivy shook Calhoune's hand.

"It's about time Jefferson gave you some real work," Philip said.

Calhoune grinned ear to ear. Built like an ox, he'd broken more than a bone or two in the training ring. If he was captured in Russia, he could simply put his head down and plow through the enemy to escape. "Glad to be out in the field again. Been babysitting politicians for far too long."

Jack offered Fielding his hand to shake. "Keep your heads down and your guns loaded."

"That's what I used to say to you when you started training. Wasn't long before you surpassed us all, despite me and Calhoune having a four-month lead on you." Fielding took Jack's hand. Built as Calhoune's opposite, his mode of escape would be to crawl between the enemies' legs. They'd never notice him.

"I'm grateful for what you taught me," Jack said.

"Sure was jealous when they sent you to Belgium last month, Vale, but Russia is bound to prove just as thrilling. Maybe even more so. This Balaur Tsar sounds like a josser off his onion."

"Put a bullet between his eyes for me," Jack said.

"No one can beat you behind the sniper scope, but I'll do my best."

Jack smiled tightly. There was always a bit of disappointment for an agent when they weren't tasked for the newest mission, but with Jack having just come off assignment it would have been unfair to send him out again before the other agents in rotation.

No one noticed but Ivy. Despite his displeasure at remaining behind, she couldn't suppress the tiniest bit of relief. The thought of splitting from him again was a hardship she'd rather not master. Especially today.

After they filed out of the room with the other agents, Philip stopped next to a pillar supporting the arched ceiling and bent down to tie his shoe. "Sure wish we were assigned to Russia. Or anywhere else in the world. Nothing exciting ever happens stateside."

"We'll be sent abroad when Washington thinks we're ready." So far she and Philip had only been assigned to stateside training practices. Tailing a suspect. Losing a tail. Surveillance. Driving and operating all manner of transport. Being dropped off in the middle of nowhere with no equipment and timed to see who could make it back to the assigned location first. All of the cloak-and-dagger darings they would need in the field, but without the excitement of a real overseas mission. "Looks like Calhoune and Fielding will have to deal with this madman for now."

"He couldn't pick a more original moniker? *Balaur Tsar* hardly takes any imagination when he's from Russia. What does *Balaur* mean anyway?"

"It's a type of dragon from Romanian folklore." Ivy leaned against the pillar. Still warm from practice and the crowded room, her skin sighed with bliss at the relief of cool stone. "Odd that it's combined with the Russian *tsar*. The principalities of Romania and Russia have been in conflict over land and power for the past two centuries."

Shoe tied, Philip stood and combed the three hairs sprouting on his chin as if to make them grow faster. On second glance, it was only two. The other was a powder streak. "This Balaur is a black-market arms dealer. He doesn't care about border squabbles, but he'll be more than interested in the fight we bring to his door. Right, Jack?" Philip threw a mock fist at Jack. "We should head up our own team. We'd be lethal."

Jack stepped aside and let the punch sail by. "We'll stay put until ordered otherwise. I wouldn't mind a trip to Russia though. It's supposed to be beautiful. Civilized and wild at the same time."

"You're better off not going," Ivy said. "You despise the cold. It's the last place you'd want to visit this time of year."

"I don't despise the cold. Merely being out in it." Jack shivered despite his protest.

"How pampered you are. Does Jefferson know you're only fit for Mediterranean assignments? With the war pushing into Africa, you could volunteer your crack shot to keep the sand in line in the desert."

A smile, a real one, tipped his mouth. "That may be too warm for my taste."

She matched his smile. "Pardon me. A nice, temperate climate where no one is too cold or too hot to be angry about anything is the perfect place for you." Actually, it didn't sound too bad for her either.

They could order those drinks with the little umbrellas in them and watch the sun set over blue waters. Share a blanket sitting on the beach perhaps.

Delightful heat brushed her cheeks at the thought. She quickly turned away from Jack's thoughtful gaze.

Climbing a set of stairs, they exited Talon's underground and stepped through a door concealed by a large painting of the War of 1812. As they passed the library, Ivy waved off calls from the books to visit their eager pages and turned into the grand entrance. Gray light filtered through the third-story windows and bathed the hall in drabness.

Philip bundled up the main stairs to the second-floor landing. "Speaking of perfect places to go, we know where we're taking you tonight for your birthday, Ives."

Ivy paused with her foot on the third step and looked between the two of them. "You remembered?"

"Of course we did." Jack came up behind her, adjusting the brace strap over his shoulder. The leather had been cut, loosening its hold.

She eyed his ruined suspender. Cut or grazed by an arrow tip? She must have shot closer than he'd let on earlier. "Last year you were too caught up watching Kid Blackie fight at the Naval Yard to remember it was my birthday. The year before that you forgot entirely."

"We tried to make it up to you," Philip said.

"For the record, baseball tickets were not my idea," Jack offered.

"It was the playoffs!" Philip insisted as if it were the most logical point in the world to make up for missing his best friend's birthday.

She'd lost interest halfway through the game, but they plied her with Cracker Jacks and cotton candy. Her silver lining for the day. "Then I'm doubly impressed you remembered while plotting to assassinate a bedlamite halfway around the world. Silly things like birthdays are easy to forget when there's so much excitement."

"No one could forget you, Ivy."

Jack's words were low enough for only her to hear. A brush to her ears like his shoulder leaning gently into hers. Truth be told, her feelings for him had only grown during their time at Talon. From initial distrust to gratitude for saving her from the streets. A friend to confide in and make mischief with. A partner to spar with, as she sharpened her skills against his own formidable ones. A fellow story lover to share and discuss the books they'd been reading, and a fellow gazer to watch the stars with. Jack knew the secrets of her heart as well as she knew his.

Their gazes met and in his she saw the same intensity that had nearly submerged them earlier. The depth stole her breath, and she had no desire to retrieve it.

"Go get yourself cleaned up. No taking you out if you look like a street urchin," Philip interrupted from the landing. He cast an incredulous eye over her general disheveled state of ripped khaki and tangled hair. "I have a reputation to uphold."

Jack ducked his head and looked away, leaving her to wonder if her imagination was acting up again. The air returned to her lungs with a prickle of disappointment. Then again, standing in the middle of the great hall for all the agency to observe was hardly the place for passion-filled declarations.

Ivy brushed a dried bloodstain on her collar. How did that—oh yes. A grazing razor star from earlier that morning when she and Jack sparred with the Eastern weapons.

"I'll do my best not to embarrass you, gentlemen, but no promises."

She executed a curtsy that would have made Dolly proud, despite the awkward trousers, then dashed to the ladies' lavatory for a quick but thorough scrub with the rose soap she used on special occasions. She buffed herself dry with a fluffy towel until her skin glowed pink. In her chamber she slipped on fresh combinations, corset, petticoat, and stockings. Saving the best for last, she reached into the hanging wardrobe and pulled out her new dress. A silky gown the color of fresh grass with a high lace collar and gentle folds that skimmed the tops of her silver-buckle shoes.

With no small amount of joy, Ivy could now style her strawberry-blonde hair in a woman's fashion with silver and pearl combs. The locks extended halfway down her back these days. No more hiding herself beneath lumpy clothes and boyish haircuts.

A soft knock came at the door before Dolly poked her head in. "Ready for visitors?" Without waiting for a reply, she marched into the room. A warm light glowed on the older woman's face. "My, my. Don't you look beautiful. Turn around—let me see the whole effect."

Ivy turned, basking in the feel of the ladylike material swishing around her ankles.

"That shade of green matches your eyes perfectly. Now, here. I didn't have time to wrap it, but every lady of Talon is gifted one. Every part of your wardrobe should be considered a weapon, particularly the pretty items. No one expects death in the beautiful." She touched an onyx-tipped hairpin securing her own bun.

The gift was a hairpin sharpened to a gleaming point with a smooth pearl teardrop topped by a tiny diamond on the opposite end. Small initials were carved into the pearl: I.O. Ivy cradled it in her hands. "It's beautiful. I'll cherish it always."

"Blind an eye and break glass with this end"—Dolly pointed to the pearl and diamond, then to the sharp tip—"jab and slice with this end. Or pick locks. Handier than a stiletto blade. You have your bully stick?"

Ivy nodded toward the hand-size club poking out of her bag. Small, but the knot on the end left an attacker dazed. "Never leave home without it." Or the pearl-handled Derringer pistol she'd slipped into her garter.

"My dear girl. I can't believe how much you've grown since you came to us two years ago. You'll make us very proud."

She gripped Dolly's hands.

"Thank you, Dolly. You being here means everything to me."

The older woman's eyes glossed over for a second before she shook off Ivy's hands. "Enough of that. Get going before those two beasts come charging up here to get you."

After dabbing a hint of rose-and-crushed-ivy water behind each ear, Ivy skipped downstairs to where Jack and Philip waited by the front door watching the automobiles motoring by. She slowed to allow her gown to move delicately over her hips and ankles as her heels clicked gracefully across the black-and-white tile.

★★★

"Good evening, gentlemen."

Jack turned at the sound of Ivy's voice. His mouth promptly dropped open. He might never be able to describe what fancy dress she was wearing, but he'd never been quite so stunned by the way his heart leapt at that moment. He only ever saw her in training clothes or simple blouses and skirts, but this . . . this was something else entirely.

"If only I had a camera to capture the two of you speechless for once. I never thought I'd see the day." Her bold words were softened by the pink tinging her cheeks. "Well? Will I uphold your spotless reputations?"

"Much better than that hideous tan you had on earlier." Not needing a moment to recover, Philip grinned. He'd changed into a tailored suit of rich chocolate with a white shirt and red tie and looked the part of a smart man about town. "Green's always been your color."

"I'll say." Adjusting his navy tie that matched his own suit of charcoal gray with a blue pinstripe shirt, Jack whistled in appreciation. "Give us a twirl." She obliged, and he whistled again when she completed her rotation. "You'll strike out the stars tonight."

He picked up a round white box from the bench next to the door and handed it to her. "Happy birthday, Ivy."

"I told you not to get me anything," she said.

Philip rolled his eyes. "As if we ever listen to you."

Popping off the lid, Ivy peeled back the crinkly tissue paper to reveal a hat nestled inside. It was made of light gray felt with a brim that tilted up to one side and a green ribbon wrapped around the crown. "How beautiful."

"You said you always wanted a hat with a green ribbon like the one your father promised to make," Jack said. "It doesn't replace the one he might have made, but you deserve it nonetheless."

"You remembered." The green of her eyes darkened, drawing him into a moment that locked out the rest of the world, threading them together in delicate understanding.

"Of course. A special birthday deserves a special gift."

"Unlike the knuckle-dusters we got you last year," Philip added.

Ivy blinked and the private moment with Jack vanished. He wouldn't mind knuckle dusting Philip right then.

"They were thoughtful, but not nearly as darling as this." She plucked the gift from its box and pinned it atop her head at a jaunty angle.

Outside, gas lamps flickered on and orange light pooled on the cobblestones as nighttime laced its way through the streets where Jack led them to an old textile building that had been converted into a dance hall on Georgetown's riverside. As they stepped inside the hall, cigarette smoke drifted between dim lights and hazed around a small bandstand where a rollicking tune played as couples spun around a crowded dance floor.

"Dolly would have a conniption if she saw this." Ivy stretched up on her toes to put her mouth close to his ear. The music nearly drowned her out, but her voice so near sent a thrill through Jack's insides. "She never teaches dancing like this in our ballroom lessons."

Eager to return the intimacy that was only acceptable in a raucous place like this, Jack leaned close for her to hear. "Yes, but in our ballroom, we dance with a gun strapped to our leg. Never know when we'll have to take down a target while keeping step to a waltz."

Ivy looked at him with her entire face beaming and giggled. When she stood this close, her scent of roses teased under his nose. It had nearly driven him to distraction earlier that day in the training room when he thought to overpower her. In the end, it was she who crippled him. One look at those soft lips inches from his own . . . then she'd jabbed her finger in his neck. It hurt like hellfire, but in his book weakness to a woman wasn't a bad thing. Especially not to this one.

"Wrong part of town, gents." A bulldog of a man with a cigar shoved between his spare teeth shouldered his way toward them. "Ain't got no use for bucks in here."

"Who you calling a dandy, you old buffer?" Philip jumped forward and started to peel off his jacket. "I'll give you an anointing with my bunch of fives you won't soon forget."

Jack yanked him back by the collar. He'd had enough brawling for one day. "We don't want any trouble."

"You don't shut him up and you'll be having trouble aplenty." The bulldog chewed on his cigar and squinted at Ivy. "She can stay. We need more skirts."

Ivy crossed her arms and returned his unabashed perusal. "You can put those eyeballs right back in your head. I'm not staying without my friends."

The bulldog took one final lingering sweep of her before shifting the cigar in his mouth. "Suit yourself, sweetheart. Come back another time, but leave the dregs at home." A waiter zipped by, catching his attention. "I told you not to fill those glasses to the top. We need people to order more than one." Shoving them aside, he hurried after the industrious waiter with his loaded tray.

Jack twisted the material bunched in his fist. "Can you for once stop thinking every encounter requires a black eye? Behave. This is Ivy's special night." Releasing Philip's collar with a shake, Jack grabbed Ivy's hand and pulled her along the side wall to the back. "Come on. I've got an idea."

Skirting the bandstand, they rounded a large curtain cordoning off the storage area of bottles, crates, cigarette cartons, broken chairs, and old sewing machines.

"There should be one around here . . . Aha!" Jack tugged her hand. "This way."

If they couldn't celebrate in the hall, he'd take the party elsewhere. Dragging Ivy up a flight of rickety stairs with Philip clomping behind them, Jack stopped at a warped door at the top. The handle was stuck. He rammed his shoulder into the flimsy door and it popped open to a flat roof. The band's next tune swelled up the stairs and spilled into the crisp autumn air.

"Where else can you listen to music with a view like this?" He still hadn't let go of her hand. He didn't dare twitch a muscle lest she realize the continued contact and release him.

She smiled. "It's beautiful."

And it was. The bright piano and floating violin notes cast a magical backdrop to the thousands of lights twinkling from windows spread across town. Out there, ordinary people prepared meals and climbed into their beds for another ordinary day on the morrow. For this night there was no war across the ocean, no raver calling himself Balaur Tsar. Tonight existed outside of all that for something special. Some*one* who had become special to him.

"Enough staring off into the distance. We came here to celebrate." Jack twirled her around. Laughing, Ivy followed his lead and they spun across the rooftop to the rhythm of the music thumping below. She was smooth and light, not merely anticipating his next step but flowing as an extension of his movements with such confidence that they might have been a single dancer. He never wanted it to end.

All too soon the song ended and Jack relinquished his hold on her. He couldn't come up with a good enough reason to keep holding her hand in between songs—at least, not one that didn't make him look desperate.

Philip took the opportunity to shuffle forward and ask for a dance. "Don't let this go to your head. I'm only doing this because it's your birthday."

"I shall enjoy it nonetheless and thank you for your sacrifice in honor of my celebration."

Philip expressed every sentiment but enjoyment. He confused quickness with confidence as he took two steps for every one of hers. Halfway through, her hat loosened from its pin and flew off her head and rolled across the roof. Jack grabbed it and set it safely aside before it nosedived into the alley below.

The song melted into a slow tune, and Philip dropped her hand as if it were poisonous and backed away. "Uh-uh. No slow ones for me."

Seizing the opportunity, Jack slipped in and took her in his arms in one smooth motion. "You don't know what you're missing." He gazed down into Ivy's face. "Best ones in my book."

With the moon winking in and out from behind a bank of clouds, their only light came from the soft golden-orange wash of candles and lanterns in the windows below. It was just enough to see the outline of her face. The details could remain hidden forever; he knew every one by heart. The thick lashes crowding her eyelids, the tiny freckle above her mouth, the small dimples curved into her cheeks when she pressed her lips together.

"I was right." His voice came out low and soft.

"About?"

"You striking out the stars."

Her hand twitched on his shoulder. "I must have hit you harder than I thought this afternoon. All this moonlight has gone to your head."

"Or maybe something else has." Something that had sparked that day he first sat with her in the library, a book across their laps, and his knee bumped hers. Since then, he'd seen her best days and witnessed some bad ones. He admired her determination regardless of the obstacle; he adored her spirit. They shared secrets, fighting techniques, orphan woes, and the acute desire to make a place for themselves in the world. A place to belong. As each day passed, his desire to share that place with her only grew.

His fingers curled around hers and a new sensation pulsed between their skin. He'd touched her hands many times before. Locked together in combat he had felt the calluses on her palms and the thundering pulse in her wrist as she tried to break his hold. She wasn't attempting to break the hold of his arm around her waist now, but this was no fighting grip. He tucked her snugly into the crook of his arm, his hand splayed across the small of her back as if it had every right to be there.

Ivy took a shaky breath. "I-I don't know this song."

"No?" He hummed close to her ear, breathing in her sweet rose scent. "'I care not what the world may say . . . if you were always near.'"

She leaned forward, brushing her forehead against his chin. His heartbeat tripled as he daringly rested his cheek on her hair, and her hand slid from his shoulder to the back of his neck.

All too soon the song came to an end.

"Ivy." He raised his head and eased back enough to find her gaze. "Ivy, I . . ."

She looked into his eyes with absolute trust. His heart twisted. What if he kissed her and ruined their friendship? What if she rebuffed him? Or worse—thought of him only as a brother, like Philip. Was he setting his sights on a target with unrelenting determination and blinding himself to any outcome other than his victory?

Lowering his head, he hesitated for a moment, then pressed his lips to her forehead. The barest of chaste touches. Taking a step back and tucking his hands in his pockets, Jack offered her a tilted smile. "Happy birthday, Ivy."

Lily-livered, gutless coward.

Her expression flashed from surprise to confusion before dropping into a wilted brow. "Oh. Thank you."

Garbage cans crashed together somewhere below.

Jack tensed and scanned the rooftop. "Where's Philip?"

Ivy looked around. More tin clanged, followed by shouts. "The alley."

Jack scrambled down the fire escape and dropped into the alley wedged between the music hall and a grocer's shop. Ivy landed next to him with her hat in hand. Ghostly light tripped down the narrow passage, cast from the street's gas lamps. The stench of rotting fruit, beer, and cigarettes clung to the chipped brick walls as Philip squared off with three chaps who looked perfectly at home in the rancid surroundings.

Of course it was a brawl.

"Get tired of the music?" Jack called. He stood loose limbed, but every muscle in his body coiled in readiness.

Philip shrugged, not the least bit perturbed at the outnumbered predicament he'd wedged himself in. If anything, he was enjoying it. "Came down to see if I could bum a smoke. These fellows have been less than obliging."

"We don't hand over good tobacco to infants." One of the fellows in question leaned forward and puffed smoke in Philip's face.

Coughing, Philip moved to go around them. "I'll forgive the slight. Once. Now, out of my way."

The man puffed more smoke. "No."

"Last warning."

"Or what? You'll wail for Mommy?"

Wrong choice of words to say to an orphan.

Philip's fist landed on the man's jaw. With a meaty *thunk*, his head whipped back. His friends jumped forward and caught him before he went down. Straightening, the man worked his greasy jaw back and forth.

"You're gonna get it now, boy." The man's arms raised in a bare-knuckle fighting stance. An amateur tactic promising more show than skill.

Jack slid between him and Philip. "We're not looking for a fight. Not tonight."

"Is that right? Well, mebbe we are." A second fellow shoved Jack's chest.

Jack's hands curled into fists. He'd worn his best suit and blood was expensive to clean out.

Ivy jumped in the middle of the boiling fray. "No need for tempers getting out of control. Why don't you fellas go back inside and finish your drinks and we'll be on our way."

The third man wormed his way forward and leered at her with yellow teeth. "I'll take you inside with me, Pretty Polly. Show you what it's like to sit on a real man's knee."

She swatted away his wriggling hand. "Don't flatter yourself. I've had better offers from a skunk. At least they smell better."

The yellow teeth gleamed. "I like 'em sassy." His hand shot out to grab her arm.

Jack knocked it away. "Don't touch her." Couldn't they enjoy one night out without someone's eye getting a half-mourning?

"Boy, don't tell me what to do with a woman."

"I was only thinking of your safety." Jack turned to Ivy and whispered, "Just so you know, I didn't plan this for your birthday."

"I'm willing to accommodate a last-minute addition." Sighing,

Ivy set her hat and bag on an overturned apple crate, then glanced down at her gown. "So much for keeping my new dress clean."

"It's still pretty—" A punch grazed Jack's nose. In instant reflex he jumped back and sent his fist flying, landing hard on the man's jaw.

From there it was a blur of arms, fists, and heads knocking around as he and Philip slid between their attackers with practiced ease. They fought brilliantly together, back-to-back, anticipating each other's countermoves and taunting their slower opponents. All those days of sparring had paid off.

Philip ducked a wild blow. "Care to join in, Ives?"

"No, thank you," she called from the sideline. "I'd prefer my dress not to get dirty."

Jack sent his man sprawling in time to see another one of the ill-bred gang clamp an arm around Ivy's waist. His filthy fingers clawed at her satin buttons. "Come on, Pretty Polly. Let's see what you got to offer."

Grabbing his wrist, she twisted the man's arm back until he hunched forward in screaming pain. Spinning around, she jammed her knee straight up to his nose. Blood spurted. Six drops of bright red on her skirt. She frowned. "Dirty after all."

Jack grinned. Still beautiful.

PART II

PART II

NINE

HUNKERING FARTHER INTO HER WHITE FUR COAT, IVY HURRIED ACROSS Blagoveshchenskiy Bridge as the frigid winter wind whipped off the River Neva. Tiny flecks of ice stung her eyes, causing them to water until frozen tear crystals collected at the corners. She brushed them away with her gloved hand and trudged on as the dying light of day slipped farther beneath the horizon. It was near twenty degrees now. She didn't want to be caught outside in Russia's capital when night fell completely in an hour.

Especially not with anarchy blistering through the streets. Anger seethed like a boil readying to burst. The war with Germany pushed the people closer to their breaking point as more men were called to fight and food disappeared. All eyes turned to Tsar Nicholas, "the Little Father of Russia," who seemed to do nothing but remain hidden behind his palace walls, unaware of the upheaval brewing across the land.

But a revolution was not Ivy's concern this night. Two months ago, Calhoune and Fielding had been sent to Russia to assassinate Balaur Tsar. Talon had not heard from them in three weeks and were left to assume the mission had failed. Their recourse was to send in

111

a second team to meet up with the in-country agent, Victory, and complete the task.

But now this Victory had gone missing as well.

Ivy turned right down a side street. The opulence of the royal palaces adorning the riverbank fell away to more practical facades and squat door stoops where people huddled together in worn blankets. At the third stoop a small fire burned brightly in a black kettle. Among those clustered around it were a woman with a baby at her breast and two children. The baby wailed mercilessly.

The mother looked at Ivy with dead eyes. "What are you staring at? Have you never seen hunger before, *printsessa*?"

"I've known it well myself," Ivy replied in Russian. She smiled at the little girl who peeked at her from behind her mother's apron. Naught but thin skin held her delicate bones together. "You have beautiful children. *Prekrasnaya*."

"Their father was dragged off to fight the tsar's war." The mother spat into the fire. It hissed in agreement. "I have nothing to feed them. It would be better if they died to feast in heaven with God. Holy Father forgive me." She crossed herself.

It was a thought Ivy had often enough when she would curl herself under a newspaper with hunger pangs scraping her empty belly. No child should live with that horror. She reached into her pocket and drew out a pouch of gold coins, then handed it to the woman.

"Love and survival are greater than death." She shrugged out of her warm coat and draped it around the little girl and boy. "For your children's sake, do not despair, *mamushka*."

By the time she reached the unobtrusive door another block away, Ivy was frozen to the core. Her stiff fingers refused to unfurl to twist the knob. She kicked the door instead, but with her boot covered in ice it turned to a thump. *Thump. Thump.* Again and again until a lock clicked on the other side of the wood.

The door cracked open. "Password."

Ivy's lips were numb. "Wh-what so p-proudly we hail-l."

The door opened and Ivy stumbled inside. Beatrix quickly shut the door and locked it. "What is the matter with you? Where is the contact?"

"Not th-there."

Beatrix boiled, her arched brow cutting off any semblance of patience. She had not been the first choice to join the team, nor the second, but as the best map reader Talon had, her value was indispensable. Unlike her personality. "What do you mean he wasn't there? He had to be there."

"Well, he w-wasn't."

"Then you should have stayed longer. I told Washington you weren't ready for an overseas assignment. Did you go to the correct location?"

Ready or not, Ivy had been thrilled to receive orders for her first out-of-country mission and had read every book in the library on Russia. Unfortunately, books and exercises were turning out to be rather different from reality.

Ignoring the ongoing interrogation, Ivy dragged her heavy legs up the creaking stairs located at the back of the abandoned apartment and pushed into the second-story room where a fireplace glowed with heat. She shot to it like an arrow to its bull's-eye. And nearly fell headlong into the flames.

"Not so fast." Strong arms caught her. Familiar and capable. She had the sense to let them carry her where they willed. Jack hauled her to a spot on the floor and a cushion he'd taken from a settee, which had long since been chopped into firewood. "Only a few hours in Russia and you've already forgotten how to use your feet?"

"E-eager to w-warm up."

"There's a better way to do that than hurling yourself into the flames." He flung a musty wool blanket around her and squatted to her eye level. Concern flared in those deep blue eyes. "Are you all right?"

At her nod, he touched her cheek with the back of his finger. It felt like fire branding her frozen skin. "If something had happened to you . . ."

"It d-didn't."

A half smile flicked the corner of his mouth as he tucked the blanket under her chin, his knuckles brushing her jaw. The cold in her belly melted. It may have been nothing more than a friendly gesture to him, but it certainly meant a great deal to her. "What *did* happen?"

Ice shifted back in her stomach. "Victory n-never showed."

Shoving to his feet, Jack bit back a curse. Ivy saw it writhing behind his clamped lips demanding expulsion, but he trapped it beneath a reserve of control. At least while there were people around. Had it been only the two of them, he wouldn't need to pretend, but in front of the others he had to carry the dignified response of calm.

Miles, their radio operator, grunted and tugged his knitted cap lower over his shaggy brown hair in his best attempt at ignoring them all. Thanks to an angry fisherman with a knife, Miles had lost his tongue as a child while trying to fill his starving belly with a stolen fish.

Now a valued Talon agent, Miles sat on the floor, yanked his encoding machine that doubled as a transmitter onto his lap, and began punching out his frustration on the keys. Ivy and the others could always decipher his mood by how fast or hard he typed.

"We have to find Victory," Jack said over Miles's incessant clacking. "Talon wired him to say we would arrive today and to meet us tonight at the rendezvous point. With Calhoune and Fielding missing, Victory is the only one left to give us updated information on Balaur Tsar and his whereabouts. Without him we'll be scouring the countryside for a ghost needle in a massive haystack."

Failure had nipped at Ivy the entire walk back to the safe house. "I'm sorry, Jack. Maybe I should have tried to signal him differently. My coat was so thick—maybe he didn't see my face." If he'd been there at all. All they needed was another dead agent.

"I'm sure you did everything exactly as we planned. A coat makes no difference to a trained— Where *is* your coat?"

"Wrapped around shivering Russian children a block down," Philip announced as he trudged into the room. Bits of ice peeled off his thick coat and pinged to the floor where they melted within seconds. Unlike Ivy and her constant need for overpreparedness, he'd taken to their first overseas assignment with nothing more than adventurous zeal and an extra pair of socks. As her second, he'd followed her to the rendezvous point with Victory in case trouble sprang up and she needed cover. "Her heart was still pinned to the sleeve."

"They were freezing," Ivy said, not the least bit apologetic. Her nose and lips tingled as they thawed and feeling started to return.

The corner of Jack's mouth tipped up, sending the tingles shooting straight down to her toes. "They're not anymore."

He paced slowly in front of the fireplace as the flames cast his shadow around the broken piles of furniture and bare spots on the faded walls. Everything of value had long since been sold by the previous tenants to buy food, and every stick left standing had been chopped for firewood. A spindly chair was keeping them warm tonight.

Apartments all across the city had been abandoned as people could no longer afford single housing or even city housing. The country seemed the best escape for many, but hardships of a different name awaited them there as war crept closer to seize their men and land.

Philip pried off his coat and leather gloves and tossed them on the floor in a wet heap. "What about the message drop box? Victory might have left a note there if signaling or meeting became too risky."

Jack spun to Beatrix. "Where's the drop box located?"

"Yusupov Garden," she replied automatically. Bundled up in a light brown fur coat that turned her red hair to copper, she hadn't shivered once since they stepped foot in the country. Then again, her blood seemed a few degrees cooler than most other people's. "Fewer military patrols in that neighborhood and relatively discreet."

A sinking feeling descended into the pit of Ivy's stomach. "Should we not try to find out what's happened to Fielding and Calhoune? It can't be coincidental that we haven't heard from them and Victory. If something has happened to all three, there won't be a message at the drop box."

"Calhoune is dead," a deep voice said. "Fielding is missing. I'm Agent Victory, but I prefer Victor. At your service, comrades." A man with a thin black mustache leaned against the crooked doorframe. He was dressed in the traditional Russian clothing of *rubakha*, loose wool trousers, sturdy black boots, *shuba*, and a Cossack hat that he wore with the cares of the devil.

Jack's Colt M1911 was on the intruder in an instant. "You're either very foolish or very certain of yourself. Password."

"*Chyort.* I knew you were going to ask me that." Victor tapped his fist against the doorframe as his eyes rolled up to the ceiling in concentration. "Listen, in complete honesty, I forgot. I realize you're probably going to shoot me because Franklin is a stickler for his passwords. There was 'lightning strikes the kite.' 'The guppy swallowed the whale.' My personal favorite was 'hark how the clergyman's daughter sings.'" His gaze rolled to Ivy and Beatrix. "Apologies. I shouldn't repeat that tawdry phrase in front of ladies."

"I know that one." Jack lowered his pistol. "Looks like I won't be shooting you today, Agent Victor."

"*Spasibo.*"

"How did you get in here?" Beatrix's eyes narrowed to glaring shards of amber. "We have a specific knock for coming and going. You're lucky we didn't shoot you."

"There is an old Russian saying: there are more ways than one to skin a mule." Grinning beneath his mustache, he walked past her and tweaked her cheek. "I jumped the rooftops and climbed in through the third-story window."

She scrubbed at the spot on her cheek while staring daggers at him. "You were on the rooftops? Why?"

"Spying." His grin broadened. "That's what I do, you know."

"That and drinking, by the smell of it."

"Correct, *kotyonok*."

"I am *not* your little kitten," Beatrix seethed. Ivy held back a laugh.

"Ah, but your little claws and twitching nose say otherwise." He closed one eye in a slow wink.

"There's no drinking on the job," Jack interrupted before those claws came out fully.

"You're in Russia now, *moy druk*." Victor clapped Jack on the back, then dropped to a crouch and rubbed his hands in front of the fire. "Drinking here *is* a job. One where you never fear unemployment."

Jack scoured a hand over his face, his common attempt to gather and strategize his thoughts as the night's events trampled his well-laid plans. "What happened to Calhoune and Fielding?"

The smirk faded from Victor's face. "I only made contact with them twice. Once when they first arrived, and the second nearly a week ago. They left a message saying they were going to a village near Kirishi where Balaur Tsar was rumored to be testing his latest weapon. I hadn't heard from them since." Victor tucked a length of unfashionably long black hair behind his ear. "Until yesterday when I went to this village myself. It had been massacred, and Calhoune was hanging from a tree with a red crown carved into his chest. I cut him down and buried him. No marker, of course."

The blanket slipped from Ivy's fingers. "Poor Calhoune." His body would never be returned to America for a proper burial in his homeland. He would never be seen or heard from again; no gravestone would signify his passing existence. Such was the inglorious death of a spy. One they could all expect if they were caught.

Jack gritted his teeth. "Fielding?"

Victor offered an apologetic shrug. "No sign of him."

"Why did you miss the rendezvous tonight? Talon wired you with instructions to meet us."

"*Da*, that. I had another event to attend."

Ivy winced as Jack surely ground his teeth into dust. "An event more important than this meeting?"

"*Da*. My own assignment to take care of. Momentarily distracted by Calhoune and Fielding, I had yet to complete my own mission, but this morning I received the invitation that would finally put my hand to the task. My very good friend, Prince Felix Yusupov, was throwing a private party this evening for a few of his select acquaintances— one of which was yours truly—and a very special guest of honor. Naturally I hoped it was his wife, the tsar's only niece, Princess Irina Alexandrovna. A raving beauty, she is." Victor slid his gaze to Beatrix, who pretended to ignore him by turning her nose away, which only seemed to delight Victor all the more. "Imagine my disappointment when I discovered she is in Crimea at present."

Philip paused in picking ice from his hair. "Don't tell me you were assigned to kill the princess."

"Of course not. The woman is a saint for marrying Felix." Victor plopped onto the floor and stretched out his legs until his boots nearly touched the fire. "My assignment was the mad monk."

Ivy gasped. "Rasputin?" Newspapers and posters with horrible caricatures of the man were plastered all over the city. The images showed the claimed holy man as the puppet master of the imperial family who pretended to heal their son the *tsarevich*, and often depicted him locked in a passionate embrace with the *tsarina*. His eyes were terrible. Wild and possessed as they leaped from the inked drawings.

Victor shrugged a disinterested shoulder. "The very one. He won't be bewitching anyone any longer. Not after we dropped him in the river."

"We?" Jack's tone clenched with incredulity.

"Me, Felix, and two of his aristocratic friends. All eager to help. After we shot, poisoned, and bludgeoned him—I swear his evilness would not let him die—they needed help disposing of the body. I suggested wrapping him up and heaving him under the ice off Petrovsky Bridge."

This man was proving himself a loose cannon. Of all the idiotic things he could have done . . . It took every ounce of Ivy's willpower not to kick his outstretched leg. And hope it bruised badly. "It's against Talon rules to involve outsiders. Did you stop to think of the implications to your cover?"

Victor's mustache twitched over a yawn. "Talon has its rules, but things change quickly and sometimes necessity wins out."

Never taken aback for long, Jack steered his team back to the mission at hand. "Right. From now on we assume Fielding is dead and proceed with the mission to hunt and kill Balaur Tsar. Victor, we need a briefing."

"First, we need to leave the city and regroup at the other safe house. There's no telling what secrets Calhoune gave up when they tortured him. Balaur's men might be trailing us as we speak. We should assume we're no longer safe at this location."

"Are you certain he was tortured before they killed him?" Jack asked.

"I've seen remnants of Balaur's handiwork more times than my stomach can handle. Never doubt what he's capable of or the lengths he'll go to for profit. Sadistic torture is his calling card."

"Calhoune was a Talon agent. He never would have talked. No matter what they did to him." Bitterness rooted in Jack's voice.

Victor's dark eyes glowed in the firelight. "I've heard of you, Jack Vale. The man who never misses. I read the reports on all your kills in Belgium and the thwarted coup in Argentina before that. You know as well as any agent what it requires to see this job done, but don't think for one minute that any previous experience or training has prepared you for this. You're in Russia now, and the whole country is burning."

"Then we count ourselves fortunate that you'll guide our steps so we don't catch fire as well."

Victor groaned as he stood. Melted snow dripped from his coat's hem onto the floor in a ring around him. "I need to grab new identification papers from the safe-deposit box at the bank. Afterward, I'll meet you at the safe house."

Talon held a private bank account and safety-deposit box in each major city worldwide so they could provide agents with funds, new identities, and small weapons. Jack wanted to avoid using the account, but when on the lam, he'd do what he must to stay alive and take care of his team. Worst case, they would steal what they needed.

"Where exactly is this safe house?"

"Southeast. An old summer *dacha*." Beatrix had pulled out one of her maps and spread it across a dry section of the floor.

Victor pointed to a splotch of inked green with his toe. "Middle of the forest just past the river. Takes about half a day on foot. Longer if this snowfall keeps up since the road is little more than a rut."

Ivy startled when Miles knocked his hand on the floor, drawing everyone's attention. He signed a string of words with his gloved hands. The fingertips had been snipped off, as they were on all his gloves, making it easier to sign and push the tiny machine buttons. His fingers were always moving, so the numbing cold never had a chance to settle in the exposed digits.

"Check drop point," Jack translated for Victor's benefit. The rest of the team had learned sign language at Talon to communicate with their radio operator. "Good idea. We'll leave in pairs to avoid suspicion. Philip, you go with Victor. Beatrix and Miles, take the gear and go straight to the *dacha*. Ivy, you come with me to the drop point. Fielding or Calhoune might have left a message for us before they left for the village."

"I'll go check out their safe house. They might have left a clue we can use to find Balaur," Philip said. "Victor doesn't need me to help pick up identification documents."

Jack shook his head. "No, we stay in pairs. They would have destroyed any evidence at the safe house before they left for Kirishi."

"Before you dismiss it out of hand, consider—"

"There is nothing else to consider. Each pair has its task and will not deviate."

Jack waited for Philip's nod of acceptance. Once given, Philip turned to gather his gear.

Ivy slipped over to Philip and gently squeezed his arm. "Learn to pick your battles, and whatever you do, do not pick them in front of the group."

"Because you're always discreet with your opinions."

"Fair enough, but there can be only one authority here. As new agents you and I are not it."

His arm tensed under her hand, then slowly relaxed. Pulling away, he strapped his pack over his shoulder. "Take care out there."

"You too."

"When you get to Yusupov Garden," Victor said as he followed Philip to the doorway, "there's a gnarled tree on an island in the center. Messages would be in a hole in the trunk. Beware the squirrels. They're bad-tempered if they think you're trying to steal their winter store of nuts."

After digging his coat out of the corner darkness, Jack slipped into the black wool and pulled a matching *kubanka* on top of his head. "Miles, before the two of you leave, code a message to headquarters. Inform Washington that we're relocating from the city with Victor and carrying on with the original mission. Calhoune and Fielding are presumed dead." He hesitated. "If they send back conflicting instructions, pretend you didn't see them. We carry on."

Ivy stood and folded the blanket she'd been wrapped in, then dropped it on the cushion. She stamped her feet to get her blood flowing amid the pins and needles in her skin. "Insubordination so early in the mission, Commander Vale?"

"A situation can appear entirely different from across the ocean than it actually is for boots on the ground. The mission is to kill Balaur, and that's what I intend to do."

"Then let's go, shall we?"

Jack's eyes narrowed with a sweep of her body. "You don't have a coat."

"She can have mine. It's stifling in here." Beatrix slid out of her fur and offered it to Ivy.

Ivy accepted it and buttoned herself in. On Beatrix the hem had hit at her knee. On Ivy it slid to her ankles. "At least my knees won't get frostbite. Thank you."

Jack frowned but refrained from comment until they stepped outside and bid farewell to the rest of the team. "It's dangerous out here. More so than we realized an hour ago."

Ivy fluffed the fur on her collar to cover the exposed skin not protected by her *kubanka* and turned onto the street. "Good thing I'm here to protect you."

He grabbed her arm and spun her around to face him. "I'm not joking, Ivy. We lost a man—possibly two, and this is your first time in the field. Blind confidence will get an agent killed."

Raw ire crossed his face and lashed over her in its fierceness. Struggling for footing in the eye of his storm, Ivy took in the classically handsome features that were as familiar as her own reflection and infinitely more precious. She looked past his blustering and roiling clouds meant to drench her in censure and uncovered the fear fissuring along his dark visage.

She covered his gloved hand with hers, willing the worry to peel from his veins and melt into her own. "I know you're worried about something else bad happening, but whatever comes our way, we take care of each other together, right?"

The cracks of worry softened. "Right. Together."

They stole silently through the quiet streets under the cloak of drifting snow. Lacy flakes peppered the grandiose architecture that had been conjured from fairy tales of ice and regality, but danger lurked on the edges of this fair tale with sinister shadows creeping beneath the surface, intent to waylay them at every turn. The city itself was like a dying beast, gasping and thrashing as revolution sank bloodthirsty fangs into its heaving sides. The glorious architecture seemed to shudder behind the bleakness of fear while the once-proud culture begged for scraps of humanity. As agents of Talon, Ivy hoped they could at least spare the Russian people the blood-soaked mayhem Balaur thrived on creating.

After what seemed like hours of Ivy's toes turning into icicles in her fur-lined boots, they made yet another turn and finally reached their destination. Yusupov Garden was a beautiful park that once belonged to one of the richest families in Imperial Russia. Frosted grass crunched beneath their feet as they entered.

Jack kept a watchful eye to the left and Ivy to the right, her ears prickling at the soft call of voices across the frozen pond. Based on the slurring words, they were most likely drunk and unconcerned with two more figures in their midst.

Skirting the central pond's perimeter, she and Jack crossed a narrow iron bridge to the tiny island where a handful of oak trees crusted in slush stood stalwart against winter's bite.

They stepped onto a well-worn dirt path meandering around the island that could be navigated in under two minutes.

"The island seems deserted." Ivy linked her arm through Jack's as they circled the path. They appeared for all the world as a couple on a late-night stroll should anyone, drunk or otherwise, happen by.

"Then why does it feel like you're trying to race me?" Jack tugged on her arm to slow her steps. "Anyone watching might think you're unimpressed with my company."

"Well, a different gentleman wouldn't have me slogging through the wet and cold."

"A different gentleman wouldn't be as much fun. Besides, you didn't refuse this excursion, so if you aren't having a good time, you've only yourself to blame." He glanced at her as they walked. "By the way, your nose is red."

"My nose isn't red." She covered the evidence with her gloved hand.

He smirked. "It is. It glows bright as a cherry when you're cold. When you stop talking I know you're close to numb, but seeing that you're willing to argue, I doubt we're close to that point yet."

At times like this she hated his ability to bypass their mirror of common reflection while still seeing her inside and out. "If I could feel my toes, I'd kick you."

"Go ahead and try. Might get the blood moving." Jack swept their surroundings with a keen eye attuned to any shift in the shadows, any hushed footstep that signaled danger. With no such danger in the vicinity, he tugged her off the dirt path. "Victor said it was the gnarled one. This is it."

They approached one of the oak trees farthest from the bridge. It slanted over the frozen edge of the lake with its naked limbs stretching to the sky in petition. As Jack began to search the tree for the hollowed-out knot that served as a drop box for communication, Ivy ran her gloved hand along the rough bark and kept an eye on the drunken revelers onshore.

"A squirrel's put his dinner in here." Victor's warning about angry squirrels rang in her head, and she surveyed the trees as Jack cautiously swept the acorns from the hole. They hit the ground in solid pings.

"There's something else." He grunted. "It's frozen to the bark."

Crunch.

Ivy's attention snapped to the walkway as her ears strained to hear the sound again. "What was that?"

Focused on his task, Jack didn't turn around. "It's stuck."

Snow crunched again. Footsteps. Ivy's hand flew to the Beretta semiautomatic pistol strapped at her waist.

"*Chem ty zanimayesh'sya?*" A figure lurched across the bridge and onto the island toward them.

Jack turned, reached for her, then pushed her against the tree, blocking the knot and frozen slip of paper peeking out. An innocent observer would see no more than a passionate embrace—one that hid Jack reaching for his pistol.

"*Privyet,*" the intruder slurred. His uneven footsteps faltered over the ground. "You out late."

"Male, late sixties. Lame right foot. Heavily intoxicated," Ivy whispered, her gaze mapping the weak points on the man's body. "Engage unprotected left side to render unconscious."

"Wait," Jack whispered before raising his voice to the old man and speaking in Russian. "Our chosen hour is none of your business. Move along."

The drunk stumbled closer. Alcohol reeked from his filthy clothes. "Your accent is not from Petrograd. You are from where?"

Jack went rigid. He spoke impeccable Russian, but Ivy often had to tutor him in regional accents. He lowered his face to the side of Ivy's neck, muffling his voice. "I said move along."

Appreciating this intimate turn of events, the drunk wobbled forward, his gray teeth displayed in a leer. "Who you got there, comrade?"

The muscles in Jack's body coiled for action, his breathing on her neck quick but steady. And despite the possible danger, she couldn't help thinking if she turned her head an inch, she could prompt the kiss she'd been dreaming of for so long. Oddly enough, her dream never involved a voyeuristic lush.

"Can you not leave two lovers in peace? The war has taken enough without boozers stealing our last minutes together," Ivy said.

The hard lines of Jack's body eased as a silent chuckle escaped and fanned across her neck. She ignored the shiver it sent racing down her spine and focused on the problem at hand—not getting caught and killed. Or breaking the old man's neck because his curiosity got the better of him.

The drunk threw his hand up in a less-than-polite gesture. "No need to be rude. I go." He stumbled away, footsteps dragging back over the bridge.

Jack leaned slightly back, shifting his hand from his gun to her waist. "You should've let me push him in the pond."

The rough bark scraped her neck as she tilted her head back to look at him. "You should work on your accent, Agent Vale."

"That's why I've got you." His white teeth gleamed in the brightness of the falling snow. Open, honest, teasing—that was Jack's smile now. Until the teasing swerved to something different as she stared into his eyes. She'd caught that look more than a few times in recent months when she'd turned to catch him watching her. The glimmer always vanished into a playful wink as quickly as she'd seen it.

Tonight there was no wink, only a look he'd given her once before when a song crooned on the October breeze. The night he could have kissed her but didn't. *Jack. Your kisses burn upon my lips.*

At least, she imagined they would.

Did he ever think about that almost kiss? That brief moment that had ignited her soul and sent her down a course from which she could never return. A course that wrapped her around Jack's heart with no hope of becoming untangled.

She'd held back a piece of herself, too long afraid of opening her heart completely. Was the fear of losing another person she cared for worth staying closed off to Jack forever? Did he even know how she felt? She dropped her gaze to his parted lips, inches from her own, and released a shaky breath. Was she brave enough to find out?

TEN

OF COURSE JACK THOUGHT ABOUT THAT ALMOST KISS AND HOW HE'D
ruined the most perfect moment by pecking her on the forehead.
Chaste and pathetic and cowardly. Not an hour passed when he didn't
dream of pulling Ivy close. From the moment his knee had brushed
hers in the library that day as they read fairy tales, he'd known she
was the only girl for him. It would always be her.

But fear of rejection held him in check.

A dirty tactic, fear, but oh so powerful. It fed on his insecurities
and kept him from reaching out for the one thing he'd craved his
entire life. Love. His parents had not offered it to him. His aunt had
died hating him with her last breath. The world was contemptuous
of his existence. A common enough tale of woe for any orphan and
one he'd learned to shoulder along with his many scars. If his own
parents couldn't spare a shred of affection for him, how could he ask
it of this woman? This woman so full of compassion and loyalty and
brilliance. How could he hope to offer her the love she deserved when
he'd experienced so little of it himself?

Unfortunately, standing in the freezing cold in the middle of
a mission was not the time or place to confess his long-concealed
feelings. They had a madman to stop, and kissing Ivy senseless was
hardly the way to go about it.

With a reluctance that tied his insides in knots, Jack released her and stepped away, redoubling his efforts to pull the message from its hiding place. It came free. Black ink splotched the paper as it crumbled in his hand.

He knocked the pieces to the ground. "Indecipherable and old."

Emotions shifted across Ivy's face. Unmistakable desire that nearly made him change his mind about stepping back, confusion at the sudden shift between them, and finally a cool mask of acceptance.

She moved away from him after a quick glance at the paper. Cold air filled the space, bridging the gap between them with professionalism as she cleared her throat. "At least it tells us someone was here."

The moment was gone, and they needed to get moving. "Yes, but there's no telling how long it sat here to rot." Jack ground the bits of paper to pulp beneath his heel. "Come on. We have a long trek ahead of us to the safe house. Then on to planning the route to our target."

Ivy linked her arm through his without meeting his eyes, and they turned back to the path to cross the short distance to the bridge and mainland.

Two figures hulked on the other side.

"Good evening, comrades." The guttural Russian voice shattered any illusion of leaving this place quietly. "Looking for Balaur Tsar?"

Jack shifted in front of Ivy as he sized up their unwelcome guests. "Well, you're an ugly beast."

The man in question looked like a big chunk of packaged meat left out in the sun too long—thick all over with ham hocks for hands and a large round head squashed directly atop his dense shoulders.

And he was blocking their exit. "Last man who came here was looking for Balaur Tsar. He ended up dead. You want Balaur's location, too, *da?*"

Jack smothered his flare of panic beneath a neutral expression as he noted weak spots to down the beast. A punch to the jaw was too obvious and unfit to cause sufficient damage. "If it's not too much trouble."

"You have the trouble, *da?*" Meat flexed his fingers with a loud pop. "Like your friend we killed. Now we kill you too."

"I'd prefer not to spill blood tonight—too cold—but if you insist."

Meat squeezed onto the narrow bridge. Glee twisted his ugly mug. "The only blood to spill will be yours."

"I'm afraid I'll have to disagree on that point."

The other man lumbered behind Meat as they crossed the bridge toward Jack and Ivy. The second man was Meat's twin except for a fishhook scar carved into the left side of his face. They reached the island in three long strides and assumed matching stances. "No disagreeing."

Ivy took a deep breath next to Jack. Her stylish fur coat and petite stature painted an oddly out-of-proportion picture amid the midnight shadows and hulking assassins.

"A moment, gentlemen. Before any teeth are knocked out, I have a few questions." She slipped off her gloves and tucked them into her pockets, then pulled off her hat to reveal the thick braid of strawberry-blonde hair coiled around her head. Glancing around for a clean spot to place the hat, she gingerly set it atop a dead bush. "Now, gentlemen, I take it you work for Balaur, *da?* Might you tell us where he is?"

Meat grinned, revealing missing front teeth. "He is here. He is there. He is everywhere."

"I see you can add poet to what I assume is a rather short résumé of thug duties. Well done, you. However, *everywhere* is not specific enough. We need an exact location, *pazhalsta.*"

Dead eyes flashed to Jack, and Fishhook's flat lips curled with cruelty. "You allow this *zhenshchina* to speak for you?"

Jack peeled off his own gloves and flexed his stiff fingers to get his blood moving as his shoulder muscles rolled in anticipation. Judging by the size of the Russians' fists, this was going to cause a few bruises. Guns were no option here. The noise would draw a crowd he'd rather avoid. "It's a favor to you really. Speaking to a pretty girl in your last minutes on earth."

"It was a mistake to bring her."

"On that point I agree with you, but telling her no is a waste of breath. Might as well let her do what she wants and deal with the consequences later."

"It's much easier to beg for forgiveness than ask for permission," Ivy said.

Jack shrugged. "See what I mean?"

Clearly Meat did not. Air hissed between the gap in his teeth as he and Fishhook stepped forward, shrinking the island by a terrible half. "I will tear her skin from her bones and make you watch. When her screams are dead, I will rip out your heart and cook it for breakfast."

"Breakfast? Oh no. This won't take that long." Jack grabbed Ivy's hands the instant she pushed off the ground into a jump. He swung her around in a half circle, and she kicked both assassins in the head before they could move, then landed gracefully on Jack's opposite side.

Meat and Fishhook recovered, centering themselves with confused twitches on their flat lips.

"Odd. That move usually works in training," Ivy muttered.

"You're not in training anymore." Jack frowned. "We'll need to dig deeper than usual for these two."

"After you, Agent Vale."

Jack lowered one shoulder and rammed into Meat's stomach, slamming him against a tree. Small branches rained down on them in a choking cloud as the thin trunk cracked. Meat shoved Jack and hammered his fists into Jack's middle, then sprang out of reach. Dropping to a crouch, Jack thrust out his leg and knocked Meat flat on his back.

A loud *thwack* told him Ivy had engaged Fishhook with a tree branch, but he didn't bother turning to look. She could handle herself. Meat rolled up from the ground and lunged, grabbing Jack's foot. He

THE BRILLIANCE OF STARS

kicked to free himself, but Meat dragged him like a fish caught on a line. Jack latched onto the nearest thing, then grabbed a rock and hurled it into Meat's head. The hulk roared like a wounded bull as red filled his eyes.

An assault of fists and blocks ensued, grunts and curses sounding as Jack tried to bloody the Russian senseless while Meat tried to rip out Jack's throat.

A small cry broke through the bloody melee.

Ivy.

On instinct Jack turned to her, and a fist caught him on the side of the head. He hit the ground in a blind of pain. Meat jumped on top of him and a bolt of silver flashed in his hand.

A knife.

"Now you will die like your friend we hanged at Kirishi. That is why you are here, *da*? Looking for him?" Meat's gaping black hole of a mouth oozed with the putrid stench of onions and ale. "You cry for mercy like him? Balaur Tsar offers eternal mercy to the undeserving."

Jack's chest suffocated under Meat's weight. He gasped, "Mercy . . . I won't offer . . . Balaur the least bit . . . when I kill him."

"Pride is your downfall." Meat slashed open the front of Jack's shirt with the tip of his knife. "First, I will carve you like your friend. Cry for me, *da*?"

Ivy's scream rent the night air. Jack twisted as the knife sliced along his ribs. Fire scorched in its wake, but fury numbed the pain as Fishhook wrapped a hand around Ivy's throat and lifted her off her feet.

She yanked the pearl pin from her hair and slammed it into the side of her attacker's neck. He howled in pain but didn't release his grip on her throat. Her face mottled red, then purple.

With a roar of terror, Jack freed an arm and smashed Meat in the nose. It crunched with a spurt of blood, and he fell back yelping, his hands jerking to his face after dropping the knife.

Grabbing the weapon, Jack drove it into the side of Meat's neck before he could react, then scrambled for Ivy. He ran behind Fishhook, grasped his head, and twisted. Hard.

The neck *popped* softly. Broken. The Russian crumpled to the dirt, dragging Ivy with him.

Jack pried the massive hand from her neck, and Ivy sucked in a lungful of air. "I . . . had him."

"I know, but you were taking longer than I liked." Jack hauled her up and held her tight as he examined the disheveled hair, torn fur collar, and scuffed shoes. No blood. "Are you all right?"

"Suffice it to say . . . I won't be singing for a while." Retrieving her hairpin, she wiped it clean and slid it back into her now-lopsided crown braid. She touched a finger to her red throat, then winced. She'd have a walloping bruise come morning.

"Could have been worse." He found her hat on the bush and fit it snugly atop her messy hair. "We need to leave before anyone decides to investigate the ruckus."

When he reached for his own coat, pain ricocheted up his side. Warm blood seeped through his ripped shirt and trickled to the waistband of his trousers.

Ivy gasped, her green eyes wide in horror. "You're hurt!"

"It's nothing." He covered the wound with his hand, but blood slid between his fingers.

"Don't play the hero with me, Jack Vale. You only grimace like that when it's truly painful." She reached under her long blue skirt and tore off a strip of petticoat. Her head bobbed under his chin as she made quick work of wrapping the bandage around his torso and tying it off. He might consider getting stabbed more often if it meant having her arms around him for a few minutes.

She nodded toward the would-be assassins. "Do we leave them?"

"Can't take them with us." Ignoring his pain, Jack grabbed Meat and managed to prop him against a tree next to Fishhook. At first glance a passerby would assume they were drunks passed out for the night.

A noise garbled in Meat's throat. He pressed a hand to the hole as life poured out in a red stream that pulsed with each movement of his lips.

"He's trying to speak," Ivy said.

Jack stepped closer. Meat's eyes, defiant with death, flicked up at him as a last hiss of words released, then he lay still. A hollowness filled Jack. He hated death and despised being the hand of Fate behind it, but the mission required sacrifice for the greater good. It was simply a necessity to keep the hounds of evil from triumphing. For that, he would never apologize.

The red imprint of a hand glared against the paleness of Ivy's throat. Anger flooded his chest. He would condemn himself to the very fires of hell to keep her safe. Tempering the sear of emotion, he pulled in a deep breath and forced his attention back to their current problem.

"Was that Latin?"

"No . . . It was Dacian, an extinct language somewhat intertwined with vulgar Latin from around AD 200. It was spoken in the Carpathian region of what we now call Romania." A thin line creased between her eyebrows as she rattled off the facts. "Why would a Russian thug be speaking a dead language? There are only a few scholars in the world who can interpret it."

"A few scholars and you." Pride crept into his voice. She knew every book in Talon's library inside and out, nearly surpassing Washington's knowledge of obscure facts and details. Nearly.

"And me." A tight smile waned across her face. "We have to find Balaur. If we don't, I'm afraid what he said might come true." Her gaze flickered to the ominous body as she reached for Jack's hand.

"'The next step is not enough.'"

ELEVEN

DAWN ARRIVED, FROZEN AND BLEAK, AS IVY AND JACK HELD TIGHT TO THE cart's sides. Jack had managed to bribe a milkman with a few coins for a ride out of Petrograd, saving them from a miserable journey on foot. The coins also kept the man's mouth shut about their tattered appearance and from eyeing Jack's bandages too closely.

"How different the countryside is from the city gloom," Ivy mused as the sagging mare plodded down the muddy track, dragging the cart and its empty crates back to a peasant village some miles away.

Jack breathed in deep. "You can breathe out here."

Indeed. No dingy clouds hovered. No auto horns beeped. No war rallies rang out from street corners. The pristine beauty of this place allowed no such disturbances. Instead, green fir trees thick with fragrant needles stood brightly amid mounds of powdery white snow. A few brave birds puffed out their feathers and trilled their songs into the crisp air as they rustled among dried bushes in search of food.

It was easy to forget the evil they hunted.

Ivy dropped her voice lest the milkman overhear. "Do you think the team is already at the safe house?"

"As long as they didn't run into trouble, they should have arrived hours ago."

"With any luck they'll have a fire going and a basket of food ready when we arrive." Her stomach rumbled.

Worry creased Jack's face. "I should have been better prepared. Keeping you out like this—"

"I'll survive. But only because I know you won't let me die."

His expression smoothed as one corner of his lips tipped up. "No. I won't."

She knew it as assuredly as she knew the sun would rise and the earth would spin. Jack would never fail her just as she would never give up on him. It was who they were—who they were meant to be together, bonded.

The cart hit a rut and jolted her against his shoulder. "And if by some horrible twist in circumstances beyond your control I do die, I'm coming back as a ghost to haunt you."

The other side of his mouth curved up to a full grin. "Only fair."

"Glad we're in agreement."

Coming to a fork in the road, the milkman pulled the cart to a stop and pointed left. "You go that way."

Paying him his dues, Ivy and Jack climbed down from the cart and struck out for the safe house by following the pocket-size map Jack kept. The six miles should have taken only an hour and a half, but the countryside's dazzling display of beauty held a darker side.

Mud, to be most accurate. Thick and oozing, it sucked at their boots and dragged at the hems of their clothing. Ivy gave up trying to keep her thick wool skirt from dragging as the sludge caked around the material and lugged around her ankles like a weight. As the clouds thinned like strands of cotton to reveal a midday sky, a silent exhaustion hovered on the horizon. They were only halfway.

"*War and Peace* made walking through the snow sound much more romantic than it actually is." She pried her foot from another icy hole.

"Those characters were all princes and nobles riding around in their gilded *troikas* with fine horses and blankets."

"What I wouldn't give for a *troika* to whisk me away right now."

Jack cocked an eyebrow. "Not a prince?"

"Only if he would let me ride on his back so I won't lose my boots in the mud."

"I'm no prince, but I would gladly hoist you on my back, my lady, if not for fear of your sodden skirts sinking us farther into the mush, from which there would be no recovery." He bowed low in a mock courtly gesture.

She mocked him right back with a curtsy that nearly sent her sprawling into the muck. "I appreciate your gallantry all the same, Agent Vale."

Two hours later they came to a river that barred them from crossing. Feet numb, legs sore, and eyes watering, Ivy glared at the swift current. If only her silent anger would force it to peel back like the Red Sea.

At its widest the river was perhaps ten feet across with deep blue water rushing between the snow-crusted shores. "Too far to jump. I don't suppose there's a bridge nearby."

"Not according to Beatrix's map." Jack pointed to the thick swath of trees across the way. "Our rendezvous point is just beyond there."

"But we're here."

"Care for a swim?" He waggled his eyebrows.

Ivy waggled hers right back. "Only if you paddle while I sit on your back."

"Making me do all the work while you stay dry is hardly fair."

"But a position I'm more than willing to agree to."

Jack walked along the shore until he came to a twisted tree that leaned dangerously into the rushing current. He waved her over. "We cross here."

Ivy trudged to him, skirts dragging with each step. "If you think

I'm going to shimmy up a tree and leap across— Oh. That could work. Is it stable?"

In answer, Jack propped his foot atop the thick limb that had been hidden behind a slight curve in the river. It stretched from one bank to the other. He shoved his foot against the fallen piece. It didn't budge.

"Stable enough. I'll go first and make sure it doesn't crack." Carefully balancing himself on the makeshift bridge, he scurried across the river with the grace of an acrobat. On the other side he jumped off, then motioned her forward. "Your turn."

Taking a deep breath for courage, Ivy climbed up and wobbled across. The river spat and drenched the bottom of her skirt; the mud on the bottom of her shoes turned to a slick sludge. She held her arms out for balance. *Please don't fall. Please don't fall.* At the end, Jack grabbed her hand and yanked her to safety. His face twinged with pain.

"Do I need to rebandage your wound?" Dropping his hand, Ivy moved to unbutton his coat. If he passed out from pain or blood loss, she'd have to drag him the rest of the way.

He squeezed her fingers as they touched the buttons. "I'll manage."

Under the thick canopy of the forest, little snow found refuge. The captured air was laden with the scent of pine needles and frozen dirt.

Dirt that crunched beneath footsteps not their own.

They crept behind a bush and pulled their pistols. Back-to-back with Jack, Ivy's heart pounded as she scanned the area for the encroaching threat. Her finger hovered a hairsbreadth from the trigger as she waited for the split second it would take to pull it.

"If you're going to shoot me, aim for the left. I got hit in the right leg two years ago and can't bear the thought of looking lopsided all my days." Victor's cheerful voice rang through the trees. Releasing a shaky breath, Ivy slid her finger away from the trigger. She moved from behind the bush to find Victor grinning at them like a Cheshire cat. "Didn't know if you were going to make it. Come on. Philip's caught a brace of rabbits for supper."

Pushing through the trees, they came to a small wooden cabin with a pitched roof—the traditional Russian *dacha* used by hunters during the summer months. The eaves were covered in cobwebs and more than one board warped away from the structure.

"It looks abandoned." Ivy's breath curled out like smoke.

"Safe houses aren't supposed to be the Willard Hotel."

"Remember the time we sneaked on top of the Willard's roof and threw pennies on the passing trolley cars?"

Jack chuckled. "The concierge chased us down twelve floors."

Ivy smiled at the memory of them racing down the polished marble halls, slipping and sliding over the slick stairs. It was the first time he'd held her hand. Her fingers had curled instinctively around his, following where he led, their mingled laughter ringing down the corridor.

Victor beckoned them onto the porch. "Come on before you two get lost down memory lane."

Inside, their team waited eagerly for an update among the cobweb-covered ceilings and piles of dead insects. With only three sagging chairs to claim as furniture, a shedding bear rug had been flung over the filthy floor to serve as additional seating. After scrubbing the mud from their shoes and donning clean, dry clothes from the small satchels Beatrix and Miles had brought from Petrograd, Ivy and Jack tucked into bowls of rabbit stew and recounted their evening of events.

"Slow down, cluck-cluck. No one's going to take the bowl away from you," Philip whispered.

Ivy paused, spoon halfway to her mouth. "Did you get enough to eat?" A habit question after so many years with nothing to satisfy their growling bellies.

"The best part about drawing the short straw for cooking duties is getting the first ladleful—and all the best meat. Like when we used to slip over to Ebbitt's Grill and steal steaks off the back of the delivery wagon when they weren't looking."

Ivy laughed. "We never could figure out how to cook them. They were always bloody or burned; no medium-well for us."

"And we always had to cook them in tunnels so the cops wouldn't see the smoke. Smoke you caused." He bumped her shoulder, grinning widely.

"Pardon me, but wasn't it you who carried in wet wood?"

"Only kind I could find, as I explained at the time." Sobering, he turned away and noticed the slight bulge under Jack's shirt and whistled low. "Lucky you made it out of there with nothing more than a scratch."

Jack glanced down at the fresh bandages he had wrapped while changing clothes. Grunting, he pushed away his empty bowl. "If we'd gotten a few answers, it might have been worth it." Standing, he moved to the fireplace. Thick tree wedges burned orange in the brick hole carved into the back wall, while the shadow of flames danced from face to face as the team sat circled around.

"We'll rest up for the night and strike out at first light. In the meantime, Victor, work with Beatrix and mark the map for every known location of Balaur. See if there's a pattern."

Beatrix pulled a map from her haversack. The freckles covering her face glowed in the firelight. "And if there's no pattern? If they're stabs in the dark?"

"Then we'll stab until we find something. And we will." The room pulsed with Jack's final words. That was the plan. And he would see it done.

But at what cost? Ivy paused as she looked at the gathering around the fire. A cartographer, weapons expert, coder, master assassins—each too significant to lose. Yet they'd lost Calhoune. Fielding was missing in action, presumed dead. How many more deaths would be required to stop Balaur?

Jack's long shadow passed over her, drawing her attention up. His eyes were hidden beneath half-lowered lids, but that didn't matter. She felt them on her, felt the words he didn't say. *Together. I promise.*

"No one ventures this far into the woods in the dead of winter." Victor's voice pulled her from Jack and back to the room. "We're safe enough."

"We'll set up watches. Two hours each," Jack said.

Victor leaned back in his chair, stretching his arms over his head. "Only thing we'll be watching for is bears." He stood and rummaged through a cabinet over a bucket that served as their sink. "At least we have enough vodka to keep us warm."

"No drinking."

"I realize you're in charge, Vale, but you've only been in the country a grand total of two days and have yet to learn the local ways. Vodka on a cold night is the way."

"If that's the case, then we part ways here. Every person on this team will be clearheaded and ready to move at a moment's notice."

"I move even better with a few slugs of Russian coffee in me." Victor raised the bottle to his lips. Beatrix snatched it away and threw it into the fire. The flames sprang up, scorching the red bricks. "Are you insane, woman?"

"No more than you," Beatrix shot back. "I won't be killed simply because you're too drunk to stand up." Grabbing her maps, she flounced behind the curtain partition that separated the women's corner from the rest of the room. Paper snapped and rustled between her muttered indignations.

"Fool woman. If I were to kill anyone, you would be at the top of the list." Victor stormed outside, slamming the door behind him.

Looking more than willing to strangle the next troublemaker,

Jack grabbed his and Victor's coats and headed for the door. "No more throwing bottles while I go cool off the hothead."

With only the popping fire to break the following silence, Ivy, Philip, and Miles stared at each other. A few hours into this journey, sanity was a prized commodity yet lacking in supply.

Never one to insert himself into the squabbles of others, Miles tugged his knit cap low over his ears and scratched notes on a torn scrap of paper. His ever-present encoding machine sat inches from his fingers.

Philip stood and pulled a bulky canvas sack into the center of the room. One by one he unloaded various size guns, ammunition, explosives, and knives. His smile widened with each addition. "If we have to fight in the woods, I'll need to change out the citified weapons. We can go bigger out here." He was practically giddy.

Recognizing the fervency of her teammates' absorption into their individual tasks, Ivy put away her and Jack's bowls for washing later and slipped into a silver fox-fur coat the team had gotten for her when they left Petrograd. She didn't bother asking how it had been obtained as she headed for the door.

"I'll take first watch." Neither man acknowledged her leaving.

The woods were warmer with the thick padding of trees blocking the bitter north winds with only patches of mud to mark the fall of melted snow. Pulling her coat close, Ivy circled the *dacha's* perimeter listening to the natural sounds of the forest and noting the surrounding landscape. All peaceful and quiet.

Odd. No sound of Jack or Victor. She circled again and found two pairs of boot prints leading to the river. Perhaps Jack had drowned him. No, at most he would've held the troublemaker's head under water until common sense cleared him out. Victor was a good man and a brilliant agent, but his recklessness put them all in danger.

Nearing the front, stomping feet snapped twigs and ground dirt.

Ivy drew her pistol and scanned the tree line. Victor broke through, tramped up the steps, and went into the cabin without looking at her.

"He's mad at himself more than anything." Jack strolled out of the trees with his hands in his pockets. "For the entirety of his assignment he's not come one step closer to finding Balaur. If he'd been able to sooner, Calhoune could still be alive."

"He can't blame himself for what happened. Calhoune knew the risks. We all do."

Jack leaned against a pine tree. Without his hat, his hair was nearly black in the light of dusk. "I told him that, but sometimes a man's guilt won't allow him to see reason. I also told him if he gets drunk, I'll hold his head under the river until the thought of taking one more drink makes him sick."

Ivy joined him at the tree. Breaking off a chunk of the fat bark, she flipped it in her palm. "What was his response to that?"

"One unbecoming for a lady's ears. What are you doing out here?"

"First watch."

Nodding, he tilted his head back to look at the sky. Bits of hair brushed the tops of his ears and curled around the slight crimp in the left one. Ivy resisted the urge to run her fingertip over the endearing dent. "Without all these trees we'd be able to see Perseus tonight."

"I don't mind the trees."

"Neither do I. They're peaceful."

She pulled out her pearl hairpin. Smooth and practical, it had a way of calming her jumping mind and putting her thoughts in order. She picked at the bark, the flaky bits chipping away as doubt had chipped at her confidence all day. Fear kept her from voicing the apprehension; once said, it could never be retracted. Instead, it would strengthen to an uncontrollable existence.

Here in the fading twilight with Jack, the fear stumbled out. "I keep thinking about what that thug said. 'The next step is not enough.' How does a common criminal come to speak a language that hasn't been uttered in close to twelve centuries?"

"Perhaps a form of it still exists in the isolated villages of Russia."

"Dacian was spoken in the Carpathian region closer to what we now call Romania. There must be a common thread." She closed her eyes and flipped through her mental pages of history, searching for a clue. "If I can find the link—"

Jack gently shook her shoulders until she opened her eyes. "The answer isn't always in a book or the folds of history."

She snorted. "Easy for you to say when you'd rather shoot first and ask questions later."

"That is entirely untrue. I have on many occasions questioned my target before pulling the trigger."

"My point being that some of us have many tactical assets to fall back on while others are better equipped with knowledge." Even that was hard won. She came to Talon with little education, so she'd worked hard to learn as much as she could, but her contribution never felt like enough. Especially now that she was on a real mission.

"You have your instinct, and sometimes that's all you need out in the field. Learn to trust it as much as you trust that astounding mind." He dropped his hands and took a step back.

The compliment nipped at her insecurities until they whimpered in retreat like the unwanted fiends they were. Warmth rushed to her face, but she didn't allow herself to dwell in the glow and instead refocused on the topic at hand.

"What if we can't find Balaur? He's like trying to pin smoke with a needle." She jabbed the air with her hairpin for emphasis.

"A man who calls himself Balaur Tsar *wants* to be found. Otherwise he would've gone with Smith or Jones or the Russian equivalent." The corners of his mouth pinched. "He wields violence to bend others to his will. He has fashioned himself into a monster to be feared."

If only she had her books, despite what Jack said. Comfort wafted between their pages, as did her father's long-lost voice. Reading had become her way to keep him close, but over the years it had also become a new way to see life. Questions and answers nestled among the cream paper and black ink, awaiting discovery and rebirth into the world they were created to explain.

Before leaving on this mission, she'd reread every book in Talon's library about Russia, as well as those in the Library of Congress, to which Washington had special access. The country's culture, cuisine, folklore, history, terrain, civil wars—every last bit of knowledge that could prove useful. Not once had the books mentioned a man named Balaur, but perhaps if she could go back and—

"Books won't help find him."

"Stop reading my mind." An impossible command. He always knew what she was thinking whether she wished it or not. Closing off her mind to Jack was like trying to shutter an elephant behind a gauze curtain. She wiped the bits of bark from her pin and slipped it back in her hair.

"I can't help it. Your face shows your thoughts so vividly, like a painting on canvas." His thumb grazed her jaw, drawing her attention up. "Happiness, anger, sadness, contentment—I know every shade and have yet to determine one more beautiful than another."

Her heart tripped over itself. She forgot all about books and elephants. Forgot everything but the deep lull of his voice and the trail of sparks igniting in the wake of his touch. "It shouldn't be a surprise to find happiness there—not when I'm with you."

"I'm sure mine betrays the same feelings—happiness, contentment, and so much more."

His throaty confidence played across her senses, beckoning her closer for a whispered reply. "Such as?"

Jack grasped her face between his hands, and his eyes met hers with absolute certainty. Ivy let go of her last bit of doubt and let her eyes show her true feelings.

Then he kissed her. Soft yet firm, leaving no question as to his claim. And claim her he did until Ivy felt the air stir from her lungs and the longing in her heart drown in her love for him. It had always been there, powerful and surging beneath the surface, but his kiss cracked the floodgates wide open. She flung away the old hesitant bits of herself and rejoiced in becoming what she'd always been: *his.* There was no going back from this moment. Not for either of them. She was his, and Jack was hers—heart, mind, feeling, breath, soul. He was home.

Jack broke the kiss and leaned his forehead against hers. His shaky breath caressed her still-warm lips. "Ivy. You scare me."

"Why?" Her voice was as breathless as his.

"Because I can tell you more without saying a word than I've ever dared say out loud." The muscles in his throat constricted. "But now it can no longer remain unspoken. Silence isn't enough anymore."

"Then tell me what refuses to stay silent."

Even in the indigo of twilight, where light hovered between waning and gone, his smile pierced the darkness. "Your arms are the only ones I want to be wrapped in. Your eyes are the only ones I want to get lost in. My resistance crumbles at your smile. I decided on you long ago, love."

★★★

The beating of Jack's heart had whispered the simple truth for years. Freed from their confinement, the words lifted to the skies and erupted across the cosmos. The forest and cold fell away until they were surrounded by nothing but stars of their own making.

"I've waited so long to kiss you. Wondered what your arms would feel like around me when you weren't trying to choke me during training—imagined your lips against mine."

"I hope I didn't disappoint."

"Oh, Ivy. You're worth the wait." A tremor of uncertainty ran through him. He'd only kissed one girl before when he was eight. It was a dare and her mother had beaten him with her bag of groceries when she saw. The look on the girl's face showed only disgust. "Did I disappoint?"

She shook her head with a shaky laugh. "Very impressive, Agent Vale."

"It's not my intention to impress you. A sunset or a bouquet of flowers can do that. I want to make you feel something you've never felt before and never will again."

"Jack." A tear glimmered in her eye as she cupped his cheek. He rested his entire world in her soft, small palm. "There will only ever be you."

She leaned into him and drew his mouth to hers. The kiss was sweeter than before. More certain than before. Her arms slipped around his neck as he pulled her close and threaded his fingers through her silky hair. Moving on, his hands skimmed down her back and circled her waist.

Her words thrummed in his heart until he felt his soul would splinter with joy. She shook him to the core—caught him alight until an all-consuming fervency blazed from within, releasing the love they'd held back for so long. And within that fervency settled a deep peace. This was right. This sense of belonging that existed nowhere else.

"How long have you waited?" she asked at last after pulling back.

"Since that afternoon in the library when we read about nightwalkers."

"All this time? But you never said anything. You never indicated—"

He brushed a loose hair from her cheek, his fingers lingering around her ear. "I didn't want to rush you at first. You were still so young and trying to find your way at Talon."

"I'm only two years younger than you."

"Still young enough, and full of innocence. I wanted our story to happen as it willed and at its own pace. I told myself I'd wait no matter how long it took. But I waited so long that I began to doubt a woman as wonderful as you could ever return the affections of a man who has been seen as unworthy of the sentiment his whole life."

"That's the most idiotic thing I've ever heard you say." She grabbed his face and pulled him close, bumping her nose to his. "The past does not determine who we are. Other people do not have the privilege of deciding if we are worthy of love. You, Jack Vale, are loved. By me. Do you need another three years to consider this, or are you quite finished feeling down on yourself?"

Grinning, he took her hands and gently kissed the center of each palm. Right where she held him, safe and secure. "Quite finished, love."

Branches snapped. The peaceful, intimate moment shattered. Danger crackled.

Dropping her hands, Jack whipped out his pistol and took aim as the crashing ran toward them. An intruder wouldn't make that much noise. "Better not be a Russian looking for his cache of vodka."

Ivy held her pistol steady next to him. "Better that than a bear roused from hibernation."

More twigs cracked and leaves rustled as the footsteps pounded closer. The patterned rhythm of a human, not the loping of an animal come to shred them apart. Hardly comforting as the pistol butt warmed in Jack's hand. The noise stopped suddenly.

Heavy panting followed. Cold tendrils of fear curled in Jack's stomach, pushing him to the edge of awareness, but never off the cliff of terror. A balance that served him well. From the sound of the breathing, the intruder was about fifteen feet away—no more than twenty—and quite possibly lost. He had the tangled canopy of trees to thank for the loss of vision. At least he wouldn't be able to see them. But that also meant they couldn't see him until it was too late.

The person moved again, barreling down on them. A figure broke through the trees like a bat from a cave.

"Halt or I'll shoot," Jack commanded in Russian.

"D-don't shoot!" The man staggered forward, rasping loudly. "I m-mean n-no harm."

"State your business in the woods at this hour."

"My-my b-business?" The man spoke as if wondering himself. He was buried deep in a coat and hat that masked any identifying features. "I w-was . . . not s-sure if . . ." Twisting on his feet, he collapsed.

Ivy rushed forward and knelt beside him. "It's Fielding! He's alive." She pressed a hand to his forehead. "But he's burning up. We need to get him inside."

Jack pulled Fielding to his feet. Sweat streamed down the agent's cheeks as the blistering fever shook through his small body. "Fielding. Can you hear me?"

Fielding's eyes cracked open as his head lolled toward Jack. "C-Calhoune—"

Jack grimaced. "He's dead. Victor told us."

Fielding squeezed his eyes shut as a single tear slipped out.

"It's all right, mate. It wasn't your fault."

"Balaur—" Fielding sagged.

Jack slipped an arm around him to hold him steady. Like holding up a boneless foal. "Let's get you inside. We'll find Balaur and make him pay for what he did to Calhoune. I swear it."

Fielding's eyes flung wide open, glassy and wild. He clawed his dirty nails into Jack's coat like a desperate animal.

"He's . . ." He gripped tighter to the fur with a shake as grimy sweat rolled down his cheek. "I-I know where to f-find Balaur."

New York Herald

JANUARY 9, 1917

ANNIVERSARY OF BLOODY SUNDAY

As marchers in Petrograd gather to remember the twelfth anniversary of the massacre, more voices call for the abdication of Tsar Nicholas II.

TWELVE

Russian countryside
January 1917

Dobryzov Castle squatted atop a rocky hill with the lowering sun brushing off its dull timber and stone walls. Weathered to a dismal brown color, a thick stone wall enclosed the asymmetrical wings and pointy guard towers with a singular drive curving around the hill to its imposing spike-studded gate. Ivy had enlightened the team, those willing and unwilling alike, that the castle was constructed in the year 1168 and had been besieged in so many wars that its medieval turrets had to be reconstructed in a Gothic Revival style.

To Jack, the castle resembled a fat toad from the pages of *Grimms' Fairy Tales*. He lowered his spyglass and melted into dense woods of larch and fir nestled in the valley at the foot of the hill. The scent of pine thickened the air like tangible sap as the long needles brushed his dinner jacket sleeves. He'd knicked the jacket from a Muscovian baron's travel trunk while on the train heading east from Moscow. It was a far cry from the clothes he was accustomed to wearing on assignment, which required a certain degree of blending into shadow.

This getup was designed to place him at the apex of wealth and gentility, though hopefully no one would peer too closely and note how the jacket fit a mite snug across his shoulders, and how the trousers were a centimeter too short of the current fashion. He'd gotten rather good at sizing up his marks, but on a train he was forced to acquire when the opportunity presented itself. Stealing for the sake of gain was not an activity condoned by Talon, but appropriating the necessary items to achieve good for all came with the territory.

He resisted the urge to tug at the starched bib and the high collar that were determined to choke him before the night was out—which would also be a good backup plan for taking down Balaur should Jack's pistol or the explosives fail: slip a starched collar around his good-for-nothing neck.

His teammates, having changed into their respective outfits for infiltration, waited for him under the thick canopy of trees.

As leader, Jack took his place in the center. "One more time, let's go over the plan. Philip will chauffeur me to the castle at eighteen hundred sharp. I'll allow myself to mingle as a minor, unremarkable aristocrat weapons buyer from Petrograd."

Dressed in a more subdued gray service uniform that he'd filched along with two motorcars when they arrived at the nearby train depot, Philip straightened from where he leaned on a crate packed with what he called party favors.

"Once I drop off His Nobleness, I'll drive the auto around back and wait to unload the explosives until the rest of the team arrives." Grinning, he tapped the crate with his booted toe. "Ivy and I will then make quick work of placing the explosives in the party guests' motorcars, all timed for a synchronized explosion when I press the trigger from a safe distance."

"And we'll arrive at precisely nineteen hundred when I chauffeur Lord and Lady Borovsky to the castle"—Fielding nodded to the finely dressed Beatrix and Victor, who'd chosen their marks with a more accurate idea of measurements—"before joining Philip around back."

After taking three days in the *dacha* to recover from his fever,

Fielding was finally able to tell them what had happened. He and Calhoune arranged to meet a black-market weapons dealer in Kirishi after posing as potential buyers. Balaur's men grew suspicious when they noticed Calhoune's American-made pocket watch—it was always the smallest detail that could trip up an agent—and captured them both.

Fielding managed to escape, but not before snagging one vital piece of information along with an invitation to a demonstration to be held at Dobryzov Castle, hosted by none other than Balaur himself. Jack now held that invitation, and tonight they would cut off the head of the snake.

Ivy spoke next, her demeanor professional and offering no hint of the romantic confessions that had passed between them these last few days. "I will then unfold myself from the suffocating confines of the trunk tied to the back of the automobile and help unload the explosives. Fielding will distract the gathered chauffeurs while Philip and I set the explosives in each of the party guests' autos. No one will be able to make a quick getaway after Jack shoots Balaur—aside from us."

Effortless in his role as a bored aristocrat from Moscow, Victor brushed invisible lint from his jacket's sleeve. Fielding had put his forgery skills to good use by creating a duplicate of the original invitation for the esteemed yet fictitious count and countess.

"At eight o'clock—because that is what a Muscovian count would say and not this military time you insist on, and I am nothing if not thorough in my character for the evening—Balaur is due to make his grand arrival." Victor smiled adoringly at Beatrix, who dripped glamour in a beaded evening gown and jewels. She proceeded to ignore him.

"My lovely countess and I will beg a private introduction, which Balaur will not be able to refuse because of the money we promise to throw at his feet for his little weapons. In the middle of said introductions, we will maneuver him into a clear position, allowing our fearless leader to put a hole right smack in the middle of his head from the sniper's nest." Pointing to his forehead, Victor made a popping noise.

A bullet to the head. Just like that. No appropriate gun had been available, so Jack and Jefferson modified existing models and pieced together parts to build a sidearm better equipped for their clandestine operation. The pocket-size body of a Walther with the .45-round firing power of an M1911, wrapped with a silencer and fitted with a device that dropped the hammer and retracted the firing pin, which allowed the gun to be shot with one hand. An elegant Frankenstein, Jefferson had called the creation. It wasn't Jack's preferred M1903 Springfield rifle with Redfield scope, but he couldn't smuggle that under his jacket. The Franken, concealed in a hole he'd carved out in the sole of his shoe, would suffice for short range.

"In the meantime, Miles will have cut all communication lines to and from the castle," Jack said. Miles held up his hands, covered in fingerless gloves, and made snipping motions. "Chaos will ensue, and no one will be able to signal for backup."

Placing the lid on top of the crate, Philip tapped it down with the heel of his hand. Another crate of similar party favors was already packed in the trunk of the designated car, which was hidden from sight at the edge of the woods. "Each explosive placed in the autos will be set to a timer activated by this device." He held up a small box with a switch and button. "Once I press the button, the explosives will be activated, and we'll have exactly ninety seconds before they blow."

Beatrix cleared her throat. "Should that not go according to scheme, plan B will have Victor and me"—she shot her escort a sidelong look—"moving to shoot at point-blank range. After which, we will most likely if not definitely be killed or corralled for torture by his guards."

"Do not fret, my dove, for I would never allow such a fate to befall you. I will shoot you myself before allowing you to succumb to the madman's clutches." Grasping her hand, Victor brushed a kiss over her knuckles. Beatrix yanked her hand back, which earned her a wicked grin from Victor. "Plan C we shoot our way out Old West style."

Jack's collar seemed to tighten. A thousand things could go wrong in ninety seconds. He didn't even want to consider a saloon-style shootout. "Everyone better make it into our explosive-free automobile and down the drive before Philip presses the button. Any questions?"

"Why can you not simply put a bullet through his brain before he ever enters the castle?" Beatrix shifted impatiently in her heels as the beads on her gown clacked. "That *is* your specialty, and it would save us all this effort."

"I won't have a shot outside the castle," Jack said. "After the archduke was assassinated in an open car, others in target positions have taken care not to expose themselves so easily. He'll expect an attack outside. Once inside and moving among his minions, he'll be more vulnerable. He won't expect an attack in a room full of comrades who made it past his guards."

As the team made final arrangements, Jack distanced himself and walked a few yards down a small slope to the edge of the Kama River. Despite the chill of January, his skin flushed with heat. It was always the same as anticipation burned through his blood. Soon enough the burn would cool into a settling peace of purpose as he stepped into the fray and his vision narrowed on the target. Hours, days, weeks, even months of preparation narrowed to a single moment of action. One minute when everything happened at once. Anything before did not exist. Everything after had no existence. All hinged on that single moment in time.

He knelt and splashed a handful of frigid water on his face. It dribbled down his neck, loosening the starched collar. Seconds ticked by.

"Careful or you'll leave water marks," Ivy said from behind him.

"It's still an improvement." Shaking his hands, Jack stood and faced Ivy. She was dressed in a black coat and black trousers tucked into high boots, her hair wrapped up and hidden under a hat—the part of a boy servant. As long as no one peered too closely, the simple lines defining her feminine shape would go unnoticed. He, on the other hand, could never fail to notice. "I look like a fool in this monkey suit. Who orders a black-tie affair for black-market dealers and warlords?"

"A psychopath who appreciates well-dressed scoundrels," she said as she walked toward him. A tendril of hair had worked its way loose and brushed her rosy cheek. He liked that her hair was never scraped back or coiffed into elaborate towers like other women's. It held a softness that begged him to run his fingers through the splendor of colors—not sunshine blonde or sunset red or nutmeg brown but a mixture of all three, their differences complemented in the changing light.

"Calling me a scoundrel?"

"Only in the best sense." She stepped close and tilted her face up to his. "Make sure you don't charm a Russian crime princess in there."

"How could I when I've got a lady saboteur waiting in an auto trunk for me?" Grasping the loose tendril, he rubbed it between his fingers. The silky strands glided over his calluses.

"Be certain to remember that—or better yet, let me come with you."

He dropped the hair. "No."

She stepped back, all charming pretenses gone. "You told me to rely on my instinct more, and my instinct informs me that you shouldn't go in there alone. I'm certain any number of these gentlemen have left the wife at home in favor of bringing along their more entertaining mistresses. I'll pinch an evening gown—"

"And play the honey for tonight? Out of the question." Dressing a woman up like a tart and parading her around as a distraction had its strategical advantages in this line of work, but no situation was dire enough to cast Ivy in such a role. She would cause *too* much of a distraction—mainly for him—and upend the entire operation. Those gray-green eyes were too much temptation for any man.

"Do you think Beatrix is the only woman capable of turning a man's head long enough to slip a blade between his ribs?" Those eyes currently snapped at him like tidal waves on a gray sea. Temptation indeed.

"Are you trying to seduce me or start an argument?" He inched closer.

"Both?"

Filtering through the trees, the washed-out sun dappled her face with shadows of dancing leaves. Ivy wasn't the classical-style beautiful with long lines and sculpted angles. Her eyes crinkled when she laughed, and her legs were a far cry from elongated, but her head tucked perfectly beneath his chin when he held her, and her smile now was different from all the others, as if this one was just for him. He didn't want to change a single thing about her; every part of her was made to fit him.

"You are . . ."

"Beautiful, talented, immensely intelligent—"

"Dangerous." He pulled her into his arms and began to hum. *To greatest heights or lowest depths, I'd go to be with you.*

"You wouldn't have to go to great depths if you'd just take me along." Her whisper dug into his neck in peeved accusation.

"But what a sweet reunion it'll make once the mission is complete."

"Amid explosions and fleeing for our lives?"

"Think of them as fireworks." He pressed a kiss into the curve of her neck where it met her jaw, then spun her away and sprinted up the slope before he was tempted to linger a moment longer. At the top he called over his shoulder, "Don't get blown up pining for me."

"Those are *my* parting words to *you*, Jack Vale!"

He grinned and turned back. She stood by the river, woodland shadows and sunlight dancing in her hair as she placed her hands on her hips and glared at him. "Come back to me."

Still grinning, he blew her a kiss before dashing off to find Philip and the auto.

"Get all your goodbyes out of the way?" Philip was leaning against the driver's door squinting at him from beneath his service cap.

"Sounds like you think I won't survive."

Philip shrugged and the shoulders of his costume bunched up to his ears. It had clearly been tailored to fit a much stouter man. "I have no doubt you will, but women give in to the dramatics of parting. No matter how long—or in this case, short—the separation is." A cheeky grin spread across his face.

Jack wasn't about to give him satisfaction for the insinuation. No matter how correct he was. "Get in."

Philip's grin only widened as he wrested open the back door. "After you, sir."

The thick stone wall flanking the drive around the hill on one side with a steep drop-off on the other was lit with torches at precise intervals. As they inched along behind the dozens of autos awaiting their turn for inspection at the gate, Jack kept his focus straight ahead and refused to look at the void of blackness creeping along their left side. It wasn't that he feared heights, exactly, but he definitely preferred staying closer to the ground where the most he could break was a leg or an arm. Keeping his neck intact proved a higher priority.

"So, Boss, got any last messages for Ivy?" Philip inquired politely from the front seat.

"Should I?" Jack was determined to keep his expression neutral. A pointless act of subterfuge since Philip knew his every tell for bluffing and never hesitated to rake him over the coals for it. Like the time he added extra gunpowder to Philip's latest experiment of explosives and then denied all culpability when it nearly took out Talon HQ's west wing. Philip had gotten him back with fiendish glee by dropping miniature caltrops in Jack's boots while he slept and ringing the fire alarm. Jack walked with a limp for a week.

"Don't act coy. We all know. There's been a running bet for the past two years. Frankly, I'm surprised it took you this long. I owe Miles three whole dollars. That brick of silence hasn't said more than ten words to me the entire time I've known him, but he's sure quick to take my money."

"This is what the agents of Talon have come to? Betting on the private lives of their coworkers." Jack tapped his fingers impatiently against the seat as the line crawled forward.

"We need to keep the excitement up between missions somehow. Of course, now that the bet on you and Ives has been called, we've started a new marker for Beatrix and Victor. Care to add anything?"

"You make a lousy chauffeur."

Philip shot him a glare through the rearview mirror. "Not the kind of addition I meant."

"It's the only one I have to offer."

"As you say, sir."

At last they pulled to a stop beneath the arched gateway as armed guards examined the stolen invitation.

A portcullis with razor-sharp teeth hung overhead in the thick stones of the archway, ready to gnash its anger on unwelcome entries, while dozens of guards with bayonet-tipped rifles stood at the ready just beyond. The men weren't wearing military uniforms designated Russian or German or any country; these soldiers wore solid black with the image of a dragon coiled around a crown emblazoned in blood red on their chests.

The guards at the gate glanced up from their prolonged examination of the invitation and stared at Jack. Mustering an expression of aristocratic boredom, he trailed a lazy arm over the back of the tufted green leather seat of the Gräf and Stift Double Phaeton, a replica of the one in which Archduke Franz Ferdinand and his wife had been assassinated. Fielding, more superstitious than a black cat crossing under a ladder, made the sign of the cross over both autos to ward off evil omens.

Finally one of the guards handed the invitation to Philip and waved them through. Philip followed the other autos circling around the courtyard to a grand set of stairs leading up to the entrance and its large door.

At their turn, he hopped out and opened Jack's door. "Good luck in there," he whispered.

Jack climbed out and took a second to adjust his cuff links that were a dull gold in the dreariness. "Try not to get yourself in trouble out here."

Shutting the automobile door with less finesse than a man of service ought, Philip gave him a low bow. "As you say, sir."

The heat of anticipation cooled in Jack's blood as purpose sharpened his senses. After entering the castle, he made a pretense of admiring the tapestries and medieval carvings while counting the number of armed guards stationed at every door and calculating a second escape route should his first be blocked.

A guard appeared in front of him. "Weapons search, sir."

Jack tucked his chin and jerked back in ruffled indignation befitting his imagined station. "I beg your pardon. Do you know to whom you are speaking?"

"My apologies, sir, but each guest is required to submit to a weapons search."

"Who do you think we are? Ruffians to bring shanks and brass knuckles to a black-tie affair?" It was laughable how close to the truth his statement was. Not to mention hypocritical, considering the guests were all arms dealers gathered for a weapons viewing. There was no doubt that Balaur preferred holding all the power.

"By order of Balaur Tsar, sir."

Jack huffed and puffed with righteous annoyance as the guard made a quick show of searching for contraband by flicking open the edges of Jack's coat and patting his trouser legs. Things would get interesting very quickly if he were asked to remove his shoes. The Franken stuffed inside one was bound to raise a few questions.

Satisfied that Jack carried nothing of interest, the guard waved him on before harassing another guest. Jack followed the flow of humanity and arrived in a great hall where he marveled not at the dozens of chandeliers, priceless paintings and artifacts, or vista views overlooking the valley; nor did he rush to gorge himself on the delicacies of canapés, vino from Italy, fruits in ice bowls, bubbling champagne, or braised whole pigs with apple tartlets in their mouths.

Instead, he swept his eyes around the perimeter and then up. On the second floor was the minstrels' gallery with heavy drapes concealing it. His sniper's nest. Right where Miles had said it would be after his scouting adventure the day before. A secret stairway located next to the fireplace would lead him up there at zero seven thirty. Half an hour to wait until it was time to slip into place.

As he looked for where Beatrix and Victor were to be stationed, voices froze him to the spot. He'd expected the Russian, along with German, Austro-Hungarian, Turkish, and Bulgarian, but he was alarmed to hear the French, the Belgian, and especially the British English. Enemies from both sides of the war had come running when Balaur snapped his fingers. A sense of despair loomed at the thought, but he pushed it away.

Some people assumed that the dirty money shuffled in the black market could only dredge up lowlife scum with missing teeth, razor scars on their faces, and deplorable hygiene. This crowd was nothing like that or any other group Jack had dealt with before. Women were draped in jewels while the men appeared in fancy suits, and more than one wore a military uniform. This was no ragtag assembly, but the cream of society jostling to fill their golden coffers from war profiteering.

They clustered in small groups whispering and casting furtive glances at their competition while an orchestra wove clashing notes of civilized gaiety amid the tension. Any moment a violin string could pull too taut and snap the barely concealed distrust. Whatever display Balaur had planned must be a prize indeed to have assembled all these people together under one roof.

Every last one of these disgusting profiteers deserved to be lined up against a wall and shot with the very weapons they used to line their silk pockets.

The pistol stored in his shoe pressed reassuringly against Jack's foot as he inched closer to the ancient hearth roaring with fire and the scent of cedar. A gold-and-pearl-faced clock throned the ornately carved mantel and chimed the quarter hour. The "party favors" should be nearly in place in the guests' motorcars. The inferno of destruction they would produce would likely surpass the Fourth of July fireworks at the Capitol Building in DC. *Understated* was not part of Philip's vocabulary.

Two men strode by whispering furiously with a touch of Belgian upper-crust derision. "Bad enough we are forced to brave this Russian cold. Now we must endure standing beneath the same roof as Germans."

"It is only for one night," the second man said as his waxed mustache twitched. "We can resume killing one another tomorrow."

"I hire other men to do the killing. Cleaner that way— Out of my way!" The first Belgian raised a hand adorned with a large ruby and knocked back a server who dared to step too close with a tray of champagne.

The tray flew straight for Jack's face. He jumped back, barely missing a crystal flute to the eye, and bumped into someone standing behind him.

"I do beg your apology, my good—" Jack stumbled for words as he took in the creature before him. "Madam."

Creature. There was no other way to describe her. Female, most certainly, but one from a sphere unseen by most except under the faded light of a misted moon. Roundly squat and brown, she seemed to have sprouted from the earth, pushing herself into existence under the moldy dampness of wet bark. Frizzy brown hair jutted out from beneath a head shawl that looped around a long face. Flat lips and a flat nose hung heavy beneath a pair of colorless eyes that sought to hypnotize him without blinking.

"Forgive my clumsiness," he said.

"What is there in life but to forgive the adroit mundaneness of humanity? Accidents are but a mere intervention of Fate." Her voice was heavy as if weighted at the back of her throat with stone, and her Russian was thickened by a strange accent. Ivy would have it pinpointed in seconds. "In this collision of Fate, forgiveness is unnecessary, for the steps to rebirth are ones we all must undertake. All steps to what must be done next."

How did one reply to utter gibberish? "Um, thank you."

"You do believe in Fate, do you not? That there is a sole purpose, and it is our destiny to fulfill it. For the righteousness of all."

"I make it a point never to express my personal philosophies with a drink in my hand." He raised his glass of now-flat champagne. Across the room Victor and Beatrix stood close together whispering and mirroring his furtive glances to size up the crowd that perfectly masked a detailed perimeter check. "They often return to haunt me with twisted falsehoods long after the glass is drained."

The woman still hadn't blinked as she gathered the draping layers of her black cape around her like diaphanous bat wings. "Yet we all drink from the cup of life. Some will thrive in its dark liquid while others are fated to drown."

Jack took a step back, smiling politely, though every inch of his skin crawled at her presence. "Good thing I know how to swim."

As he moved away, his eyes caught on what looked like an over-large red fan embroidered in gold and pearls bobbing above the crowd. It floated along disembodied like a balloon until the black jackets and evening gowns parted to reveal a very real body attached beneath a headdress and decked out in the traditional attire of a Russian woman brandishing a serving tray.

Jack stared in disbelief as a very real fear hit him. "Ivy?"

Something had gone terribly wrong.

THIRTEEN

Two hours earlier

Why must people assume that just because a person is on the petite side, she must have no qualms about squeezing into tiny spaces?

"Well, you couldn't have gone as the chauffeur," Philip argued as he pulled a crate of explosives from the storage trunk tied to the second motorcar. He'd parked discreetly in the far corner with two rows of autos blocking their nefarious labors from view of the other chauffeurs who'd clustered around a small brazier glowing pathetically in the center of the courtyard. Busily occupied with staying warm and sharing cigarettes, the other drivers gave them no notice. "There is no possible way I could have folded myself as nicely as you did into that tiny space. My legs would stick out."

"I could break them if that would ease your qualms." Ivy stretched her arms. Freedom fluttered down her cramped muscles.

"Me crawling and dragging broken limbs to place explosives would hardly help our mission. Think of the greater good, Ives."

"I will as soon as the blood returns to my brain."

Tugging a shapeless cap onto her head to hide her hair, she glanced over the automobile roofs to where Fielding stood in the middle of the chauffeur cluster passing around a bottle of vodka topped off with bawdy tales. Nothing quite like booze and coarse laughter to distract the men as she and Philip slipped their deadly packages into their employers' back seats.

They worked quickly and silently, moving farther away from the chauffeurs and toward the stone walls surrounding the courtyard. Ivy squeezed between two Rolls-Royces on the last row. A rat shot in front of her. She managed to cut off the scream hurtling up her throat before it escaped.

Philip caught the explosives that tumbled from her arms and frowned. "I spent a great deal of time packing these, and I'll thank you not to set them off over a little mouse."

"It was a *rat*, not a mouse."

Rolling his eyes, Philip squatted and gingerly set the crate on the ground between them, then added her leftovers to it. "You said the same thing that time we crept through the underground passageways of the Capitol Building."

A squeak echoed from under one of the autos. A chill that had nothing to do with the freezing temperature grabbed the back of Ivy's neck. Mice and spiders were disgusting, but rats existed on a realm beyond terrifying. If one came tearing at her again, she couldn't be held responsible for the amount of screaming to follow.

Philip, being of the male variety with that inevitable interest in all things slimy and rabid, held no qualms about encountering lurking or scurrying beasts. "At least those tunnels were a smidge cleaner than this place. There's enough sludge on these cobblestones to fill the Potomac River."

"That's because the Capitol Building is a spritely ninety-seven years old while Dobryzov Castle is seven hundred forty-nine and was built during the reign of Andrei the Pious. A castle like this—"

Philip gave a ripping snore. "Unless someone died in a fierce battle and his vengeful ghost now haunts all who trespass its lair, save the history speeches for Jack. He's enraptured no matter what you say."

Ivy dropped to a squat next to him between the autos. "I don't know what you mean."

Still floating in the trance of utter happiness, neither she nor Jack wished to expose their intimate declaration to the prying attention of others. She'd lived with Philip as a brother for most of her recollected life, which spared little room for secrecy. He knew her habits as well as she could predict his moods. But the fragile newness between her and Jack was something Ivy wished to hold tight and protect as something of their very own.

"I mean"—Philip gave her a pointed look—"he can't utter a complete sentence that doesn't include your name, or think straight without his attention wandering to you. And he's shaving more than usual. Only one reason a man aims to keep a smooth cheek."

"Because only wildebeests look admirable with full facial hair?"

"Because he hopes to get close to a particular lady. That particular lady being you." He rolled his eyes. "Come on, Ives. It was bound to happen. You deserve a good man, and that's Jack."

She should've known she couldn't keep a secret from Philip. He knew them both too well. "You're a good man too."

"Don't say that. It's taken me years to build up my rakish reputation, and I won't have you ruining it in a weak moment of sentimentality." He pulled out a few sticks of dynamite and handed one to her.

"As your dearest and oldest friend, I tell you truly, no one considers you a rake. I'm afraid you miss the mark of a libertine as well." She laughed at his crestfallen expression and rushed to console him. "Take heart. There is ample room for those seeking improvement. Work hard, loosen your morals, and I'm certain some woman out there will be more than willing to slap your face after your skills have sharpened to match Don Juan's perfection."

His chest puffed out the tiniest bit. "Your confidence is appreciated."

After placing an explosive in the last auto parked in the courtyard, they slipped through a squishy, lichen-covered passage that connected to another square courtyard where gray snow had been shoveled against the walls to accommodate the later arrivals, now parked in the center. On the far side two armed guards were standing post before a set of iron-hinged doors built into the stone wall of the castle's central tower.

Lowering the crate to the ground, Philip flattened against the passage wall and peeked around the corner. "Now what do you suppose they have hidden in there?"

"Something they don't want anyone snooping around, or guards wouldn't be posted."

"Let's do some snooping then. I don't see other guards on the rampart."

"The cliff is on the other side. They must assume no one would be foolish enough to scale it; therefore, no guards are needed to patrol so high up."

Philip pulled the knife from his boot. "I'll take care of the henchmen by the door. You wait with the crate and keep watch."

"Our mission is to set explosives in the autos. Not take down guards."

"Guards who will grow suspicious when a chauffeur and errand boy waltz in carrying a crate. They'll want to know what's in the crate. I'll refuse. They'll demand. Blood will spill. Easier to avoid all that and go straight for the kill."

She was trained to kill. As Talon agents they all were, but there had to be another way. Death should only come as a necessity, a last resort. Flinging off her cap, she slipped past Philip. "You keep watch. I'm going. And I won't need a knife."

"Wait a minute. I said I was going."

"You had your daring idea with the explosives. It's my turn."

Eyeing her for a long second, he finally relented, twirling her hat on his finger. "Have it your way. Just sing out when you get in trouble and need help."

Taking a deep breath to calm the blood pounding in her ears, she sashayed across the open courtyard bold as brass, chin tipped demurely down and lashes suggestively up. *"Prosti menya, gospoda!* I'm so glad to have found you. Could you gentlemen possibly help me? I'm hopelessly lost in this great big castle."

"Stop right there!" Rifle muzzles glinted as the guards roused from their frozen stupor and aimed at her.

A quick intake of fear halted her forward motion. Covering her hesitation, she reached up and unpinned her braid to coil over her shoulder. "My mistress, Princess Vronsky, will have my head if I'm late to help her dress. Could you be sweethearts and point me in the direction of the ladies' sitting room?"

One of the guards lowered his rifle as he took in her boyish uniform at odds with her long braid. "Princess Vronsky?"

"Da." Of course, there was no such person, but she doubted either guard was literate enough to have read *Anna Karenina.* "She's ever so fidgety about her hair. I want to tell her the newer styles don't suit a woman of her age, but I can't afford to lose this position even if she does force me into this hideous travel outfit. She doesn't like the maids distracting attention from her, you see."

The guards exchanged a silent look of argument that ended in a shrug. What threat could a woman of her size possibly hold? Their second mistake. Their first had been not to shoot her on sight. "Go back the way you came to a door marked—"

Ivy grabbed the end of his rifle and jammed the butt into his stomach. He doubled over and she rammed her knee up and into his nose. *Crunch.* Blood spurted over the cobblestones as he fell to his knees in agony. Swinging the rifle around, she aimed for the second guard's head, but he ducked and pulled a knife from his belt. She thrust forward to strike him in the neck with the muzzle, but he pivoted and flung the blade straight at her heart. At the last second she twisted and the knife sailed past.

Knees or head? Which would be easier to crack?

The guard saw her hesitate and leaped with a second knife ready.

Philip was behind him in an instant and flicked a blade across the man's throat. He then made quick work dispatching the other guard.

"That wasn't necessary." The rifle went slack in Ivy's fingers. "I could have knocked them unconscious and tied them up."

"No witnesses."

She'd hoped to avoid it, but he was right. Talon taught them to kill only when necessary, which in their job proved rather frequently, and above all no witnesses. The sentiment soured in her stomach. *Nothing about fighting is fair when only one person can walk away.* Jack's voice drilled into her survival at any cost. It was an easy enough notion to boast in training sessions but quite another to stare it in the bloody face. If she couldn't handle that truth, she didn't belong here.

A focused calm returned to her mind as she dug through the guard's pockets and found a key. She slid it into the lock on the door. It popped open. "Time to find out what they're hiding."

Philip hauled the two bodies inside and out of view before shuffling in himself with the crate. Ivy had taken one of the guard's canteens and splashed away the blood funneling between the cobblestones. One last glimpse toward the empty ramparts and the darkening late-afternoon sky, then she closed the doors.

Musty darkness sealed them in. The air pressed against Ivy's skin, weighting her to the blackness, until a beam of light hit her face.

"There you are." Philip held a flashlight that had recently been attached to one of the guard's belts.

Ivy blinked to clear the dizzying red dots from her vision and followed the thin shaft of light. The tunnel was large enough for a small delivery truck to squeeze through. The walls were roughly hewn stone, and the dirt-packed ground gave evidence to tire tracks and footprints.

Philip handed her the other guard's light, then hefted his crate and started walking down the sloping tunnel. His light bounced without cadence in front of them.

Ivy aimed her light away from the bodies as shadows pressed in.

"I shouldn't have hesitated back there. I'm sorry." Her beam caught a black blob shaped suspiciously like a bat, and she quickly pointed the flashlight elsewhere. "We went through all the training and scenarios, but it's nothing like I thought it would be. Nothing can prepare you for what's required out in the field. The amount of subterfuge, one decision away from death, delivering the fatal blow. Don't you feel in over your head at times?"

"Sure, but sometimes you have to take a chance and trust your gut. Washington thought we were ready for the big time, so if nothing else, trust him." Philip stopped and looked back at her. "Do you know why I enjoy demolitions so much?"

"Because you like blowing things up."

He smirked. "That's the easy answer. The real one is because it lets me be in control. My entire life has been at the whim of deprivation. I don't have memories of loving parents and a warm home the way you do. I was born alone and to nothing, and the orphanage made sure I knew my place and never rose above it. Then you came and finally I wasn't alone. It was the two of us against the world. You and me, we've shaped our own destiny." He flicked a smile at her, then ducked.

Years of shared pain and loss passed between them. Some things were better left unsaid. "I couldn't have survived without you either."

He continued walking. "After we left the orphanage and thought we could finally do as we pleased without a headmistress screaming at us, we still had no control. Every day was about scrounging for a scrap to eat and a dry spot to lay our heads. And we were just kids. Never once were we able to rise up and seize a moment and say, 'This is ours and no one can take it from us.' Then we came to Talon and for the first time someone took care of me, gave me a task and told me to make something of it. Make something of *me*. For once I felt like I was in control of success or failure, and I won't ever go back to failure. I won't let you either. This"—he rooted in the crate and held up a stick of dynamite—"protects us. We don't have to live in fear anymore, Ives. We can fight back now."

What a pair of discarded misfits they were, but it was a bond she would never relinquish. "I'm glad we're fighting together."

"Always." He shifted the weight of the crate, then turned to continue down the tunnel. After a couple of steps, he tossed back a grin with an impish light dancing in his eyes. "Otherwise you'd be forced to bore the enemy to death by reciting some historical fact known only to musty old scholars."

She kicked a dirt clod at the back of his legs. "See if I help you next time you need to decipher an ancient text to open a cell door and save a pair of hostages."

"Open it? Nah, I'll blow it. Quicker." He laughed as he rounded a bend in the tunnel and fell silent. Ivy nearly ran into him as she made the turn and found him stopped dead in his tracks.

She gasped at the sight before them. A cache of weapons. Mounds of dynamite. Hoards of guns. Slews of knives. Piles of grenades. A treasure trove of death, none of which dared to be traded in the legal market.

And it all sat directly beneath the castle.

"He's stockpiling an armory," she said.

"More like preparing for a global takeover. There has to be over eight tons of explosives in here. Millions of dollars' worth of weapons. Do you know how much this collection would go for on the black market?"

"To blazes with the black market!" The walls pressed in, drawing in their last breaths of hope and poisoning the stale air with doom. "Philip, all those explosives we set in the autos . . . ."

He cursed. "When they go, there will be no controlling the blast from reaching this cache."

"What if we remove all the explosives? Abandon that plan for another option. We can come up with something else—"

Cursing again, Philip slashed a hand through his hair. "We don't have time to gather all of them, and it's far too late for an option B. If I don't set off the explosives, there's nothing to stop all those killers upstairs from chasing us. And if I do, there's a very real possibility of us and our team getting caught in the explosion."

The unspoken implications screamed between them.

Jack.

Upstairs, he, Beatrix, and Victor were positioning themselves for Balaur's arrival. They had no idea . . . There was no way to warn them of the deadly disaster they'd waded into.

No. She would not lose Jack. Not now.

She whirled and sprinted back up the tunnel, yelling over her shoulder, "Set the auto explosives as planned and inform Fielding of the situation. I have to warn the team in the castle."

Philip shouted after her. "Ivy! Stop! You can't just waltz in there! Ivy! We need a new plan."

"I'll come up with something!"

The cold indigo of night had begun to fill the courtyard as Ivy exited the tunnel. Snow had begun to fall, lacing over the frozen slush and clinging to her eyelashes as she checked for guards, then raced across the cobblestones. She slowed her pace to avoid drawing attention, then stepped inside and walked with purpose as maids and servers in traditional Russian folk costumes scurried about with trays of hors d'oeuvres and bottles of champagne. Above the din of moving feet, she heard pots clattering and shrill instructions screeched in Russian.

"What are you doing down here?" A man built like a barrel drum squared himself in her path. Emotionless eyes cut her from head to foot. "You're not dressed!" Ivy absorbed his appearance in a split second: black evening suit with tails, impeccable bearing, condescending glower—he could be none other than the butler.

She scrambled for a response. "Forgive me. One of the ladies upstairs required my help and I—"

His spiked eyebrows snapped together like two angry beetles. "Silence with your excuses. Get into uniform and pick up a tray."

"Right away, sir."

Lip curling in disdain, he pointed to a rack of clothing shoved into a corner. "Over there—and stay away from my male servers. Their tasks on this important night will not be veered off-kilter by giggling maids."

Bobbing a quick curtsy, Ivy snatched one of the ensembles off a hanger and ducked into a broom closet to wrangle herself into the embroidered satin material. No simple black and white to help a girl blend into the background for this grandiose affair. Rather, she found herself holding a beautiful traditional Russian *sarafan* of red and white with gold trim and a matching *kokoshnik* to perch atop her head like a crown, held in place with ribbons tied under the hair at the back of the neck. The attire seemed to herald her straight to the imperial court of Tsar Nicholas himself.

Except this night, she hunted a different tsar.

Orchestra strings guided her up a spiraling stone staircase worn smooth over the centuries to a service corridor congested with attendants jockeying to have their trays refilled with drink and food. Ivy grabbed a tray arranged with finger foods and slipped through a connecting door into a world the likes of which she'd never seen.

A medieval great hall with timber arches, detailed paneling, master stonework, priceless sets of armor, Gothic paintings, and dazzling chandeliers greeted her. It was as if the pages of *Grimms' Fairy Tales* had fallen open and spilled forth their magical contents. But just as those stories were never as they first appeared, so, too, was the masquerade before her. These men and women in their dazzling diamonds and starched collars were no knights of the realm or princesses fair but monsters parading in disguise as the hour ticked closer in which the world would be consumed by their weapons of destruction.

Where was Jack?

Keeping her expression serene and tray steady, she weaved between couples and groups, offering the dainty bites while scanning the crowd for a familiar head.

There. He was standing by the hearth with a woman who looked as if she'd stepped from another world of marshes and toadstools. A squat polliwog out of place and all the more coarse among the fine ladies and chandeliers. Ivy swerved away from a rotund man reaching for seconds when Jack caught sight of her. His expression betrayed nothing, but she knew the flash of horror in his eyes.

Before she could take another step toward him, a *balalaika* and *gudok* keened through the air with a tune from the Russian countryside. The crowd surged back, cutting her off from Jack, to make way as dozens of feet pattered into the room with the gentle *whoosh* of skirts swishing. Dancers.

Their feet began to move in time with the music. The tempo increased and the women twirled with their colorful peasant skirts flinging out like flower petals in bloom. The audience pushed forward to watch the entertainment. Ivy wormed around the bodies, careful to keep far from the dancers, and maneuvered toward the fireplace where she had seen Jack.

He remained there, his gaze fixed on the dancing as if it were the only thing to occupy his attention.

"*Piroshki*, sir?" She stopped at his elbow and offered her tray.

He didn't look at her. "Yes, thank you." His mouth swept close to her ear as he leaned over the delicacies with great concentration. "You better have a brilliant reason for being here, love, and not simply because you missed me."

She made a show of pointing to each of the delicacies. "There is a mountain of explosives beneath the castle. Philip has no way to keep the blast from the autos from reaching the cache. If it blows, there won't even be teeth to identify us with. I need to warn Victor and Beatrix." She started to turn away, but he subtly grabbed her arm.

His lips pressed together. "We proceed."

The music shimmered like suspended drops of silver rain, a breath of freshening notes as a *gusli* thrummed in a roll of ominous thunder. The dancers bowed gracefully to a roomful of applause, then scurried away with satin skirts and dreadful anticipation billowing in their wake as the instruments drifted on with a new tune.

Ivy covered Jack's hand on her arm with her own, her cold fingers brushing his strong and reassuring pulse. "If you don't get the shot and Philip is forced to blow the explosives early, we'll never make it out of here alive."

"I'll make the shot."

"But, Jack—"

Movement at the corner of her eye caught her attention. The strange woman draped in a black cape watched them with open interest. Ivy pulled back her hand. The woman's lips slitted to a smile and then she was gone like mist sucked back into the wet earth.

"Who was that woman?"

Jack looked over his shoulder. "What woman?"

A gong crashed.

Wide doors that blended seamlessly into the paneled wall flung open. The music stopped, its last notes shivering in the silence of the vast hall. Two rows of men dressed in black with the red crown-and-dragon symbol emblazoned on their chests marched in and fanned out in precise intervals to form a circle around the space the dancers had left vacant. Unlike their rifle-wielding counterparts at the gate, these men carried pistols, and curved blades as long as a man's forearm were strapped to their belts. A show of force without direct threat.

The moment seemed to take a deep breath, the last of its anticipating kind, for the spectacle was finally upon them.

In walked Balaur. The air stilled, amassing its weight around him and forcing all other matter to shrink in his presence. A brown robe trimmed in brown fur enfolded his tall, long-limbed frame, while pale hair snarled loosely over his shoulders. The stale scent of wine and dirt hung on him as if he'd been scraped down the sides of an abandoned cave.

"It's *him*." Jack muttered a curse. "And he's early. He was supposed to arrive at zero eight hundred."

"Who 'him'?"

"Yuri." Jack's whisper was filled with acid. "Two years ago he came to the States in hopes of recruiting supporters to his Russian revolution, which was little more than a dream at the time. Jefferson feigned interest in the crackpot scheme so Talon could extract further information, but the plan was foiled by a bit of rain and two overly curious orphans." His mouth twitched in her direction. "Seems old Yuri fled back to Russia and took up the pretentious moniker Balaur Tsar. Guess he found his supporters after all."

"Why do so many men follow him?"

"There's a fortune to be made in black-market arms dealing. The dregs of society will always flock in droves to that amount of obscene wealth."

She had been too scared and upset to remember any of the details, but at his nearness she was confronted with a long face, jutting cheekbones, flat nose and lips, and pale eyes—unusual eyes that appeared to have been pressed from their sockets into horizontal dashes as if they sought to see well beyond their physical limitations. He was severe. As if the failings of youth had been knifed off to leave hard bone in their place. How many murders had it taken to sharpen him into this treacherous monster?

He stopped in the center of the hall, raised long arms in the air, and tipped his head back a fraction.

"*Dobro pozhalovat*." His voice, loud and sharp as a blade, cut the silence. The crowd fell back, hushed into submission.

"Friends. Comrades. We have many obstacles that drive us apart. Politics, religion, country borders, tsars, and kings. Yet there is one thing that brings us together with a power greater than any force on earth. Money. In times of war a great deal of profit can be made, as well you all know; otherwise you would not be here. The longer this war drags on, the more riches to be acquired—and the bigger the gun, the greater the riches."

"I need to get into position. You get back outside with Philip." Jack's gaze darted around the room. "Where are Victor and Beatrix?"

They were penned against the far wall behind a crush of people and an impenetrable line of guards. They would never be able to reach Balaur in time from where they stood or put him in line for a clear shot.

Jack cursed again. "I'll have to shoot without them."

He moved toward the hidden minstrel staircase, but Ivy cut him off. "Too late." She nodded toward Balaur's men blocking the path to the steps and every other potential exit.

Trapped.

Balaur continued to command his spectacle. "As you have observed by now, this castle is filled with primary customers tonight. No shadow buyers on your behalf to hide your identities. I want you to stare into the eyes of your competition. These are the lords you make war against. For your bravery, I have designed a special reward. A new weapon of which the common mind could never dream. Its ingenuity and deadliness will make your enemies tremble before you in fear. Bayonets, flamethrowers, poisonous gases"—he sneered— "children play at such pathetic toys."

With a flick of his summoning hand, ten men pulling a large cart entered the room. Their faces flushed red with exertion and the ropes creaked against the weight of the deadly mortar poised at their backs.

Larger than an automobile, the cannon mortar gleamed a dull gray along its sleek body down to the tip of its pointed nose. A perverse nightmare crafted in understated grace.

Dear God in heaven. Half the world would be annihilated.

"Weighing more than a rhinoceros, this shell and its brothers belong to the White Wolf, the largest cannon-gun machine ever made. A gun so enormous it cannot be moved from its location far from here and can propel mortars such as this across no-man's-land and beyond with its owner never stepping a foot outside his country.

"Let the earth shake beneath your feet, the hot metal fill your nostrils, and the horrifying boom burst your ears! It will be the last sound your enemies will ever hear. At last, you will claim supreme triumph!"

The hall erupted in a cacophony of buzzing voices in several languages.

"I have learned that if it sounds too good to be true, then often it is not," said a man near the front of the crowd. Russian. "How do we know this White Wolf fires?"

"Do you think I would dare to present an offering that does not exceed all expected and promised?" Balaur's gaze slid around the room and stopped on the Russian. The man paled. "My Wolf has been tested with great success. Judge for yourself by the city-block-wide craters it has left in the Ottoman Empire and Romania."

"I'll pay you twenty million rubles for White Wolf," a German voice shouted from the back.

"Thirty million!" cried an Italian.

"I will not limit this magnificent weapon by naming a price. Not this time." Balaur's dead eyes gleamed. "Tonight, the highest bidder walks away with the prize. The White Wolf is the only weapon of its kind."

A portly man with the royal sash of Denmark harrumphed from the front row. "How do we know there *is* a White Wolf and not simply this shell we see before us? Where is this one-of-a-kind gun?"

Balaur stroked his beard as it hung like a dead thing against his chest. "Being the length of a blue whale and twice its weight, the White Wolf is not travel friendly. Forgive me if I did not take on the trouble of hauling it from Crimea for your inspection. The winner may claim his prize at my facility at Swallow's Nest on the Crimean Peninsula and witness for himself the power I have harnessed. The bidding starts at thirty million rubles."

Voices clamored over one another as enemies shouted to outbid one another in an unholy purchase of hellfire until at last a victor was appointed.

"Congratulations to Captain Glišić. You will no doubt find sufficient use for your newly acquired prize, and I look forward to seeing it put to action."

Ivy grabbed Jack's sleeve with her free hand. "Glišić is the leader of the Black Hand. They were involved in the assassination of Archduke Ferdinand. An unstable weapon in the hands of a terrorist group . . ." Her stomach churned. After taking down Balaur, they needed to destroy this White Wolf before it destroyed half the world.

"Auctions and prizes, bah! What sort of game are you twisting?" A man with a thick Ottoman accent and a dozen medals swinging from his chest shoved through the clamoring crowd. "We came here with a promise of weapons for sale—not just one fantasy gun."

Balaur cocked his head at the brazen defiance. Greasy strands of hair stuck to the sides of his neck. "And so there were. Only, you lost. I control the weapons; I make the rules."

He pushed his curved-toe reindeer boots—often worn by the indigenous Sami people north of the Arctic—against the man's polished shoes. "Do you not appreciate the way I do business?" His voice was deadly low as the room fell silent.

"You give these weapons to the *russkiye* and the Serbs. Those of us left do not stand a fighting chance against them."

Balaur tapped a bony finger against the İmtiyaz Madalyasi hanging from its place of prominence around the man's neck. *Tap. Tap.* His long, dirty nails clicked the embossed black.

"*Da*, there is truth in what you say, but I have never professed commitment to the truth, and I honor no loyalty beyond profit. I do not care if you are Turk, Serb, British, or Indian. The highest bidder wins the prize, and you are not the winner." Sweeping his long robe aside, he pulled a knife from his belt and sliced it across the man's neck.

The crowd gasped and shrank back in horror, a din of chatter building around the room. Jack quickly knelt beside Ivy and fiddled with his shoe. Rising, he nudged his way to the front of the crowd. Right behind him, Ivy dumped the delicacies from her tray and quickly palmed the knife she'd strapped to her arm.

Balaur's piercing gaze lingered on the body at his feet. Blood drained across the gleaming wood floor to fuse into a singular shallow pool of extinguished life. Lifting the hem of his robe off the floor, Balaur wiped blood specks from his boot on the back of the dead Turk.

"Is there anyone else in disagreement with my distribution of my weapons? Anyone else foolish enough to challenge my methods?"

"You drone on, you lunatic." In a flash Jack whipped up the gun and leveled it at Balaur's head. "I'm tired of listening."

A loud bang exploded from the side of the chamber where Victor and Beatrix had been trapped. Smoke engulfed the room. Not quite the plan B they had discussed, but it would do.

People screamed and stampeded for the exits. A guard with a fixed bayonet rushed at Jack. Ivy struck him with her tray, then swept her foot under his. He hit the ground hard but jerked his bayonet to rip through Ivy's sleeve as she came at him with her knife. The bayonet sliced her skin. She hissed in pain as he then swung the butt around and knocked Jack in the thigh.

Jack dropped to his knee, his bead on Balaur lost.

Ivy jumped behind the guard, grabbed his head, and twisted. *Pop.* Dead. "Get the shot!"

Jack took aim and fired.

Balaur, his appearance ghoulish in the smoke, spun from the bullet's impact and dropped to a heap, smothered in shrouds of roiling gray smoke.

A dozen languages shrieked in terror as people clawed and trampled one another for the door. Grabbing Ivy's arm, Jack hauled her to her feet and knocked people back as they pushed through the fray. She clung to him, her barricading wall of protection. Smoke coiled thick, choking out sight and muffling sound to garbled moans of panic.

Until a high-pitched voice rose above the deafening clamor.

A woman's cackle. Ivy twisted her head around and saw the strange woman who'd been standing near Jack earlier. She now stood in the center of the great hall, over Balaur's body, with the chaos building around her. And she was pointing straight at Jack.

Jack yanked Ivy in front of him, and just as he pushed her through a side door, she saw the woman vanish.

They burst into a narrow corridor and slammed the door behind them.

Jack frowned at her bloodstained sleeve. "Your arm."

It stung like mad, but this was hardly the time for an examination. "I'll manage."

"If we survive this, you're going to get more than a piece of my mind for abandoning your post." He glanced up and down the hall as cries of panic crashed toward them like a tidal wave. "Ready to make a run for it?"

Guards rounded the corner. "There they are!" Guns aimed and fired.

Ivy raised her pistol and grinned. "Ready or not."

FOURTEEN

"Of all the reckless, stupid things you could have done, sneaking in there like that is at the top. Hold still." Jack gritted his teeth as fury boiled to his lips. He'd managed to squash it during their escape, but they were more or less safe for the moment. He tore the sleeve off Ivy's dress. Blood trickled from the slash angled across her bicep, the bright red drops marring her white skin and glowing in the campfire light.

The flight from Dobryzov Castle had nearly killed them quicker than any assassin's bullet. Smoke had streamed from the medieval windows and doors. Aristocrats and dignitaries screamed and tore in all directions for escape. Bodies had been strewn about the stairs and courtyard after being pushed down and crushed under stomping feet.

While the frightened masses fled to their rigged autos, Philip and Fielding idled in the only working motors and sped off as soon as their teammates threw themselves into the back seats. Unlike Ivy and Jack, Victor and Beatrix had managed to race out among the crowd without a single bullet fired at them. Careening down the drive, the team had barely made it to the bottom of the hill before a fireball exploded into the night sky behind them. The stone wall blasted into the air as the driveway cratered to a blazing pit. Not a soul followed them to their rendezvous point deep in the woods seven klicks away.

They had intended only a brief pause to collect their breath before pushing on to Crimea, but first Jack was forced to tackle the fight brewing in front of him. And his opponent knew right where to hit him.

"My stupidity has nothing on yours most days." Flipping open the first-aid kit, Ivy unstopped the iodine bottle and squeezed three yellowish drops across the bayonet cut. "You told me to start thinking beyond the pages of a book, so I did."

"When I said to rely more on your instinct, I did not mean for you to throw common sense out the window."

Ivy rolled her eyes. "Make up your mind. Either you want me to use it, or you don't."

"I want you to use it the correct way."

"The correct way according to you, perhaps. Much to your current dismay, I have a mind of my own, and I will put it to use in the way I see fit." Recapping the iodine, she returned the bottle to the kit. "Correct me if I'm wrong, but was that not one of my quirks you once found so endearing?"

"Under normal, non-life-threatening situations, yes. Right now, I find it irritating." Jack unraveled a bandage from the kit and wrapped it around her arm. "You had an assignment and you abandoned it. You were to remain outside with Philip. Those were your orders." Anger seethed, shaking his fingers as he tied off a double knot.

"And I obeyed those orders until something greater was at stake—your *life*. And the lives of Beatrix and Victor. Don't tell me you wouldn't have done the same. I happen to know you risk personal safety for others on a frequent basis because that's who you are."

It was precisely what he would have done, but if he was to lead a successful team, each member had to follow his orders. Not take matters into their own hands and twist his heart with more fear than he'd ever known. "Do not turn this back on me. The mission comes first."

"*You* come first." She gripped his fingers. "We vowed to protect the lives of others, and in that moment your life needed protecting."

"Don't twist the meaning of our vows to Talon to suit your purpose."

"I'm not. I'm simply interpreting them to include my team."

"This isn't some training exercise in the middle of Nowhere, Maryland, where you can try again tomorrow if you make a mistake. This is the field. It's deadly and requires every whit of sense an agent possesses. How can we as agents be protectors when you're constantly putting yourself and other agents in danger?"

"Danger is what we *do*!" Intensity sparked in her fire-lit eyes.

Let it spark. Let it turn to rage. Let it burn through him until he all but quivered at the thought of losing that flame. "Don't do that. I need to be furious at you right now." His voice was ragged, harsh from battling the fear inside him. A fear that wanted to shake sense into her until her teeth rattled, while he simultaneously burned to kiss her until time itself stopped.

"Then be furious. At least you're still alive to do so." Her eyes sparked with defiance.

Jack pulled his hand from hers and shoved the first-aid supplies back into the kit, then slammed the lid closed. Curious eyes from the rest of the team glanced their way. Could they not at least pretend to offer a semblance of privacy?

He stood and turned away from them and stared into the surrounding darkness of oak and pine. High above the frosted limbs, a ball of orange glowed against the black vastness of night, the scent of ash curling among the needles of heady evergreen in a strange dance of destruction and fresh life. Dobryzov Castle would be little more than medieval ruins come dawn—and Balaur's bones to resurrect no more.

He looked to Ivy in her torn dress with her bandaged arm. Yes, they had killed the intended target, but at a cost that was nearly too much.

His life had always been a survival of lone wits. His parents found him worthless, and his aunt thought even less of him. By six he could properly define love as everything he was not and did not have. So he ran away and sought to fill the emptiness inside by fighting and trying not to die on the streets of DC. Jefferson had found him in a bloody mess after a boxing match and taken him to Talon. There he found the purpose and loyalty he'd craved all his life. Yet despite their acceptance, a shadow of fear hovered. Would they, too, find a measure of failure in him and cast him off?

Then Ivy attacked him and his world changed. She gave him so much more than existence. How dangerous it was to finally have something worth losing.

He turned back and knelt before her, then took her hands and kissed her fingertips. Small and delicate, they were capable of exquisite tenderness or determined death.

"If something ever happened to you . . . I couldn't go on."

"Yes, you could. You're too stubborn not to." A smile eased across her face.

His hands tightened around hers. "I mean it, Ivy. Don't disobey orders again."

Leaning forward, she pressed a kiss to his knuckles, then broke away before giving him the chance not to care who saw him kiss her. She stood and handed him a blanket. "Privacy, please."

He dutifully held it up and turned his head away. Clothes rustled and dropped to the ground. "I promise I won't disobey orders again. Unless I have to get to you, because that's a promise I can't keep. And I won't. Just like you wouldn't for me."

Jack hissed beneath his breath. "You don't fight fair."

"Nothing about fighting is fair. Don't you remember telling me that?"

"I'm regretting teaching you anything."

She leaned across the blanket and kissed his cheek. Her lips were cold on his chilled skin. "Your dimples show when you scowl." She buttoned her jacket and took the blanket, then folded and stored it in the duffel bag with the last of their spare clothing. The Russian serving uniform she gathered and dropped into the fire. No evidence left behind. "A shame. It was pretty."

A burst of warmth flared from the charring white-and-red satin and highlighted the faces of his team members.

Except for one. "Where's Philip?"

Victor, having changed out of his formal wear, jerked a thumb over his shoulder. "Said he was going to do a perimeter check."

Jack hadn't issued a perimeter check. They had stopped only long enough to regroup and change clothes. He wanted them gone from the region before Balaur's surviving men, if there were any, had a chance to scatter in search of the culprits. He pulled Undertaker from its holster hidden beneath his jacket and checked the pistol's chamber before moving beyond the edge of light. The last thing he needed was to play hide-and-seek in the dark after his best man decided to go rogue.

"Get the gear packed in the autos. Beatrix, find me coordinates to the Black Sea. Our mission was to kill Balaur and we did that, but now we have a new goal. Find and destroy the White Wolf. Miles, wire headquarters when she has the route and inform them of the new target." *And tell them I might have to kill one of my agents for going off on his own. Again.*

Miles signed, "Headquarters won't appreciate you changing targets without consulting them first. They like to give the orders."

"When the assignment was first ordered, Balaur was the only mark. Discovering he was building a cataclysmic apocalyptic gun in a secret facility requires the mission to evolve. We are not finished until every last trace of his fingerprint is erased," Jack said.

Washington and Jefferson could bark all they liked, but no one would argue against a completed task.

"Here's something better than fingerprints." Like a champion of battle announcing his triumphant moment, Philip pushed through the trees grinning with achievement. Two of Balaur's men marched in front of him at rifle point. "Found them hugger-muggered down the road."

Dressed in the heavy black uniforms of death, the captives had belligerent eyes that had witnessed too few winters and far too much evil. Boys fighting in a war of men's making in hopes of pocketing gold for themselves.

The dull ache of an ill-sought burden lodged itself on the precipice of Jack's collapsing patience. "We have no need for hostages."

Per usual, Philip had shrugged over the line of caution and barreled straight into disregard. "They'll have important information." He prodded the hostages in the back with the rifle muzzle and barked in Russian, "On your knees."

They must have sensed they were not in a position to bargain because the captives did their best to upset the balance by scowling furiously as they knelt. Those expressions hid a multitude of emotions. Fear, anger, denial, jealousy, hatred, and the inexperienced notion of summoned bravery.

Jack searched their faces and selected the two most viable emotions. "Were they running or searching?"

"Running."

Fear it was, then. Good. A faster trigger to pull rather than wasting precious time dealing with two thickheads set out to make a name for themselves in memory of their recently deceased leader. It also meant no one tracked his team. Yet.

"Tie them up and break camp. We leave them here." Exposure to the night cold would kill them quickly enough without wasting bullets.

Philip didn't budge. "They can give us information. Plans. Accomplices."

A jagged piece of Jack's patience cracked off, exacerbating his sour mood. "Balaur is dead. We know where his facility is. Not to mention these are low-ranking lackeys if their cheap boots and inability to overpower a single man on a deserted road are any indication. They likely haven't been granted pertinent intelligence. We don't have all night to launch an interrogation for answers that will never come."

Firelight clawed against Philip's face with red raking over his stubborn brow and hardened jaw. "We came all the way to this forsaken country, nearly getting ourselves blown up, and you won't take ten minutes to break them for information that might be of use to this mission?"

The insubordination exploded Jack's remaining fragments of tolerance. Challenging him as a friend was one thing, but challenging his call as leader in front of the entire team was another insult entirely.

"In the woods. *Now.*" Jack snatched the rifle from Philip's hands and tossed it to Fielding. He nodded to the prisoners. "Get them tied."

He stalked deep into the privacy of the trees, far beyond the camp, where the only captive audience was made of icicles and tree branches too bothered with their winter nakedness to notice the humans trespassing their frozen domain.

Philip's breath blasted the air in a crystalline puff of smoke. "You're wasting an opportun—"

"One was opening doors when I walked into the palace. The other was checking invitations at the gate. I'm not basing mission facts by the make and model of automobiles they screened at the party." Blood seethed in Jack's veins.

At Talon he excelled at every task thrown his way and got along well enough with other agents, yet he remained apart. Until Philip and Ivy came along. He envied their closeness, their history, and the ease with which they knew each other, and without warning he found himself drawn into their circle. Ivy stirred his mind and heart, but it was Philip who offered him an understanding that could only exist between two beings of similar interests and pursuits. A brotherhood. They had respected each other without resentment of the other's talent. Or so he thought. A man could not ask for a better friend.

But at that particular moment, Jack was ready to knock his friend's head off and be done with it. A man's frame of mind was always clearer after a good brawl.

"I went through the trouble of marching them here—in the dark, I might add. The least we can do is interrogate them," Philip said.

Seething shifted to boiling. "You went off on your own without permission looking for trouble when I explicitly ordered a regrouping to change clothes, assess damages, and discuss routes before getting out of here in half an hour. Not once did I mention taking hostages—or doing a perimeter check."

Philip stepped forward, inches from Jack's face. Challenge sparked in his eyes. "Why can't you admit when someone else has a good idea? Why not try things my way for once?"

"What do you think this is? The training room where we can sit around discussing tactics? Despite your best efforts to forget the obvious, you are in the field, and I am in charge here. I am responsible for this entire team." Jack fought the burning in his veins as his anger at Philip's insubordination and fear for Ivy's life collided. He took a deep breath. His duty was to the team. Not his own arrogance or the pangs of his heart.

"You leaving to do as you saw fit endangered all of us. Talon agents live by a code of honor, and I will not put a single life at stake on account of your selfish recklessness."

"Selfish? For wanting to take action instead of hiding out in the woods? Talon's codes exist to keep us from sitting on the wrong sideline of a righteous fight." Philip swatted at a fir tree. Needles scattered across the ground. "Come on, Jack. We don't run away from a ready brawl. Avoid it if possible, you say, until it comes swinging at us."

Why was his team so determined to twist Talon's ideals to their own means tonight? How could they hope to continue upholding those sacred pillars when they were constantly putting the entire team in danger?

"Our fight here is done. Balaur is dead. Our next task is to finish taking down his operations before those mortars are launched straight at the front line of the war."

"We'd be foolish not to gather as much information as possible and terminate lingering threats."

"I won't kill those men in cold blood."

"You did with Balaur."

Jack's fist strained. One punch. That was all it would take. He had to maintain control. "Balaur was the target. An assassination to prevent the spread of further bloodshed."

Frozen dirt crunched under light footsteps. A small form melted through the darkness and took shape into Ivy. "You do realize that we can hear every word you're saying, right?" She plucked a dead leaf from a withered branch and twirled it between her fingers. "Not enough leaves to provide adequate muffling."

Another cloud of irritated air blasted from Philip. "If you're so keen on arguing with those trying to help, why not yell at her for abandoning her post?"

"He already did while you were gallivanting down the road." Ivy blew the leaf from her hand. It caught on a brisk wind before spiraling to the ground in a slow dance of decayed beauty.

"Both of you. With me. Now." Jack stalked back to the campfire and stood wide legged as he stared down each of his team members. Even if their actions were justified, this was a challenge to his authority that no self-respecting leader would dare allow. To do so spelled disaster. "If any of you want to run around with your own interpretation of how an assignment should be managed, do it elsewhere. As long as you're here, you will operate under my command. Put another insubordinate toe out of line and I'll boot you right over the Russian border to find your own way back to Talon, where I can personally guarantee the only assignments will be scrubbing gunpowder from the floor cracks."

Tension crackled hotter than the fire. No one met his eye. He hated standing there hurling threats, but defiance could not be tolerated if they were to advance this mission with any degree of success.

Hauling in an unsteady breath, Jack gouged his hands through his hair, digging along his scalp. Tension rattling the length of his bones settled into submission. "All of you will drive me into an asylum before this assignment is done."

Across the fire, Philip was the first to meet his eye. A smile ghosted his expression. "Wouldn't be a mission complete if someone didn't fall off the deep end of sanity."

Jack's lip twitched. Not quite a smile, but enough to snip the strain coiling around the group. In that quiet exhale, the captives made their move. The one closest to Victor wiggled his hand free of his bonds and pulled a Luger pistol from inside his trousers, jumped to his feet, and ran.

Victor dove after him, but the man turned and fired. Victor fell, clutching his bleeding leg.

Fielding took aim and shot the escapee dead while his friend grabbed Beatrix and wrestled her into a headlock.

Jack yanked his pistol from his belt and took aim. "Release the woman."

"*Nyet!* I go and she comes with me." Eyes darting with terror, the man jerked Beatrix against him, using her as a shield. No open spot to shoot.

Philip lunged from the side. The man spun sideways at the surprise attack, taking Beatrix with him and exposing the right side of his body. Jack aimed for the head.

Bang!

The man dropped dead. Splattered in blood and exploded matter, Beatrix screamed and pitched forward. Philip caught her, but she pushed out of his arms and flung herself next to Victor. "Devil ragger!"

"Such language from a lady." Pale in the yellow glow of the fire, Victor gritted his teeth as Ivy rushed over with the first-aid kit. "It's not as bad as all that."

Glaring through blood-streaked hair, Beatrix snatched the kit from Ivy and flipped it open, knocking bandages, scissors, and iodine tablets around like bocce balls. "You've been shot, stupid man. It doesn't get any worse than that."

"I would endure such pain gladly if only to steal a precious moment of your company."

The sweet metallic scent of spilled blood choked the fresh pines.

"Gah! Fire and hell stone! Must you pour that vile brew on me as I lay dying?" A squirming Victor was held in place by Miles and Ivy as Beatrix dabbed iodine around the oozing wound.

Twisting the cap back on the small brown bottle, Beatrix grabbed the same roll of gauze Jack had recently used on Ivy's arm and wound it around Victor's gunshot. "You're not dying, but you need a doctor. Perm is ten kilometers from here. The closer villages employ the local butcher for bullet extraction and suturing if you prefer."

Victor had the presence of mind to look affronted. "I am not an animal upon a block to be hacked at."

"Sometimes I wonder."

Ivy clamped Victor's ankle to the ground as he bucked against restraint. She tore her gaze to Jack. "We have to take him to Perm. It's not a clean shot. The bullet is lodged in the femur. One of us can dig out the slug, but the bone is shattered and needs to be reset by a professional. There's also the risk of infection, and we don't have medicine on hand."

The femur. The longest and strongest bone in the body. It didn't forgive unwelcome intruders easily. From the sweat dotting Victor's brow and the ashen tinge of his cheeks, the injury was retaliating with the full brunt of pain. To his count, Jack had removed precisely two bullets from people before while simultaneously recognizing surgery was not his calling. He would do it again if life hovered in the balance, but this instance might prove good intentions often caused more harm.

"Finish binding the wound, then put him in the back of the auto." Jack bundled the spent weapons into their carrying case and hauled it to the parked autos a few yards away, hidden behind brush. "After the doctor we'll find a safe location to rest before continuing on."

Fielding handed the rifle to Philip and marched after Jack. "I'll take him to the physician in Perm and get us back to Petrograd where we're needed. You go on with the assignment."

"It's too dangerous for you to return there. I'll wire Talon and tell them—"

"You'll tell them Balaur is dead, but the mission isn't complete yet. This they don't need to know about just yet."

"An agent is down. Headquarters must be informed."

"Jack, you've been in the field long enough to know what will happen." Weariness tinged Fielding's voice. "They'll send a replacement, or worse, order a stand-down until they can scramble together a new plan. Men who spend too long in the office and not on the ground cause delays. You and I both know we can't afford delays." Moving to the auto without the stash of weapons, Fielding opened the driver's door and slid onto the front bench. "Somehow I knew I'd never be the one to take down that madman. Losing Calhoune, well, it shook me. Then you came along, and I knew. Great Ichabod, did I hate you for that, but let's face it. You've always been the better agent. Steady as the Buffs, you are."

Jack shrugged off the compliment. He didn't feel nearly as calm as others perceived. "We only got this far because of you and Calhoune. Without that invitation we might still be twiddling our thumbs in Petrograd."

Fielding's expression sagged. "Calhoune might still be alive as well."

Scratching a dirty hand through his hair, Jack weighed his obligations and split them down the middle. Headquarters could scold him when the mission was complete and they were all stateside again.

"I'll wait twenty-four hours to give us all a head start before wiring Talon. They need to know about Victor, but it'll be too late for them to interfere by then."

Grunting with every step, Victor hobbled over supported by Miles and Ivy. Sweat dripped down his face and soaked his collar as he lumbered into the back seat and collapsed against the leather, shaking from head to toe. Shock had set in.

Beatrix tossed a blanket over him, tucking folds around his chest while carefully draping it over the injury. She brushed a strand of hair from her forehead and flattened her lips. "Don't die."

Victor rolled a grin up at her. "Would you mourn me all your lonely days? Knowing that, I might die a contented man."

"Insufferable." She slammed the door and stomped away.

Jack leaned down to catch Victor's eye through the window as the auto sputtered to life. "All right there? We'll get you to the doctor and by morning you'll be enjoying a hearty breakfast of *kasha* and *butterbrots*."

Victor lolled his grin at Jack. "And vodka."

"No vodka."

"I won't be on the clock, so *da*, vodka." Victor's head tipped back as a shudder tremored along his limbs. Bright red blood seeped through the bandage.

Jack banged on the side of the door. "He's losing blood. Get going!"

The wheels crunched over the frozen grass, headlights slicing through the darkness as the motorcar weaved through the woods to the main road and disappeared out of sight.

The last sounds of rubber on gravel faded to the hushed sounds of night, reverent and untroubled by the foils of man. Jack turned back to his team standing silently behind him.

"That is why we don't take hostages." He took a deep breath that settled in his lungs like a magazine of lead bullets and strode past them to the other auto, brushing Ivy's fingertips as he walked by.

"Pack it up. We've got a train to catch and a weapon to destroy."

The Washington Post

FEBRUARY 1917

AMERICA FACES BREAK WITH GERMANY THAT MAY DRAW THIS NATION INTO WAR

Notification of renewal today of illegal submarine warfare brings on an unexpected crisis.

FIFTEEN

HOW APPROPRIATE FOR THIS TO BE THE TSAR'S PATH.

The woodland path was built for the privileged use of tsars and their glittering tsarinas nearly sixty years ago. They holidayed in the warmer climate at their summer retreat, Livadia Palace, where the therapeutic trail curved its way through the shadow of the Crimean Mountains with breathtaking views of the Black Sea far below the wind-buffeted crags and ended at Swallow's Nest Castle. How many times must the grand duchesses and tsarevitch have splashed in those blue waters? Salt sticking to their skin and sun shining on their faces with no thought to royal decorum.

With Russia seething in cries for revolution, and hatred for the tsar burning like torched tinder, would the imperial family ever live in such luxurious escapism again? Likely not when Balaur had commandeered the compact castle for his own nefarious purposes.

A midday sun glazed the milky blue sky and washed out the Mediterranean colors of sand, scrub green, and sparkling water to a mild winter palette. Crouching on an overlook near the end of the path next to Jack, Ivy unbuttoned the top of her jacket and inhaled the fresh sea air. She'd opted for a hat with a small brim to shield her skin against the sun, but she'd not accounted for the bright reflections off the surrounding sand cliffs and felt the slight tenderness of exposure on her nose and cheeks. A far cry from the near frostbite of the previous week. If only more of their missions took them south.

Jack tapped the tip of her nose. "Getting sunburned."

"Better than icicles dangling off." She tipped her head so the brim blocked the cliffside glare. She wore a moss-green travel suit that allowed for movement of her legs should the need to kick or run arise, but she looked the perfect nonchalant tourist. Except that she carried a three-inch blade up her sleeve and a Beretta strapped to her leg with a garter.

"A rare day indeed when fifty-five degrees is considered pure tropics."

He tilted his face to the sun. "I'll take it any day. I'm just glad we escaped the twenty-degree weather of the frozen tundra."

Leaving the rest of the team in a safe hiding spot farther back on the path, she and Jack crept away from the trail and down the hillside to the scrub of trees and scraggly brush overlooking the square castle. Swallow's Nest Castle boasted a wraparound observation deck and three-story tower where four turrets perched on the corners. She'd heard that the average man could circle the large deck in under a minute if he were running. The castle itself was built on a hunk of rock that jutted out over the water like a ship's bow or a forlorn lover awaiting her love's return.

"Can this *schwalbennest* truly be where Balaur built his giant gun?" A chill clipped down Ivy's spine as she remembered the size of the mortar shell that lunatic had paraded as enticement before his guests. "A single gun of that size could take down an entire city in one shot, but I see nothing to indicate the weapon or testing."

Jack stood and brushed the dirt from his knees. He wore dark blue trousers tucked into high black boots and his brown leather jacket. Dashing yet rugged, her favorite combination.

"Things are not always as they seem at first."

"Well, it seems like he chose a rather small enclosure for a rather extraordinary creation."

"I've found that true in my own preferences." Slipping an arm around her waist, he pulled her into the hollow of his side and nuzzled her neck where her pinned-back hair provided ample exposure. "Extraordinary in every possible way."

"Except perhaps in height."

"What do I need height for in a woman? Nothing speaks more to a man's innate sense of being than taking a woman in his arms and having her head tilt back as he lowers his to kiss her mouth. He sees everything in that tilt. Soft lips with soft promises. Thick lashes fanning over green eyes that beg him to take her so they might get lost in their vastness together. Her vulnerability is his strength, yet in that fortitude he finds himself completely at her mercy. Particularly if he's unendingly and implicitly in love with her."

She circled her arms around his neck and toyed with the hair clipped just above his collar as his lips hovered enticingly over hers with promise. Her breath hitched as she awaited the imminent fulfillment.

She met his strength with her softness, his lips against hers unyielding as they tipped her heart off balance. Never did she want to find footing again, not when Jack held her like that—like she was a shining star and he the night sky holding her up. She smiled against his mouth. *Finally.*

Every time they kissed, every time his hand reached for hers, her breath settled into that sigh of *finally.*

"At my mercy, you say?"

"And happy to be so." Jack leaned his forehead against hers, those deep blue eyes a fraction away and filled with wonder for her. The corners of his lips curled. "Mercy."

She kissed him again, quick and hard, then reluctantly stepped away from the temptation of his arms and forced her mind back to the task at hand. "For now," she said with a wink and took another step back. Just to be safe. "Time to make a plan."

When they rejoined the team back down the path where they waited in hiding, Jack settled into his command stance of loose hips and feet braced apart, all business—and rather alluring—as he detailed the plan of attack. Ever since he'd put them in line after the Dobryzov debacle, the grumbles and defiance had given way to his authority as each team member settled into their respective roles. Ivy wouldn't go so far as to call the team harmonious, but perhaps respectably cohesive.

"We wait for midnight when there should be fewer guards on duty. Ivy and I will take lead with Beatrix and Miles at the rear point. Once inside, we'll provide cover for Philip to set explosives around the White Wolf. We take down any and all opposition. Once Philip gives the signal, beat a retreat to the tree line and pick off any surviving guards."

Philip scoffed from his perch on a rock as he twiddled with fuses. Outwardly, he was easy smiles and jokes, but Ivy sensed something below the surface. Something that prickled inside him since the night he'd brought in those captives. Then again, a bruised sense of pride could be difficult to shake.

"There are no survivors with my dynamite. Add in the ammunition bound to be stored nearby, and we're going to have another thrilling night of fireworks."

Miles raised his hand to get their attention and started signing. "Why not place the charges around the perimeter of Swallow's Nest?" he asked. "We don't need to go inside."

Jack shook his head. "Given the size of the castle, the weapons facility is most likely subterranean. Blasting the castle from the outside would be like slicing a freckle off a nose. We cut off the head of the beast with Balaur; now we go underground and attack the heart. It's the only way to ensure the group never rises again."

"Which is why I brought this beauty." For the first time in days, true excitement danced across Philip's face as he reached for his bag of tricks. Which could mean only one thing: he had a new dangerous invention ready to be unleashed. True to form, he pulled out a rectangular metal box with two coiled antennae and a clockface. "I call her Time of Death."

And true to form, Beatrix spiked an unimpressed eyebrow. "It looks like you put a clock into a shoebox. How clever."

"Oh ye of little imagination. Securely snug inside are ten vials of ammonium dinitramide and silver azide—highly explosive compounds. By pressing this button"—Philip pointed to a black button under the clockface—"magnetic waves stimulate the chemicals. We retreat to a safe distance where I press a corresponding button on my receiver"—he pulled out a flat, rectangular piece of metal with a matching coiled antenna and black button—"and the magnetic waves connect to stimulate the countdown on this beauty box. And then— *boom!*—the mountainside is now a crater. It packs more heat than six crates of grenades."

Beatrix's other eyebrow spiked to form an expression of incredulous horror. "You've been carrying that around the entire time and didn't think once to tell us? Or use it back at Dobryzov Castle?"

"Only because I knew you would react this way. Dramatic as always. Besides, exploding automobiles requires a different approach. A more delicate touch, if you will, to keep the blast under control." The corners of his mouth flicked down. "Except that plan backfired on us at the castle."

Ivy glanced at the duffel bag he'd used to store Time of Death. A thousand scenarios all ending in fiery deaths flashed through her mind. "I used that bag as a pillow on the train," she murmured.

"And nothing happened, did it? It's perfectly safe as long as no one presses both buttons and the safety switch is on, which it has been"—he frowned and peered at the side of the flat receiver, then flicked a switch—"which it is now."

"Comforting." She grimaced.

Ignoring his teammates' terror, Philip continued pulling lethal rabbits from his hat—the next was metal balls the size of billiards. "I also brought these. I call them Porcupines. They're made of non-heating metal, so you simply pull the tab, roll them across the ground, and take cover. Three seconds after impact they discharge smoke and needles."

Silent as a cat, Miles had given up his isolation and crept closer. He picked up one of the balls and examined it from every curved angle before pretending to throw it overhand with a questioning look at Philip. Explosives always captured even the most solitary man's attention.

"Yes, you can throw it that way."

Miles curled his arm around his back and pretended to throw it again before glancing back at Philip.

"Yes, that way as well."

Philip snatched the ball as Miles started to wind his arm like a baseball pitcher. "Yes! Any way you wish to throw it. Any more questions about the devices that are going to save all of your lives?" Cradling the ball to his chest, he rubbed it against his shirt as if to buff off their mockery.

"One more." Jack slanted his brow in a look of earnest serious-ness, which indicated he meant nothing of the kind. "I'm not partial to porcupines. Any chance you have something more akin to a pan-ther? Or any animal that doesn't lumber about."

Philip stared hard for a moment as the prickle inside him seemed to shudder its bristles before retracting.

Slowly, his brow shifted to match Jack's slanting one. A light Ivy knew all too well flashed in his mischievous eyes. "You think a bear doesn't lumber about?"

The same light flickered in Jack's eyes. Matching bullets in a chamber preparing to spark off. "I've never gotten close enough to find out. Too terrifying."

"Are you saying my Porcupines aren't terrifying?"

Jack shrugged as he wriggled the bait. "I'm saying when was the last time you quivered in your boots about the impending attack of a porcupine? When he at last lumbered close enough to you, that is."

"You're going to regret jesting about my porcupines."

"No, I don't think I will if only to watch you riled up." Jack did smile then. A mere curl of the lips that would taunt a saint to utter blasphemy.

Philip was no saint and greeted the devil's challenge in appreciation. As casually as drawing the stopper from a drain, he pulled the tab from the ball and launched it at his grinning friend.

Jack kicked it with the flat of his foot into a tangle of bushes. Seconds later, it made a popping sound and rattled the bushes with needles piercing leaves and smoke billowing.

Having paid the mischief-maker his dues, Philip grinned at Jack in little-boy delight. Ivy smiled at the lightness it restored to her soul. At least she wouldn't have to knock their heads together to make them speak to each other again. Apparently all men needed was the imminent threat of danger to draw them into communion.

Settling on a patch of grass, Jack pulled a long knife from his boot and a whetstone from the utility pouch attached to his belt. He spat on the gray stone and slowly worked the blade up and down its gritty surface in ritualistic strokes to buff away nicks and sharpen the edge.

"How many of those can you juggle at once?"

"Four," Philip boasted without hesitation.

"I'll bet my best scope you can't do five."

"You're on."

Jack flipped the knife over and worked the other side against the stone. "They have to stay in the air a total of ten seconds. You lose and you shine my shoes for a month."

Having drawn her eyebrows back to their normal level, Beatrix huffed with an amount of disapproving haughtiness only she was able to obtain. "Children. Oblivious to the seriousness of our situation." Snatching her bag of maps, she stormed away.

Ivy quietly followed and found her sitting on the pale grass below the rise of the path with the view of the cresting blue of the Black Sea before them. Beatrix had one of the maps unrolled across her lap, but her gaze traveled far from the printed countries and coordinates to the distant horizon.

Not holding her breath for an invitation that would never come, Ivy sat next to her and drew up her legs to her chest. A breeze swished her skirt gently around her ankles, and for the briefest moment she imagined indulging herself and slipping off her stockings and shoes to run her toes through the grass.

"I think they're very much aware of our situation. This is their way of releasing the anxiety. Much like I try to take in a moment of scenery from all the unique places I've never been before. The world is trying to destroy itself in endless battles, but nature remains true. Ice in winter and flowers in spring, no matter what else is going on around us, and we have the privilege of experiencing it in countries all over." Ivy leaned back on her hands and reveled in the simple glory of the sunshine. "I never imagined seeing so many different kinds of sunsets."

"From here the sun sets over Romania." Beatrix pointed west to the land unseen beneath the dropping sun's orange light.

Romania. A land cloaked in myth and tradition since the most ancient of times. "Where the undead will awaken and roam the mists of castles whitewashed by moonlight." At Beatrix's small, strangled noise, Ivy rushed to explain. "Bram Stoker perpetuated the vampire myth, but his story merely built upon Emily Gerard's collection of Transylvanian folklore and a liberal dose of Vlad the Impaler's nefarious reputation."

She didn't precisely care for Beatrix's good opinion—if the woman ever decided to have one—but if Ivy was going to receive judgment, she'd rather it come with full facts in hand. Then at least it was honestly earned.

Beatrix lifted her eyebrows in a silent cry of *you poor pathetic creature* and slowly shook her head. "You spend far too much time in the library."

Though the comment was meant as a slight that books weren't the sort of weapons most prized among Talon agents, Ivy saw it as a compliment. Knowledge was the greatest weapon anyone could possess, and she intended to be formidably armed. "True, but how else could I impart such fascinating, if occasionally useless, historical minutiae?"

"Indeed. How would we ever manage without it?" Despite her best attempt to repress it, a smile tugged the corners of Beatrix's mouth up. Then like a wish on a shooting star, it was gone. A perfectly coiled, bright red barrel curl slipped over her shoulder as she looked down at the map on her lap, finger hovering over the grand capital city of imperial Russia.

Worry and wistfulness furrowed her brow. A conundrum Ivy well understood.

It was a maddeningly wonderful and frustrating thing to care for a man of danger. The complexities could cleave a girl in two. Half thrilled at his prideful swagger as he charged forward to meet a threat armed with naught more than arrogance and a smirk. That was her man. That recklessness, ferocity, and bravery fought for her, and it was her arms he would seek when the deed was laid to rest.

The other half at war with that prideful visage was the never-ceasing worry. Would he one day depart her arms toward danger and never return? Would he remain the same man her heart first beat for, or would the goodness be strained from him like impurities through a sieve, leaving behind only the hardened bits of who he once was?

These were not questions Ivy allowed herself to dwell on often. Not until the firestorm came and the bullets reached for them. When the shouting screamed like agony in her ears and black hopelessness seized her. There was Jack. Blazing with the brute strength of will to pull them through. If a sieve existed, they would enter its trials together.

"They wouldn't have made it to Petrograd by now," Ivy said softly as Beatrix's finger still hovered over the map. "Word will be sent once they do. Victor is strong. He'll mend and be back to his reckless self in no time. Hopefully with less vodka."

The moment snapped like a wire stretched too tight for too long.

Beatrix surged to her feet. Pink splotches blazed high on her pale, freckled cheeks. "Who said anything about him? It's the mission I'm concerned for." Snatching her map, she marched up the rise to the path with her skirt whipping about her slim ankles.

"I only meant— Beatrix, wait!" Ivy's plea fell like dust on cracked earth. She turned back to watch the gentle swell and fall of waves as they rolled across the sea to touch the shores of Romania, Turkey, and Bulgaria. A magnificent sight that thrived on its inhospitable reputation. Sighing, she dropped her chin to her knees. Perhaps this sea had more in common with Beatrix than Ivy ever could.

By nightfall, the plan of infiltration had been reiterated once more, the guns checked and rechecked, knives sharpened, and explosives carefully packed. With little left to do besides counting the cartridges in her Beretta's magazine, Ivy changed into dark fitted trousers, a leather jacket with scarlet satin lining, and boots that were never shined—to avoid a reflection signaling the enemy—and climbed to a high point above the trail where the trees broke apart to offer an unguarded view of the land falling away. To the right,

Swallow's Nest stood sentry on its rocky outpost. Far to the left and tucked out of sight, Livadia Palace, summer home to the tsar himself. And Ivy herself somewhere in the middle where the moon's light shone silver across the sea.

The sound of familiar bootsteps reached her ears. He'd found her. He always did. She could be on a glacier floating in the Arctic and he would find her.

"It's nearly time," Jack said.

A chilled breeze ruffled the water and swept up the cliffside, tugging at the edges of Ivy's jacket. She buttoned it closed and crossed her arms.

"I hate this part most—the long wait before the push."

"The soldier's breath."

That was what the men in the trenches called it. The minute between all ready and charge. One minute to consider all that had passed and all that was to come. One minute in which nothing existed, yet all seemed possible. One minute to say farewell, gather a final breath, and plunge forward into Fate's waiting arms where mettle would be tested and bravery emboldened. Ivy had never had much use for the notion of bravery. It was a braggart term flung around to inflate egos and compliment heroic feats, when really those feats comprised nothing more than overthrowing fear in a moment, making a snap decision when called upon to do what was right. No sentiment claimed more worthiness than doing what was right for the people and the principles she held most dear.

Beginning with the man standing behind her.

Jack stepped closer and wrapped his arms around her waist, then rested his chin on her shoulder. "What are you looking at all the way up here?"

"An unspoiled view of beauty before we set fire to it."

"We won't set fire to all of it. Only the corrupted parts. Like cutting down a diseased tree before it sickens the entire forest." His breath stirred the loose hairs curling over her collar and caressed her skin with shivers.

"I'm relieved the sickness hasn't stretched all the way down the road to Livadia Palace. It's too beautiful to destroy."

"My girl has a tender heart. Always wishing to preserve every lovely thing she finds in the world." He pressed a tender kiss to her neck. "Where might this magical palace be?"

She pointed east to where a soft glow of lights from Yalta melted into the darkness. "The hillside there blocks it from view, but I've seen photographs in books and on postcards when we pulled into the train station. Perhaps someday when peace reigns we can return and spend a day at the beach. No explosions. No sinister weapon. No one trying to kill us. Just you, me, sand, and a picnic."

"So simple."

She curled her hand over his, dragging her nails through the rough hairs encircling his wrist and delighting in their differences. His coarseness to her smoothness. Opposites yet perfectly complementary. "I don't need extravagance. Not with you."

"What if I were to offer you a postcard palace on a silver platter?"

"Postcard palace or tent under the stars, it doesn't matter. Not as long as the entrance opens to you at the end of the day."

His chest expanded against her back as if her words stirred something deep within him. "I was hoping you'd say that."

"Anything else you hoped I'd say?"

"That you love me."

"But you already know that."

"Doesn't mean I don't like to hear it."

She twisted around in his arms and brushed her palms up his chest and around his neck. The ink of midnight blotted out the deep blue of his eyes, but she didn't need light to see their depth or the way the color ringed to the outer edges when he looked at her, as if he were trying to pull her in all at once.

"Then kiss me and I'll adore you under the light of a thousand stars."

He obliged, softly and gently. A lingering taste of home while far away on unfamiliar land. With one arm still anchored around her waist, he cradled her right hand and began to rock side to side in their comforting rhythm, sealing the world away for a last moment of tenderness.

"'Beneath the heaven's blue and all else is as naught to me, the breath of life is you,'" Jack sang in her ear. "You make me weak in the knees."

"I'll do my best to catch you should you faint in my stunning presence." Ivy rested her head on his chest. His strong heartbeat filled her ear, steadying the anticipation of what was to come. This she would cling to. This moment of stars and waves and embraces. Without them, what were they fighting for?

All too quickly the moment passed and Jack pulled away. Angling his wristwatch to the moonlight, he found the arms pointing straight up.

"It's time." Before her eyes her tender lover shifted into the man of danger, the warrior.

Ivy pulled her gun from its holster. One round waited patiently in the chamber. Gone were the starlight and the gentle lull of the waves below.

The soldier's breath exhaled.

SIXTEEN

THE SENTRIES POSTED OUTSIDE WERE DEAD BEFORE THEY HAD A CHANCE to fire a shot. Four more inside had the gumption to put up a fight, but it didn't end well for them either.

Snatching the uniform off the last fallen guard and slipping it over his clothes, Jack motioned his similarly uniformed team past the first level of rooms in Swallow's Nest Castle. The rooms were empty save for a few sticks of furniture, a stone fireplace, and two dusty tapestries that hung in the corridor depicting swallows in their nest.

A telling sense scuttled across Jack's awareness. A telling, he assumed, that would manifest itself into awful being as they descended farther down into the madman's lair. They passed a staircase leading up to the other levels, including the observation deck at the top of the tower, and then a short hallway with views to the sea on one side and a single locked door on the other.

Beatrix holstered her sidearm and retrieved a hairpin from her bun that doubled as a pick. A few quick twists and the door lock sprang open. Salty air stung Jack's nostrils. His trusty Undertaker at the ready, he crept down the stairs and through a short tunnel where the scent of brine clung to the walls. He signaled a halt to the team as he came to the end of the tunnel. Pressing close to the wall, he peered around the edge. The passage opened to a four-story-high cavernous chamber carved out of the cliff's volcanic rock with jagged stalactites hanging from the ceiling like fangs. Hundreds of gas lights rimmed the walls and flooded the floor with a sickly yellow glow. Along the far back wall was a bank of glass windows with a single door sandwiched between them. Most likely the control room.

An army of Balaur's men scurried around like ants carrying crates, pulling carts loaded with metal scraps, and tamping powder into canisters. Sparks hissed as torches welded metal together. Men shouted frantic orders in Russian, sizzling the air with urgency that revolved around the masterpiece in the center of the floor.

The White Wolf. One hundred fifteen feet long, thirty-nine feet high, weighing close to fourteen hundred tons—if Jack had to venture a guess. The machine was capable of firing the eleven-feet-long, self-propelled siege mortars that were insidiously lined up next to it like soldiers awaiting orders. Its enormous muzzle with gaping black hole from which it spewed its deadly fire pointed out of a roughly cut window in the cave's wall through which open sea air drifted. Judging by the number of stairs it took to reach from the top of the cliff to this lair, they were just above water level.

"Keep low and follow me," Jack whispered behind him. Creeping out from the tunnel, he ducked behind a rack of grenades and launchers. One by one, his team joined him. Peeking between the racks, he estimated the number of men at fifty. Each one armed. His team would be massacred if they took one step toward the White Wolf.

His eyes drifted to the gas lamps along the walls.

"Beatrix and Miles, ignite three of those lamps to draw attention away from the White Wolf." He kept his voice low as he pointed to the far corner.

Beatrix glanced at the network of light fixtures. "What a brilliant idea. If that much gas catches fire, it's liable to burn the whole place down around our ears."

"Then keep it under control. The fire will be enough of a distraction for us to get to the gun and set the explosive."

"And if there's a security measure in place to keep them from combusting?"

"Get creative." Jack ducked as four men marched by pulling carts loaded with ammunition rounds. Smaller than White Wolf shells, but enough firepower to take out a slew of artillery. It would be a miracle if his team wasn't blown sky-high once the firestorm erupted. "Ivy, stay here and cover me and Philip when we run for the Wolf."

Philip rummaged through one of the two knapsacks he'd brought and pulled out two oblong grenades.

"If all else fails, use these." He passed them to Miles, then pointed at a squatty rack ten feet from the control room windows. "Throw them at those racks. Get them close enough and it'll spew a wall of fire that can only be smothered with baking soda."

Miles handed one to Beatrix, who examined it with dubious acceptance. "I doubt they have baking soda on hand, unless there's a kitchen nearby."

Philip grinned as if she'd played directly into his hand. "Precisely. They'll go immediately for water or sand, which only makes the flames hotter. Like ancient Greek fire but improved."

Not the least bit impressed, Beatrix placed the grenade in a pocket on her utility belt. "As ever, your devilishness soars to new heights."

"His devilishness fuels the success of this operation," Jack said.

Ivy peered between the racks, her stolen cap slipping low over her brow. "If we could grab those three guards standing next to the—" She stopped, her brow furrowing as two shadows darkened the light filtering through the rack slits.

A man dressed in tailored civilian clothing and wearing an irritated expression of assumed authority stood on the other side of the racks. He pulled out a gold pocket watch with a chain that was buttoned to his waistcoat and squinted at the numbers.

"How much longer will this take? Captain Glišić will be arriving in one hour to inspect his prize, and I want a demonstration before then. Dobryzov Castle may have ended in disaster, but the White Wolf will not."

The second man, dressed in the all-black uniform of Balaur, removed his head covering to reveal a bland face and darting eyes. "Captain Glišić will not be disappointed, sir. It is a miracle he survived the explosion."

"Rest assured, the saboteurs will be found and executed for what they've done, but that is not your concern. Get me a demonstration with coordinates on Ankara. There is enough unrest between Russia and the Ottomans that none will think to question an attack."

A line of sweat appeared on the guard's lip. "Sir, White Wolf's size makes it a monster of destruction up to five hundred kilometers away, and it requires forty men to load the mortar. That alone can take thirty minutes."

"Then get eighty men." Slipping the watch into his waistcoat where the chain dangled free like a looped tail of gold, the first man leveled the guard with a dead stare. "If it's not fired in the time I've given you, I'll cut you and your team to pieces and use you for wadding. The White Wolf must be successful if we are to make more of its kind and sell them to buyers all over the world. We cannot and will not fail." He then said words in another language that triggered a cold memory.

Wiping the sweat from his upper lip, Balaur's man repeated it. An ancient language. Draconian.

Ivy's round eyes bored into Jack's as the men walked away. Not Draconian. Dacian. *The next step is not enough.* The same words uttered by Balaur's assassin in Petrograd when he attacked them at the drop.

"Beatrix. Miles. On my signal." Jack peered over the wall. Balaur's men scurried about with their attention diverted to their own tasks as orders to hurry were shouted. "Go."

Miles and Beatrix took cover behind carts, boxes, and gun racks as they darted to their destination, then slipped into the black recess of safety.

Or so they thought. As Beatrix's fiery hair dove behind a large crate in the corner, a guard did a double take and decided it was worth investigation. With his gun held loosely in front of him, he skirted around the crate. Jack's heart pounded out the seconds. The guard never emerged.

Minutes ticked by in excruciating slowness, yet time seemed to leap with impressive doom toward the detonation. How difficult was it to shoot a gas line? A crackling echoed across the cave, and the next instant a ball of fire erupted from the corner where the three lamps now burned out of control. Panic erupted as Balaur's men raced to contain the fire.

Jack nudged Philip. "Ready?"

"Today's as good a day to die as any." Philip adjusted the sacks across his back.

"Destroy the gun first. Die later, but whatever you do, don't get caught." Jack looked to Ivy, who propped her rifle into position.

"I've got you," she said.

Tucking away Undertaker, Jack fixed Reaper with a bayonet. It was more than enough protection, but Jack felt a bit safer knowing she had his back. He tossed her a wink. "Try not to shoot us."

"Questioning my aim?"

"I've got a scar or two setting the precedence."

"Watch your sass or I'll add a third."

Nothing like a woman's confidence to send him hurtling into danger. Particularly when her dead shot nearly rivaled his own.

Philip ran out with Jack right behind him, dodging between guards who had frozen in the pandemonium. Skidding to a halt at the Wolf's base, Jack and Philip flattened themselves against the metal. How had this beast not sunk Swallow's Nest into the sea by now?

"Men on the firing platform aren't moving." Philip pointed to the station above them.

"Let's give them a reason to." Grabbing a Porcupine from Philip's knapsack, Jack launched it up the ladder that led to the platform. It clattered around among cries of surprise. Seconds later, smoke billowed and screams were cut short. Bodies hit the ground.

Philip scrambled up the ladder while Jack took a defensive position below him. Reaper was solid in his hands, a rifle of lethal beauty that molded to his grip like an extension of himself. Its weight was perfectly balanced with a walnut stock fitted tightly to his shoulder and a customized silencer; he swept the barrel side to side, inch by inch, with sight fixed for possible attackers.

Men shouted across the chamber as guns suddenly turned toward the bank of windows along the back wall. Beatrix and Miles must have ducked into the control room for cover. A gun fired, shattering the glass. Fragments sprayed into the air. Jack's finger hovered over the trigger. Shooting men in the back was a dirty business, but he wouldn't hesitate if Beatrix and Miles were up against a firing squad. An object hurtled from the shattered window and hit its mark of canisters.

Boom! A ball of orange fire exploded the rack of weapons. More gas lamps burst into heated fury, throwing the chamber into a chaotic storm of flames, screams, and gunfire. So much for keeping the fire under control.

"Hurry up!" Jack shouted. "We need to get to Beatrix and Miles."

"Thirty seconds," Philip called.

Gunfire erupted from Ivy's position as she took out three men trying to ambush Miles and Beatrix. Muzzles swung her way before the guards realized there was no way to take her out without hitting the racks of grenades and blowing them all to kingdom come. A few men branched off to come at her from each side of the low wall. Jack picked off those closest to him and earned himself a rapid return of bullets from the men who joined the attack as they realized that despite the matching uniforms there were enemies among them.

Even with the cool sea air sweeping in from the open gun portal, sweat dripped down Jack's back, making his shirt cling to his skin. "Now, Philip! We're out of seconds!"

"You can't rush a masterpiece."

"I can when I'm being shot at."

Philip dropped one of his sacks at Jack's feet. "Use a few of those." Porcupines and Liberty Fires—torches that spewed fire from both ends.

Choking smoke, needles, and blazing fire punctuated by gunfire filled the chamber. Water was thrown, but the fires roared brighter and hotter. Men swung around the short wall, forcing Ivy out the other side.

"Philip! Now!"

Philip slid down the ladder, but Jack didn't wait for his feet to hit the floor before sprinting to Ivy. She met him halfway and together they barreled through attackers toward the back room where Beatrix and Miles hid. Philip kept close behind, picking off attackers from their tail.

Armed guards swarmed down the spiral stairs, blocking their escape. The guards were easy enough targets to pick off in single file, but how many more waited at the top? There had to be another way out.

Heat blazed against Jack's face as more buckets of water were dumped on the flames. The fire hissed in anger and soared to lick the distant ceiling with hungry tongues of orange and red.

"Get in! Quick!" Ivy's short legs pumped to cover twice the distance of his. Into the control room she flew, followed by Philip. Jack hurled himself in last as a spray of bullets clipped the heels of his boots. He slammed the door shut.

Panting hard, Ivy discarded her spent magazine and inserted a fresh clip. "We're trapped."

"Look for another way out." If a second door couldn't be found, they'd be forced to retake the spiral stairs. That would be a death sentence.

As Philip and Miles returned gunfire through the shattered windows, the rest of the team banged around in search of an exit. The room was long and rectangular—a control room with multiple panels of buttons and knobs and blinking lights. On the back wall hung a bulletin board with maps and charts tacked to it, shadowed by eerie red flames. Black Xs were stamped over city capitals located around the Black Sea on the first map labeled Testing. The second map extended the Xs over every major city and capital in Europe, Britain, Asia, and the Americas. Balaur had been planning to take over the entire world by annihilating the power points of each country. And it all started here by testing the White Wolf on the unsuspecting residents around the Black Sea.

Jack's fingers curled tight around Reaper's stock as his gaze cut to a flag hanging over the maps. It was solid black with a silver moon rising above a golden star in the dead center. Under it, words were scrawled in an ancient language he couldn't read.

"Does that say what I think it does?"

"'The next step is not enough,'" Ivy translated. "Balaur's motto."

"Are we certain?"

Ivy spiked her eyebrow in reproach of his doubt.

"I found something you're not going to like." Beatrix held up a briefcase. Her hairpin was still jammed into the sprung lock. "White Wolf blueprints, rosters of potential buyers, and a list of supplies to be sent to a second facility."

"He has another facility? Where?"

Beatrix lifted an annoyed eyebrow. "I didn't have time to translate the directions. There's been a spot of excitement these past few minutes if you failed to notice, but I did find this." She held up a torn ticket stub for the Trans-Siberian Railway.

"As fascinating as that sounds, might we get back to the problem at hand?" Philip jerked his head to the madness exploding outside the room. "Like finding an exit before this room becomes our grave?"

"Here!" In the far corner, Ivy shoved aside a wheeled chalkboard depicting Romania with a silver circle drawn around it, to reveal a ladder leading up into a wide round pipe that cut through the ceiling. "A safety door. It probably leads outside the Nest."

"Or straight into a waiting death squad," Beatrix muttered.

Jack ignored her and took up a defensive position at the broken windows where Philip and Miles were holding off the guards as they inched closer and closer. He would ensure his team made it out first while he remained to cover them.

"Philip, take the lead. If they are waiting, throw everything you've got left at them."

"Three Porcupines and a few good ol'-fashioned grenades I swiped from the rack earlier. Follow me, ladies." Hoisting his one remaining bag, Philip raced across the room and climbed up the ladder. He disappeared into the tube, quickly followed by Beatrix.

As Ivy stepped on the first rung, the door burst open and two guards charged in, their black uniforms backlit with fire and bullets bursting from their rifles. The shots went wild, pinging off the metal tube and shredding maps like confetti. Jack stopped the men with single taps to the forehead.

"Go!" He shouted at Ivy and Miles. Grabbing the last Liberty Fire from the floor where Miles had left it, Jack hurled it at the open door. Flames exploded into a thick inferno that choked the air black. He sprinted to the ladder.

The pipe was dark and narrow around Jack as he pulled himself to the top where Ivy's anxious face awaited him. He climbed out and landed on a pile of rocks and brush on a hill twenty feet away from the Nest with the moon shining bright as a new nickel.

"A little parting gift." Philip pulled the pin from a stolen grenade, tossed it down the pipe, then slammed the lid shut. Seconds later a *boom* thudded below, shaking the rocks beneath their feet.

Yards ahead, Beatrix and Miles scrambled over rocks for the cover of the trees. Two hundred yards was the distance Philip had calculated for their safety before he could blow the bomb attached to the White Wolf. An easy enough distance to reach—until Jack saw men suited in black crawling out of Swallow's Nest like ants from a disturbed hole.

Rocks shattered all around his team, pelting cheeks and foreheads. Two paces in front of him, Ivy stepped on a rock. It exploded beneath her foot. She twisted sideways and slammed to the ground.

Philip turned back at her cry, but Jack waved him on. "Go! I've got her." Jack tucked his arm around her to scoop her up.

"My foot is stuck." Ivy half crouched against the boulder she'd fallen behind. Her foot was sandwiched between two large rocks.

Gunfire and shouting moved closer. Thirty seconds and Balaur's men would be on top of them.

Philip plunged behind a rock next to Ivy. "You two don't stand a chance without me." He raised his rifle and returned fire. "Get her foot out."

Jack grabbed Ivy's ankle and yanked. She winced, but her foot didn't budge. If he pulled any harder, he'd risk breaking it entirely. Jack settled into a squat and gripped the rock atop her foot. The bugger looked to weigh close to eighty pounds.

"On three I'm going to lift this. One. Two. Three." Jack lifted and quickly realized the weight was closer to one hundred pounds. He held it up just long enough for Ivy to snatch her foot free. Jack dropped the rock and dusted the broken grit from his hands. "Can you stand?"

"It's not broken if that's what you mean." She pulled a modified grenade launcher from her utility belt and attached it under the barrel of her Beretta before loading a miniature grenade and firing over the top of the boulder. A direct hit to a pack of men attacking on their left, but there were too many to fend off for long.

Jack threw his rifle to his shoulder and picked off attackers one by one with no hesitation. "Philip, make a run for it. Ivy and I will hold them off until you get to the trees."

Philip snorted impressively loud enough to be heard over the gunfire. "And leave you here to have all the fun? I think not."

"The White Wolf must be destroyed. You're the only one who can blow it. I promise to save the next death shootout for you. Go!"

"Jack. You're too close. If I blow it—"

"I said blow it!" Jack grabbed Philip by the collar and shoved him back.

Indignation cut sharp as a blade across Philip's grimy face. His jaw worked back and forth as he likely considered slugging his best mate before recognizing said mate spoke the truth.

"Fine. Take the last of these. Put 'em to good use." He flung his second pack of explosives to Jack. "Don't get killed without me." He turned and hopped up the rocky slope like a goat and fled into the trees.

Balaur's men ate up the ground. Their rifles spat streaks of red. Bullets punched into the rocks surrounding Jack and Ivy. Their assailants swung around them like a sickle, squeezing tight for the cutting blow. Jack took the left flank while Ivy fired down the right. Exploding fireballs and slugs ripped through flesh. And still more came.

Ivy's shoulder braced against his as she fired round after round. Powder was smudged across her cheek and nose, and loose hairs flew about her mouth, set in grim determination. Then she had the charming audacity to glance at him and wink.

Jack's heart drummed with singular purpose. He would fight for her. Die for her again and again and again. In that moment as death hovered near, there was no other place he wished to be than at her side.

He jammed new cartridges into the magazine, slid the bolt home, and took aim at a shadow racing from a grenade's lingering smoke. "There's a good chance we won't make it out of this alive. The last thing I'd like to hear is 'Yes, I'll marry you.'"

Ivy's firing hesitated before tripping off four rounds. "That sounds like a top-drawer send-off. Shame you haven't proposed."

"Haven't I been saying it for months?"

"A girl would remember something like that, and to date I have no recollection of you bending on one knee."

Jack glanced down at his firing position and grinned. "I'm on one knee now."

"And you still haven't asked."

Taking the last grenade from the knapsack, Jack lobbed it straight down the middle of the guards less than ten yards away. *Bang!* Rocks shattered, orange raged, and curses screamed. He took Ivy's left hand and slipped the grenade pin ring over her third finger where it hung ridiculously large.

His entire life had been a series of hard knocks. Existing from one day to the next with nothing more than the talent of his fists. No loved ones watching over his shoulder to care if he survived or not. He'd bloodied more men than he cared to count and had himself been bloodied more times than he could remember. He could dis-assemble a weapon underwater with his eyes closed and snap a man's neck with one hand without batting an eye. Never once had his hand trembled—not until this moment when he held Ivy's dirty, scratched hand in his with that ridiculous pin sliding around her finger. His entire world converged to her.

"Share my life with me, for however long we have left. It's yours. Always has been and will be until the moment I die." He squeezed her fingers. The metal pin dug into his palm. "But know this, death will not stop me from loving you."

Balaur's men closed in, swinging their deadly sickle around Jack's and Ivy's backs to cut them off completely from escape. Only a tiny gap remained, small enough for them to retreat through and make a dash for the tree line if they moved now. They would be shot from behind. There was no more dishonorable way to die. They had made their choice to give Philip time to press the detonator and Jack would never regret sacrificing himself for his best friend so he could spend his final moment with the woman he had loved for so long.

Ivy's expression softened as their inevitable situation blazed in her eyes. "Then in death shall we be together." She gave him a swift, fierce smile. "Yes, I will marry you."

Jack grinned, nearly splitting his face in half. He kissed her hand one last time.

As one, they stood and pressed back-to-back before firing off the last of their rounds. The enemy charged shouting a battle cry amid the acrid gunpowder whirling between the burning brush of charred black and bright orange.

Jack's blood pounded with anticipation for the bullet that would end his life. At this range it would tear through him and straight into Ivy. There was a small comfort in that. He should have told her he loved her ages ago. Should have kissed her more. Told her how precious she was. Built her a home with a family they could call their own. Now it was too late.

A black-masked man came screaming at him. Jack pulled his trigger. It clicked empty. Tossing the gun aside, he yanked his dagger from its sheath. He would go down fighting for her.

The ground trembled, then with a mighty force that staggered the night to its knees, the earth tore open and the pits of hell were unleashed in an all-consuming torrent of fiery destruction.

PART III

PART 10

SEVENTEEN

URAL MOUNTAINS, RUSSIA
FEBRUARY 1917

IVY PEELED BACK THE RED VELVET CURTAIN FROM THE WINDOW OF THE
sleeping quarters she shared with Beatrix. They were traveling on the
brand-new Trans-Siberian Railway. She'd read that it was completed
only last year and was known as the longest railroad in the world
and already carried a reputation of mysticism that attracted travelers
seeking their own adventure from Moscow to Vladivostok where the
great Russian empire touched the Sea of Japan.

Beyond the frosted window the landscape was coated in white.
Thick flurries poured from the sky and covered the ground, while a
frozen wind spun delicate hoarfrost around the forest of pine trees.
The train clacked over the tracks at a snail's pace of thirty miles
per hour to avoid derailment as they climbed steadily up the snow-
blanketed Ural Mountains that divided west Russia from the wild
Siberian plains.

Their final destination was yet to be determined. Ivy had translated the papers they'd found at Swallow's Nest, but they hadn't
uncovered a single clue about the latest target in their ever-evolving
mission—Balaur's second facility. Except for the torn railway ticket.

She pressed her face to the glass. With any luck, the lunatic had hung a sign next to the tracks reading "Secret Evil Lair. Assassins Stop Here."

She slumped in her seat and let the curtain fall back in place, then glanced in the gilded mirror propped over the tiny vanity table that Beatrix had liberally cluttered with beauty products and hair combs. Ivy's reflection caught her attention. Day after day of hard travel and near death, and she could scarce believe the image she saw in the mirror.

A woman wearing a deep green gown trimmed with a fox-fur neckline, her curled hair pinned up, and simple pearl earrings adorning her ears. Her most treasured possession, the grenade pin engagement ring, she wore around her neck on a silver chain, tucked safely out of sight. A lady of means. Or so her story went, which was decidedly at odds with the scratches and bruises on her face.

Battle scars from their near-fatal escape from Swallow's Nest. The earth-shattering explosion and consuming fireball had taken out most of Balaur's men. The few who had survived were shot down by Philip, who had circled back for her and Jack after detonating the bomb. The blast had knocked them off their feet and thrown them behind the cluster of rocks they had used as their last stand. The boulders saved their lives by blocking the worst of the flying rocks, earth, and fire spitting from the surge. They'd limped away a little worse for wear, but they were alive.

Afterward, the team had traveled from Swallow's Nest in Crimea—heavens, was that only a week ago?—to Moscow in the back of a railway box that had been converted from a cattle transport into a third-class car. It was covered in filth and grime that seemed to have soaked several layers into Ivy's skin.

Once in Moscow, they went straight to the bank where Talon held a private account before purchasing first-class tickets on the Trans-Siberian. Such exclusive accommodations prompted a quick trip to a bathhouse, a lady's dress shop for her and Beatrix, and a tailor for the men before they were ready for their pristine accommodations.

Leaning closer to the mirror, she gave her face a once-over. The cuts from the explosion were healing somewhat, and thank goodness after the incident at the dressmaker's. The woman had nearly fainted when she saw Beatrix and Ivy covered in bruises and scratches. She'd quickly crossed herself when they explained that they were attacked by peasants trying to steal their gold coins. After they'd pressed a few of those coins into the woman's fleshy palm, she assisted them and asked no more questions.

Glancing at the pot of rouge, Ivy felt temptation calling to her. Her finger hovered over the red cream, then quickly dipped into it. She patted the color on her pale cheeks—just enough for a pinched look—then hurried from the room before the eyelash mixture snagged her attention. Enough primping for the day.

She stepped into the shared sitting space and closed the door firmly behind her. Jack looked up from the papers he was studying, smiled at her, then went back to reading. Ivy's heart fluttered as it did every time he looked at her like that.

From her chair near the settee, Beatrix tore her attention away from filing her nails to spare Ivy a glance. "You look like the undead. Go add some mascara."

"My eyes have enough black and purple under them without that goop drawing more attention." That and she was uncertain how to use it despite the saleswoman's avid demonstration. Ivy moved across the space and joined Jack and Miles at the table.

They'd been fortunate to acquire the private accommodations with two separate sleeping quarters and a common sitting room that boasted a table with four chairs, one settee rolled in red damask, and two plush accent chairs. Large windows draped in red velvet with gold tassels ran the length of the area, allowing the cold winter light to pour in.

"I'm telling you, not one of those powder monkeys was left alive. If not from the initial blast when the fire touched all that gunpowder, then when I set off the bomb strapped to the Wolf." Dressed in a gentleman's suit of black, Philip reclined on the settee, clearly not caring the least bit about the wrinkles he was causing by throwing his legs over the armrest.

He'd been constructing a fresh stockpile using the small arms they'd found in the Moscow bank account along with some newly purchased parts from the funding. The satchel at his feet suggested he'd managed to engineer quite the arsenal.

"Frankly, I'm surprised the two of you made it out alive. I thought for sure I'd find nothing but crispy bones when I circled back."

"You almost did," Jack murmured, reaching across the table to give Ivy's hand a squeeze. He wore dark gray trousers, a burgundy waistcoat, white shirt, and navy pindot tie that had loosened around his throat. No doubt from his agitated fidgeting. He looked as handsome as could be with one lock of reddish-brown hair waving over his forehead. Ivy held back a lovesick sigh as she touched the ring hidden beneath her fox fur. Her fiancé.

"If you hadn't made it to that boulder before the second blast, you'd have been goners for sure. Not even a dental filling left to identify you with," Philip said.

Ivy turned in her chair so he could properly absorb her eye roll. "How grateful we are that you decided to wait for us before blowing the White Wolf, but you can't milk this indefinitely."

Linking his hands behind his head, Philip nestled into the plush cushions. "Oh, I intend to milk it as long as I can, but my point is, the blueprints are in hand and we've destroyed the only White Wolf Balaur managed to build. Now we've got a briefcase with a roster full of potential buyers we can start picking off."

"That's a task for another day. The second facility is our current target." Jack swiped a hand through his hair, causing more waves to forgo the restrictions of their pomaded flatness. "Wherever it is."

Philip adjusted a pillow behind his head. "Balaur intended to sell White Wolf blueprints to arms dealers worldwide. If every country had a gun of that firepower, they would destroy each other in a bloody mess. Millions annihilated. We need to find out how many of those blueprints he already sold instead of worrying about some other facility out in the middle-of-nowhere Russia."

Miles had been minding his own business as he wielded a small screwdriver to repair his transmitter. It had been damaged during the firestorm at Swallow's Nest. Now he held up his free hand and signed, "I alerted Talon headquarters. They are scouring the underground markets for news of blueprints for sale."

"Good. Talon can create another task force for hunting blueprint buyers while we focus on locating the second facility." Jack passed a few pages to Ivy. "I need your help with that."

"Happy to oblige, but I've looked these over a hundred times. There isn't a single mention of where this place is located. All we have to go on is part of a ticket stub for a railway that stretches over nine thousand kilometers." She thumbed through the pages of a supply list for chemicals, syringes, test tubes, propane, and a number of other items and ingredients for a mad scientist's lab. Whatever Balaur had been brewing was sure to be pure poison.

Near the end, two pages stuck together. Odd. How had she missed that? Pulling them apart, she scanned the last one. It was another list of poisonous chemicals, similar to the previous list but with a few substitutions. At the bottom a note was scrawled in Russian. She peered closer at the scratchy handwriting, which was different from that of the list.

To be delivered where the queen gathers her ice.

"Russians don't use the title *queen*. Their female ruler is referred to as an empress, and before 1721 a tsarina."

Miles looked up from his transmitter and waved a hand to get her attention. "Did you translate it wrong?"

She shot him a quelling look that sent him ducking back to his machine. "'Where the queen gathers her ice.'" Ivy slid the pearl pin from her hair and twirled it between her fingers as she flipped the words around in her memory from the pages of books. An ice-gathering queen. Snow and ice. Northern queen. Icy queen.

"The Ice Queen! Where the Ice Queen gathers the ice for her throne. Jack, do you remember that book we read from Washington's library? The one with the *moroi* from Romania."

"It was *The History of Folklore from Around the World*." He smirked. "Of course I remember. I got to sit close to you for hours on end without drawing suspicion. Why do you think I kept wanting to read one more page?"

Ivy fought the urge to lean over and kiss his dimples. "There was a Russian legend about an Ice Queen who built her scepter and throne from ice every winter on a large lake." She tapped the hairpin to her chin, then sprang up. "Beatrix, what's the largest lake in Russia?"

"Lake Baikal," their map connoisseur answered without hesitation from where she sat buffing her nails. Climbing the rocks in Crimea had turned them into a jagged tragedy. Ivy's too. "It's also the world's deepest and oldest lake and measures roughly 636 kilometers long and 79 kilometers wide in southern Siberia."

Beatrix reached into her bag and pulled out a rolled-up map. Ivy had once asked why she didn't fold them, only to be met with an icy scowl and a gruff reply about creases distorting accurate lines. She unfurled the map on a low table next to her and pointed to a large blue crescent in Russia just above the Mongolian border.

"Here. Nearly a four-day trip from Moscow. This time of year the snowfall will add at least one, maybe two days more."

Philip leaned forward and scanned the map over Beatrix's shoulder, then looked back to Ivy. "From chemical supplies to a frozen royal. What else did you lovebirds read in this book that might help us?"

Ivy practically bounced with triumph. "Baikal must be the fabled Ice Queen's home. She's the only mention of a queen in Russian literature." At last, all those hours reading in the library, many nights spent well past one candle's lighting capabilities, were finally put to good use. Her knowledge was a contribution to the team and not a bluestocking bon mot.

"Unlike Dobryzov Castle and Swallow's Nest, to which Balaur was willing to send out invitations to fill an entire room with black-market weapons dealers, this facility was meant to be kept secret," Philip said. "Otherwise he wouldn't have been so elusive in naming it."

Beatrix tapped her nail file against the map. "Assuming Baikal is our new destination, how do you propose to find Balaur's secret lair? The shoreline of that lake is close to fourteen hundred kilometers. We don't have time to scour the entire thing. Can your encyclopedic knowledge of Russian folklore be more precise?"

Ivy shot her a cool look. "Incidentally, Dostoevsky forgot to include coordinates in his tales. Appreciate the fact that it's one step closer than we were before."

Beatrix ignored the barb as she carefully rerolled her map and tucked it safely away. "Siberia is one of the most remote places in Russia, not to mention miserable. There's a reason they built the *gulags* there for their prisoners and dissidents. I have no intention of skating around a desolate lake only to be eaten by a polar bear."

"We'll figure out the exact location. Once we arrive we'll gather more clues. Surveillance. Tracking. Whatever it takes until we have him." Sitting back, Jack shuffled through more of the paperwork. "Here's a report dated three months ago: 'More tests conducted on Risers. Dosage nearly accurate. Instability remains a concern. Begin adjusted injections by first full moon.'"

Beatrix snorted. "Well, that's not worrisome."

Returning her hairpin to its proper place, Ivy stood and paced. "What does that mean, 'Risers'? Is it some kind of army or a new weapon like the mustard gas the Germans released into the trenches? Or perhaps an antidote to chemical gases? Soldiers wouldn't need a gas mask if they consume a potion to keep them safe."

"It's not a gas. He's injecting a chemical dosage into something." Jack angled the paper to her.

Ivy leaned over his shoulder and read. Subject mortality rates and toxicity reports were listed. "Subject mortality—he's poisoning some kind of animal with this chemical. Or people!"

"Poisoning them to find the correct dosage to create these 'Risers.' Look here." Jack pointed to a notation in the margin. "He made a list of the chemicals experimented with. Mind alterations, he's calling them."

"Balaur could make a staggering profit from the highest bidder," she said. "If the Germans got their hands on such a chemical, they would be invincible. The Allies wouldn't stand a chance."

Jack made a disgruntled noise. "According to these reports, he was yet to be successful, which explains why he referred to the subjects as unstable."

Miles signed, "Dead more like."

"Yes, but he couldn't very well say that to a room of potential buyers back at Dobryzov Castle. He presented White Wolf to them while secretly taking time to perfect his poison. A bad product would mean no profit for him."

Keeping her eyes trained on her nails, Beatrix spiked an eyebrow. "What does a killer care about perfection?"

Philip stretched his long limbs from where he lounged on the settee as snowflakes clustered around the window behind him. "How many reasons does a crazy person need? If the man couldn't blow people to bits with his gigantic gun, it seems he turned his attention to drugging them. Profit was his end game."

"Profit means little to a dead man," Beatrix added over the scratching of her nails. "Why was he experimenting with psychotic mind alterations, and to what end?"

"Why else?" Jack squeezed his eyes shut and pressed his fingers to his temple. "A new form of weaponry."

Squealing train wheels interrupted as the hulking train lurched to a stop, flinging Ivy sideways into Jack. Miles dove for his transmitter as it slid to the edge of the table. The papers took wing and scattered over the walnut-stained floor.

Righting herself in the chair when the train was still, Beatrix smoothed her purple skirts into order. "What on earth is the upset? This is hardly the way to pull into a station."

Flung to the ground from the settee, Philip quickly gathered the bombs and rifle shells that had rolled across the floor and stuffed them back inside his satchel, tying the bag securely closed and shoving it under the settee. He dusted off his knees and stood to peer out the window. "The station's still a mile away. There's another train ahead of us. Bunch of men in greatcoats and tall furry hats moving around with shovels. Hold up! Those are Cossacks."

Ivy moved to stand next to him and pressed her face to the glass. "It must be a troop train going to the eastern front. My, they look fierce."

"Savage warriors. Wouldn't want to go up against them in a fight."

A group of three Cossacks with shovels slung over their shoulders stood some yards away sharing a cigarette. With grim expressions beneath long mustaches, they were impervious to the harshness of the land they called home, or so she'd read.

"Look at the double eagle on their *papakhas*. They must be part of the tsar's White Army going to fight the Bolsheviks."

Philip braced an arm against the glass as the men ground out their cigarette and trudged through the mound of snow toward the other train. "Should've chosen their side better. According to this morning's paper, riots have escalated in Petrograd. Committees are calling for the tsar's abdication."

A knock rapped on their door, quickly followed by the train conductor's entry. He was a short, slender man with clipped movements. "Apologies for the delay, *damy i gospoda*. An avalanche has hit the tunnel three miles past the station. Soldiers from the train ahead have been sent to clear the way with the rail crew, but it will take three or four days for the passage to be safe once again. In the meantime, we ask all passengers to find accommodations in town until the track reopens. Our deepest apologies for any discomfort this may cause you."

Jack reached for his dark gray jacket and slipped it on. "We can help clear the tunnel if there are shovels to spare."

The conductor's mustache bristled in offense. "*Nyet, ser*. Trans-Siberian Railways never allows gentlemen to lend aid to menial work. That is why we have Cossacks. Manual labor and killing are all they are good for." His compacted eyes jumped to Beatrix and Ivy as he realized the blunder of his coarse talk. "Pardons, *damy*."

Playing her role as the affronted gentlewoman, Ivy pressed a hand to her presumably shuddering heart. "Killers among us. How dreadful."

"This is my thinking, *mem*." The conductor returned his attention to Jack to resume explaining the tactics of departure. "*Ser*, these delicate *damy*. It is best to move them quickly into town. Red Chalet is the finest establishment on offer and will appease your finer tastes. All third-class passengers will go to the Golden Mule where they cannot bother you."

Nodding gravely, Jack placed Ivy's hand in the protection of his crooked arm. "Peasants and killers. We'd find ourselves in certain trouble without your kindness in looking after us, sir. *Spasibo*."

Bowing his way out, the conductor continued to the next car to pass along his prolific insights on the human character.

Grinning with all the cheek he possessed, Philip tipped an imaginary hat to Ivy and Beatrix. "Well, ladies. I believe it is our moral obligation to whisk you away from the ne'er-do-wells loafing about lest they taint your fine upbringings."

Miles honked through his nose, which was as close to a laugh as he could muster. The uncharacteristic noise startled them more than the lurching train. Controlling himself, he signed, "They're more tainted by our nefarious schemes than any Cossack. Those men are at least honest about what they do. None of this cloak-and-dagger business."

For a troupe dealing in the cloak-and-dagger business, they certainly made a fine show parading through the small town on a sled that had been commandeered from the postal office. Cradled in a stout valley between rocky slopes of the Ural's foreboding range, the tiny town was a dichotomy of old and new.

Weathered shacks with rocky gardens and animal skins stretched tight over decaying wood frames stood in the shadow of a magnificent Orthodox church with its onion domes painted bright white, red, and green. They resembled Christmas tree toppers more than a place of worship. Buzzing telegram wires were strung from pole to pole across the slushy streets and up the mountain slope, providing news east to west. Plodding mules pulled milk carts that looked as old as the hills themselves without the slightest interest in the world beyond the route their muddy hooves trod each day.

"Once this was a trade village," their driver explained as the sleigh skimmed over the snow-rutted street. He was the local postman but offered rides to stranded train passengers when they were willing to make it worth his while. That, and he didn't have much post to deliver. "Old ways have been pushed out. Now the train brings telegrams and places called hotels. Tell me, what is so wrong with staying in a hayloft?"

Worn faces peered through grimy windows as the sleigh passed, while outside wizened men doffed their hats and chapped-cheeked women, hunched from carrying firewood on their backs, stopped to watch the strangers passing by. Ivy glanced neither to the left nor the right. If she dared to look these people in the eyes, she knew what she would find. Hunger. Coldness. Loathing. Such feelings had crawled within her once, too, beasts of insatiable appetite that prowled the gutters and slums, never allowing victims the freedom of humanity. *Traitor*, the beast called to her. *Fraud*, her heart pounded.

Jack leaned close. The silver fur trimming his overcoat brushed the thin netting she had pulled over her face to cover the scratches. "All right there?"

Nodding, she touched the small lump under her coat where her ring rested. "Just eager to reach the hotel."

"I know it takes a toll pretending to be something we aren't, but there is purpose in what we do. Even if it goes unrecognized."

As always, Ivy's thoughts were laid bare before him. She despised the transparency at times, particularly during training exercises when he anticipated her next move, yet mostly it was a comfort.

She smiled up at him. "Can't hide from you, can I?"

"Never, my love." Taking her gloved hand, he kissed her ring finger where one day a true ring might rest. "I'd find you because you belong with me. Always."

A coughing fit erupted from the bench behind them. Philip. "Ahem. Your love-birding heads are blocking my view." His gloved hand wriggled over Ivy's shoulder and wedged them apart. "And do I really have to be the voice of decorum and remind you that proper ladies and gentlemen do not canoodle in broad daylight?"

Ivy frowned at the lead-lined sky puffing out snowflakes. "I hardly call this daylight."

"Semantics and weather do not change the rules of social modesty."

Twisting around in her seat on the sleigh's middle bench, Ivy raised a dubious eyebrow at him. "Since when have you cared for rules? Or modesty for that matter?"

"Only since he's the one without a girl to be immodest with." Jack turned around with a grin.

Stuffed on the rear bench with the luggage, Philip braced his arms atop the trunks and settled back with the air of a man at leisure. Snowflakes laced the brim of his black homburg while his soft sandy curls peeked out from under the rim.

"Never has a truer word been spoken, but until I can find the right girl who's willing to put up with me like Ives does with you, I'm content to have fun with all the wrong ones."

"We should find you a nice strapping milkmaid to keep you in line," Ivy said.

Philip shuddered. "Who's likely to have chapped hands and a face uglier than the cow's. No, thank you. Leave my matchmaking in my own capable hands, which are in the meantime fully occupied chaperoning you two. Now, eyes forward, lips apart, and no patty fingers."

The Red Chalet held court at the end of the main street, the only street, in fact, as all other thoroughfares were no more than muddy ruts darting between the solemn buildings. The hotel was built of whitewashed aspen trees with four golden onion domes perched atop the third-story roof and two red front doors. It truly was the most opulent structure in the vicinity.

What looked like apple orchards were planted on each side and come summer they must blossom with mouthwatering sweetness. Two boys rushed down the wide steps to gather the luggage as Jack escorted Ivy inside, where the scents of aged wood, beeswax, and baked bread lingered. The floors were polished and cozy hallways were lined with thick velvet to ward off the cold.

"*Dobro pozhalovat!*" An older man with a great gray mustache and a belly that bulged beneath his jacket came around the front desk to greet them. His rheumy blue eyes roved over their fine clothes and the number of trunks being carted in, and his smile widened.

"Welcome, ladies and fine gentlemen. The Red Chalet welcomes you. I am the owner, Mr. Borensky. You are from the train, *da?*" His wide Russian vowels proved him a native to the Ural Mountains region.

Jack removed his hat and tucked it under his arm. "*Da*. We'd like two rooms, *spasibo*."

Questions flashed across Mr. Borensky's face as he took in Jack's bruises, but he wisely chose discretion and quickly smoothed his expression. The promise of money from a wealthy patron often did that. "How long?"

"Until the track is cleared from the avalanche."

"Many fine views to explore if you stay longer. I arrange picnic or ski trip, *da?*"

Jack shook his head. "I'm afraid we don't have the luxury to remain any longer than the train's delay."

The two underage bellhops trudged in carrying more luggage and tracking mud over the polished floors. Mr. Borensky leaped around the desk to scold them before directing them to carefully deliver the trunks to rooms 3A and 3B.

"I should help them." Philip started after the boys as they struggled up the stairs. The weapons were well concealed and padded in their newly constructed false-bottom compartments, but it wasn't worth the risk with two clumsy boys jostling them about.

Mr. Borensky held out an arm to stop him. "*Nyet*. They earn their keep this way." The sternness faded from his wrinkled face. "Grandsons. My boy was killed in the war fighting for the tsar who makes life miserable for us all. My boy was a brave soldier. My grandsons are all I have left now." A wet sheen coated his eyes, despite his attempt to remain professional.

Murmuring her sympathies, Ivy followed Beatrix and the boys up the stairs to room 3A.

It was a lovely space with two twin beds covered in colorful quilts and a thick rug spread across the floorboards. A wide window offered an expansive view of the trees climbing up the mountains, while a stone fireplace warmed the room.

"Here you go." Ivy placed two gold coins in each of the boys' hands after they had deposited the trunks at the foot of the beds. "We're lucky to have strong men like you to carry these heavy things for us."

Their little eyes widened at the treasure, then, grinning in delight at each other, they thanked her profusely and skipped out.

Beatrix unwrapped the white silk scarf from her hair and tossed it on one of the beds. "You gave them too much." She peeled the netting from her face held in place with a hair comb and dropped it on top of the scarf.

"They're orphans."

"As are we."

"And someone once showed us kindness."

"Teaching them to survive would be more useful."

"Living here I assume they learned that lesson long ago." After unbuttoning her forest-green wool coat, Ivy carefully draped it over the foot of the other bed and smoothed down the trim of black beads that glittered like polished onyx. She stepped to the window where thin icicles clung to the eaves like frozen tears. Dark clouds heavy with moisture melted to a thin silver with the palest of light probing the icy creations and magnifying air bubbles caught within. "It's stopped snowing. Perhaps we'll see sun later today."

"One can hope. The dreariness is tiresome." As if to prove her point, Beatrix patted a hand over her yawning mouth. The mid-morning light washed away what little color there was in her face and drew out the dozens of freckles like specks on milk. She pulled the long stickpin from her hair, which also served as a lock pick and general stabbing armament, then shook out the long copper hair that nearly brushed her waist. "I'll have a lie-down."

"Don't you wish to explore the hotel?" As a child Ivy had dreamed of staying in a hotel. She would sit for hours staring at the tall buildings on Pennsylvania Avenue, watching the expensive carriages arrive with elegant women and dapper men who seemed to glide up the front steps rolled with red carpets and whisk through the revolving doors into a perfumed world of refinement. As a paying customer now, she had no reason to fear being swatted at with a broom.

"I imagine the only thing to observe in this rustic outpost are murals of Ivan the Terrible and bowls of cabbage in the kitchen." Beatrix unbuttoned her heeled boots, slipped them off, and tucked herself under the quilt. "Go find Jack and discover a dark corner or two. Do you both a world of good."

"I believe that's the most scandalous suggestion I've ever heard from you. Aside from when you told that man you would knife his brains and fork them down his throat if he thought to whistle at you again."

"Lifting my skirt to step over a mud puddle and inadvertently flashing an ankle is not an open invitation to unwanted male attention." Not bothering to cover her next yawn, Beatrix pulled the quilt up to the garnet earbobs dangling from her ears and rolled over to face the wall. "You have a fiancé who adores you. Enjoy what time you have. Our tomorrows are never promised. Not in this game."

Dwelling on such dour thoughts offered no reprieve for joy, and since the world spun on an axis of madness and death, Ivy would seize what happiness she could.

But her happiness had left without her.

"What do you mean Jack went out?" she asked when Miles answered the door of his shared room. "Where did he go?"

Miles scratched the top of his knitted hat, slanting it side to side. It clashed horribly with the tweed suit he'd purchased in Moscow, but he'd rather lose an arm than remove the ratty head covering. "Out," he signed and shrugged.

"He didn't say where he might be headed?"

His attention snapped from her to the dented transmitter abandoned on the table and back to her, as he unloaded the full brunt of his annoyance at being bothered with questions about a missing fiancé. "Just out. Philip too."

"Both of them?" The door closed in her face. Miles was not a man to be distracted from his wires and gizmos. Or by questions. Or people in general.

She frowned at finding herself with no one's company but her own, which was no sad thing most of the time as she considered herself content in solitude. But on this rare day when she and Jack might find a moment away from the eyes of their ever-present teammates, he'd run off with Philip.

She started for the stairs and nearly ran into him bounding up.

"There you are," she said.

"There *you* are." Excitement danced in his eyes like blue flames as the dimples around his mouth carved deep. "Go back to your room and gather your things. Hat and gloves and any other mysterious contraptions ladies need to venture out of doors. We don't have much time before the stupor comes to claim him again."

Stupor? "Is Philip in the cups already?" That boy. He never could say no to the opportunity for a good time.

Jack prodded her back down the corridor. "No, it's not Philip. Hurry!"

"Shall I tell Beatrix and Miles to pack?"

He shook his head, goading her past the first set of doors. "It's just you and me, and you don't need to pack."

"But you said to gather my things. Has the train started again?"

She spun around with sudden fright. "Have we been tracked?" They would need to leave the hotel before the other guests could come to harm. They'd have to get out of town really, and trudging up a snow-covered mountainside was hardly ideal.

"No, we're perfectly safe, but the clock is ticking." Exasperation strained his dimples.

"Jack, you're not making any sense."

"All will be made clear, I promise." Catching her face between his hands, he kissed her firmly, then turned her toward her door. "Meet me in the lobby in half an hour. Not a minute later."

EIGHTEEN

WHAT SHOULD A GIRL TAKE FOR A SECRET OUTING WITH UNKNOWN possible hostiles? No, it couldn't be hostile with Jack grinning from ear to ear. He reserved a certain smirk for impending danger. Still, it was best to be prepared. Whirling into her room, she placed her white rabbit-fur *ushanka* atop her head, slipped her Beretta into the hidden pouch of her matching muff, and added a knife to the garter above her knee.

"There is no point in attempting a nap with you swinging in and out like a hotel door." Beatrix flung aside the quilt and clamored out of bed. Yawning widely, she sat before the small rectangular mirror positioned over the writing desk and employed a pearl comb to hold a single ringlet trailing down her back. "Going somewhere?"

"There's apparently a man in a stupor, and I've been instructed to come prepared with a lady's trimmings." Grabbing her gloves, Ivy stuffed them into the muff next to the gun. "Jack is being secretive, and Philip has gone missing."

"Is that so? Wait, you cannot possibly mean to go out looking like that. You look positively dreadful." Twisting out of the chair, Beatrix held out a small powder-blue box. "Add a bit of this to your lashes."

Ivy took the box and lifted the lid. Inside was a waxy black substance pressed into a square with a tiny brush. Mascara—the new

all-the-rage cosmetic made from petroleum jelly and coal powder—
had begun creeping into the treasure boxes of beauty enhancers kept
under the counter at drugstores a few short years ago. The salesgirl
in Moscow had looked over her shoulder twice before pulling the
box out for Ivy's and Beatrix's enchanted oohs and aahs, even while
dowdy old ladies walked by whispering insults of harlots and, horror
upon horror, no-good actresses, for they were the only women who
painted their faces with such filth. Thank goodness the old biddies
didn't linger long enough to watch them select a pot of rouge.

Putting aside her pristine muff to avoid smudging it, Ivy sat
in front of the mirror and rubbed the brush bristles over the thick
black mixture, grateful she didn't have the scorched eyelashes that
inspired the creator's original concoction of burnt cork, coal powder,
and Vaseline intended for his sister who'd burned off her lashes while
cooking.

Taking a deep breath to steady her hand, Ivy swiped the brush
through her lashes. What was once a light brown fringe over her eyes
was now a sultry swath of black lace. She blinked in disbelief at the
image staring back at her. Black smudged her lower rim.

"Oh no! I ruined it when I blinked."

"Here. We'll wipe it away." Beatrix took the lace hankie from her
sleeve and dipped it in the water pitcher, then blotted it under Ivy's
eye. "There. Good as new. Try not to blink until it dries."

Ivy widened her eyes and fought off the urge to blink as the seconds ticked by. "Where did you learn to do this?"

"You were standing there with me at the cosmetics counter in
Moscow when the saleslady showed us."

"No, I mean this." Ivy swept her hand to indicate the feminine
arsenal of bottles and boxes. "Powders and kohl and colored paste to
line the eyes. Other than a dab of rouge when Dolly isn't looking, I've
always been too scared to try my hand at it."

"I used to watch my mother. She was an actress at Ford's Theatre.

She would put her stage makeup on, then touch the powder puff to my cheeks and nose. It always made me sneeze," Beatrix said quietly. "She died from consumption. I was twelve."

"I'm sorry."

Beatrix paused, then gave a curt nod. "Me too."

Ivy touched the tip of her finger to her lashes. It came away clean. She carefully blinked and looked in the mirror. No smudges, merely a pair of bright green eyes transformed from innocent to sophisticated without a harlot in sight. "Well?"

"It'll do. Try not to cry."

"Do I have a reason to cry?"

"Of course not." Snatching the mascara box, Beatrix spun away and busied herself rearranging it next to the rouge pot and tray of earrings. "Wear these." She thrust a pair of blue sapphire earbobs at Ivy.

"My pearls will suffice. Wherever we're traipsing to, I doubt we're attending a ball."

"Those pearls don't bring a hint of color to your cheeks. A corpse has more complexion." Beatrix pushed the pieces into Ivy's hand. "Emeralds are about the only color you can pull off, but one can always appreciate something blue."

Ivy nearly fell off the chair at the ludicrous position in which she'd been placed to accept a favor from the woman who considered thoughtful cooperation a fatal flaw to human personalities. Which was how she found herself removing her pearls and slipping on the sapphires. More out of cautious confusion than excitement for the beautiful gems. "Thank you."

Rolling her eyes as if the words disgusted her, Beatrix flicked a hand in dismissal. "Just don't lose them. I want them back."

And with that bit of familiar snootiness firmly rooting her, Ivy returned her gaze to the looking glass. She then gathered her muff and felt for the reassuring outline of her ring beneath her fox fur. Nothing. Heart rate spiking, she flipped her fingers beneath the material and around her neck. It wasn't there. Her ring was gone. Blood now pounding, she dropped to her knees and crawled over the floorboards, ransacking her travel case and patting down the bedding.

"What are you doing?" Beatrix jumped out of the way as Ivy rushed to the vanity table, dislodging hairpins and knocking aside brushes.

"My ring is missing."

"Perhaps it slipped down your corset."

Stripping down to her satin knickers out of sheer desperation, panic washed over Ivy more chilling than the cold air against her exposed skin. Not there. Beatrix helped lace her back into her stays, then made somewhat of an effort to check under her own bed.

"Where could it be?" Panic was fast becoming despair as Ivy slipped back into her green gown.

"Are you certain you put it on this morning? Search your toilette case again."

"I've never taken it off." Ivy scanned the room once more. She wasn't falling into despair just yet. Not without a proper fight. It wasn't lost, merely misplaced. Anything misplaced could be found. "I'll check the hall and downstairs. Perhaps it got caught when I took off my coat."

Half an hour later Ivy had searched every nook and cranny of the Red Chalet to no avail. She had even gone through the kitchen, much to the cook's consternation, even though it would have been quite the feat to find it there considering Ivy had not stepped foot in the area before.

Sitting on a bench beside the register desk, Ivy tugged on felt boots over her more stylish leather ones. Russian peasants wore these to keep their feet warm and dry in the rugged, snow-covered lands, and she'd bought a pair three sizes too large from a stallkeeper in Moscow to protect against slush seeping through to the leather.

Mr. Borensky hovered, wringing his chapped hands. "I will send the boys to bring a sleigh for you."

"The postman said he had a new plow to deliver several kilometers away to a Farmer Vashi. I suspect he's not due to return anytime soon, and I can't wait." Ivy stomped her heel to fit it snugly into the felt boot.

"I cannot allow a lady to walk alone in the street."

"I understand and appreciate your concern, *ser*, but I take full responsibility for my actions." Standing, Ivy stamped her other foot to slide the boot fully in. Jack would be here to collect her any minute, but she couldn't tell him. Not yet. Not until she had searched to exhaustion. "Please inform Mr. Vale that I have gone out and will return shortly."

The dining room door creaked open and a maid with ruddy cheeks stepped out carrying a vase arrangement of ribbons, snowdrop flowers, and small evergreen branches. "Mr. Borensky, Cook asks where you put the vase. On the table or next to the cake?"

Mr. Borensky's eyes darted from the maid to Ivy and back to the girl. "Back! Back inside. Go, go, go! I will deal with details later." Seizing the distraction, Ivy slipped out the front door and down the steps before she heard him calling from the porch. "Wait! It is no good for you to leave without a chaperone!"

Ivy waved over her shoulder and tucked her fox stole closer around her neck as she trekked down the street. Irrational. Panicked. She knew the loss of the ring paled in comparison to other horrific events in the world. Assassinations, massive guns of decimation, the bloody Somme, yet fear and grief hung black over her. It was only a grenade pin made from cheap metal and might as well have been a tab from a tuna fish can for all the differences between them, but she would not part with Jack's gift for all the gold under King Midas's thumb.

"Where are you going?" Jack called from across the street where he emerged between two squat buildings, which seemed to be standing upright only by the sheer amount of mud caked over their slats. A frown slanted his brow as he jogged over to her. "I told you to meet me in the lobby."

"I'm returning to the train." She clamped her lips together to keep the words from spilling out and kept walking.

He glanced back at the hotel, then joined her and matched her stride. "I appreciate your willingness to toss in a new twist to my already-planned-out adventure, but I'm afraid we've a schedule to keep." She shook her head. "Is that a no to the adventure or the schedule? I'll grant you, schedules have never been my forte, but I did make an effort with this one."

He was trying to lighten the mood, but it wasn't working. She shook her head again. *Don't open your mouth. Don't let him know he's engaged himself to a girl who can't keep track of his precious gift.*

He grabbed her elbow and pulled her to a stop. "Ivy, slow down. Tell me what's wrong, love."

Keep your mouth shut. She very nearly succeeded. She'd been trained in the secret arts of silence and defense. Then he had to go and use that word. That one confound-it-all-to-fire-and-brimstone word. *Love.*

She broke like a paper target under buckshot. "I lost my ring. I looked everywhere except the train. That's where I'm going now. I'm so sorry, Jack."

"Is that all?" His frown shifted into that easy yet presently irritating smile.

At least she had the presence of mind to be outraged for both of them despite his startling lack of alarm. "'Is that all?' How can you say such a thing when that ring means the world to me?"

"It's a piece of metal. If you want, I'll get Philip to pull one off the grenades we packed without exploding everyone."

"I don't want another one. I want the one you gave me."

Jack rolled his lips inward and studied her for a moment. He only did that when trying to decide the proper course of action that wouldn't set her off. Like pulling the pin from a grenade. "Come with me first, then I promise to help you search until the ring is recovered."

Stubbornness told her to wave him off and keep looking. Common sense stopped her short. Jack was right, loath as she was to admit it—and she certainly never would do so out loud where he might hear it—but it was simply a piece of metal. *He* was her fiancé. The actual man and her one true love, and he was standing directly in front of her. *He* was her priority with or without a piece of metal. Besides, she would be grateful to have the extra help later when they searched the train.

She accepted his offered arm, and he led her down the alley he'd emerged from. Frost crunched beneath their feet as they turned down one path and then another, the buildings sagging into one another like wizened old men whose bones had become brittle long ago. The scents of cabbage, mashed beets, and wet animals clung to the air with cloying incivility until the shacks gave way at the edge of town where a lone church hunkered next to a frozen pond surrounded by scraggly trees.

Made of moldy brown clapboards, the church's roof struggled upward, its slopes like a pair of collapsed praying hands. Two broken windows had been covered with burlap sacks. A sunken graveyard with crooked headstones sat in silent somberness next to the church. The very air of the place languished in abandonment.

Despite the shabbiness, Jack could barely contain his excitement as he led her toward the entrance with a grin splitting his face. "Ready?"

"Dare I ask for what?" Ivy shifted in her oversize footwear that made walking more like galumphing. "I'm not dressed for digging up bodies."

The church's front door swung open and out walked a middle-aged man dressed in a priest's black robes. Throwing his hands in the air, he approached them with billowing sleeves flopping to his elbows to reveal skinny arms covered in black hair matching the hair that tumbled to his shoulders.

"*Dobro pozhalovat*, lord and lady." He squinted hard and held up his pale hand to block the watery sun. "Why is it so bright?"

"Because it's three o'clock in the afternoon, Father." Philip sauntered out behind the priest and put a hand on his shoulder. "Come back inside where it's more to your liking."

The priest scowled and shook off Philip's hand. "Liking? It is cold as a donkey's hoof in there."

"Yes, but it's also dark like the bottom of a freshly poured beer."

The priest's expression lifted. "Is there beer?"

Ivy's brows lifted in surprise. This must be the man Jack meant when he talked about needing to keep someone sober. From the look of his bloodshot eyes and sallow skin, the priest didn't appear to come up for fresh air very often.

"No drinking until afterward, Father. We told you there was to be none before." Philip pulled a silver flask from his coat pocket and wagged it in front of the priest. "In the meantime, I'll be safeguarding this for you."

The priest scowled again. "It is medicinal." He made a swipe for the flask, but Philip held it out of reach.

"You've had enough medicine to fell a cow. Sobriety is the game we play for now, as agreed." Philip pocketed the flask.

Casting a final longing look at where his flask now hid, the priest gathered his tattered cloak and turned back to the inward gloom. "Come. I cannot start the ceremony by myself."

Belying its outward state, the inside of the church had been swept clean with only a few cobwebs dangling from the uppermost reaches. The air was thick with the smell of aged, damp wood, while several dry pews had been chopped up to feed the tiny furnace near the altar. Tallow candles glowed brightly from four tall candelabra at the front of the church as they cast their warm light against the faded icons of Mary, Jesus, and various saints painted between the windows. As the priest donned a ceremonial moth-eaten stole, Jack kept Ivy outside the rim of candlelight at the back of the room.

"What is all this?" she asked.

"Have you not realized by now?" Jack's voice was soft, reverent almost, as he looked at her and reached for her hands. "I would marry you in a cathedral filled with jewels if I could. I would fill it with harp music and thousands of candles and dress you in the finest lace."

He stepped closer and brushed a finger over her cheek. "But shall I tell you something, love? All that matters is that you said yes, and I would go to the ends of the earth and beyond to make you my wife. A cathedral is nothing without you. Jewels have no value compared to you. Music is soulless and candles shine no light if there is no you. The longer I must wait to call you mine is an agony I can no longer endure. Will you marry me here, Ivy Olwen, love of my soul? In this crooked little church that is far from the wonderment you deserve? Yet no place could be truer than the one where I pledge my undying devotion to you."

If she'd been able to breathe after such a declaration, she might have offered a reply. One filled with her own reverent words of love and devotion, but her emotions were too overcome, her eyes too tear-filled for her to do more than stare into the wonder reflected in his eyes. All she could manage was a simple kiss to each dimple cornering his mouth.

He reached for her for what she anticipated was to be a real kiss, but the effort was cut short by a loud clearing of the throat from the priest.

Jack stepped back to a respectable distance, which, sadly, was not within kissing range. "I take it your response means there's going to be a wedding."

She took a deep breath to steady her nerves. "Well, you did go to the trouble of lighting all these candles."

He nodded. "I did, or Philip did rather while I left to fetch you, but my sentiment is in every lit stub of wax."

"And the priest is sober."

"For the most part, yes."

She unbuttoned her wool coat and draped it over the back of a pew whose front legs had been sawed off, then placed her muff on the seat. The *ushanka* she kept on for warmth as the small fire did little to banish the cold this far down the aisle. She had also read once that it was customary for women to wear head coverings in Eastern Orthodox churches.

She brushed a hand over her deep forest–colored gown that nipped in tight at the waist and fell in heavy folds around her ankles. Stylish and warm, but hardly what she had dreamed of wearing on the most important day in her life—the day she had dreamed of radiating in pearls and lace with a frothy veil cascading down her back and a bouquet of peonies for a touch of sweetness.

"I only wish I'd worn something more bridal."

His gaze swept her from head to toe in approval. "Green has always been my preference for you. A white gown would pale in comparison to this one and the way it brings out your eyes. You are a vision."

Her dreams of pearls and lace vanished at the utterly bewitched expression on his face. Had a man ever before looked at a woman like that? Had a woman ever managed to resist growing weak in the knees from being looked at like that?

She tossed him a wink. "Charmer."

"Only with you, love."

Heat flushed her cheeks at the unspoken promises burning

beneath the surface of those darkened blue eyes to a depth in which she could drown and never resurface.

"Your attention! Ready, *da*? Stand around on your own time or I will be forced to chop another bench." The priest pointed to wood splinters and an axe next to the furnace. "An exertion for which my soul requires fortification by holy water." The priest glared at Philip, who feigned obliviousness to the problem.

"I better take my place before they call out each other for satisfaction. Standing as a second is not how I want to spend my wedding day," Jack said. "In case you're wondering, I'll be the one standing up front *not* looking for a fight." Dimples carved deep on each side of his grin as he started down the aisle.

"Jack." She caught his hand. Her heart beat fast, but not from nerves. Never nerves with Jack. He was her constant and comfort. "I would've married you on that rocky hillside with bullets flying over our heads."

He reached for the gun hidden in his jacket. "I can fire off a round if you like."

"This place couldn't handle any more holes, and I don't want to worry about ducking from ricochet when I promise to love you until the day I die."

Jack leaned toward her, his eyes fixed on her mouth. She eagerly counted the seconds until his lips touched hers. *Three, two—*

Philip cleared his throat mere inches from them. Given the proximity he sounded a bit like a staccato fire of gunshot. "There'll be none of that until there's a ring on that hand." He wriggled between them and held out his hand palm up. "Speaking of which, I'll be taking it from you now."

Gloom dashed all lovely thoughts from Ivy's head. "I-I'm afraid I don't have it."

"Dry your tears, love. It's safe enough." Jack reached into his inner jacket pocket and pulled out the grenade pin. Except it had

J'NELL CIESIELSKI

been snipped in half to form two separate rings, one large and one decidedly smaller. "I had it cut and resized to fit."

Ivy's mouth fell open. "You had it all this time?"

With his customary audacity, Jack grinned. "Nicked it off you on the ride to the hotel."

"You cool liar! All this time it was safe in your pocket and you let me go on and on—"

"I was touched to see your devotion to my gift."

"If I wasn't so relieved, I might summon the nerve to be very cross with you just now."

In half a blink, Philip snatched the rings and slid them into his pocket. "If you two don't quit yammering and moon-eyeing, this wedding will never happen. I've put too many rubles in that priest's chapped hands to let it go to pot now. Get to the front, groom." Jack trotted up the aisle, and Philip shoved a sloppy bouquet of evergreen leaves and snowdrops into Ivy's hands. "I got a lot of sap on my hands arranging those for you."

The bouquet would never pass muster for a funeral, much less a wedding, but she wouldn't trade it for the most artful of floral enticements. "I appreciate every leaf and stem of it." Ivy pulled out a snowdrop blossom dangling from the bottom and rearranged it at the top with the other bell-shaped petals, then inhaled deeply the clean, sweet scent. "My something new."

"Eh?"

"The old wedding-day saying. 'Something old, something new, something borrowed, and something blue.'" A smile fanned across her face as she touched one of the sapphire earbobs dangling from her ear. Something borrowed *and* blue. "Beatrix must have known."

Philip nodded. "She volunteered to stay behind and oversee the post-wedding celebrations, and Miles, well, weddings delight him no more than forced conversation. I'm hoping he'll be found lurking around once wine is served."

"Well, I suppose that leaves 'something old.'" She cast about to fill that line of the tradition and came up short. Every article on her person had been purchased recently in Moscow, save for the trusty knife strapped to her thigh. It had been with her for two years, so perhaps it could be the 'something old.' Probably not the first choice for most brides, but in a pinch one did what one must.

"How about me?" Philip offered.

His devil-may-care expression softened to one she had not seen in some years. It was the look of the little boy who had huddled next to her in alleyways as carriages rolled by, the occupants giving no concern to the two orphans who had only each other.

"Our friendship. It's the oldest thing I have to offer you. We've been together a long time, Ives. I hope"—he blinked and cleared the heaviness from his voice—"I hope that never changes."

"I'm not going anywhere." Ivy threw her arms around his neck, careful not to crush her bouquet, and hugged him tight. "You are my dearest friend in all the world, Philip. Would you give me away?"

"Proud to."

"She is marrying the other one, *da?*" The priest wheezed into his stained handkerchief as he trudged down the aisle toward them with the effort of a man slogging through mud. "Or has she changed her mind to you?"

Ivy pulled away and dabbed at the tears dotting her lashes. No telling what the mascara would do if exposed to full waterworks.

"She's marrying the first one."

Without so much as a by-your-leave, the priest flung a lace cloth over her head. "The veil costs four kopecks extra."

Philip snorted as he righted the questionable veil over Ivy's *ushanka*. "Two. It's a tablecloth you ripped off the altar."

The priest hemmed and hawed but finally relented to two kopecks. A bargain really; judging by the handiwork and musty smell, the makeshift veil was likely stitched in a previous century.

"Lucky you find me." The priest wheezed as he pocketed the coins. "I remain the only pious Christian soul performing non-orthodox ceremonies. All the other zealot mouthpieces of the Orthodox Church forbid dabbling with unrighteous heathens—that is, you—and ran me to the edges of the village. My unbiased services will be an additional two kopecks."

Philip shook his head. "We'll keep to the originally agreed-upon price, and that's only if you manage to stay upright for the whole ceremony. You pass out and you get nothing."

"Pass out at wedding, *nyet*."

"Then it remains in both our interests to follow through with the deal. After you, Father." Philip tucked Ivy's hand in the crook of his arm and winked at her.

The priest trudged to his position up front, using the bare altar to sag against while Philip escorted Ivy. There was no sweet music to swell among the rafters, no teary eyes or familiar faces in the pews, and no light glowing through stained glass windows. Instead, her bridal march was conducted by the sound of water dripping from a hole in the roof to a metal pot. She didn't need violins or pillars of scented flowers. All she required was here. Breath in her lungs, a good friend at her side, and the man she loved before her.

Jack's face outbeamed the sun when she reached his side. The edges of the world blurred, drawing in a singular existence of hushed stillness around them. Ivy plucked a single snowdrop from her bouquet and tucked it into the buttonhole of his lapel—her gift of hope for all that was and all that was to come.

For being only half sober, the priest managed to assume a calming voice as he gave the marriage sacraments, while forgetting more than once that this was a nonorthodox ceremony and scattering in a bit of Russian tradition. He was particularly affronted when no crowns were presented for the crowning portion of the ceremony, which caused him to mutter about *yazychnik*, or heathens to the Church, and then proceeded to lead them around the analogion three times to symbolize the pilgrimage of their wedded life together. Prayers were said, vows and rings exchanged, and a final benediction offered, ending with the priest demanding his flask be returned.

Jack whooped with joy, pulled Ivy into his arms, and bent her backward for a mouth-searing kiss that might have curled her toes if they hadn't been frozen together.

"Mrs. Vale. At last." He kissed her again.

She gazed into the face she adored above all. Her husband's. "Took us long enough."

"Only because I'm old-fashioned in thinking sixteen is too young for a girl to receive a proposal of marriage. At least in this modern age."

"A proper gentleman you are."

He leaned close and whispered, "I sincerely hope you're not so old-fashioned as to think my gentlemanly behavior will continue later this evening, Mrs. Vale." With that husky promise, Jack swept a kiss along her neck to sounds of Philip's celebratory whooping and the contents of a tin flask being gulped down.

NINETEEN

"TO THE BRIDE AND GROOM!"

Schnapps and vodka sloshed around the Red Chalet's festooned dining room as another celebratory toast was offered to the happy couple. Jack had thrown back his first shot of the burning liquid hours before with the first toast but waved off any more. Falling down drunk was not the memory he wished to cherish from his wedding day.

His bride—*his wife!*—leaned into his side. "I think they're trying for last man standing."

Jack pulled her closer, relishing the way she curved perfectly into him. "I think most of the folks here are professional drinkers."

The celebration had to go down in the books as one of the oddest wedding parties ever thrown together. In addition to the merry band of Talon assassins, three more couples from the train's first-class compartments were gathered, along with Mr. Borensky and his grandsons—who pinched the vodka when their grandfather wasn't looking—the hotel staff, and a handful of high-ranking Cossacks. An entire table was littered with empty glass bottles, yet not one wedding guest swayed on their feet. Russians.

"*Muzyka!*" Mr. Borensky, already three sheets to the wind and sailing ever onward, waved at the musicians lounging in the corner.

He twirled in the center of the room with an expectant smile on his withered face. *"Muzyka!"*

The band consisted of the postman, the butcher, a farmer, and one of the underage kitchen hands. What they lacked in cohesive timing they more than made up for with their enthusiasm for playing the traditional Russian instruments. The lively melodies leaped off the strings in a dizzying thrumming that plucked straight from the heart of Russia.

"Come!" Mr. Borensky spun around like a top in his colorfully embroidered kaftan, which he assured Jack only came out of storage for special occasions. The man had practically wept that morning when Jack told him he was arranging a secret wedding and asked if the cook had time to make a small cake. The hotel owner had knocked the soon-to-be groom aside and dashed to the kitchen with orders to whip up a wedding feast, ensuring nothing was made with vanilla that might offend Ivy's taste buds. Before Jack knew what was happening, decorations were being planned, musicians called, and bottles of vodka frosted. If Mr. Borensky ever needed to earn money on the side, he would cash in handsomely as a wedding consultant.

Whirling around Jack and Ivy, Mr. Borensky pushed them into the dancing space where tables and chairs had been cleared away. "Dance!"

"It's similar to a mazurka," Ivy shouted over the music.

They had danced a waltz, several polkas, and even a polonaise over the course of the evening, but not this. Jack thumbed back through his dusty catalog of dance lessons with Dolly and plucked out the Polish folk dance. His feet had always found the steps tricky, but he doubted any of the vodka-smothered guests would notice. Taking Ivy's hand, he swept her around the floor.

A Cossack had snagged Beatrix into the fray, and she seemed to be marginally enjoying herself, while Philip attempted his steps with a blushing chambermaid. Miles remained perfectly content sitting in the corner with a bottle of red wine.

The music thrummed faster and faster as Jack and Ivy ducked and spun under the evergreen boughs strung across the timbered ceiling. With each pass, green needles shed onto their heads and tumbled to the floor to be crushed underfoot. They wafted up rich scents of fresh spice and thick woods.

Without warning, the music halted to a single *balalaika* strumming wildly. The dancers shuffled to the perimeter of the dance floor as a single Cossack dressed in red and black with a bushy blond mustache took center stage. He started slow, clapping his hands and tapping his heels. As the tempo sped up, so, too, did his movements with acrobatic jumps and spins. One by one the other instruments waded in, summoning forth the other Cossacks. Around and around they moved to the frenzied music, no two steps alike yet all complementing the footwork of their proud ancestors.

"It's wonderful, isn't it?" Ivy squeezed her arm around Jack's waist. Her eyes were as bright as glowing emeralds as she watched the spectacle with awe. "I never thought I'd see a traditional *hopak*."

"A man who can dance with that much stamina must make for an indomitable foe in battle." The Cossacks squatted and jumped, squatted and kicked out their legs, squatted and trailed around in circles. Their leg muscles alone would send an enemy tearing in the opposite direction. "They put my waltzing skills to shame."

"I would still rather waltz with you." Candlelight wreathed her face as she tilted her head to him. Her skin glowed like warmed cream and was complemented by the delectable perfection of the golden-strawberry curls that had slipped loose from their pins.

His mind hummed with anticipation as he glided a finger over her shoulder to the fox trim of her collar, curving through the fur to the soft skin hidden beneath. At his touch, her warm neck flesh rippled.

"That can be arranged." How soon could a couple sneak off from their wedding reception without appearing rude? He'd shared Ivy enough for one day, a lifetime really. Tonight, they belonged only to each other.

Before his fingers could trace the delicate bones along the back of her neck, his wife was torn from his side by a passing Cossack who tossed her high in the air to be caught by his compatriot. If Jack considered himself a jealous man—which he did not, being firmly rooted in the knowledge that his woman loved only him—he might have stormed across the floor and demanded her back with his fists.

Instead, he crossed his arms over his chest to ward off the ache of her absence and leaned against the wall to watch his wife grinning ear to ear and laughing with obvious delight as the Cossacks paraded around her.

"Not going to steal her back?" Philip clapped him on the shoulder.

"She's enjoying herself. The woman has created a lifetime habit of going unnoticed. It's past time for others to witness how brilliantly she shines."

"If that's not the most lovesick notion I've ever heard, then apparently I'm not the romantic I once thought myself."

Jack grinned as Ivy twirled past. "That chambermaid didn't seem to mind you placing second to my superior skills. Practice your lovesick poetry on her."

"A waste of time as you and Ives have spoiled me for flings and flirtations. I have only the best to surpass." Philip's expression twinged as Ivy waved at him. "You should have asked me first, you know."

"Asked what?"

The twinge on Philip's brow creased to irritation. "Permission to marry her. As her oldest and closest friend, a brother really, my blessing is required."

Jack laughed with surprise. Since when had Philip cared about such trivial matters? "With all the bets you placed on us stepping out as a couple, I assumed your blessing was guaranteed."

"There's that Vale confidence cutting through the unnecessary."

"I knew what I wanted, and she was it."

"Like I said, a confidence the rest of us can never hope to match. It's why you take the lead on missions. Why the instructors adore you. Why you get the greatest girl. Luckiest man in the world, you are. Glad we're friends and not adversaries. I wouldn't stand a chance." He slapped Jack on the shoulder and skirted around the dance floor toward the door. Before he could make a clean getaway, Ivy caught his hand and forced him into a dance.

Jack's humor faded. Philip had always carried a certain moodiness with him, pulling it on and tossing if off at his whim like a cloak. By now Jack thought he knew every punch his friend could serve, but tonight Philip walked in an unrecognizable cloud.

After one decent turn around the floor, Philip bent his head close to Ivy as she said something, then pecked him on the cheek. He nodded and touched her shoulder, then left.

The Cossacks ended in a sweating flourish and gave way to an easier strain of music that brought more couples to the floor. Mr. Borenksy extended Ivy a gallant bow, and she politely accepted his offer. She waved at Jack over the old man's shoulder, and he smiled back.

She was the most graceful woman he'd ever seen. Her hair a crown of rose gold, her ears adorned with winking blue jewels, and her figure nestled into a green gown, rustling soft as wings as she swept around the floor. His own fairy queen come to shed her light of love on him, a mere mortal of a man. Never in a lifetime could he hope to be worthy of her, but by all that was good in the world he would endeavor to become so.

As his radiant bride twirled and smiled, Jack's attention wandered back to Philip. His friend never left a party in full swing. Then again, his friend had never seemed so out of sorts.

Jack left the dining room and looked up and down the corridor, then marched to a set of double doors at the back end of the hall and pushed out into the frigid night air—a welcome relief after the heated confines of the dining room. It was barely past six, but the sun disappeared early during Russia's winter; it would have its time again as the season crept slowly toward the White Nights of summer. The crisp scents of pine trees and cold snow drifted along under the bright watch of an inky sky and crystal stars.

"They say the best fizz comes from France, but these Russians are on to something if the war keeps up for much longer." Philip's voice drifted from the dark corner of the veranda. "Nothing like cutting off supply lines to force a person into home brew."

Jack strolled toward him. "'Necessity is the mother of invention,' as they say."

Philip's profile came into view. He was holding a bottle with a label that appeared Russian in the moonlight. "Care for a swig of Russian-brewed invention?" He tipped the bottle to his lips, made a sour face as he swallowed, then thrust the bottle at Jack.

Jack shook his head. Why did people insist on imbibing drinks that twisted their faces to disgust? No amount of thundering hangover was worth the effort. "No, thanks."

He joined his friend at the rail and leaned his arms against the old wood that chilled like ice through his shirtsleeves. He'd discarded his jacket earlier in the overheated dining room and hadn't thought of it when he left to find Philip.

Moonlight glowed white across heaping mounds of snow, crisscrossed with tracks from animals scurrying about, before losing its brightness in the shadows of the mountainsides. Foreboding and jagged with stone, the ancient range ripped through the earth like towering giants and forced all within its vicinity to stand in awe of its violent beauty.

"A man could lose himself up there," Jack mused. "Nothing but his wits and courage for survival."

"Can't be any more difficult than our hike in the Allegheny Mountains."

"The Alleghenies don't have vertical faces and weren't covered in ice and snow when we went. We'd more than likely get ourselves killed trying to scale the Urals, if we weren't eaten by bears or wolverines first."

"A challenge that makes it all the more fun." The prospect of danger and death lit Philip's expression with anticipation.

Any other time Jack would have met that call to danger with unbridled eagerness. The risk of demise had a way of whisking a man's blood to action, but on this day of days something else stirred his blood more than defying death ever could, and she was inside, warm and soft and waiting for him. "Married not four hours and you're already trying to get me killed."

"Just trying to make sure you don't settle into the slippers-and-pipe routine yet."

"Nothing about our life says slippers and pipe. Unless you're Franklin. He once shuffled into a classroom on a Monday morning with his ratty slippers and smoking the rancid tobacco he's so fond of."

"I once caught him raiding the icebox at two in the morning in nothing but his pantaloons. I'd take the tobacco over that sight any day of the week." Philip shuddered and took another swig, presumably to chase away the disturbing memory.

Such a simple state of being—the freedom to walk around completely unmindful of one's surroundings. The liberation it incited in him was wholly unaccounted for by those who lived daily with the privilege. No threat of a knife to stab their pillow while they slept. No followers of a Russian madman hiding in the hedgerow. A peaceful home of one's own. It was a dream to aspire to—after the thrill of danger racing in his pulse cooled. But that wouldn't be for some time yet. Not while he remained a Talon agent.

"Someday I'd like to have the privilege to shuffle to my icebox at two in the morning and parade around my house in holey slippers or sleep without a gun beneath my pillow." A wry smile twisted Jack's mouth. "Or at least trade off with Ivy on that last one. One night it's under hers and the next under mine."

The thought of resting his head on a pillow next to Ivy's shot heat through him. On any given day for as long as he could remember, he'd found himself distracted by the desire to pull her close and kiss her under the lingering heavens, but it had always been that—a distraction, a fantasy never indulged for the sake of her virtue. He would never give chance to regrets between them. After today, regrets no longer held sway. He glanced down at the silver ring circling his third finger and thanked God for blessing him with the woman and the promise it symbolized.

"Men like us will always sleep with a gun under our pillows. It's who we are. Never resting while danger prowls, not when there's another Balaur waiting around the corner." Philip rolled the bottle between his hands, blackened by dynamite and gunpowder. He'd done his best to scrub them clean, but years of handling explosives were reluctant to relinquish the residue beneath his short nails. "Sure would've been nice to be there when you buried a bullet between his eyes instead of crawling underground like a mole."

"Was blowing up the White Wolf not impressive enough of an accomplishment for you?"

Philip rolled off the feat with a careless shrug. "Just another day on the job."

"You tell me another job where we could chase bloodthirsty lunatics around foreign countries while setting off hundreds of pounds of explosives."

That at least earned a spark of amusement from his friend. "Speaking of which, who's our next lunatic? I hope he's plotting destruction someplace tropical instead of in this frozen tundra."

"I think we're out of luck on that. At the moment, the only considered lunatic is the Kaiser and he's sitting pretty in Berlin—hardly tropical—and from what I hear, he's naught more than a shadow king attending more award ceremonies and troop inspections than making battle decisions. The entire world is watching him." Arms growing stiff from leaning on the icy rail, Jack straightened and crossed his arms over his chest. "No, it won't be the Kaiser, despite the number of lives it could save. Talon's targets are the outliers. The threats no one sees coming."

Philip scraped a black thumbnail under the edge of the bottle's label. The corner curled tightly away from the cold, green glass. "It didn't take specialized Talon agents to see where you and Ives were headed."

"I thought we covered it so well." Jack held back a laugh. Keeping a secret in the middle of a secret agency designed for ferreting out lucrative information was as pointless a task as carrying an unloaded gun. They only fooled themselves at the effectiveness. Besides, Jack no longer wished to hide his love for Ivy. She blazed across his life like a hail of stars. What man in his sane mind would obscure such a glory?

"I started a betting pool the day after I found the two of you sitting pretty in the library with a book across your laps. Most folks lost out on her eighteenth birthday. They thought that would definitely be the day you'd whisk her down the aisle. Dolly lost after pegging you for an elopement. Jefferson bet it wouldn't happen until after you returned from the mission. Personally, I think he's holding out hope his best agent doesn't ever hang from the noose of matrimony."

"How nice our little romance has kept you all so well entertained. What did you bet?"

"Before the mission was out. Danger surrounds us here. My gut told me you wouldn't allow that danger to catch up before seizing your opportunity at happiness. Even if that brief spark of hope"—a match struck in Philip's hand—"lived in fear of being snuffed out." The tiny flame wavered, hissing to a brightness that burned down the stick. With a flick of his hand, he launched the match. It cartwheeled in an orange circle of fire and landed in the snow, doused to charred black.

"Congratulations on your winnings."

"Thank you. I plan to spend it unwisely." Striking another match, Philip touched it to the curled edge of the champagne label. The flame flickered, turning the paper tip to ash, then died without the lingering grace of a puff of smoke.

Taking out his pocketknife, Jack slid the slim blade under the remaining bit of the label and pried it from the spare bottle. "I would expect nothing less. Just as I expect today never could have been managed without you." He pricked the tip of his knife into the center of the sticky paper and slowly twirled the blade in his hand.

"I'm thinking of turning a side job for wedding planning. Flowers, bridal escorting, priest wrangling. I do it all."

"The only job I would have you for is best man, which you've always been."

"Don't turn sentimental on me. This is my first wedding, and I don't intend on adding to the cliché of crying." Philip struck yet another match and reached over to touch it to the twirling label where it burst into a blur of flaming orange.

"I wouldn't tell anyone if you did."

"You'd hold it over my head."

"That I would do." The label crumpled to ash and flecked the top of Jack's hand in wispy bits of gray. He blew them off to suspend momentarily in the still air before trembling to the snow below. "You and I have gotten into too much hot water together over the years. No point in ratting each other out now."

"You say that, but things will change. They always do." Philip tapped Jack's wedding ring with the end of the spent match. "Mark my words. One minute you're out having a few drinks and laughs with your pals, next thing you know, you've made a few vows and suddenly you can't leave the house without the chain of wedded bliss slung around your neck and all your friends declared ill-suited reprobates. You'll stop sparring with me in favor of long walks with her. I'll be forced to pick fights by myself because you won't be there anymore. You'll be with her."

"You may still be the one to pick a fight, but I'll always be at your back." Jack returned his knife to his pocket. "It should ease your conscience to know my bride already thought you a reprobate long before today."

Laughing, Philip tossed the charred match into the snow. "Don't I know it. She's told me often enough. Told you as well a time or two."

She had. Particularly those nights when he and Philip had slipped back home in the wee hours of the morning covered in muck from the night's clandestine activities, some sanctioned by Talon and others by the brawling ring.

"Ivy is the furthest thing from a ball and chain," Jack said.

"Marriage changes people. Changes their priorities."

"Change isn't always a bad thing."

Grimacing as if the words disagreed with him, Philip popped the bottle to his mouth and took a deep swallow to wash them down. "That's because you've bought into the institution hook, line, and sinker. Drowning in love, while I'm abandoned to paddle about in a tide pool on my lonesome."

Under that detached facade one might find the detriment of alcohol lurking, which boasted in loosening insecurities sitting on men's tongues, but Philip could hold his own. One bottle of sour grapes was no match. Clearheadedness was his weakness—the fog of delusion rolled back to reveal stark regrets. Regrets not for himself but for what once was and what would never be again.

Jack knew the dread as well as he knew himself. It was a feeling you never escaped after realizing there was no one left in the world who cared for you, no hope of a better life beyond the streets upon which you'd been dropped, and no survival beyond what your own hands were capable of clawing out. If you were one of the rare few to find a sliver of constancy, you clung to it, fearing abandonment once again. While Jack was one of the fortunate few to find a home with Ivy, never more to roam, Philip still clawed when he thought attentions were diverted elsewhere.

Jack dropped his hand to his friend's shoulder. "We won't ask you to swim around in our ocean of love, but we're not abandoning you."

"Once it was just the two of us. Me and Ives against the world. I punched bullies for her, and she stole bread for me. We've kept each other from the nightmares even while we lived them. Then we came to Talon and you belonged to the misfits ring as much as we did. All three of us together. Now it's back down to two, only it's you and Ives. I'm the odd man out. But how could she resist choosing you? You're everyone's choice."

"We'll be here like always, the three of us."

"A toast to your misguided but well-intentioned optimism." His friend took a slug from the bottle. "Me and Ives have been through a lot together. She's the only family I've ever had, and there's nothing I wouldn't do for her. Including knocking your lights out if need be."

"I hope I never give you reason, brother. She's my family too. You both are."

With the tip of a smile, Philip's fog of dispassion rolled into place. He shrugged off Jack's hand and shifted ever so slightly. He might simply have been shuffling his tired feet or stretching his back muscles, but Jack saw the nearly indecipherable message as clear as a brick wall closing him off.

"Stop standing out here in the freezing cold listening to me talk from the bottom of a bottle. Go back inside to your wife."

Jack shook his head, desperate to chip out bits of the mortared wall between them. "And leave you to the company of misery?"

"No, you leave me to the sparkling companionship of *Novyi Svet*. A very good year by Russian standards." To prove his point, Philip gulped down half the bottle in one go, then wiped golden drops off his chin with his cuff. "Go on, Jack. I didn't spend my entire day decorating a decrepit church for you to marry the woman of your dreams only for you to spend the evening giving me that long face of good intention."

"Return with me to the dancing. It's not a celebration without you."

"Maybe so, but it's already your wedding night, and for that I doubt you need me."

With a pointed glare, Jack pushed off the railing and stamped his feet to circulate the freezing blood. "No. I most certainly do not."

Nor did he need assistance in locating his wife, who barreled toward him the moment he stepped in from the cold night.

Giggling, Ivy grabbed his hand and tugged him to the stairs. "Hurry before they kidnap me."

"Kidnap you?" Jack tripped along behind her to keep up as they mounted the steps. What kind of wedding had this turned into?

TWENTY

"Apparently it's tradition to kidnap the bride during the reception and force the groom to pay a ransom for her." They teetered into the wall as they rounded the second landing. Ivy smothered her laughter in Jack's hand and continued upward on unsteady feet. "I'd rather you kidnap me yourself than spend hours searching and finally find me shoved into a cupboard."

"In that case, I shall happily oblige, Mrs. Vale." Grinning, Jack caught her in his arms before she swerved into the rail and took the remaining steps two at a time.

Candles shimmering in brass wall sconces lit their path down the corridor. Past his door. Past her door. Leaving behind all they had been and entering the door at the end of the hall no longer separate, but one. Dozens of candles warmed the chamber to an orange glow while a fire crackled cheerfully in the brick hearth, its blaze reflecting in the window where cool, blue-tinted moonlight filtered through the glass. Snowdrops were draped over the edges of mismatched vases set on each side of the bed, adding notes of fresh greenery to the otherwise wood-flanked room.

Turning his back to the bed and the anticipation beckoning from its softness, Jack gently set his wife on her feet. He'd loved Ivy for so long that his heart knew nothing beyond her, but those feelings from before were no more than a specter in the art of dalliance. He'd never known such an utter stripping of love to its truest form, the complete way it changed a man and brought to life parts of his soul that had slumbered too long in complacency.

A smile hummed across Ivy's full lips as the corners tilted up at him. Desire swept through him like fire set to underbrush, sparking and blazing as it threatened to consume the last morsel of his rational thoughts.

Not yet.

He resisted the blaze with a determination to savor this moment in time. To drink in all she was, every glorious inch of her.

He brushed a hand over her flushed cheek, along her smooth jaw, to one of the curls that had freed itself in all the dancing and fallen over her shoulder. Soft as silk, it glowed a golden red like champagne caught in the firelight. Jack pressed his lips to the looped strand and earned an indulgent sigh. He raised his head a fraction to press a kiss to the sensitive skin behind her ear—a liberty he had never taken before, but one he found himself desperate to repeat. His lips skimmed lower, brushing the spot where her neck met her collar. She rewarded him with a giggle.

"I didn't realize you were ticklish." His voice was muffled in the fox fur surrounding her delicate neck, where an enticing scent of fresh flowers lingered.

"Neither did I, but it seems you have a knack for discovering my secrets." Gliding a hand under his chin, she tilted his face to catch the gleam in her eyes, where a spark teased from the depths of her darkened green-and-gray irises, like a firefly dancing on the surface of a lake after the rain. "Any hidden talents you wish to declare?"

"I'm a deadly marksman."

"Hardly a secret." Her nails grazed his lower lip.

"Superior hand-to-hand fighting skills."

An eyebrow hitched. "Debatable."

"Not debatable, but I'll allow the slight since it's your wedding day."

Her other eyebrow raised to join its twin. "Gracious me. Be sure to add magnanimous generosity to your list of aptitudes. Is there anything else I should stand in awe of?"

More likely he was the one standing in awe at the feel of her as he brushed his hands down her sides and hips, a leisure he'd been unable to engage in—outside of training sessions, which were little more than a means to tackle her and in no way comparable—but a decadence he was now permitted to linger upon in full appreciation.

"My dancing shoes, which have swept you off your feet many times."

"So they have, although I'm looking forward to being swept off my feet tonight more than ever."

"In that case, I shall happily oblige you, Mrs. Vale," he said, using the name he'd given her hours before. *Their* name.

The need for words fell away as they came together in a melody that played only for them. Sweet and hopeful and filled with every tenderness he wished to lay at her feet.

He circled his arm around her waist and sang as they swayed. "'I swear by all the stars I'll be forever true.'"

"No need for lyrics about frowns and jeers anymore." She slid her hand up his arm and over his shoulder, and her cool fingers parted the hair at the nape of his neck. Every nerve stood at attention to her gentle command.

"Then I'll skip to the best part." He bent his head to hover his mouth just over hers. "'All I want is you.'" The kiss was soft and full, and every beat of his heart cried for more.

Keeping rhythm to the sway as he hummed, Jack began to unfasten the buttons of her green jacket but stopped more than once to kiss her as a distraction from his trembling hands before the jacket fell in a soft *whoosh* to the floor. Ivy's fingers whispered over the nape of his neck and glided beneath his collar to undo his tie. She gradually stripped it from around his neck and tossed it to the floor. Her fingers trailed a path of pleasant fire down his throat before she unlatched the clasp holding his collar stiffly in place, then freed the top two buttons of his shirt.

Deliberately, she peeled the material back. Her eyes flickered hesitantly to his.

"I've always loved this part of you." Her words were faint, as if caught in a spell that promised to undo them both. "This hollow at the base of your throat. The muscles playing on the sides of your neck that dip down into a V, forming a perfect basin. I've noticed it many times during training. You wondered why I would so easily allow myself to be pinned." A coy smile parted her lips as she traced a fingernail around the indention.

"It's also the easiest place to slay a man." Jack swallowed hard. Concentrating—*breathing*—was becoming rather difficult. "Straight to the jugular."

"There'll be time enough for that." Unexplored wonders glittered in her eyes, unraveling him further. "When we were training, I'd find myself imaging how perfect it was." Her eyes were again focused below his chin.

"Perfect for what?" His voice was little more than a rasp.

She leaned up and pressed her lips to the V-shaped hollow. Firecrackers shot through him, exploding and blinding him to all but the ecstasy she branded him with.

As she withdrew, her breath curled against his heated skin like a lingering breeze. "Perfect."

"Turnabout is fair play." The buttons down the back of her gown were deftly managed, and he praised the fashions of fate that she hadn't worn a frilly contraption to trip him up; necessity demanded swiftness. He peeled away the silky material to reveal a tantalizing expanse of shoulders glowing like warm cream in the firelight. He kissed the curve of skin between neck and shoulder.

Their tune hummed deep in her throat and tingled against his lips as they lingered on her velvet skin. Beneath the hum, like a tide rushing below the surface, her pulse quickened to a pace all its own.

"Nothing about your current actions is fair, yet I find it difficult to resist at all."

"Delighted to hear it." His hands traveled up her back and into her hair, where he pulled out the dozens of hairpins. They pinged to the floor like a shower of raindrops. Their confinement now breached, locks of golden-red hair spilled into loosened glory over her shoulders. "All's fair in love and war. And, Ivy, I plan to love you for a very long time."

"Do you promise, Jack?"

He lowered his head, as if he were a knight bowing to his lady in one of those fairy tales they used to read to each other, and touched his forehead to hers. "Until the day I die."

★★★

Later that night, Ivy stole from the bed, too restless from the day's excitement lingering in her bones. She pulled on Jack's discarded shirt and walked to the window. Moonlight washed the world in pale silver and silence, save for the fire's dying crackles and her husband's deep breathing. The night was stretched velvet of deep midnight with shimmering white snow and a heaven full of stars as far as the eye could see.

Cold crept through the glass, chilling her still-flushed skin. Jack had been so tender. Gentle, patient, thoughtful, teasing, demanding, with nothing held back. That was her Jack. She had known him to be all these things, but never in the light through which she saw him tonight. Unashamed and wholly vulnerable, they had peeled away the veneers and given all to each other.

Perhaps heat should have flooded her cheeks or her hands should have trembled as she enjoyed her husband and held nothing back from him. After all, ladies of good reputation were expected to faint dead away lest the raptures of enjoyment overcome them. Being a spy, Ivy had never regarded her reputation as noteworthy.

Even now she could not conjure a blush as her reflection gazed back at her from the frosted windowpane. She looked the same, but nothing could be further from the truth. Loving Jack had taken the specter of herself and flooded the hollowed crevices until she no longer knew where she ended and he began.

Behind her, the bed creaked and the quilt rustled. Ivy held her breath as she counted the seconds until two strong arms enveloped her.

"Why did you leave our bed?" Jack murmured into her hair. "It grows lonesome without you. Like the moon without its stars."

"I see yellow Pollux and white Castor shining from their celestial seats of Gemini." Ivy leaned against his broad chest. "Sirius is just there. Bright as always on Canis Major. Though none are brighter than the sun today. I'm glad it was out to smile on us."

"I begged it to shine so I might observe your glory on full display, but now I'm relieved for the veil of stars. They've always been our constant."

A constant, yes, but never had she felt so bright as she did in that moment, never so fully alive. Like two flames of light unpinned from the earth beneath them, wrapped in timelessness where only lovers dared to dwell.

His wedding band winked in the glass. Ivy dropped her hand to rest next to his, their rings glittering like a matching pair of silver stars. "A shame we can't wear these."

"We can until we arrive at Lake Baikal. After that they'd draw too much attention." He rubbed his thumb over her ring. "If it were up to me, I'd proclaim to the highest of mountaintops that you're mine, but such is the life of a secret agent. I won't give anyone reason to use my feelings for you to our detriment."

"Secrecy equates to safety."

"Don't worry. We'll find a way to remind each other who we belong to." Jack kissed her shoulder and up her neck to a spot that evoked a sigh of pleasure. Ivy tipped her head back to rest against his opposite shoulder and offered full exposure to his exploration. "I once had the arrogance to think I knew all your sounds and expressions, but I quite like these new ones."

"I've been keeping them for such an occasion."

"What occasion might that be?"

"Now. When I'm enjoying all the different ways you tell me you love me."

His eyes flamed in the reflection of the glass. Blue as the heart of a burning star. His arms tightened around her.

"There is no name for what I feel for you. No sequence of letters that can convey my feelings. *Love, adore, worship*—all words too simple and common. Let what I feel for you have no name. It is enough as long as we know it exists."

He kissed her. Softly, reverently, and with final claim.

"Mercy, Jack," she breathed.

"Not tonight, love."

TWENTY-ONE

As honeymoons go, Jack and Ivy's euphoric time of disappearance from the world ended all too quickly. They'd enjoyed two glorious days tangled in quilts with a warm fire, snow-crusted view, and each other. On the fourth morning, after they'd finished a leisurely breakfast while reclining on the foot of their bed, Philip had the audacity to knock on their door and announce that the tunnel had been cleared and the train was set to depart at noon.

Jack and Ivy had lingered as long as possible in their sanctum of wedded bliss before venturing out to rejoin their team and finally climbing aboard the train, thick smoke pouring from its black stack. When they returned to the team's private car, Philip and Miles chose to sacrifice their sleeping compartment for the newlyweds and slept in the shared sitting space, while Beatrix lounged comfortably in the compartment she had shared with Ivy.

Daylight hours were spent poring over the maps and documents they had taken from Swallow's Nest as they attempted to form a plan without the slightest firm detail. Then again, it wouldn't be a Talon mission if it were easy, which was all well and good with Ivy. Her mind seemed incapable of focusing on the most minor information.

That spot on Jack's neck where she'd pressed a lingering kiss that morning proved too great a distraction. As did his hands, wide and blunt-tipped and lethal in capability yet oh so gentle in caressing her. While she was good and distracted she might as well admit to studying the curve of his mouth more than the Dacian language she'd been tasked with translating. From the stolen looks Jack sent across the table, his mind was tripping down the same rosy path as hers.

Nighttime was their time. Within the confines of the sleeping chamber, the outside world and its cares fell away as they slipped into a dream all their own with no eagerness to rouse come the first streaks of dawn.

But the next day always came with its tolls of purpose, and on the third day the train chugged into Irkutsk, the largest city near Lake Baikal. From there, they commenced a bone-numbing journey on the back of a cart through slush and mud to the thick woods surrounding a rural coastal settlement of tired wooden buildings, inhabitants hunched over as if the harsh elements had worn them down, and fishing boats marooned on the rocky beach waiting for spring's warmth to thaw their frozen domain.

Not daring to enter the village lest news of their presence scatter to enemy ears, they crammed into an abandoned, dilapidated hunter's cabin several miles from the settlement. The structure boasted more holes than an actual roof, but it would serve well enough to keep out the elements for one night.

"Now what?" Philip set the trunk of explosives in a corner on the dirt-packed floor. He'd cobbled together an impressive arsenal while stuck at the hotel.

Jack flipped open one of the travel cases and pulled out a map. "We find Balaur's remaining facility."

"If you hadn't distracted your 'brilliant girl's' mind with honeymoon nonsense, we would know where to find it by now." Beatrix huffed and turned to Ivy. "Dig past your newlywed fog into that mental library for some long-lost fairy tale or ancient Cyrillic text. I'd prefer a location where X marks the spot. I tire of this mission."

"Perhaps you should contribute more to this search than complaining." Ivy burrowed her cold hands farther into her muff and tried to ignore Beatrix's acid. Tempers were short enough as it was after stumbling around in the woods for close to an hour in search of shelter. "The lake itself was the only reference for where the queen gathers her ice. The old folklore failed to mention exact coordinates."

"First things first. We need transport." Jack squinted at the map through the fading light of day. "Traversing the lake will be impossible on foot. Not to mention, the ferry has been commandeered by the Red Army to convey machine guns and cannons to their headquarters across the water in Mysovaya."

Philip snorted. "Transport to where? You heard the ladies. We have no leads. We'll have better luck searching the area for a flagpole with Balaur's little flag waving high in the wind."

"We didn't come all this way to hunker down in a cabin and wait for them to come to us. We have to search around the lake."

"This lake that Beatrix claims would take us days if not weeks to go around in the snow? Balaur's cronies might be long gone by the time we stumble across his lair."

Jack's mouth flattened into a tight line. Ivy knew he had nothing to go on for a plan of attack, and that rendered him immobile—a state akin to cruel torture for a man of action. They had all pored over every single paper from that briefcase multiple times, but not a single detail gave away the precise location of Balaur's facility on the lake. They would find it, that much was certain, but what would be lost in the amount of time it took them to comb the area?

"Send up a flare and let them come to us. It's about as useful a plan as we've drummed up thus far," Beatrix said with just the right amount of sarcasm to further frost the atmosphere. She was huddled in the corner, her pale lips peeking out from her upturned collar.

Jack swung his attention to Miles. "Is your transmitter working?"

"Somewhat," Miles signed and pulled his gear from his sack, then set it atop the explosives' trunk. After a few switches and knobs were turned, two lights blinked on. Soft crackling filled the air. "There's a wire that needs new threading. I need copper."

"I have a few pennies in my coin purse," Ivy offered. "You can melt them down and hammer them into new wires."

"It might work."

Ivy dug through her travel case, then passed the coin purse to him. At least she could contribute something useful to the stalemate.

"Once Miles has everything up and running, he can bounce the signal around and try to pick something up," Jack said. He was grasping at straws. "A nearby facility will be putting off signals we can use to track them."

Miles shook six pennies into his gloved hand. "The mountains and tree coverage disrupt clear signals, but I'll see what I can do."

"See what you can do?" Philip tucked his hands into his armpits and stamped his feet as another breeze knocked a clump of snow through the roof. "We're the most skilled assassins in the world, and all we have to go on is hammered pennies and a flare gun?"

Jack frowned, knuckling his hands atop the map. "If you have a better idea, now is the time to speak up. If not, make yourself useful and go chop wood."

"We should ask around the villages dotting the lake. They'll have better insight into suspicious activity than we can dredge up on our own," Philip said.

Jack shook his head. "We cannot risk being seen by locals. If Balaur's facility is nearby, he may have spies about and we'd lose the element of surprise."

"There are ways to inquire without giving ourselves away." Philip kicked at the pile of slush, spraying mud against the wall.

"These are rural villages. Most of the inhabitants have never stepped foot away from these shores. A newcomer will be deemed a threat."

"Not if we go about it the right way."

Jack pulled himself to his full height. The towering leader set to knock away any threat to his command. Ivy, or anyone for that matter, rarely saw this side of him, and she had to admit that she much preferred his easygoing manner. It was more in tune with his true nature, but dissension in the ranks fueled chaos, and a leader could not afford to allow a group of cantankerous assassins to lose control of what little patience they possessed.

"I will not risk a single member of this team or the mission itself for an unnecessary venture."

"So we sneak around here in the woods instead of blazing out with the courage of Talon agents?" Unfortunately, Philip's patience couldn't be bothered to back down out of respect nor to save his skin.

Which Jack took as a challenge and squared off toe-to-toe with his opponent. "There is a difference between being wisely strategic and arrogantly rash. I have not confused the two, and neither should you."

Ivy grabbed a small, saw-toothed seax from the weapons bag and made for the door as her irritation spiked. If she didn't leave now, she was likely to spear her teammates with the sharpness of her tongue. "I'll get the firewood."

"Ivy, wait," Jack called, but she yanked the door closed behind her and trudged through the woods in blissful silence. Everyone was on edge, and she had no desire to hurl over the precipice with them. In no time at all, tempers would cool and they would agree to a plan. For now, she would seek her own reprieve among the snow-dusted firs and crisp air that burned her lungs and smelled of sharp evergreen. And something else.

The air shifted, bringing with it a crystalline clearness. She pushed through the trees and found herself at the edge of the woods where the ground sloped down to the sandy beach of Lake Baikal.

Pebbles set in motion by her sturdy boots rolled downhill as she walked to the solid edge of the lake with chills prickling her skin at the wintry magnificence. Framed by snowcapped mountains, the frozen lake dazzled in mystical shimmering lights of blue, white, and gray. In the distance, plumes of water crashed against the land and swirled in frothing eddies, though the water did not move. A single motion frozen in time like pearls strung along winter's frigid necklace. Slabs of ice jutted upward like dragon scales rising from the depths.

"Queen brought her fury that day. Violent ice pieces."

Ivy startled at the rough Russian voice. An old man hunched over a fishing net sat a few yards away staring at her with a dispassionate gaze. He was draped in a gray sealskin coat, his weather-bitten face difficult to separate from the animal's skin. A young boy, nine or ten years old, sat next to him draped in a matching sealskin coat. They were most likely from the nearby village, and neither seemed the least bit surprised to find a stranger standing on their remote shore.

Admonishing herself for the slip in observing her whereabouts, Ivy quickly scanned the beach and surrounding trees to find they were quite alone. The old man appeared harmless enough, but she tucked the seax close to her side, her grip tight.

"What queen do you speak of?"

"Ancient one. Goddess of ice. Ice Queen of Baikal. She was mad that day. Struck her staff, out spewed water in warning." His Siberian accent was as harsh as the unpredictable terrain, as if he'd had to fight for every vowel since birth against a bitter wind snatching it away. There was nothing of posh Petrograd or hearty Moscow in his speech, merely survival, here at the edge of civilization. He looked up from his repairs with two bright blue eyes shaded under a heavy brow and stared at her.

Concluding his assessment—probably wondering why a woman, clearly not of this region and scandalously dressed in men's trousers, was trespassing on his beach—and finding her unworthy of questioning, he pointed back to the lake.

"She was content there."

The love for fairy tales and lore piqued her curiosity. She glanced up and down the beach once more before taking a cautious step toward the man and boy.

"What makes her angry or content?"

He shrugged, his seal jacket moving as if part of his own skin. "Bah, fickle like all women."

Putting aside his patched net, he pushed himself off the rotting tree and stood to a hunched stature resembling one of the fishing hooks dangling from his coat. Bending over, he whispered in the boy's ear. The boy nodded and took off running straight across the ice as quickly as if he were gliding on skates.

Ivy started to call after the boy, but he had already disappeared. "Will he be safe out there? It's too dark for him to see."

The old man ignored her concern and shuffled toward the ice. "Come."

A tightness clutched in Ivy's chest. The ice was beautiful, but her mind also saw it as death, for it nearly had been. Two years after her family died, the Potomac River had frozen over in one of the coldest winters ever to hit DC. She had watched the other children with their shiny skates gliding across the ice as their parents waved from the shore.

They had looked so happy. Ivy had run out to join them, waving at the smiling faces as if they were her own family and she could capture that fleeting blossom of joy that existed only in her memory. She must have found a thin patch. The ice cracked. To this day she still heard that awful sound in her nightmares. Philip had pulled her to safety. Not one of the happy families had even noticed.

Well onto the lake by now, the fisherman turned back and gestured abruptly. "Come."

"I prefer to stay here."

"You come with me. I will show you the queen. Her palace, throne, and scepter."

Where the queen gathers her ice.

"Wait!" Ivy rushed forward as Balaur's cryptic words rang through her head, but the man was several yards out on the ice. Her feet slid and she wobbled to remain upright until at last she reached his side. "Tell me about the queen's scepter."

"The Ice Queen builds her castle here each winter where she gathers snow and ice for her cold reign. It melts away when a warm south breath arrives and turns frozen palace to water. Look close. Her breath you can see." He pointed at the ice beneath their feet. Bright white bubbles stacked atop one another in the clear teal water like thousands of strung diamonds. The breath of a queen.

"Where does she gather ice for her scepter?"

"Her throne is served by seals. When they die, she takes their skin and sews it to her gown made of frost. Gown becomes longer and longer, gathering more frost until it stretches wide as the lake."

"It sounds lovely, but tell me of her scepter, *pazhalsta*."

He frowned at her persistent interruption of his tale and reluctantly pointed northeast. "Barguzin. She gathers ice from its highest peak. Powerful magic dwells there. She captures all who go and casts a spell to transform trespassers to *upyr* who protect the mountain."

Ivy's heart pounded at the translation. "She transforms men into the undead to protect this place. Have you seen one of these creatures before?"

He gave a jerky nod, his gaze skittering about the ice as if the predators stalked close. "Risen dead. *Ubiytsa*. You go. You see." His eyes hardened before he turned and disappeared across the thick ice.

Superstitions had never held sway over Ivy's rational mind, but as the light faded to indigo and a crescent moon sliced through the sky, her penchant for fantasy came into itself. Suddenly, the bubbles beneath her feet began to move and the trees along the shoreline sharpened to fangs.

Risen dead.

Risers.

She scrambled off the ice and raced through the trees, using her seax to hack away limbs that dared to impede her speed. She crashed through the cabin door and nearly stepped into the fire someone had started without her forgotten firewood. Her teammates sprang to their feet, knives and guns at the ready, for what they could only assume was some wild woman with twigs and leaves in her hair.

"Ivy?" Jack lowered his pistol and stepped around the fire to her. Tempered fear sprang into his eyes. "What's happened?"

She grasped his arm as her lungs wheezed with frigid air. "The queen with the scepter." Pain jabbed every intake of breath. "A man and risen dead. Barguzin."

"You're not making sense. Come sit down. Philip, hand me that canteen of water."

Ivy grabbed Jack by his jacket lapels and forced her words to overcome the bitter cold freezing her tongue. "Barguzin."

He shook his head, not comprehending. "What is Barguzin?"

On the other side of the fire, Beatrix unrolled a map and tapped her finger to a northeastern quadrant of the lake. "A mountain range."

Ivy nodded, her frozen fingers kneading Jack's chest. "It's there. The facility. The Risers. We found it."

"My brilliant girl. I knew you'd figure it out." Jack grinned, catching her gloved hands in his bare warm ones as the flames in his eyes burned away the fear and sparked a gleam of danger. "No flagpole required."

TWENTY-TWO

PERHAPS IT WAS STRATEGY. PERHAPS IT WAS A DEATH WISH. MOST LIKELY it was downright stupidity.

Jack swiped the falling snow from his eyes and stared across the moon-glazed darkness. Lake Baikal stretched through the night like a sheet of glass, dark blue and terrible. Midnight. When all manner of danger shook off the trappings of daylight and safety and took on the hidden world.

Standing on the beach, Jack snatched off his wool hat and rubbed the back of his neck as he resigned himself to the task ahead: cross nearly fifty miles of ice to reach the eastern shore with naught more than shaky patches of starlight to guide them. Waiting until daylight might be the smarter option, but they couldn't risk being seen.

Boots crackled toward him over snow and pebbles. Philip stopped next to him, his breath puffing white over his red nose. "You've had more than one bad idea over the years, but this one might be the worst yet."

Jack might have laughed if it weren't true. No mission was without uncertainties and each one held the anticipation of danger, but tonight the air was quiet, a stillness to disguise the unrest lurking in his mind. He'd be glad to put this cursed lake far behind them and sign off as mission complete with near failures put aside and Talon's trust in him as a leader intact.

"It's either this or we spend the better part of five days trekking around the lake on snow-covered land inhabited by wolves."

"Nothing like keeping things exciting right up to the very end."

"Seems to be our lot."

Philip sucked in a deep breath and smacked his lips. "The air tastes off."

"It's only the souring of fear that comes the hour before a battle."

"Well, that's what we're going into, isn't it—a battle?"

"A battle is one thing. You can anticipate the frenzy, but this"— Jack indicated the ferocious blackness—"this is an unknown beast, and I fear its jaws are angled to devour us."

"So we cut the teeth before it bites." Philip unbuttoned his coat to reveal a vest with rows of pockets. Each pocket held a grenade, or what closely resembled grenades. He had an inventor's habit of disassembling objects in perfect working order to fill in with guts of his own creation. In other words, he made them ten times as deadly with an artful construction of detonation.

"I made them on the train after swiping a few parts from those Cossacks. These beauties are all connected by a single wire that I can access through a slit in my coat pocket. One tug, ten-second delay, and boom! I can unhook the wire and use it for remote detonation as well."

Insides jolting, Jack took a step away. As if another foot could save him from obliteration. "What compels you to wear such a thing strapped to your body? Do you wish to go up a croaker and not have your pieces collected for proper burial?"

"If I'm going out, it might as well be in a blaze of glory."

"And taking all of us with you."

Philip buttoned up his coat, concealing his deadly compatri-ots. "I'll be careful to fling it far in the opposite direction for your protection since you're more often in need of it." He punched Jack on the arm.

Jack rolled his fingers into a bunch of fives, then thought better of it. No telling what those grenades would do should they encounter a punch. "Keep up your tosh and you'll be the one in need of protection." He put his hat on his head and tucked it over his ears. The temperature hovered dangerously close to zero degrees and was bound to sink further before the sun climbed the mountain peaks. "Are we ready?"

"Nearly. Miles won't allow anyone to touch his precious transmitter now that he's got it working again, but the static is making the reindeer jumpy. Is it just me, or is he surlier than usual?"

"I wouldn't know. I've never met a reindeer before."

Philip rolled his eyes with enough force to freeze them to the back of his skull. "Miles."

"Lack of sleep and food. Deadly cold. Lack of precise coordinates. Take your pick as to what would make a man surlier." True enough for any person in their given situation, but Miles feared a different beast. A past come haunting.

Farther back on a deserted stretch of shore far from the village, Ivy, Miles, and Beatrix packed the last of their supplies and gear onto the commandeered sleigh. A torch of dry driftwood was wedged into the sand, snatching at shadows and casting the brown pebbles in burnt shades of orange. The equally commandeered reindeer twitched against his harness. He was none too happy to be stolen from his warm stall in the dead of night.

"Did you compensate the poor farmer who's going to wake up come morning to find his sleigh and animal missing?"

Philip nodded, huffing out another smoky breath. "I left the coins in the center of the empty stall. Can't miss them, although we sure will. That was nearly the last of our funds. We'll be lucky to afford a pint when this is done."

"I doubt they have many public houses where we're going." Jack stamped his feet against the crusted pebbles, chipping off ice crystals from his boot tips. Blood prickled sluggishly in his toes. As soon as this mission was over, he and Ivy were finding the nearest beach with the warmest sand to sink their feet into.

Next to him, Philip shuffled. "Listen, I've been meaning to— that is . . . the night of your wedding when we were outside, I don't remember much of what I said due to a walloping amount of chilled Russian bubbly, but I'm sure it ranked along the lines of idiotic."

"It was honest and between us; that's all."

"Still, I vaguely remember something about loneliness and reprobates swimming in a pool. Things I'd rather remain in the fog of a stupor."

To remain forgotten so he could believe it untrue. Philip's pain had been raw, scratching into the most honest conversation they had ever shared. Relegating it to a drunken whim was disloyal to all they had been through together.

Jack opened his mouth to argue, but one look at his friend's shuttered expression stopped him cold. There was no mischievous glint or sly tip of the head, but a hardness that had begun to grate along his jaw after the incident with the captives at Dobryzov. Further prying would lock him up forever, so Jack was forced to remain content in the truth that had passed between them.

Nodding, Jack clapped him on the back. "Time to get a move on. We've a long night ahead."

Turning his back on the chilling fate to come, Jack joined Miles at the sleigh as the last of the guns were loaded. From here on, they would carry no superfluous baggage, only weapons.

"All right there?" Jack asked, taking advantage of the moment alone.

Miles nodded distractedly from where he sat on the sleigh's last bench, eyes trained on the transmitter cradled on his lap.

Jack lowered his voice. "With the water."

Miles's eyes flickered to the dark lake then back to his machine. His fingers moved quickly before anyone else could see them. "I'll manage."

"It's frozen. There are no fishermen here."

"No, but he's here." Lips pressed tight, Miles pointed to his head and then to his mouth. "And here."

Childhood horrors could never be scrubbed away no matter how old one grew or how many targets one had trained to shoot. The mind captured those traumas and held them prisoner for a lifetime, allowing just enough length of chain to rattle in torment when faced with the origin of the fear once more.

Each member of his team was bound by different chains. Torture. Abandonment. Death. Demons of all shades.

Jack shook it off. Best thing he could do was keep his team focused on the task at hand, not the past nipping at their minds. "Able to pick up any signals yet?"

The white line of Miles's lips eased slightly. "Still testing frequencies. More static than up on the hill."

The machine hummed erratically, frightening the reindeer to prance sideways into Philip and his armload of explosives. Dynamite and magazine clips spilled onto the pebbled beach.

Philip cursed. "Devil beast! See if you don't end up on my breakfast plate." He swooped down and gathered the ammunition.

"Here. I'll help." Beatrix knelt and scooped the clips and grenade parts into a canvas rucksack she'd pinched from one of the Cossacks.

No one moved.

Jack frowned. "What is she doing?"

Ivy shuffled over to stand next to him. "Helping," she whispered, looking inordinately pleased for such a disconcerting situation.

"I can see that. Why?"

"Because Victor is alive."

A few hours before, Miles had hammered out a new wire and fashioned an antenna from a broken fishing rod they'd found beneath a tangle of rotten rope. A bit of moving pieces around mixed with a few smacks of the hand and the transmitter blinked to life. They immediately sent a message to Talon headquarters with the latest updates, much to the relief of Washington and Jefferson who were ready to list them as daisy shovers, or at the very least missing in action. Washington had then informed them that Fielding and Victor had returned safely to St. Petersburg—he refused to acknowledge the city's name change to Petrograd—and that Victor was expected to make a full, if not slow, recovery.

"A relief to be sure," Jack said slowly, "but why would that invoke such a complete change in character? She's almost . . . pleasant."

The quirk of his wife's eyebrow told him he'd lost a notch of credibility in her estimate of his capabilities. "For a man with an eagle's sniper eye, you certainly are blind."

"From the expression on your face I take it the answer is obvious except to male eyes or concern."

"In that you are correct."

A notch of capability for female insight was not one he mourned the loss of. No man alive or dead claimed to possess it in the first place. Shrugging off the odd scene, Jack leaned over the sleigh's side and checked the safety on Reaper, a habit as soothing as sighting down the rifle's long barrel that centered all his thoughts to a single point.

"Then all I have to say is Victor should find a bullet more often if only to spare us from her moods."

"For her happiness, you mean."

He flipped the safety lever. On. Off. On. "All they did was bicker. You call that happiness?"

"Bickering is often the flirtatious language of undeclared love." Ivy leaned against the sleigh, resting her shoulder against his. Or what would be their shoulders if twelve inches of coat padding weren't in the way. No need for coats on a warm beach.

"We never bickered."

"That's because we had our own language."

On. Off. On. "And that would be . . . ?"

Quicker than he could blink, she had a blade pressed to his throat and a glint in her eye. A move he much preferred to that of any a blushing bride could offer.

Lowering Reaper to the bench, safety on, Jack wedged his finger between Ivy's lethal knife and the vein it hovered over and slowly pushed it away. Love language indeed. Born of necessity, tested by survival, and perfected beyond the mere use of words. "How I adore you, Mrs. Vale."

The suggestive smile curving her lips was interrupted by a loud clearing of the throat from Philip and his impeccable timing.

"If you two are done basking in your marital bliss, we're ready for this mission that will most likely freeze us into ice chunks of regret." Philip assisted Beatrix—who smiled and offered a thank-you, to his utter amusement—into the middle seat before clambering onto the front bench. "And don't presume to tell me that your love will keep you warm. I'll push you under the water myself."

Jack helped Ivy to her seat with Beatrix, then climbed up next to Philip to take the reins. "Your foolish mistake in thinking we would sink when our hearts are so filled with the airs of undying love that we would float right back to the surface."

Philip laughed, puffing out great plumes of white breath. "Stick to bullets and blades, Jack-o. You do no favors to the words of poets."

The ice hissed as the sleigh trespassed its silent domain, the metal runners shaving icicles that splintered into the air and stung their hands and faces. For a mangy beast, the reindeer trotted with the confidence of having traversed the throes of winter his entire life and required little more than a tug of the reins to set him on course.

Far in the distance hulked the Barguzin range. The sharp granite tips stabbed the sky like knives, impaling the heavy clouds and dragging them down as imprisoned snowcaps, frozen in fear along the blades' edges.

Somewhere in that devilish fortress of rock was their target. The night wore on as hour after hour they drew near, Jack's eyes fixed ahead on the frozen surface to the sole point of their target.

He flicked the reins, driving the reindeer onward as he twisted his head to look back at Miles pinched between the explosives and guns. "Any new signals?"

Miles wiggled the antenna this way and that as the transmitter whirled with indecipherable static. "Still trying," he signed. "Difficult in this landscape bowl."

Jack shifted his next question to where his wife huddled next to Beatrix. They were like two frozen rabbits in their thick coats. "Your stranger on the ice didn't give coordinates to where this mystical queen gathered snow, did he? Or suggest how many henchmen she had on hand to ward off attackers? Anything more helpful than a mountain range?"

Ivy shook her head, her face barely visible beneath the fur hat and collar drawn up to her nose. "I already told you no."

"I was hoping for you to suddenly recall a vital piece of information."

"Sorry to disappoint."

Jack had never been one to turn away from a challenge. The more danger to be found, the more the thrill of pursuit chanted in his blood, but combing over an entire mountain range in the dark went far beyond a grand adventure and straight to the point of no return. A thought not so daunting for himself, but one he could not allow to befall his team. Most especially his wife. Ivy would follow him to the deepest circle of hell, but he would cast out his own life before sacrificing her unwavering loyalty.

The transmitter crackled. A voice.

Jack yanked the reins, and the reindeer jerked to a stop, slinging the sleigh sideways as the rails lost their forward momentum. Jack whipped around on the bench. "Turn that up."

Miles twisted the knobs as all ears strained for another sound, a spark of hope that fruitless desolation was not the only thing ahead.

The wires hissed. A lone voice, ancient and guttural, came from the darkness of centuries before in a language long since unspoken. Yet it now resurrected itself from death to haunt them all. "The next step is not enough."

A light flickered on the horizon. A pinprick of orange springing from the black. Another. And another until bursts of flame lined the awaiting shoreline a mere three hundred yards away.

"Come forward," the voice droned through the transmitter, this time in Russian, harsh as the rugged land from which it clawed. The voice spoke through a memory of smoke and screams and a singular bullet.

The voice of a dead man.

"The next step is not enough for you."

More fires blazed in the darkness, fanning out from the shore and ringing around them on the ice. A trap. One light detached itself from the shore directly in front of them and glided forward.

They were surrounded. If Jack tried to turn the sleigh and make a break in any direction, the ring would close in on them like a noose to cut off all possible escape routes.

Tossing Philip the reins, Jack leaped out of the sleigh. "Form a perimeter. Wait for my command." Rounding the sleigh, he pulled Reaper from the back bench and aimed at the light as it gained ground. "They set up for a performance. Let's not disappoint." He squeezed the trigger.

Bam!

The light wavered. Echoes of the shot crackled off the ice. The wavering light split into three and started forward once more, not gliding but bobbing. Their host for the evening came to greet them on foot.

"*Da*, there is the man I remember. Quick to the trigger." The voice.

Chills ricocheted down Jack's spine. He nudged Reaper tighter to his shoulder to steady himself. "Plenty more where that came from."

"Then be certain to kill me this time. I detest failure." The body that belonged to the voice stepped out of the darkness, unshrouding itself from a memory of billowing smoke, panicked screams ripping through a castle, and a single bullet lodging into skull and brain.

Torchlight carved his cheekbones to razor points, hollowing out the skin beneath like dried parchment stretched tight over jutting bones. The pair of dead, pale eyes, relentless in their terrible stare, now gathered their foulness into one ocular orb as a black patch clouded the other.

Balaur Tsar. Very much alive.

TWENTY-THREE

JACK CURLED HIS FINGER AROUND THE TRIGGER. NEXT TO HIM, IVY TOOK aim at a flame creeping toward their rear. "I suppose it's true when they say evil refuses to die."

"Not for lack of trying on your part." Balaur tapped his eye patch with a long, dirty fingernail.

"A rare failure. One I won't commit again." If he had succeeded at Dobryzov Castle, his team wouldn't have fallen into this death trap. He had to get them out, and this time, failure was not an option.

"Two millimeters more and I would be cold as this lake. A fate you will be plunged into before this night is out."

From the corner of his eye, Jack saw the circle tighten around his team. "Anticipating our demise, were you, with this little trap? How did you know we were coming?"

Balaur raised a hand and motioned with two of his bony fingers. A small figure climbed from the sleigh behind him and inched into the torchlight.

Ivy gasped. "The boy who was with the old man."

"What boy?" Jack frowned as he calculated how to get the child away from Balaur.

"He was on the ice with his grandfather, the man who told me the story about the Ice Queen. He whispered to the boy and the child ran off across the ice. In this direction."

Balaur laid his hand on the boy's head. The child flinched but didn't move. "The villages around the lake belong to me. Not a hair twitches without my command, and no stranger passes through without my knowledge." The boy trembled all over. "Their loyalty in reporting to me is vastly rewarded by being allowed to live another day."

A trap. And Jack had led his team straight into it. How could he have been so foolish? How would his team ever trust him again if this was where his leadership brought them?

Reaper was solid and heavy in Jack's hands, steadying him to the spot as he forced down the onslaught of failure. His mind raced frantically for a plan. Even a bad one was better than sitting like ducks for the kill. "You terrorize the locals into submission."

"I cannot afford to be without eyes and ears everywhere. They also make useful subjects for my experiments." Balaur twisted the boy's head to look at him. "Is that not right, *kroshka?*"

The boy whimpered but did not resist.

"Let the child go." Jack fitted Balaur's head through the front sight. One bullet to the brain. It might not stop the guards, but it would offer a second of confusion. An opportune moment, slim though it was, but a chance all the same for his well-trained team.

Balaur held the child's terrified stare. "I will not harm you—not so long as you are useful to me. Now tell the man to put down his gun or I will slit your throat."

The boy's lip wobbled. He tried to turn his head to Jack, but Balaur gripped it still. "Put down gun. *Pazhalsta.*"

Jack could not disobey. He dropped his rifle and pistol and motioned his team to do the same with their weapons. Steel clattered across the ice.

Balaur smiled at the boy and released him. "Return to your

grandfather. Tell him you may live this day for his fealty in reporting the intruders to me."

The boy took off running, slipping over the ice as his feet sought to make purchase against the slickness.

"The lake is too wide and dangerous for that child to cross!" Ivy cried. "He could die out there."

Balaur shrugged. "That is not my concern. His purpose was complete. Bind their hands and bring them."

He motioned forward the two torchbearers standing behind him. They were dressed in the solid black uniform with the red crown symbol blazoned across the chest to signify Balaur's private guard. The men held bits of rope.

Outgunned and outpositioned, but Jack wasn't going to be led like a lamb to slaughter. "You should know we won't go down without a fight."

"I have seen that you are not a man who will needlessly send his men"—Balaur's pale eye flickered over Jack's shoulder to Ivy and Beatrix—"and women to their deaths. Not without attempting a desperate escape, for which you will bide your time, awaiting the opportune moment. Am I correct in this thinking? There is no need to answer, for I know I am right. My spies tell me all from Dobryzov Castle and Swallow's Nest."

"We killed all your cronies," Philip spat. "Not one henchman survived that blast."

"You have seen that not all of my followers wear a uniform." Balaur's gaze roamed the ice beyond Jack where the child had disappeared. "While your mind is contriving a doomed escape, let us talk."

"Never been much for talking." Jack pushed Ivy behind him as he shifted into a fighting stance.

The snake's lips peeled back, his teeth gleaming brown in the torchlight as he looked past Jack's shoulder. "For her then. She is the one you protect, *da*."

Guards, quick as shadows from the rear, sprang from the rim of darkness with their guns pointed at Jack's team. One man leaped at Ivy, grabbing her hand. She pulled a concealed gun from her coat pocket.

Bam! Her shot skewed, the bullet slicing the man's cheek. He knocked the pistol to the ice and yanked her away from Jack. With Balaur's guard holding a gun to his wife's head, Jack could only watch as another guard quickly tied her hands before pushing her into the circle of Balaur's torchlight.

"The *prekrasnaya* maid from my party. *Da*, I heard all about you and your whisperings. A servant girl and a supposed nobleman. Did you think you would remain unnoticed?" Balaur grabbed Ivy and jerked her alongside him, his filthy fingers digging into her sleeve. "Come with me, *kotyonok*."

Jack rushed forward. A nearby guard grabbed Reaper from where it lay on the ice and shoved the butt into Jack's chest, knocking him to the ground.

Balaur paused and looked back. No indication of life flickered across his bony face. "Hear me clearly. Another move of that kind or any resistance and I put the bullet you intend for me into her head. Like this." Reaching into his brown robes, he whipped out a revolver, aimed at the guard closest to him, and shot. The man crumpled to the ground without a twitch as blood splattered from his head to the red crown blazoned across his chest.

Horror retched across Ivy's face as she trembled in Balaur's grip. "Monster! He was your own man."

"All for the good of a cause greater than self."

Jack was jerked to his feet, his hands bound behind his back. The guards followed suit with Miles, Beatrix, and Philip. Despite the dead man's blood spilling dark and thick across the ice as warning, Jack refused to acknowledge there was no way out.

Yet the ice proved a dangerous foe should they try to run, to say nothing of being surrounded and outmanned by at least twenty guards while Undertaker lay on the ice several feet away and Reaper was in the hands of a goon.

Balaur had spoken true. Jack would be forced to wait for the unexpected to make a move.

The eastern shoreline spread out as thick as oil with the Barguzin mountains rising high and formidable as giants against the predawn darkness. The ring of torches drew closer, the flames dancing over the silver mirror of ice in a hypnotic frenzy. Balaur sat, pulling Ivy down next to him while Jack, Philip, Beatrix, and Miles were made to sit across from them on the ice.

Balaur crooked his finger and two guards entered the ring with an oversize auger. Driving the sharp tip of the tool into the ice, the men gripped the long horizontal handle and began drilling. The frozen water cracked and popped up shards.

Settling comfortably as one might before a fire at the end of a blustery day, Balaur bent up one knee while stretching out the other leg. His brown robes, trimmed with decayed squirrel fur, flopped against Ivy's leg like cesspool sludge mucking over unsuspecting territory.

"You've been a nuisance to me for some time. Arriving unannounced at Dobryzov Castle, destroying my prized gun in Crimea, and now sneaking into my home at Baikal."

Cold saturated Jack's trousers, yet anger boiled in his blood in a maelstrom of shivering sweat. He dared not look at his wife lest the barely contained storm lash out and doom them all. Rashness would kill them faster than a firestorm.

"What can I say? We wanted a round-trip tour of Russia. Chasing you hasn't disappointed yet."

"Alas, you will not be around long enough to continue your travels to my newest facility. Siberia was ideal for its remoteness to keep my secret experiment hidden, but it is compromised now with your arrival. You have no doubt alerted your handlers—a ragtag team such as yours must have them—to this location. So I am forced to move on."

"My 'handlers,' as you put it, will chase you to the ends of the earth."

"Why, precisely, are you chasing me?"

"Because we want you dead."

Balaur's lips peeled back in a perverse display of amusement at the brutal honesty. "Who is this 'we'?"

The cold dug through Jack's flannels and burrowed into his bare skin. He set his jaw against the chattering of his teeth. "Defenders of righteousness. Protectors of the weak. All of which you seem hell-bent on destroying. I'm afraid we can't allow that kind of anarchy to persist."

"Anarchy, you call it."

"Is there another way to phrase murder, lawlessness, war profiteering, and brutality?"

"*Da.*" Balaur leaned forward, catching the orange light in his pale eye. "Opportunity."

A single word spoken with the conviction of derangement. A belief shattering the sanctity of life with no care to consequence or moral obligation. The man had no soul.

"You're off your chump." The maelstrom boiled with fury in Jack's blood. He twisted against the bindings holding him back, the rope burning around his wrists. One good lunge and he could cleanse the life from that murderer. "Blasting seven-ton mortars against cities around the world is genocide. Millions of innocent people killed while you make a profit playing both sides of the war."

"I only create the weapons. It is up to my buyers' discretion how and where they will be used."

"You crammed sworn enemies, warlords, and the world's most dangerous underground criminals into the same room at Dobryzov

Castle, and you expect them to use any kind of discretion? They will stop at nothing to achieve supremacy, not only by destroying one another but by murdering millions of innocent bystanders."

"I care not for lives lost. They are nothing to me, like dogs scrambling for scraps of land and power, but I hold the weapons. I hold the true power." The skin stretched taut over the razor bones in Balaur's face. A skull ablaze in fire. "Understand this: I do not care if the world burns."

Numbing coldness crept to the rim of Jack's lips. Soon enough he wouldn't be able to move them. "You will care if you have no one left to sell your weapons to. Weapons we've seen fit to dismantle for you."

Air hissed through Balaur's flat nose. "You may have destroyed my White Wolf, but that is only the surface of the destruction I intend to wreak."

"You mean these chemical experiments? Poisoning people into what you call Risers? We know all about them, and by this time tomorrow it will be another failed experiment just like your Wolf."

"You will never stop them because you will never sense them coming, not with a raging war to distract you. Poetically convenient, do you not find?"

Jack smirked to return feeling to his lips. "You disappoint me. Megalomaniac is hardly an original concept for a madman. I expected something a bit more astounding, considering your theatrics. The self-imposed title of Balaur Tsar demands showmanship, not to mention, the eye patch adds a rogue touch. Or outcast. I can't decide."

Ice popped and cracked as the auger drove deeper into the lake. The men grunted with exertion. Balaur cut his eye to the labor, his lips pulling back on one side before he sliced his attention back to Jack.

"And what are you but outcasts from your society? Good people of standing do not plot assassinations, nor do they carry trunks of explosives. They don't steal across a dangerous lake in the decline of winter for a man they believe dead. Tell me, what drove you from your home to pursue the inescapable mire of sabotage? What demons haunt the depths of your souls that you are no longer fit for polite society?"

Spittle leaked down Balaur's chin into the scraggly beard dragging across his chest. It glistened there for a moment before frosting into the tangles. "Russia is not even your home. You can tell by the eyes. Russians are proud but wary. Your eyelids are carved with obstinacy and pupils brightened by fervency."

Nose still running, Philip sniffed. "You've got it all wrong. This brightness is a glaze of boredom from listening to you drone on."

"Rest assured, soon you will hear nothing at all but the calling of cold eternity."

Balaur uprooted himself like a mushroom from its mud pit and walked to the reindeer, crooning low in his throat. "Magnificent creatures. Little but capable of a mighty load." He pulled a rust-flecked knife from his boot and stroked it over the sand-colored fur. "They are pure and serve as the spirit guides for wisdom and cleverness. Is that not so, *krasotka?*"

A grunt rumbled from deep in the reindeer's chest. Accepting, obliging, unknowing as the dirty blade wove through its thick hair.

"Animals with their pure intent are too good for this world. We trap their noble spirits in these hides and chain them for our labors. Reverence is lost on mankind. We are called to honor them. We are called to set them free from earthly bonds." He curved the knife around the beast's throat.

"No!" Ivy's scream stabbed the air as she struggled to stand.

Balaur paused, his blade pressed to the animal's cheek as his tangled hair curled around the antlers. His flat eye pressed farther into the horizontal slats of his cheeks. "You are not in agreement."

"There is no reason other than the evilness of your heart to murder this animal as it stands tethered before you."

"That is precisely my point. It remains chained, and I intend to set it free." With a vicious thrust, the knife sliced through the leather harness. Bits of rope, leather, and metal fell to the ice. After a swift pat on the rump, the reindeer shook himself and trotted off into the darkness, into the forest, and far beyond their reach.

Balaur kicked aside the trappings, then turned the blade to Ivy, pressing it flat against her shoulder and driving her down to the ice. "You weren't told to stand, *kotyonok*."

"Animal spirits?" Philip scoffed, driving the attention away from Ivy. "You must have gotten that mumbo jumbo from the mushroom patch you eroded from."

"Bold words filled with ignorance, but then, that is to be expected from the unenlightened." Shoving his knife into his boot, Balaur walked to the back of the sleigh and scraped his nails over the guns and ammunition. "You came well prepared. That is smart but will do you no good in the end."

Crack. The last bits of ice severed beneath the auger. The men retrieved the drill from the black depths, then sank large hooks into the floating chunks of ice, which they hauled out to reveal a hole large enough to snare a grown seal.

"I am a man of simple pleasure, preferring the old ways to the contrived entanglements of this day. Yet I will not deny uses of the modern. A cannon proves more effective than a *sovnya* polearm." Balaur plucked their transmitter from the back bench and twisted its knobs as static warbled out.

Miles strained against his ropes, his eyes bulging beneath his shaggy hair and never once wavering from the machine—the one thing in the world that made him who he was—now cradled in the palms of the devil.

"You may have destroyed my White Wolf, but my coming weapon is too brilliant and well guarded."

Jack continued twisting his hands as the rope cut into his skin. If only he could reach the blade strapped to his waist. Or the one in his boot. Or in the folds of his sleeve. What use was being armed when he couldn't reach any of them?

"More brilliant than destroying one-third of the world's population with a single shot? For all your lunacy, it was a master stroke in satiating your thirst for blood money."

"Nothing can stop what I am creating now. A pity you will not live to see it. You would have made a fitting addition." Balaur's eye bored into Jack with all the supremacy of a conqueror. He strode to the hole and tossed in the transmitter. No more than three seconds passed before it hit water. A six foot drop, at least.

Miles released an outraged cry as his pride of creation drowned beneath the ice.

"The operator, *da*? What, no tongue to speak of? Or should I say *with*?" Balaur opened his own mouth wide and stuck out his flat tongue. "I knew a mute once. Made the same pathetic noises before I put him out of his misery. Come. Show me your misery."

Miles stared hard, clamping his jaw. Air shot from his nostrils as Balaur stirred the tormenting memory of a reprehensible fisherman. Balaur flapped his ugly mouth open, taunting the man who had no way of defending himself.

The storm seethed within Jack. Unlike the burning fury that prompted him to lash out at Ivy's distress, it now roiled cold and hard. Patient death. "That's enough."

"A man should face his truth. Not shy away with undisciplined cowardice, miserable from his own existence."

"Cowardice is taunting a man you've bound to keep him defenseless against your attacks. Here I thought Balaur, the terror of Russia, feared no man." Taunting any leader in front of his men was foolish, for he was then bound to defend his honor, if he had any to speak of. In that rash haste to prove himself, he was bound to trip headlong into a mistake. That mistake would provide Jack's opportune moment.

Tucking his hands deep into the rotting squirrel fur of his

sleeves like a priest at benediction, Balaur fixed his eye on Miles. "Release him."

A guard cut Miles's ropes. Miles jumped to his feet and ran headlong at Balaur with a guttural war cry.

"No!" The opportune moment was gone before it began, and Jack's warning came too late.

At the last second, Balaur smiled cruelly and stepped aside. Miles pitched forward toward the ice hole only to be stopped by Balaur's bony hand around his neck. With his free hand, Balaur pushed up the knit cap, then placed his festering mouth to the hair covering Miles's ear. "Show me your wretchedness."

With the tips of his toes brushing the ice and the upper half of his body leaning over the hole, horrifying noises garbled from Miles's strangled throat.

"*Glupyy*." Balaur released his grip.

Miles's arms flailed, but for only a second that proved not enough. Down he plummeted, striking the water with a sickening splash.

Jack cursed but heard nothing beyond the desperate thrashing in the frigid water deep within the black hole. He lurched to his feet and was immediately hit in the back with the end of a rifle. He toppled to the ground, his cheek scraping ice as Philip and Beatrix suffered the same fate for their efforts on either side of him.

Balaur watched with detached interest as Ivy crawled on her belly to the edge of the hole, crying out to Miles and imploring for his rescue. Hands still tied, she swung one of her legs around and lowered it, but it was impossible for Miles to reach.

Balaur stamped a heavy black boot in the center of her spine. She cried out in pain. "There is no room for two. Wait your turn."

Seconds passed until the water grew silent, and the air became charged with wrath and revenge.

"Murderer," Jack spat. "Treacherous, belly-crawling demon. I'll take pleasure in destroying you."

"I will drown everything you care for first, and then you will die. No better than an unwanted dog. No better than him." Balaur dug his toe under Ivy's belly and shoved her away. "We'll go in order of least important to you, saving the best for last. Bring the other woman."

Quick as a cartridge dislodged from its chamber, Philip sprang to his feet and threw himself into the center of the torch circle. "Have a go at me first, boys. I've got twenty pounds of dynamite strapped to me, and it's getting awful uncomfortable. What do you say I put us all out of our misery right here and now? A nice send-off since we missed you bastards the last time."

It wasn't the moment Jack had expected, but he knew never to underestimate Philip. Opportune or not, the moment had arrived.

"Call off your guards, Balaur, or he'll blow us all. And don't think about testing him. I've seen him pour gunpowder in his coffee for an extra kick."

"Gets the blood pumping," Philip said, wriggling his hands for the hidden trigger up his sleeve.

The white of Balaur's eye swallowed a sliver of fear and blazed with inhuman devilry. "You lie. Your hands are tied, and you are surrounded."

With a dozen rifles pointed at his heart, Philip took a step toward him. "I anticipated your old-fashioned method of tying our hands behind our backs without properly checking for weapons. I have a release trigger attached to my wrist. Come closer and I'll give you a peek."

Balaur laughed, a sound straight from the pits of evil. "To deserve life, you must first welcome death. You must welcome me. But I see the fear in your eyes, the frantic impulse to live."

"An impulse felt by most if I dared to guess." Philip wriggled his hand up his opposite sleeve. His brow creased in concentration as the element of surprise slowly ticked away from them.

"And deserved by none. It remains my duty to dispatch you

from this earthly burden. Order of importance no longer excites me. Bring the other woman. This ends now." Balaur snatched Ivy by her hair and threw her to the edge of the hole.

"Blow it, Philip!" Jack lurched to his feet and started toward Ivy. Live or die, he was getting to his wife.

Philip jerked at his coat sleeve. "I'm trying. The release is caught on my cuff link."

A guard dragged Beatrix kicking and screaming and shoved her down next to Ivy.

Balaur planted a boot on Ivy's shoulder, pinning her in place as she bucked against him with murder in her eyes. "Any final words to the man who has failed to save you?"

"*Stoy!*" a voice shouted from the black-shrouded shoreline, followed by the unmistakable clicks of rifles. "In the name of Comrade Lenin and the Workers' and Peasants' Red Army, you are ordered to surrender!"

TWENTY-FOUR

THE COMMUNISTS HAD ARRIVED. TO JACK, THEY WERE AS WELCOME A sight as the cavalry. Two dozen soldiers dressed in dingy brown and sporting red armbands rushed from the mainland. The steel of predawn light glanced off rifles with bayonet tips.

"They are White Army! The tsar's men!" Jack shouted, flinging the damning accusations at Balaur. If there was anything the commies hated more than the tsar, it was his devoted followers. Of which Balaur was not, but the Reds need not know that. "We are with you, comrades!"

"Glory to the Red Army! Glory to the people!" Ivy cried, picking up the only leverage they could muster in such a situation. If they could strike the two sides against each other, Jack's team might stand to see the next day.

Chaos exploded. Shouting and cursing collided in a hail of bullets as Red Army soldiers poured onto the frozen lake in a bitter rush to kill. The girls had disappeared. Philip needed help with the wire. If he couldn't get the remote detached, Jack might not be able to reach Ivy before the explosion went off. Cursing, Jack made his decision and low-crawled—an extremely difficult maneuver using the sole force of leg muscles while his useless hands remained tied—straight to Philip as bullets bit into the ice around them.

"Get the knife from my boot." Jack pressed his foot into Philip's bound hands, and Philip yanked the blade free, gripping it between his palms. Spinning back-to-back, Jack clutched the knife and sawed up and down until his ropes cut free. He made quick work of freeing Philip. "Get that vest off and set the charges to remote detonate. We'll blow the ice and run south. I'll untie the girls and get the guns." He made to rise.

"Wait!" Philip snatched his wrist. "The wire is tangled around my cuff link. I can't remove the trigger to detonate remotely if it's still attached to the vest."

Jack shoved up Philip's sleeve. A thick black wire was coiled around his cuff link, which was stamped with the Talon seal. "We lost just about everything, yet you managed to hang on to these?"

"They're magnets dipped in gold. Handy when I need to crack a safe."

"Don't let the commies see them. Wealth, industry, and capitalism at their finest."

"You're the one making friends with them."

"The enemy of my enemy and all that rot," Jack muttered, untwisting the wire. No matter which way he twisted, it refused to come free.

Metal whizzed through the air. Philip ducked sideways. "Don't mind me and the stray bullets coming at my head. Take all the time you need."

"You've tangled it right good." Jack reached for the knife in his boot. "I'll cut the sleeve off."

Cold metal dug into the side of Jack's head. "On your feet." One of Balaur's guards.

Jack slowly rose to a half crouch, knife gripped in his hand ready to slice. The man's face went slack, largely due to the hole from a lead round-nose bullet punching through both cheeks. He crumpled without a sound.

Lowering his pistol from the killing shot, a Red soldier rushed over and kicked the dead man aside. "We are here for you, comrades. Fighting against the privileged tyranny—"

His intent, too, was cut short, this time with a bullet to the chest that dropped him on top of his victim from seconds before.

"If these Russians trained to fight more and talk less, a few of them might actually survive this war. Whichever side they belong to." Philip jerked Jack back down. "Get this wire off me, or it'll be us next!"

All pretense of finesse gone, Jack yanked the wire, ripping off the cuff link, which bounced several feet away.

Wire now free, Philip unbuttoned his jacket. Sweat beaded his brow despite the frost puffing from his lips. "It'll take a minute to get the vest off and detach the remote from the wire. Cover me."

Diving for Undertaker, Jack crouched next to Philip and scanned the melee for Ivy. The line of Reds clashed with Balaur's guards in a seeping river of blood on ice. The soldiers ducked and stabbed as trained warriors, but the guards were ruthless. The chance of Jack's team escaping dwindled with every second.

"We don't have a minute."

"Half a minute then."

A scream ripped through the storm of bullets. A woman's scream. At the opposite side of the torch circle, Beatrix yanked a knife from the heart of a guard and crawled toward a small head and hands clawing the rim of the ice hole.

Jack's heart stopped.

Ivy.

He raced to her, mindless of the bullets and Philip's shouting and the ice slipping beneath his feet.

Until a bullet slammed into his shoulder.

He jerked sideways with the impact and collided with the very guard who had stolen Reaper from him. Undertaker spun out of his hand.

The guard rammed the rifle's muzzle into Jack's gut and leaned his weight against the stock. Ignoring the pain in his shoulder, Jack grabbed Reaper's barrel and shoved, bashing the stock into the guard's eye. The ocular bones crunched, and the guard keeled over with a howl of pain.

Jack put him out of his misery with a single shot, courtesy of his newly returned Springfield. Jumping to his feet, he grabbed his pistol and ran.

Shoving past knots of guards and soldiers, Jack skidded to his knees beside the hole. Ivy was nowhere to be seen. Neither was Beatrix. No forms were floating in the water. No air bubbles surging to the surface.

Jack angled himself over the edge, ready to dive in. "Ivy!"

"Jack! We're here!" Crouched beside the sleigh looking glorious, ice crusted, and alive were Ivy and Beatrix.

Jack rushed to them and gathered Ivy in a lung-crushing hug. "I thought you were a goner."

"It takes more than knocking me into an icy hole to ensure my demise." Pushing him away, her gaze dropped to his shoulder. "You're shot."

"A graze. Time enough later to worry about it."

A purse of her blue-tinged lips was all the chastisement she gave before nodding to the bundle in Beatrix's arms. "We got the guns."

Beatrix hitched her brace of pistols and looked back at the ice hole. Sorrow twisted her face. "But Miles—"

"It's too late. Miles is gone. We have to move, or we will be too." It ripped his insides apart to leave a man behind, but there was nothing he could do now except survive and get the rest of his team to safety. "On my count we make for Philip, then get off the ice before he sets the grenades. There's a ten-second delay once he presses the trigger, so move fast. Go!"

They jumped out from behind the cover of the sleigh and raced across the ice. Gun smoke choked the air, punctuated by flashes of orange from spitting rifles.

Jack's eyes watered as the acrid bitterness clawed his throat and his shoulder pounded. Bullets cut the air all around them, stabbing into the ice and punching through bodies as the hellishness of battle raged.

As quick as the snap of a magazine into a chamber, the scene stilled, like a target seen through the distorted glass of a fogged scope.

The smoke of gunpowder rolled back.

Philip's vest of explosives lay abandoned, the trigger nowhere in sight.

"A parting gift to you." Several yards away, Balaur's arm was locked around Philip's throat. He was dragging him away as three guards surrounded them.

No!

Balaur held up his other hand. Clenched between his fingers was the trigger.

Jack's stomach plummeted to his feet.

"Catch me and save your comrade. Or save yourselves—if you can." Evil contorting his face, he pressed the trigger.

Ten seconds.

Jack would never make it to Philip in time. Not with the vest ticking down between them. A pain far worse than his gunshot wound tore through his heart.

He had no choice but to leave him, his best friend. Or blow himself and the rest of his team to smithereens.

They had to live. It was the only way to rescue Philip another day.

He spun and shoved Ivy and Beatrix away. "Run!"

Before the sound of his shout ended, the explosives detonated, and the earth imploded with a shattering crack of ice and rushing water.

PART IV

The Evening Star
DECEMBER 1, 1917

ROMANIA SURROUNDED!

As Russia abandons the only point of light in the East to fight her own civil revolution, Central Powers close ranks around Romania. Armistice to be signed in Focşani on December 9, 1917.

TWENTY-FIVE

THE PAST TEN MONTHS HAD PRODUCED NOTHING BUT DEAD ENDS TO FIND-
ing Balaur. Jack and Ivy had followed every rumor about weapons
dealing trickling from the black market. They'd traveled from Bulgaria
to the Bay of Biscay, gotten caught behind battle lines and trapped in
bombarded cities for weeks at a time, and still the man they hunted
eluded them.

Until a single tip from a dealer in Moscow let slip—or perhaps was
forced to reveal—that Bran Castle had become an underground safe
house for White émigrés. Yet the most interesting detail was that the
ancient castle reportedly sold weapons to certain zealots who wished
to return to Russia with an army to roust out the Reds. It could be
a long shot to hope Balaur was putting his deadly skills to use once
more, but it was the only lead they'd had since the disaster at Baikal.

Since Philip was taken.

Talon had insisted they return to headquarters immediately, but
Jack refused. By his judgment, the mission wasn't complete until
every last member of his team who could be was accounted for. They
would return after they found Philip and not before.

Jack and Ivy had parted ways with Beatrix, who returned to Petrograd to rejoin Fielding and Victor for an overdue reunion, which she vehemently denied. He and Ivy had assumed new identities as Russian nobles fleeing the revolution overtaking their country. On their journey south, they had huddled with other White émigrés in train stations and disclosed the vast number of jewels they'd managed to smuggle out from under the Bolsheviks' noses.

Wealthy people were always eager to brag about who had suffered the most by being weighed down with diamonds. The gossip chain did its work and by the time they stepped off the train in Braşov, Bran Castle had issued a formal invitation to Lord and Lady Turgenev, recently of Moscow.

Jack took in their surroundings as he and Ivy entered the castle. If only the night was dark and stormy, the setting would be perfect. Bran Castle, the fabled home of Count Dracula, stood in silent reflection against the dull light like a Gothic king on his mountainous throne. Jack felt the slightest twinge of disappointment to discover clean limestone walls, dark crossed timbers, and fine artwork instead of moldering stone dungeons and blazing torch-lit corridors. Not even a display of wooden stakes was present to humor visitors.

Still, it was the most interesting place they had trekked to in their search.

A servant led Jack and Ivy down a short corridor and through a set of heavy oak double doors to the castle's ground-floor receiving hall where a man awaited them.

"*Willkommen!* Or as they say here in Transylvania, *isten hozott.* Though I am certain for you, baron and baroness, *dobro pozhalovat* is more welcoming to your ears." Klaus Saltzmann, emissary from the Austro-Hungarian Empire for the newly acquired Transylvania territory, greeted Jack and Ivy. If spouting off in German, Hungarian, and Russian wasn't enough to impress, he'd gone the extra mile to slick back his hair with enough oil to burn every lamp in town, to shine his shoes enough that Dracula himself would think it was daylight, and to wear a suit woven from the finest spoils a war could offer. He was, in other words, a politician.

"We speak many languages, my good man." If Jack was going to play a baron, he might as well make the most of the usual arrogance associated with the privilege. As a gentleman, he would resist mentioning that French was the language in which he should be addressed and not Russian. Or so Ivy had instructed on the snowy ride up to the castle. Speaking Russian in Russia was for the dirt peasants.

"For you I shall keep it simple and settle on German." He gave a stiff nod and affected a bored continental manner.

With a subservient smile, Saltzmann bowed respectfully over Ivy's offered hand. "As you wish, Lord Turgenev. My lady. This way, please." He escorted them past the grand dining hall, gleaming in dark wood and rows of windows, to a smaller antechamber with rounded limestone ceilings and a large fireplace tiled in exquisite blues, reds, and greens.

Light crowded through the recessed windows and floated over the dark mahogany floor where a small table with four chairs sat in the center of the room. The table had been elegantly laid for afternoon tea with cakes and cookies and a steaming brew, and the cloying musk of Old World hung in the air.

Saltzmann pulled out one of the intricately carved chairs and beckoned Ivy forward. "Lady Turgenev, at your pleasure."

Ivy lowered herself to the seat with all the grace Dolly had mustered into her during deportment classes.

"Danke." She peeled off her white kid gloves and draped them over her lap, then crossed her feet at the ankles. A perfect depiction of the proper aristocrat she was pretending to be.

"I hope you take tea?" Saltzmann sat after Jack and reached for the silver filigree teapot.

"Ah, tea. How I have missed the civilized simplicity." Jack sighed dramatically. "Ever since the baroness and I were forced into exile by those vile Reds, we have barely scraped together any comforting notion of home."

"Indeed, and there is nothing so heartening as tea with dark cherries picked from the fields of Bakaldy." Ivy matched Jack's sigh.

Saltzmann poured the steaming amber liquid into the delicate cups painted with vines of flowers. "I sincerely apologize, my lady. We have no cherries today, but my personal chef in residence has spiced the brew with delicate cloves. I do hope you find it a suitable exchange." He handed her one of the cups with its matching saucer, then offered one to Jack.

Jack hated cloves, but he sipped the brew and smiled, as required of a polite guest, while the liquid tumbled horribly down his throat.

Ivy fared much better as she swallowed the swill without so much as a flicker of disgust. "Your chef has quite the touch. Of course, we always served our tea by samovar. Another tradition it seems we must sadly leave behind."

Saltzmann's hand fluttered about the table as if searching for the ancient contraption for heating water. Coming up at a loss, he grabbed at the plate of crescent-shaped cookies and offered them to Ivy instead. "*Vanillekipferl*. Delicate and buttery with hints of vanilla. A culinary creation of celebration for when Austria defeated the Turkish army in 1685. They mimic the shape found on the defeated flag."

Ivy had started to reach for a cookie until the mention of vanilla, her old scent nemesis. She quickly withdrew her hand. "It was 1683, was it not?" The history book in her refused to remain silent.

Saltzmann frowned. "Far be it from me to correct a lady—"

"Then don't." Her mouth flattened.

"We are grateful for you taking us in," Jack hurried on before his wife could launch into a history lesson and throw off their cover. "It is so difficult to know who is friend or foe in these times, and your open door has been a welcoming beacon to our ravaged souls."

Saltzmann leaned forward, all interested concern. Sconce light bounced off his hair like small spotlights. "The madness rampaging through your homeland is almost incomprehensible. You and your compatriots will always be welcome here, protected from Lenin and his blood-crazed henchmen."

Ivy pressed trembling fingertips to her temple. "Please do not speak of blood."

Jack took one of her hands and pressed a kiss to her fingers. "Please forgive my wife. We have seen enough blood running through the streets of our beloved homeland to fill a lifetime of nightmares." Ivy may have been acting with enough theatrics to put Theda Bara to shame, but the truth of the statement was heartbreaking.

"Forgive me, my lady. I do not mean to cause you distress."

"We were lucky to escape with our lives." Ivy leaked tears into her performance. Not bad considering she'd been practicing for days. "Forced to flee in the middle of the night—I barely had enough time to pack my box of jewels. Nothing could be more devastating than losing the Turgenev emeralds to those peasant communists."

Saltzmann's eyes widened for a fraction of a second, but it was obvious enough. She had captured his full attention. Or rather, the prospect of adding Russian jewels to his Austro-Hungarian coffers held his interest. He'd created the perfect con of opening his doors to war refugees only to skin them for all they were worth. "However I may be of assistance, you have only to ask, Lady Turgenev."

Ivy smiled graciously, like a cat counting the feathers of the unsuspecting canary. "Your magnanimous hospitality is more than enough for the baron and myself."

"Anything you require, I am at your command."

Jack leaned forward. "There is one pressing matter I should like to discuss. You must forgive my bluntness since we've only just arrived, but I fear the matter cannot wait."

He pushed aside his teacup as if it might block his words and dropped his voice.

"It is of the utmost importance that our presence here goes strictly unnoticed. The Bolsheviks have their spies everywhere with the prime mission of tracking down Russian nobility and those with ties to the tsar and dragging them back to Russia for execution."

Ivy let out a whimpering moan and groped for his hand. The tsar and his young family were being held as prisoners by the Red Army. Nobles, wealthy citizens, and monarchists were hunted like dogs under the new communist thirst for the so-called liberation from tyranny.

Saltzmann rushed to prove his stalwartness. "We here at Bran Castle are the silver service of discretion. There are four other guests who have sought asylum with us after being forced to flee your homeland, and I can personally assure you that your privacy and safety are our gravest priorities." He offered a sympathetic smile.

"Perhaps tomorrow after you have rested and settled in we might schedule a time to discuss any other matters that remain pressing to you. Travel documents, new identity papers, safe passage, or currency exchange. I am at your disposal."

Currency exchange, indeed. The only exchange he was interested in were all the jewels Lord and Lady Turgenev were reputed to have smuggled out of Russia.

Saltzmann was a master of his duplicitous craft at this point, and Jack silently congratulated the man on his restraint from appraising them for lumps of gems sewn into Ivy's corset or a hidden ruby bulging from Jack's pocket. Saltzmann had more than enough time to practice his game, considering the number of refugees who had trudged through these ancient gates.

Jack settled back in his chair, conveying ease at the fine treatment he was receiving. "Your thoughtfulness is much appreciated. I know I speak for all my displaced countrymen when I say how grateful we are for you to have opened your doors to us."

Ivy nodded her agreement, which set the jeweled pin in her fancy hat to sparkling. "Indeed, a castle is made to shelter the weary. I cannot imagine these grand rooms stand desolate without guests for long."

Eyes flitting from the jewel to the chamber, Saltzmann shook his head. "On the contrary, this pile of stone was left to decay for too long. Since coming to reside within its cold walls, I've done what I can to requisition its meager comforts, though my post here has been a rather quiet one." He adjusted his tie, a rather serious affair of oxblood pindots, and sighed wistfully to the room.

"This region is not known for its thriving entertainment, but it is an important territory acquisition for our war efforts. We fought hard to capture this land, and now that it rightfully belongs under Austro-Hungarian rule, it is my duty to enforce the peace. To prove to the people of this principality that we are benevolent conquerors."

Bullies and opportunists, more like, no matter how they tried to dress it up. Jack tamped down his disgust. "From what I hear the kingdom of Romania is set to join your growing list of conquered lands. Congratulations."

Saltzmann preened as if he'd single-handedly stormed the line of defense. "They have fought long and valiantly against our Central Powers, but surrounded now as they are, the Romanian army has no choice but to lay down their arms in a truce. An agreement was reached just last week."

No doubt with Russia having once been an enemy to the Central Powers before pulling out of the war to tend to their own revolution, Austro-Hungarian officials hoped that a peace treaty would entice former enemies to their side by offering refuge to their fleeing wealthy. Wealth that would plump Austro-Hungarian funds nicely.

"Tell me, will peace truly be achieved? It's heartening to hear when the world has seen nothing but war for so long."

"The armistice is set to be signed the day after tomorrow in

Focşani where the main defense line of the Romanians is located. Rather symbolic I find."

"Quite." Pretending to sip his tea, Jack took note as the man rattled off the names of the attending diplomats, generals, and leaders jockeying for power, noting whom he was personally connected to and hinting at who could provide an advantageous introduction. Tomorrow would be time enough for discreet inquiries about a weapons dealer that would hopefully lead them to Balaur.

"Of course, if I can persuade Lord Hapstein"—Saltzmann was still talking and building castles in the sky—"who is attaché to the Austrian councilman of foreign affairs, of the peace I've managed in this backwater, I might be reassigned to Vienna. Torte?"

"*Ja, danke.*" Ivy accepted a plate with a small slice of chocolate cake. Her fork paused halfway into the dessert. "My, these are interesting markings on the rim. I confess that my Romanian is rather limited, but these seem to be a most unique dialect."

"Dacian," Saltzmann replied as he offered a slice of cake to Jack, who declined. "An ancient language that was once spoken in this region but died out centuries ago, though the villagers find it chiseled into tunnels from time to time out in the mountains. Leftovers from an extinct age that are often placed on wares to honor their past. Of course, a lady of your breeding wouldn't be interested in such primitive practices. You would have been educated in the classical and romantic languages. None of this barbarous tongue with no place in the modern world."

"How right you are, Mr. Saltzmann." Ivy smiled tightly, dragging her attention away from the plate. Jack suppressed a grin, knowing it must have taken Herculean effort considering the history notes likely fluttering out of control in her mind. "There is only so much education suitable to a lady's delicate mind. An archaic civilization is of little use to me."

Jack took Ivy's hand and squeezed before she bent her fork in half. "My wife is accustomed to gentler pursuits like those we had on our country estate near Lake Ilmen. Isn't that right, *shatz*?"

Ivy smoothed out her smile and nodded. "How I miss the serenity of our estate after the terrible ordeal of fleeing Russia. It was so quiet and surrounded by woods. The serfs spent half of the morning dispersing those awful birds from the trees, but the peace to my ears was well worth their effort." She took a deep breath that relaxed her shoulders. "I know I shall rest soundly here for the first time since spending weeks cramped into train boxes. You cannot imagine what it has done to my silks."

Acknowledging the cue, Saltzmann placed his napkin next to his plate and stood. "Then by all means, I shall show you to your rooms where you may rest before supper and meeting our other guests. This way, please."

★★★

Snow fell thick across the orange roofs and cobbled streets of the ancient city nestled in the valley below Bran Castle's imperious glare. Streetlamps flamed to life in flickers of red and yellow protected by soot-stained glass. The light pooled in shallow circles, its depths never reaching farther than the blankets of snow hushing its brightness. Not a single spark dared glimmer toward the darkness of the castle skulking on high in its shroud of night.

Ivy dropped the damask curtain over the window and turned back to the warmth filling the chamber. No boasts of fine luxury as so many castles held, but the room was well enough situated for the cover of a minor nobleman and his wife.

Ivy slid off her dressing gown and tossed it on the large four-poster bed, then donned the merlot-colored evening gown. It shimmered in the firelight, the silver silk threads weaving between folds of velvet like shimmering rivers. She had bartered it from a fugitive countess for a loaf of bread on the outskirts of Paris a few weeks prior.

The truth behind their convenient cover story of fleeing Russians was a tragedy beyond comprehension, but after months of traveling over ice and rock with the barest of ablutions available, she couldn't contain the small joy of feeling clean fabric against her skin and a warm blanket to pull over her at night.

She presented her exposed back to Jack. "Will you help with my buttons?"

When her "lord" husband didn't respond, she turned to where he sat in a wingback chair next to the fireplace. Shadow and flame chased across his expression, one instant smooth and light, the next dark and intangible. A fair representation of his inner turmoil of late.

"Jack."

He stirred as if surfacing from a deep dive. "I'm sorry, love. What did you say?"

Kneeling in front of him, she placed a hand on his knee. His trousers were a rich woven black paired with polished black shoes, the perfect ensemble for a nobleman—or at least a man posing as one—but he had yet to change from his day shirt to the starched collar and waistcoat lying forgotten on the bed. "You're lost again."

He placed his hand on top of hers, an intuitive reaction but hardly more than a gesture of acknowledgment of late. Especially when he drew into himself.

"We've scoured most of Europe without a single clue. This is the only thread we have. What if the path turns out to be another dead end?"

She moved her other hand atop his and squeezed with a summoning of conviction to eclipse the sorrow of her husband's voice. "We *will* find Philip. Balaur must have gone deep underground to regroup and strengthen. He's biding his time to strike again, and when he does, we'll be ready."

"Unless he's already killed Philip. Or the Reds did. For all we know he may be in one of their prison camps. Philip and Balaur together." Jack's fingers twitched against her palm as defeat overtook his expression. She knew he would never give in to it, would run himself into the grave before admitting loss, but unguarded moments came when the darkest of possibilities seduced his soul.

Perhaps it should have frightened her to see him like this, doubtful and without direction, but in truth, it didn't. She met him where he was with no illusions or expectations, no guns or plans of attack or coddling, but with simple honesty. As a husband and wife must to withstand the darkness together. And she had every intention of weathering every storm at his side.

"Balaur has weapons and plays both sides of the war," Ivy said. "If the Reds had captured him at Baikal, it would have made front-page headlines. Beatrix promised to send word if she hears the slightest murmur of a rumor."

"Philip wouldn't have made headlines. My best friend, who I abandoned on the ice to a madman."

"He's my best friend, too, and we did not abandon him. We had no choice but to run, and we went straight back to search for him."

Jack lurched out of the chair—Ivy slanting out of the way just in time—and slammed his forearms on top of the mantel, leaning his forehead to the wood. "We were too late. Balaur knew we were coming. He must have abandoned the Baikal facility before meeting us on the ice. There's no knowing where he might have escaped to."

They had barely escaped that day. The ice had cracked beneath their feet as they raced for the safety of shore. Red soldiers and Balaur's guards were swallowed into the splitting fissures and dragged down into the freezing depths of the lake where the Ice Queen claimed her victims for eternal slumber.

When the chaos cleared, only a handful remained to drag themselves to shore. Ivy, Jack, and Beatrix had combed the area with no trace of Balaur or Philip. They trekked into the mountain and found the lair buried deep inside Barguzin. Abandoned. Empty cells and broken syringes were the only remaining evidence of the evil that had been performed there. Setting the last of the dynamite, they destroyed the facility. Ivy had wept while Jack stared glassy eyed across the damage to the lake.

Rising from her kneeling position, Ivy touched his shoulder. "Do not lose hope."

"Hope." He spat the word as if its vileness poisoned his tongue, then shook her off. "I have nothing but anger and revenge burning inside me."

"Fanned hotter by self-loathing. It does not become you, Jack." Honesty came in many forms. Mercy was one; harshness another. She took a step back and crossed her arms over her velvet bodice. "I married a man, not a pity-lapping recluse."

"Miles is dead and Philip might as well be, and there is no one to blame but me—their leader, the man who swore to protect them."

"You may have served as their leader, but that did not make you their lord and master. They were agents of Talon. They understood and accepted the burdens of the job when they took their oaths. To live or die fighting for justice. What happened at Baikal was a terrible tragedy that no one could have predicted."

"It was my duty to predict it!" Eyes blazing, he slammed his fist against the mantel.

Ivy didn't back down. "How could you? Do you suddenly possess the infinite knowledge of the Almighty? If you think so, then your pride has gone willfully out of control, and I wouldn't be the least surprised if a lightning bolt streaked from the heavens and smote your arrogance."

"My arrogance. What is truly to blame in thinking my way was the only option to consider."

"You are the leader, Jack. It is your responsibility to make the decisions, and you did so to the best of your ability. No one faults you for that."

The fire in his eyes smoldered to crumbling coals. A flicker of red heat and then ash. "Not even for abandoning Philip when he needed my protection?"

If there was one thing she admired Jack for most, it was his ability to stare failure in the eye and not shrink away. A man with less honor would duck in search of excuses with pathetic attempts to salvage his reputation. Jack took it square on the chin, perhaps walking away with a bruise or two, but always with his head held high.

He had told her once what had happened—why he'd left Philip and the explosives. Because of her. It was instinct for a husband to rush to his wife's screaming—mission be damned—as she would have done for him. Though he'd never given voice to the incident again, it stretched between them like a weighted charge on a taut rope.

On more than one night when sleep failed to claim her, her restless mind turned over every action of that day. Balaur surrounding them. Miles's silence beneath the ice. The Red Army springing from the shoreline. Jack and Philip with the vest. A Red soldier knocking her into the ice hole as he lunged for the enemy. The water inches from her dangling feet. Her own screams filling her ears. Beatrix grabbing her hands and hauling her to safety. Jack crushing her in his arms.

The look of utter abandonment on Philip's face as he was dragged away.

Her heart throbbed against the confines of her corset and tight bodice. That night could have ended so differently. Abandonment had always been Philip's greatest fear. Was it not every orphan's? After already suffering from it, whether through rejection or death, to trust again was a monumental feat in overcoming the self-preservation of solitude. Then to have that trust shattered in a moment of need . . . a moment her scream and Jack's instantaneous reaction had severed.

Even as she told herself it all could have—should have—ended so differently, the ugly truth coiled deep in her soul. A truth she hated herself for. Between Jack and Philip, she would never wish Balaur had taken Jack in Philip's place.

Her emotions, which she fought to keep on the cool path of logic and reason, gave way to the sinister weavings, spooling out of her grasp, leaving her to scramble as they surfaced with anger and blame. Before she could stop them, the words spilled out.

"Why did you not stay with him?"

Jack's ruddy eyebrows slanted down as her accusation sliced between them like a knife. "Because you screamed. Nothing else mattered."

Insecurities from old wounds festered to the surface and boiled out. "Did you not think I could manage?" She couldn't stop the hurt her words inflicted, like poison being lanced from a wound. If she had reacted quicker, if she had not screamed, Philip would be here with them now.

"I didn't stop to think beyond getting to you."

"I have been dangled over the sides of buildings, thrown into a river with a twenty-pound pack strapped to my back, and dropped off in rural Virginia in the dead of night without a compass. Pulling myself from an icy ledge was nothing in comparison."

"And yet you screamed." Flames danced orange shadows across the tips of his shoes. As if he stood in the fire itself. "Is that what this sudden anger is about? You think I doubt your capabilities as an agent? What in our history together has ever given you pause to doubt my confidence in you?"

Her pain exorcised, shame flooded the gaping hole throbbing inside her. "Perhaps the times I proved too weak to defend against attackers."

"Weaker, yes. Weak, no, and that is all the difference because your strengths must be applied differently than mine. I don't have this"—he tapped the side of her head—"but you do. In spades, and it's what I find most alluring about you." He dropped his hand to cup her chin.

"Never once have I thought you incapable. In that moment I was forced to choose between saving my wife and saving my best friend, but I was damned either way. I will never apologize for going to you, but I will forever live with the regret of abandoning him. If I had stayed, Balaur never would have captured him."

"Or both of you might have been captured. Or Beatrix might have fallen in and drowned saving me. We cannot know what might've happened because a hundred different things could have gone wrong. And did. The past is unchangeable no matter how much we wish it otherwise. All we can do is go on searching." The heat of emotions cooled as rationale ebbed back into place. "And not snap at each other when the guilt begins to gnaw. I'm sorry."

A sad smile ticked the corner of Jack's mouth. "Just my luck. Adding 'terrible husband' to my growing roster of disappointments."

"You could never be a terrible husband, not to me."

He picked at the hoof of a ceramic lamb decorating the mantel. Its once glossy white coat was crackled beige from years of presiding over a roaring flame. "I never thought I deserved you. Your clever mind and kind heart. All I have to offer is how to break a nose in a single punch or shoot a moving target."

"Admirable traits in our profession."

An unamused noise rumbled in his throat. "What about outside our profession? A home with a roof, and a front door that squeaks differently from the back, yet it's somehow comforting because it's the sound of *our* front door." His finger hovered over the lamb's pink ear as he stared into the fire. "A family."

A longing near the surface, but tucked safely away, tugged inside her. In the calm moments when the world slowed its spin around the two of them, they would share such whisperings of their hearts and drift into dreams of possibilities.

"I love our life together in whatever form it takes. Hopefully someday it will encompass all of those wonderful things, but for now I'm content to travel this path as long as I am beside you."

"Some days I feel as if I've lost my way. As if I'm far away somewhere and the path has crumbled to dust. I am no longer myself and everything real—you—has been parted from me."

Grasping his shoulders, Ivy pulled him around to face her, offering his loneliness no quarter. "How can we be apart when we exist beneath the same sky and moon and stars? We will see the same shapes, the same lights, and it will be as if we're standing next to each other. The stars will always lead us home to each other."

"Even if that home is currently a rented room in a war-torn country that isn't allowed to determine its own allegiance?" The shadows lifted from his eyes and he brushed the backs of his fingertips over her cheek.

"There, or a train car speeding through frozen Siberia, or a fancy pile of bricks hiding a weapons cache below its floors. Home is not a place to me. It's here." She rested her hand over his heart. "Wherever this is, there I am also."

He wrapped his arms around her and rocked her in a slow sway as he had a hundred times before and every night in her dreams. A movement their bodies knew by instinct as all the sharp edges of the day were smoothed into a blurred union of togetherness.

It lasted for a minute, no more. As Ivy pulled back, her burdens stretched not so taut as before and her strength was restored.

"My buttons, if you please, or we'll be late for supper." She turned and presented the gaping back of her dress to him. "I wonder if Saltzmann will go through the effort of trying to impress us by cooking borscht."

Jack's fingers worked deftly—thanks in part to all the tiny bullets he was accustomed to loading—up the row of pearl buttons as he sealed her into the velvet. The heavy fabric molded to her limbs like a warm kiss, every inch of her skin aware of its fitted touch as if it had become a part of her.

She traced a finger along the silver thread swirling over her hip. Silk was preferable to the bare skin and certainly in summer as it floated about like butterfly wings. Velvet, with its languid regality, was made for the powers of a woman.

Jack unbuttoned his shirt and dropped it carelessly on the bed next to her dressing gown before reaching for his formal shirt that had been starched to within an inch of standing upright on its own.

She looked at her husband, and the chills of December thawed to warm delight pooling in her stomach. Jack slipped his arms into the crisp sleeves, then reached behind his head to adjust the collar that had flipped up, his stance offering a fine view of his muscled chest and the masculine swath of dark hair that tapered down his flat stomach.

"You're staring."

Ivy dragged her gaze from the impressive view that never failed to please and met his eye. "So what if I am? A wife has a right to admire her husband."

She seriously considered doing more than admire but remembered the fifty pearl buttons on her dress and how long it would take to unhook them.

The clock on the mantel chimed the bottom of the six o'clock hour. Supper was to be served at seven o'clock sharp. Arriving fashionably late was one thing, expected even among the upper echelons of society, but arriving tardy with buttons missing from her gown and an all-too-pleased husband was quite another.

She sighed with resignation. "You may finish dressing."

With a wicked grin, he flexed and the fabric of his sleeves strained against the hulk of his biceps. In that smile she saw her Jack again, the carefree man who flirted audaciously with her and knew precisely how to exploit all of her weaknesses.

For that unhurried tick in time, all was right in the world.

"Shameless." She laughed.

"I wasn't the one staring with my jaw sweeping the floor." He smoothed his collar, then began buttoning his shirt from the bottom up.

She stepped closer and brushed his fingers aside, then took up the buttoning task. "*This* time. I've caught you ogling me on many an occasion, Mr. Vale." Pausing before the edges of the shirt pulled together, she traced a finger over the black interlinking circles branded on his chest.

"Only because my wife is worthy of admiration on *all* occasions, Mrs. Vale." His skin rippled with gooseflesh as her finger slid over the tattoo.

Since they were unable to wear their wedding bands while on a mission lest their connection be used against them, they'd had their grenade-pin rings locked together and strung on a necklace for Ivy, while Jack had their likeness inked over his heart at a port in Athens three months ago. Ivy placed a palm to her bodice where the rings rested peacefully beneath the velvet. She never took them off.

A deep breath hitched in Jack's chest. "You keep doing that and we'll be forced to send our regrets for spending the night in."

She toyed with a button. "Not the whole night, as we don't want to be rude to our host, but perhaps we could be fashionably late."

His mouth caught her grin, and he quickly proved that buttons and velvet served as poor impediments to an obliging husband.

Precisely twenty-two minutes later they were properly festooned in furs, borrowed jewels, and a silk cravat and slowly made their way down the lonely tower's steps.

"Bit of political genius inviting the refugee Russian nobility here, whom mere weeks ago they were shooting at in the trenches," Jack said as he moved down the twisting staircase ahead of her. It was narrow and built to keep invaders from advancing upward with their armor and weapons.

Ivy smoothed the heavy skirt over her legs as the cold whisked through the tower's arrow slits and circled her ankles. "Now that the tsar's supporters are being hunted and killed in their own country, the Central Powers want to scoop up them and their wealth before the Reds do."

"Bully for the Austro-Hungarians. Machiavelli would be proud." Jack ducked beneath a smoking torch sconce that looked to have been nailed to the wall centuries before if the thick layers of soot were anything to go by. "Did you bring the chirper?"

"I wish you would stop calling it that. My gun does not chirp. And yes, of course I brought it. This isn't my first scouting expedition." Ivy patted her evening bag, which perfectly matched her gown. Along with the pistol she had a knife secured in her garter, one tucked in the special pocket on the front of her corset, and her pearl hairpin sharpened to a point. A light evening for weapons as they searched about the castle for signs of Balaur.

"We should skip past the scouting and go straight to the source that can give us the information we need. If I have to spend much longer with that sycophant Saltzmann—"

"No assassinations tonight. He's the best lead we have to finding Balaur, and if you put a gun in his face we won't have any answers."

"It would be fitting. Blood spilled tonight at Dracula's castle."

Ivy paused on a landing before the corkscrew staircase continued down another level. A narrow arched window had been carved out of the stone wall and offered a view of the snow falling across the fortress's thick walls. "I can't stop thinking about that tea."

"It was the cloves that threw it off."

"No, not the actual tea. The inscriptions on the plates were written in Dacian, the same language Balaur uses for his motto, 'The next step is not enough.' It can't be a coincidence that he and this place are linked somehow."

"Perhaps his people came from this area long ago and he revived their language to make himself appear more mystical. It would certainly add to the blood-soaked myths of this place."

Freezing air gusted through the window and straight through Ivy's layered garments. Jack tucked her close and she tried to focus on the castle's orange conical turrets instead of his distracting warmth.

"Did you know it's only a rumor that Bram Stoker used Bran Castle as the inspiration for his vampire's home?"

"Rumor or not, this place seems to attract bloodsuckers. I have no doubt Saltzmann would latch onto a neck or two if he thought it might draw him riches."

"Please stop. That is hardly the image I wish to entertain over soup."

Jack brushed his fingers over her fur collar. "Then be sure to keep this close or you never know what might happen." He ducked and nipped her neck.

She squealed and shoved him. "Beast."

Sadly, supper was not served on Dacian dinnerware for further investigation. However, the guests were stuffed with gossip about the upcoming treaty signing and lamentations of wealth lost. Saltzmann barely contained his disappointment at not getting those lost riches into his pockets first.

Not a single bullet or blade was required throughout the duration of the meal nor coffee afterward, despite Jack fiddling with his knife under the table. By the end of the evening, Ivy was delighted to report that everyone's neck remained bite free, including her own.

Much to her husband's disappointment.

TWENTY-SIX

THE FOLLOWING MORNING DAWNED DULL AS DIRTY DISHWATER. AFTER A breakfast of tasteless yellow maize flour thickened into a porridge called *mamaliga*, Jack met with Saltzmann to discuss the security of their supposed smuggled gems and to inquire about weapons for the retaking of their homeland. Ivy went snooping.

She carried a book to make it appear as if she were searching for a quiet place to read while discouraging others who hoped for a potential chat. She searched the highest towers, roamed the crumbling catwalks, and clambered down into the cellars.

All she managed to uncover was a nest of mice, dozens of cobwebs, and what looked like a once extensive wine collection now full of empty, broken bottles. Not a single clue to unearth Balaur—or the Russian jewels Saltzmann was reportedly keeping safe. The rat must have stuffed them under his mattress to paw over at night.

"Baroness, what brings you down here?"

Ivy jerked from the cell she was peering into and banged her arm on the metal door. Her book went flying and sprawled on the earth-packed ground. Speak of the rat and he appeared. Saltzmann stood behind her frowning. Rubbing her throbbing elbow, Ivy smiled sheepishly.

"Forgive me. I did not mean to intrude."

"It is no intrusion, but I wonder why a dignified lady would bring herself to the dungeons."

"Dungeons? Oh dear."

Saltzmann held up a hand as if to alleviate her distress. "Do not fear. These old cells may have once caged criminals, but they are used merely for storage now. I came down to retrieve the eighteenth-century painting Prince Olav expressed interest in last evening over supper."

Prince Olav. Ah, yes. The portly, whiskered man who complained about everything while boasting of his prowess in slipping past the Red Army.

Opening one of the cell doors, Saltzmann selected a painting wrapped in oilcloth before frowning at her once more. "Can I be of service to you somehow? Escort you back upstairs perhaps?"

"Yes, I think you'd better." She retrieved her book and dusted the dirt from its cover. *The Castle of Otranto.* "Isabella's frantic attempt to navigate the castle's labyrinth inspired me to explore. I was carried away by the fantasy and became lost among the twisting passages."

Smiling benevolently at the presumed witless female, Saltzmann magnanimously offered his arm and brought her back up to ground level. "Tea?"

"No, thank you." Tamping down her irritation at his bothersome presence, she lurched for an excuse to be rid of him to continue her mission. "I'll take the air."

"I shall join you as I've been rather cooped up this morning." He handed the painting to a servant, along with Ivy's book, for which he didn't bother asking permission before snatching it away. He then motioned for their outerwear to be brought.

"I thought you were meeting with my husband this morning?" Ivy slid her arms into the warm coat held out by another servant, then tugged on her gloves.

"We finished our business some time ago. He and Count

Borgasi are now situated in the library discussing the count's business in iron manufacturing—an enterprise that was stolen by the Red Army for their own nefarious warmongering, I'm afraid to say. The count is hoping to build a new facility for weapons manufacturing nearby."

So Jack had found a new angle for their search. Hopefully he would have better luck than she'd had.

Outside, the asymmetrical courtyard was smaller than she'd expected and rather claustrophobic with its towering limestone walls, cracked by age and crowned by orange slate-roofed catwalks, all supported by rotting timber beams. A few gnarled trees stood in scattered corners scratching their way toward the weak sunlight, while uneven flagstones jumped up to catch the feet of unsuspecting walkers. It was charming in its dilapidated manner.

Saltzmann turned up his coat collar as they ambled around a pool of green mold dripping from a broken roof tile. "Forgive the derelict appearance. As I said, the structure has been abandoned for some years and renovations have not extended this far. I would have offered the gardens, but Bran Castle does not boast in the way of fine flowers and lush grasses. It's more of a steep, rocky drop-off meant to deter invading hordes."

"This castle must have seen its fair share of war." Ivy snuggled deep into her rabbit fur scarf and wished she had a matching *ushanka*, but the more fashionable gray-felt toque with its contrasting purple feather would have to suffice.

"Built in the fourteenth century, it has withstood the Mongols, Turks, Wallachians, and Romanians. She's defiant in her survival. Come, look at this." He led her to a raised part of the courtyard tucked against the northwestern walls to a well that looked as if it had been hewn from one solid white rock. Filigrees, feathers, and other designs of regality were carved around it while a wrought iron arch swooped over the top, lacking its chain and bucket. "A wishing well. The builders were required to dig through sixty feet of solid rock before they reached the water source at the base of the cliff."

Ivy leaned over the lip and gazed down into the yawning black. She repressed the overwhelming urge to call out hello for its wallowing echo.

"Just above the water level they built a secret room of refuge as a last resort should the castle be overrun. All the treasures of the castle could be ferreted away there for safekeeping." He leaned closer as if imparting a secret not to be overheard by the protection detail discreetly patrolling the catwalks. "It's empty now that the castle has sat abandoned, but we'd like to revive its usefulness, a nod to the past, if you will, to wish away possible invading hordes."

"What nod is this?"

"All who pass by must surrender an object of value to its depths."

Why, you brazen tomato. Coming right out and asking for it.

Surely he wouldn't ask her to toss in a coin. A lady never carried such a vulgarity as money, much less a baroness. "Alas, I was forced to trade my loose gems for train passage out of Kyiv."

The eagerness slipped from his face. Clearly the invading hordes of modern day were kept at bay by pocketing the discards of foolish visitors. Well, she'd come this far. She might as well play along. Removing the jeweled bird holding her hat feather in place, she gave it a playful kiss and tossed it down the well. A moment or two later it hit what sounded like a bed of coins.

"There. We are safe from invaders."

The man grinned with anticipation. How long would that grin last when he discovered the jewels were paste and not worth a lump of coal?

Prying his attention from the treasure below, her guide swept his gaze around the courtyard, then turned back to Ivy. "It surprises me that you have not asked about the castle's most notorious claim to the echelons of fame."

Ivy stepped away from the well before he had the chance to eye the pearls dangling from her ears and studied a half-moon window cut at the bottom of a wall and crossed by rusted iron bars. A lookout from the dungeon, perhaps?

"If it involves a certain Irish author and his fanged creation, then I'm afraid I'll have to disappoint you. I'm quite aware that any connection between this castle and the fabled blood-draining count has been spun from glorified myth by those wishing to bring their Gothic horrors to life. Or would it be to death, as vampires are by definition dead? Either way, it's an avenue of indulgence led by the mystics and tourists hoping for a proper scare."

"Here I thought Russians enjoyed a good story."

"Stories of romance and tragedy, yes. Claptrap, certainly not."

"*Dracula* is not entirely claptrap. It's said to be inspired by Vlad the Impaler, or Vlad Dracul. His horrors of blood and tyranny still stain the history of the Wallachia region, over which his family reigned for a number of years before they, too, were killed. It's said he was imprisoned in Bran Castle for a time."

Saltzmann shrugged as if the local lore held not a candle to a pistachio and marzipan Mozartkugel awaiting him in Vienna. "The storytellers seemed to love this whiff of interest and Bran Castle has been Dracul's castle ever since, but it was never his true home. For that you'll need to look farther afield to Poenari Castle." He pointed west, or what would be west beyond the towering walls. "About eighty kilometers from here, as the bat flies."

Ivy managed to cover a snort. The poor man had been stationed here for far too long.

She'd read every book in Washington's library, even his private collections, not to mention the monthly trips to the Library of Congress, but not one margin note of where Vlad had shucked off his boots after a long day of impaling the locals.

"If Poenari was the Impaler's true home, why do the stories not proclaim it of interest rather than Bran?"

Saltzmann doled out an indulgent smile most often bestowed upon women who asked silly questions. "Because Bran is intact, mostly, while Poenari is little more than a ruin of the original dragon's lair. Hardly a place for the nobleman Count Dracula to call home."

Ivy stopped short. "Dragon's lair, you said?"

"Certainly. Vlad Dracul, also known as Vlad the Dragon, referred to his monstrous fortress as a lair. In fact, local legend claims that you can still read an inscription he hand-carved into the cornerstone himself, in Dacian no less."

Dragon's lair, home of Vlad the Dragon.

Balaur. A Romanian dragon.

Why had it taken her so long to put two and two together?

She grabbed Saltzmann's arm. "What does the inscription say?"

"I beg your pardon, baroness." Eyes widening in shock, he tried to wriggle from her grip, but she held tight.

"What. Does. It. Say."

"Something about the next step." He yanked his arm free and smoothed the wrinkle from his sleeve. "But do not take the inscription at face value. Most of the locals are illiterate, and no one alive can read that dead language any longer—baroness! Wait! Lady Turgenev!"

Ivy didn't stop as she raced across the courtyard and into the castle in search of Jack. They had a dragon's lair to hunt.

TWENTY-SEVEN

POENARI CASTLE, WALLACHIA
DECEMBER 1917

"THERE MUST BE AN EASIER WAY TO TRAVERSE THIS TERRAIN." IVY DUCKED under a tree branch sagging with snow. Puffs of lingering flakes drifted from the afternoon's dull sky and coated the mountain's steep incline, bristling with pine, ash, and oak trees stripped of their foliage.

Poenari Castle towered high above on a rocky precipice like an aged, stubborn king on his throne of decaying stone. As long as one stone remained, he would not relinquish his precarious seat.

"Now's the time, if you have a better idea," Jack said.

"If I had, I would have offered it long before we started this neck-breaking climb. Have I mentioned how much I detest hiking? Walking, strolling, even a jog should the occasion call for it is preferable to this uphill torment."

Jack hopped over a rock like a proper mountain goat. The annoyingly perfect foil to her logical argument. "Are you still grumbling? This is what happens when you only get two hours of sleep in three days."

"At least I'm attempting to sleep, unlike you. If you pass out from exhaustion, I am not carrying you or your rifle."

He shrugged as if lugging Reaper was the least of his concerns. A new vigor had stolen over her husband three days ago when she'd burst into their chamber at Bran Castle and announced Poenari Castle as their next target. It had to be where Balaur was hiding.

Jack's eyes had burned bright and before she could so much as show him a map, he was tossing knives and bullets into a pack. They would have left that very day had a snowstorm not buried them in the castle. Once they managed to dig themselves out, their remaining funds went toward procuring train tickets to Curtea de Argeş and then hiring a farmer's cart to take them to Arefu. The rest of the way they had trudged on foot.

"Tell me again about this connection with Dracul and Balaur's dragon," Jack said.

"*Dracul* is the old Romanian word for dragon and became the sobriquet of Vlad Dracul, which he then passed on to his son Vlad III, more commonly referred to as Vlad the Impaler. It is the son's former residence that we plan to infiltrate once we reach the top of this mountain."

"I thought you said *balaur* meant dragon in Romanian. Now you tell me it's *dracul*."

"Without confusing you more with etymology and the shifting language that we now know as Romanian, suffice it to say that *dracul* translates to dragon while a *balaur* is a specific type of dragon in Romanian folklore. Balaur Tsar uses the likeness on his guards' uniforms."

"The dragon circling the crown."

"Yes. The connection I've drawn is that the motto he uses, 'The next step is not enough,' contains the same words our dear friend Vlad inscribed into this fortress over five centuries ago. Both are in the Dacian language." She paused and stared up at the foreboding edifice towering high above them. "Unless I've wrongly connected things simply because I want them to fit."

Jack flashed her a smile. "Your brain would never allow such a travesty. It may work in mysterious and confounding ways, but I'm not about to start questioning it now. With any luck, the bastard will be waiting for us at the top. I'll fire off a round or two straight into his skull. Then we'll find Philip and be on our way home by Christmas Eve."

"And what if this is another wild-goose chase and he's not here?"

"Then we keep searching. This is the closest we've come to finding an actual clue connecting a place to where that madman is probably holed up conducting experiments. We will not fail. *I* will not fail again." He cocked his ear to a far-off sound. "Do you hear that?" Jack moved around a scrub of brush.

Ivy followed and they stood on a rocky overhang. Jack pointed to the moving strip of water far in the valley below. "Ice chunks floating in it."

Ivy peered over his shoulder. "Watch your step. That's a long way down. If you managed to survive the fall, the water would kill you."

"I've been in icy water before."

"You go in that river and you're not coming out. Be sure of that." Ivy kept walking. "No one is going swimming today."

"I wouldn't mind swimming with you. Somewhere with blue water and warm sand." Matching her short stride, her husband leaned close and lowered his voice. "Maybe you could wear one of those new bathing costumes that are causing such a stir. Although if I'm allowed a preference, I'd prefer you out of one."

Ivy bumped his shoulder for censure as much as to control the delightful images her own mind conjured.

"Keep your mind on the mission. We'll talk bathing costumes later. Or lack thereof." Then she yanked him to a stop, grasped his face, and pressed a deep kiss to his lips. Censure was highly overrated. She released him and kept walking.

"That is not helping me keep my mind on the mission." His voice floated behind her.

"Consider it last-minute bravado."

"I'll be considering something all right."

She glanced back long enough to catch the smirk on his handsome face, then quickly turned ahead to the task at hand of not tripping over roots on this hunt for a murdering devil.

An hour later, her toes frozen in her boots and the tip of her nose glowing red, she felt the warm beach sands calling to her like a siren's song, but she pushed away the thought as they reached the top of the mountain. Snow fell lightly, coating the ground and dusting the tops of evergreens that clung to their richly scented needles.

Poenari stood cold against the gray sky, its weathered stones decaying like rotten teeth on an ancient skull, stained with mold and rust that too closely resembled dried blood.

"There's no one here," Ivy said as they crouched within a screen of trees some yards away.

Jack shifted restlessly beside her, a giveaway that his mind was ticking through every eventuality and countering it with attack. "There's someone here all right. It's too quiet. Stay here. I'm going to do a perimeter check." Hunched over, he took off through the trees.

Ivy kept watch, scanning the area and fortress for signs of movement, but all remained serene. It set her nerves on edge.

Soon enough the bushes rustled and Jack silently appeared next to her. "On the south side there's a faint whiff of charred wood from a fire that was recently put out."

Her eyes shot to the southern walls looking for signs of smoke. "Guards?"

"Most likely." He checked his rifle chamber. "On the western corner there's a small grate at the bottom of the wall. A drainage hole.

It's clogged with sludge, but just wide enough for a man's shoulders. We'll go in through there."

Lovely.

When they reached the spot, Jack kicked off the rusted grate and set it aside, then scooped great globs of muck out of the way. Ivy tried not to think about what she was crawling over and in as she slithered through the hole after him. With just enough room to stand, they entered a low stone corridor lit by smoky torches and festering with the stench of putrid water and human foulness. Vlad had probably crowed in fiendish delight to store his victims in such a place.

Ivy drew her pistol and slipped quietly behind Jack as they made their way down the passage to a squat closed door set at the far end. Yellow light flickered beneath it, and she heard the faint sound of boots ascending steps.

Ivy and Jack rushed forward and braced themselves on either side of the doorway as the footsteps drew closer. At last the door opened and a man appeared. He took two steps past the door before Jack slipped behind him and drew a knife across his throat.

The guard crumpled without a sound. He wore all black with Balaur's insignia on his shirt. Jack sheathed his knife, favoring his pistol Undertaker over the rifle in the narrow space, and motioned Ivy to follow him through the low door and down a winding set of stone steps, many of which were broken or missing from centuries of neglect—*or* to make unwanted visitors trip. The latter, Ivy concluded, after one gave way beneath her foot.

The stench was eye-watering at the base of the stairs where another corridor stretched out slick with mold and rough with sharp points, as it had been hewn straight from the mountain rock. Wisps of black smoke choked the air from a single torch wedged into a crack on the right wall. On the opposite wall, small chambers had been carved out. Batches of molded hay and rusted chains were scattered on the cell floors like dead carcasses.

"My God." Bile rose in Ivy's throat as she caught sight of the black splotches on the walls. Blood.

Jack flicked a concerned look over his shoulder at her. She shook her head and motioned for him to keep going. The deafening quiet was punctuated by dripping water and scurrying rodent feet. Where were the rest of the guards? If Philip wasn't being held captive down here, where was he? She gripped her pistol tighter and tried to keep her worst fears at bay.

The end of the dark, deserted corridor took a hidden bend and opened into a chamber slightly larger than the others. Dozens of candles lined the walls, dripping wax to molten pools on the floor and throwing orange shadows against the sharp stones.

A low table sagged in the far corner, lined with dull instruments of all shapes and sizes resembling crude instruments from a medical bag. A row of syringes varying in size and clear bottles filled with a thick white fluid rested on a tray on the edge of the table, which was within easy reach of the reclined crude wooden chaise propped in the center of the room where Philip lay strapped down.

His head lolled from side to side as he mumbled incoherently.

"Philip!" Ivy rushed forward.

"Stop!" Jack cried as a hulking shadow unfolded itself from a dark corner and crept to the chair.

Ivy jerked to a halt as the monster materialized.

★★★

"At last you are here. My loyal spies informed me you followed the breadcrumbs scattered across Europe. I knew it would not be long before your cleverness led you to me."

Balaur sidled up to Philip and pressed his cheek to Philip's with a malicious grin, blocking any kill shot. If Jack wanted to shoot, the bullet would have to pass through Philip first. "You have come to see my work."

Jack calmly raised his pistol. "I've come to blow your head off."

Balaur pressed his fingers against the space above Philip's ears. Philip screamed.

"Do you want me to stop the pain?" Balaur crooned.

Philip whimpered and nodded as his arms and legs strained against the leather straps binding him.

"A wonder, is it not? To see the human form bend and obey a will stronger than its own. We have awaited this moment for a long time." Releasing the pressure on Philip's skull, Balaur raked long, stained fingernails through Philip's matted hair.

"I don't care what you've been waiting for. It's past time I put a bullet in your other eye and rid the world of your evil." Jack took aim. "Step away from my friend."

"The world is crying. The world bleeds itself dry in the mud of war. The world battles for power among the undeserving. The world is infested with avarice. Who shall live and who shall die? Governments, politicians, and kings spill their tripe, planning more battles while each hour passes in senseless slaughter."

"Here I thought a ruthless arms dealer such as yourself would bask in men killing one another," Ivy said, her eyes locked on Philip.

"Is that what you think I have been doing?" Balaur hissed. "This war is a petty scrambling for scraps of land by power-hungry old men. I seek to set this earth free from its own destruction. To achieve this purpose, the unworthy must die, *da*, but balance will be restored for rectitude."

Jack kept his sight locked on Balaur. The man was as slippery as an eel and Jack would not miss his shot this time. "Planning to achieve world domination all on your lonesome? Last time I counted, most of your men we killed at Dobryzov and Sparrow's Nest and Baikal. If I had to guess, you're operating on nothing more than a skeleton crew. Doesn't seem the odds are in your favor."

"How limited your views are. I am but one small tick in the winding of time set to strike in a new era after centuries spent gathering strength from the shadows. A new era of chosen ones is upon us, but first the earth must be purged of filth. For generations the atrocities have gone unchecked as mankind is allowed to pillage the earth for his own greed and sin, never believing he is accountable for his selfish deeds. This war has set the wheels in motion as it rids the world of the existence of unbelievers while pushing us, the steadfast, toward the appointed hour."

"You, sir, are a hypocrite if ever there was one. Denouncing the very actions you stand guilty of while using the war as a smokescreen for your own purposes."

"The Order of the Rising Moon has used many world unfortunates such as war and assassinations to gather our strength until the opportune moment strikes for us to seize power once more."

"The Order of the Rising Moon . . . The black flag we saw at Swallow's Nest with a silver moon rising above a golden star. The map of Romania." Ivy's voice shook as she recounted the pieces to the puzzle. "'The next step is not enough.' Is that what your Order believes?"

"How dare you speak our sacred words. They are meant only for the chosen few." Balaur's eye widened, the white bright as marble. "Foolish *devushka*. You will regret speaking of what you do not know."

She stared back, not cowed by his unblinking malice or insults. "I have a talent for compiling dusty, and quite frankly useless, information. Including dead languages with occult undertones."

The corners of his flat mouth knifed back as spit leaked with each jabbed word. "Occult. A dirty word for spiritual enlightenment. Caretakers of the honorable cause."

Jack moved forward, gun leveled straight at Balaur's remaining eye. "Outcasts with too much time on their hands is more like it."

"We are a force to bring about the world's reckoning in blood and ash." Balaur bared his teeth in primal rage next to Philip's neck, draining spittle down his captive's throat.

"Is this the part in the narrative where you twirl your mustache and tell us all about your dastardly plan for world annihilation?" Ivy took a step toward Philip. "Speak plain. I tire of philosophical riddles. What is the Order of the Rising Moon?"

He considered her for a long, murderous moment. His eye bored into her with deadliness. "An ancient order begun centuries ago when the world was in chaos, leaders scratching over lands for power, warring to instill peace, and corruption gouging the hearts of all. For all the advancements we have made as a civilization in the name of art, medicine, music, literature, architecture, and transportation, humans have been unable and unwilling to cut the venality from their souls. It has become a disease that sickens the world, crippling it to weakness. Except for the few who would stand against it. Those who would vow to cleanse the earth of its sickness to restore order and begin again without borders or nationalities to confine us."

"That's why you play both sides of the diplomatic fence." Jack sidestepped to circle around the chair and gain a clean line of sight without Philip being in the line of fire. "Selling weapons to your enemies so they might destroy one another and leave you to sweep into power in the aftermath. The White Wolf and these drugged assassins you've been testing, that's what it's all about."

"For the sake of formality, I prefer you use the term 'Risers.' The term 'assassins' conjures evil intent when their work is a gift to mankind."

"Risers, as in Rising Moon," Ivy drawled. "I can't decide if that is clever or indolent. My speculation is indolence as you plan to use these so-called Risers to do your dirty work so you and your little band of followers can rule. Genocide in the name of cleansing. Is that the gist of things?"

"How clever you are, *devushka*. Simple is best, I always find. As did Dracul when he began our order in 1461 by massacring an entire village and leaving only two witnesses, the initial members of Rising Moon. Since that day our ranks have swelled into thousands bound by the vow to finish what Dracul began when he spared the two found worthy of his vision."

"That's why you're here," Ivy said, astonishment tinging her words as if a fog had been lifted from a maddening question. "Not selling weapons to displaced Russian aristocrats but because of an allegiance to a dead man more bloodthirsty than you. From Dracul's castle to the dragon-and-crown emblem—even the name *Balaur* gives homage to the Order's founder. I couldn't begin to understand why you decided to sell weapons in this sleepy land, but I see now. Because this was Dracul's home—or Dracula, or Vlad the Impaler, or however your coven refers to him."

Jack snorted. "I doubt these troublemakers deal in specifics when their leader is a dead sadist who used to impale the locals for sport."

"Vlad Dracul was a ruthless genius, but never could he have imagined what I have created here." Balaur's eye traced the length of Philip's restrained body before glancing over to the syringes.

"My mind is made for weaponry, and all that I create is for the benefit of the Order. Always seeking better methods to inflict death while my brothers and sisters have their talents to serve our cause. Infiltrating seats of power, leading armies into suicidal skirmishes, ensuring the infirmed never awaken from their hospital sickbeds, even scrubbing the stairs at your hotel. We are nowhere and everywhere, forever moving one step closer, and you cannot stop us."

"For a man about to die, you certainly have a highly unwarranted opinion of yourself," Ivy said.

Balaur's stare didn't leave Jack. "Upon occasion I do not mind allowing a woman to speak her mind, but only when she has a thought significant enough to contribute. Keep your woman silent, or I will."

Jack grimaced. "Ah, see here, we have a problem. I don't take well to threats. In particular threats to her, so I'll give you one chance to apologize before I put a bullet through your other eye. The lovely lady will follow up by shooting off your ugly lips for the insult, and last but certainly not least, Philip here can take the kill shot. He's more than earned it. A group effort, as it were. A notion your communist comrades can appreciate."

"Your speech is much inflated for a man who does not stand a chance of winning this fight."

"What can I say? I like an underdog." Jack moved forward, his trusty Undertaker unwavering in his hand.

Balaur's lips peeled back to reveal rows of gray teeth. "You must watch for the back teeth belonging to the dog who is under. They bite while you are busy watching the fangs."

Two guards ran into the chamber with guns raised. Ivy whipped around and shot, hitting one of them in the shoulder. She fired again and hit him dead center.

Jack downed the other one with a single, unwavering shot to the head before swinging back to confront their target.

"Where's Balaur?" Jack's gut twisted. The man had disappeared.

Ivy rushed to Philip and sliced through his bonds before helping him sit up.

"Philip? It's me. It's Ivy and Jack. We've come to take you out of here."

Philip moaned and covered his head with his hands. His knuckles were scabbed and bruised, as was most of his body, visible through his tattered clothes. Black circles smudged under his eyes and his bones jutted through his sallow skin. He pushed away from her and staggered to his feet, then stumbled to the table and grabbed at the liquid-filled bags.

"The pain. Stop the pain!"

"Calm down." Jack rushed to Philip's side and seized his hand before it swept over the syringes. "You're going to hurt yourself."

"Don't tell me to calm down!" Philip knocked him back. An unrecognizable light burned in his eyes, shuttering out the easygoing friend who had stood at his side for so long and ushering in a stranger. "Where is he? He promised to stop the pain." With the shout of a wounded mad bull, Philip charged into the dark corner and disappeared through a hidden door.

"That fool. He's going to get us all killed." Jack cursed and took off after him with Ivy close on his heels.

They sprinted up a twisting tunnel that at last broke free into the open air outside the fortress walls that rose up behind them like an impenetrable shield. Before them was a scraggly line of pine trees standing as sentinels leading to a precipice with a sharp drop-off that plunged far below to icy torrents.

Half a dozen rifle bolts slid into firing position. Balaur's only remaining men. They surrounded Jack, Philip, and Ivy. Balaur stood among his guards, his ratty robes cloaking him like a king who had crawled through the bowels of his exterminated kingdom.

"Surely you did not think escape would be that easy." A breeze crusted with ice whipped from the lead sky, clawing the decayed squirrels of Balaur's robes into a hideous dance with black nails and eyes clacking together. The man's singular pale eye was nearly colorless against the leached winter landscape. Cruel and cold, it calculated every muscle twitch, every ragged intake of breath, every second before he gave command to open fire.

"You will never leave this mountaintop again of your own free will. Take them back inside."

Never one for subtlety when direct action would suffice, Jack leveled his pistol directly at Balaur's remaining eye. "No need. We already got you out here and the inside is nothing more than a sludge hole, so you'll excuse me if I decline your offer."

"How tedious you make this." Balaur's eye flicked to Ivy. "Take the woman. She's of no use."

Jack saw him too late. A beast of a man shot from the tunnel and snaked his arms around Ivy, jerking her off her feet. She screamed.

Jack lunged. Two guards blocked his path. He fired, killing them on the spot.

Two more rushed to stop him. He put a bullet in one and a knife in the gut of the other.

The beast had Ivy by the throat. She kicked and clawed, but her struggles grew faint. Her head lolled to the side like that of a rag doll.

Jack raised his pistol to the man's head and squeezed the trigger. A remaining guard slammed into him and the shot went wide.

The beast tossed Ivy to the ground where she lay motionless on her stomach.

"Iv—" Jack's shout was cut short by a rifle butt to the belly. He doubled over in pain and was dragged backward to kneel beside Philip on the icy ground. After kicking his and Ivy's guns out of reach, the two remaining guards aimed their rifles at the back of Jack's and Philip's heads.

The beast, sheathed in solid black, braced an enormous leg on either side of Ivy and toed her cheek with his filthy boot.

Rage consumed Jack. "Get away from her!"

The monster ignored him and continued to prod Ivy's cheek. She moaned and twisted her head away. Blinking rapidly at first, her eyes opened and scanned the ground until landing on Jack.

The panic dissipated from her face as she offered him a fragile smile. He sagged in relief. Their current positions were less than desirable, but they were still alive and that was enough to change the status quo when the opportune moment came.

"Magnificent, isn't he?" Awe oiled Balaur's voice as he stared unblinking at the hulk of a beast looming over Ivy. He raked a dirty hand through his beard, wrapping the scraggly bits around his thumb until they knotted at the ends.

"A paragon of strength, brutal and cruel without the fetters of conscience to weigh him under suffocating morals. My Riser is the perfect controlled specimen. He obeys every order without question. Carnage is his hunt and death his shadow. He was created for it—his mind warped with the single thought—and trained never to stop until the task is complete."

Despite kneeling before his enemy without a weapon, Jack assumed a portrait of calm, going so far as to tip his head to the side in boredom. Anger and defiance would keep Balaur on alert, but calm was likely to fluster him. And flustered men made mistakes.

"Seems we did you a favor by blowing up White Wolf. This specimen"—Jack nodded to the man-beast—"is bound to be easier to use than lugging that enormous metal contraption around."

Balaur yanked free a knot of hair. He rolled it between his fingers, the flaxen strands packing into a tight ball before he flicked it to the ground and smashed it beneath his toe.

"My beloved White Wolf matters not. I have created a new weapon. My Risers. Assassins capable of more destruction than a single White Wolf or army of soldiers. Those are for show and able to leave survivors, but a Riser is a spear tip. His kills are precise. The enemy will never see him coming as he slips among the world of shadows and ushers in a new order. The Order of the Rising Moon."

"A shadow assassin?" Jack scoffed. "Looks more like a lumbering ox to me."

Balaur kicked his boot into Jack's face. Bones crunched. Jack toppled backward, blood spraying from his nose to the crust of ice.

"No!" Ivy's scream was rewarded with a kick to her side from the beast. Crying out in pain, she grabbed at her ribs. Broken most likely.

Jack spat out the blood in his mouth. "Don't touch her!"

Balaur raised his hand to signal another kick for Ivy when Philip suddenly lumbered to his feet. "Here!" He was kicked down by the guard behind him. His lean face splotched red with anger. "Finish what you started and kill me. Let them go."

Barely turning his head an inch, Balaur considered Philip with pitiable disinterest. "You never could have been a true Riser. You're nothing more than a weak sack of bones to harden my true killers on. You are lower than a dog to kick."

"You filled our veins with your poison until it eroded our ability to think for ourselves. You are the one who made us dogs. Begging and scratching to stay alive."

After flipping back the edge of his mud-caked robe, Balaur pulled a rusty knife from his belt. He held the knife close to his face as if performing a sword salute, and his eye traced the grimy blade from tip to hilt in a wondrous caress before he curled his fist tight around the blade. Slivers of blood squeezed out between his fingers.

"What better way to control loyalty than by force?" He lunged and stabbed Philip in the arm.

Philip keeled sideways, howling in pain as he clutched his arm. Thick red blood flowed between his fingers. "No better way to ignite hatred in your Riser creations. Enough of it will build in them until they finally turn on you." With a curse, he gritted his teeth. "I want nothing more than to be there when they tear you to shreds."

"I should worry more for the sins heaped upon your own soul. The Order of the Rising Moon under the Silver One's guiding hand is bringing a purge. Only the true believers in our righteous cause will remain. Those who survive the purge of fire and rise to create a new beginning, an incorruptible existence, as it was meant to be."

Jack wiped his bleeding nose against his shoulder, smearing blood onto his jacket. "So you're not the big fish after all. This Silver One is.

I'm disappointed, but it's nice to know who I have to track down next since ol' Vlad's been moldering far too long to be giving you orders."

"Is that your dying request? To know the master of our order?" Balaur pushed the stained handle of his knife against Jack's busted nose, inciting a wail of pain, then wiped his bloody knife on Philip's ripped sleeve, not heeding the dull edge as it smeared against the fresh well of red.

"It may come as a shock to learn that you have had a previous introduction. A shame you will not live long enough for a reacquaintance."

Jack spat the blood dripping from his nose to his mouth. "We'll see you to hell first."

"That is fair enough, but I shall give it to you first. Break her neck." Balaur flung the command at his beast. "It will be the last thing these two see before I plunge a blade into their hearts."

Ivy scrambled onto her hands and knees. The beast clamped a hand around her legs and dragged her back.

In one swift motion, Ivy pulled the pearl pin from her hair and rolled to her back. The beast's boot went toward her face, and she jammed the sharpened pin into his femoral artery, then ripped it down to his kneecap.

Jack saw his moment. He twisted sideways and grabbed the rifle muzzle, jerking it down. It fumbled out of the guard's hands. Jack swung it around and cracked the gun against the side of the man's head, then followed the hit with a punch to the jaw and another to the stomach.

The guard shook himself as if to right his senses, then swung his arms out wildly. Jack stepped aside, aimed the rifle at the man's chest, and fired. He fell to the ground dead.

Philip grappled with the last guard, the rifle tugging between them as they grunted for control. Jack swung the rifle he held and shot. The guard dropped dead and Philip fell backward from the sudden lack of resistance.

Turning his aim to the beast, Jack's finger curled around the trigger and squeezed.

Nothing. The chamber was empty.

He threw it aside. His own pistol was nowhere in sight.

Ivy lay on her back with the brute crouched over her, his hands reaching for her neck. Bending her knees, she slammed her feet into his stomach and launched him over her head. He'd barely hit the ground before Ivy was on her feet with her knee to his chest.

She lifted her fist and drove the hairpin straight into his neck. Blood gurgled until he lay still.

Jack rushed over and eased her to her feet. "Are you all right?"

She nodded, swiping blood from her cheek. "Where's Balaur?"

Jack scanned the area. Gone.

"A-as soon as Jack moved for the guard, Balaur disappeared." Philip gasped as he clutched his bleeding arm. "He went through the trees."

Cursing a silent string for not keeping his eyes on the target, Jack tore through the needled boughs of scraggly pine trees. "Balaur! This isn't finished."

Standing on the empty precipice with the river churning far below, Balaur stood waiting. "Indeed. We have only just begun." He looked Jack up and down like a prized stag. "We have been waiting for you. Strong, quick, deadly. What a splendid Riser you will make."

Jack smiled. "You drone on, old man." He lunged.

Balaur met him like a mad bear. A fight to the death. They beat each other with a flurry of fists and kicks, neither giving ground. Jack with his fighter prowess and Balaur with feral rage as they matched blow for blow.

Blood poured from Jack's broken nose, but he ignored the pain and grabbed the knife from his belt. With a sharp uppercut, he sliced down the left side of Balaur's face, severing his eyepatch to reveal the mutilated knot of skin beneath, now bleeding afresh.

A vicious snarl erupted from Balaur. He knocked the knife from Jack's hand. It skittered toward the frozen cliff's edge. Jack landed a punch to Balaur's jaw that dropped him to his knees. Jumping on his back, Jack wrapped an arm around his neck and grabbed his jaw with the opposite hand.

Balaur clawed for the knife at his fingertips. He snatched the blade and swung it up, slicing Jack's forearm. Jack grunted in pain but didn't release his hold.

The pine limbs rustled. Ivy and Philip burst onto the precipice. Philip's stabbed arm hung limp at his side while in his other hand he held Undertaker. He was shaking too badly to aim straight.

Jack tightened his grip.

Ivy, pale and bleeding, reached for the weapon. "Give me the gun, Philip."

"No. He's mine. For what he did to me." Philip raised the pistol with a shaking hand and pulled the trigger. Nothing.

Balaur sliced Jack's other hand. Jack yelped and released his hold.

"Give me the gun!" Ivy yelled.

Balaur shot to his feet and twisted behind Jack, snaking an arm around his waist.

Philip smacked the gun with his palm. "It's jammed." His fingers fumbled to release the clip to sort the cockeyed bullet.

Ivy lunged for the gun as metal flashed in Balaur's hand.

"I would not think to take another step." Balaur pressed the cold blade to Jack's throat; his other hand clenched Jack's wounded arm. Jack felt drops of blood pulsing from a vein and running down his neck. He tried to calm his racing heart to slow the trickle of blood, a nearly impossible task.

"The predicament has changed for our lovebirds. It is you, *devushka*, who will be rash for him now, while still the other remains useless and oblivious to the sacrifices of love." He took a step back. Toward the ledge.

Jack dug his heels down, but the ground was frozen and his feet slid over the dirt.

"Let him go." A hidden blade slid out from Ivy's sleeve into her palm. Her voice shook. "Philip, hand me the pistol. *Now.*"

"He's mine," Philip said. Metal clicked and scraped together. Bullets thumped into the snow.

"Shoot! This is what you have wanted!" Spittle flew from Balaur's mouth, grazing Jack's cheek. "From your days mewling in that dungeon for revenge. The moment is upon you and you fail to rise to its demand. Shoot!"

"Shoot, Philip!" Jack twisted against Balaur. "Shoot him now!"

Bam!

The bullet slammed into Balaur's chest, knocking him backward. His arms flailed for balance. His clawing fingers dropped the knife and latched onto Jack's shoulder as his feet stumbled over the edge. Jack tipped backward.

His eyes caught Ivy's.

Time hung suspended as a thousand longings that could not be put into words arced between them. He saw them burning in her eyes as a cry rushed to his lips.

And the air opened up behind him.

TWENTY-EIGHT

Ivy screamed, filling the void of open air and rushing water. "Jack!" She raced to the edge of the cliff.

Jack clung by his fingertips to a rock two feet below the drop-off. His body dangled in the air. Throwing herself flat, she squirmed her upper body over the ledge and grabbed his arm.

"I've got you. I won't let go. Dig your feet in and push up." She clamped her hands around his wrists and pulled. "Philip! Help me."

But Philip didn't come.

Jack's toes scrambled to find leverage. Securing the tiniest bit of traction, he pushed as she pulled. Inch by inch his body hoisted up until he was able to grab hold of the ledge and fling himself onto firm ground in a sprawl.

Ivy collapsed next to him, one hand still locked around his wrist. "Don't. Ever. Do that. To me. Again." Panting hard, she scooted her cheek onto his chest. His beating heart pounded reassuringly against her ear.

"Have to keep you on your toes somehow." Out of breath himself, he patted her head. "Complacency kills the romance in a marriage."

"So does flinging yourself off a cliff. Effectively for all time. In future should we require spontaneity in our relationship, surprise me with theater tickets. What happened here?" She pointed to his crooked nose.

"Ah, that." Grasping his nose between his hands, Jack cracked the bones back into place. "Good as new."

"A few more breaks like that and it'll be good as putty." She sat up slowly and pushed the hair from her face. It came away sticky with blood. Thick flakes of snow drifted down and melted against the warm red. She pushed to her feet and her ribs shrieked in protest. She grabbed her sides with a gasp as the ribs crunched over one another.

Jack was beside her in an instant. "You need to move slow."

"We can't move slow. We need to get off this mountaintop." She looked around and found Philip rooted to the same spot where he'd been standing when he shot Balaur. The gun dangled from his fingers. Was he injured and unable to move? "Philip, are you all right?"

"We stay the night." The gun dropped from Philip's hand. Emptiness filled his eyes as he stared at them. "Snow's coming."

Frowning at the flakes falling from the darkening sky, Jack shook his head. "It's too dangerous to stay here."

"The only danger is fumbling down a mountainside at night during a snowstorm." Philip glanced blankly at where the dead guards lay behind the scraggly trees. "They're all dead now anyway. No more will be coming." Turning, he stumbled back toward the fortress.

Ivy laced her arm around Jack's waist and leaned her weight against him. "Perhaps he's right. It might be best to rest here overnight and strike out in the morning once the storm clears."

A fierce line settled on Jack's brow as he brewed for an argument. "You need a hospital."

"Patch me up as best you can, then tomorrow I'll let you sweep me in your arms and carry me off to the nearest infirmary. Where's my hairpin?" Her mind went woozy then, and her body softened.

Then she was falling, falling, falling.

★★★

Hours later, the surrounding woods lay silent and dark with tufts of snow snarled in the pines' dead branches. Tucked into a pocket on the fortress's west wall, where a steep path led up to the entrance and inner bailey, they took shelter under a watchtower sticking out from the corner that provided an overhang of protection from the snow.

Jack tossed a few more branches onto the small fire. Orange and red flames glowed against Poenari's walls and reflected back a warmth to battle the night's frigid temperature.

If only he could so easily battle the agony within himself. What he wouldn't give to shift the world back and set it all right again. Before the guilt and dishonor. Before his failure.

Stretched on the ground next to him lay his wife. She still hadn't roused after passing out in what he knew was the body's way of protecting itself after major shock. She was bruised from head to toe with gashes and cuts sliced across her.

He was grateful she'd been unconscious when he wrapped bandages torn from his undershirt around her torso to keep her broken ribs from causing further harm. He feared deeper injuries undetectable to his eyes. Clutching at her stomach, she moaned and shifted, sending up the sharp scent of pine needles from the pallet he'd piled together for her.

"Rest now, love. I've got you." He gently stroked her cheek with his bandaged hand. She needed proper tending at a hospital, but the mountain's descent would prove impassable until morning. For now, she rested in his care.

Branches snapped. His hand flew to his gun. Seconds later, Philip pushed out of the white storm and dropped a load of wood next to the fire. Black smeared under his friend's eyes as purple and green bruises marred his skin, the likes of which hadn't existed since their training days when every exercise inflicted brutal punishment to his body.

Jack had never batted an eye before at the tenderized appearance, whether in training or in the field, but this was something different, something more that penetrated deeper than pummeled skin and exhausted muscle. It was as if his friend's insides had been pulverized, leaving a hollowness behind.

Philip sat across the fire with his right side exposed to the woods. "Quit looking at me like that. It's pathetic."

"That's how I feel." Jack placed his gun on the ground next to his feet within easy reach should something less friendly make its way through the woods. Remorse heavy as a black curtain and hung by his own hand settled between them. The only way through was to cut straight to the truth.

"I never should have left you on the ice. It's my fault Balaur captured you. I am so very truly sorry, Philip."

Philip didn't move, didn't blink as the red veins on his eyelids quivered from the intensity.

"Do you feel guilty?" A thousand emotions fired across his face like arrows in the midst of battle.

Jack forced himself to meet them head-on. Honor demanded it. He would never be caught running again. "Yes."

"Ashamed?"

"Yes."

"Despicable?"

"Yes."

"Good." Philip blinked, severing the black curtain from top to bottom. The ghost of its division lay in tattered remains around them, no more than bits of debris to be swept away.

"You did what you had to do. For Ivy. She's worth more than either of us. There's nothing more to be said of it."

"I failed you. You and Miles. Abandoned both of you to death. You trusted me as your leader to keep you safe, and I failed."

Philip grabbed a twig and snapped it. "There you go again. Taking all the responsibility on your shoulders. Tragedies happen. It's part of the game we play. Miles knew it, as did Calhoune. We all signed the dotted line knowing our sins and the payment required for them."

Bygones may be where his friend intended to sweep the past, but Jack could still feel the guilt as it clung to his shoulders and hands. "It should've been me. If anyone had to be taken, it should've been my life forfeited."

"And where would that put Ivy? As a widow. I've watched her suffer enough hurt and loss in her life. For her sake, stop demanding to be the heroic martyr."

As he reached for another stick, the ripped cuffs of Philip's sleeves rode up and exposed his arms. Red grooves circled his wrists as if he'd been chained with manacles. The strips slashed through his shirt offered a glimpse of welts scored across his skin from lashes.

"Are you in pain?" Jack asked quietly.

Another branch snapped. "Did you know the human body can be taught to suffer pain without actually feeling it?"

Everything fell away. The snowstorm. The dark woods. The foreboding fortress. His need for atonement. All that mattered was the fallout from that night on the ice.

"What happened, Philip? What did Balaur do to you?"

Philip stared down at his knees. "I thought I was dead. They dragged me to a dark and cold dungeon. I don't know if it took days or weeks to get here. I was half delirious with only a tin cup of water and a moldy crust of bread to nibble on once a day. Then the torture started. Over and over to the brink of oblivion. It never stopped."

"Did he question you?"

"At first, but in the end all he wanted was an experiment. A lab rat for the evil he's brewing." Philip picked at a loose thread uncoiling from a tear over his kneecap. "I've never seen anything like it. It's a master plan nothing short of annihilation. Not by using weapons or marching armies, but soldiers created to kill."

"Soldiers." Plural. The implication dragged out like a fuse firing toward a mound of black powder.

Absorbed by his task, Philip pulled the thread, unraveling the material until his entire left knee was exposed. "He was breeding a killing force like the world has never seen before. This war that France, Germany, and Russia are fighting will be nothing in comparison."

"How was he manipulating you to turn you into one?"

"At first through starvation until your stomach was screaming like a wild animal and there was nothing left but the primal will to survive for a crumb, even if the hand that fed you the crumb was the same hand that beat you. Once the body was broken, he lunged for the mind. 'Psychological reordering,' he called it." Philip gave a humorless laugh as he wrapped the long thread around his finger.

"See the clever wordplay he did there? Re*ordering* for his Order. The mind was suffocated with the most horrific experiences imaginable, uprooting every good piece of you and twisting it into a nightmare until it was no longer the darkness you feared, but yourself. Because you were no longer yourself. You'd become what he'd made you."

"A soldier for death." The ramification hung heavy, morbid and rotting the air.

"Risers. Trained to think no longer, but to follow his commands. To kill those unworthy of the Order, much like he intended the White Wolf to accomplish, but more precise, like a blade when that enormous hunk of metal proved too unstable."

Jack snorted with disgust. "And human beings always prove the model of stability."

"Stable enough when he pumped drugs into our veins. We would've snapped our own necks if he'd commanded it." Philip shrugged dismissively, as if he'd accepted the horrifying repercussions long ago.

"How many of you were there?"

"Ten or so. He scrounged up vagabonds and army deserters. Dregs that would go unmissed by society. By the end, me and that hulking fellow Ivy stabbed were the only ones left."

"What kind of drugs did he use?"

"I don't know. A thick white substance—like when you leave a marshmallow out on the hot pavement. It burns through your system, scorching out all rational thought. Then the trigger comes. Sights and sounds and smells he's planted in your head, and once they're released"—Philip snapped his fingers—"you're his to command."

"He conditioned you."

"Like Pavlov's dog. Only these dogs were trained to bite with no recollection of what we'd done. Cold, hard assassins with no ability to control our own minds because he controlled them for us. I would wake up in a filthy cell covered in blood and bruises with no memory of how I'd gotten them—or how I'd killed the man lying dead next to me."

He snapped the thread. It uncurled from his finger like a silken serpent. "Sometimes snatches of memory would filter in, and I would almost beg for the drug to send me back into oblivion. Balaur was always happy to oblige."

Fury gnashed through Jack's veins as the blackened shreds raked their guilt across his skin. "Brother, I cannot tell you how sorry I am. It should have been me they captured to spare you the inconceivable pain you now have to carry. What can I do?"

Philip went silent, his jaw working back and forth. He didn't meet Jack's eyes. "The Risers weren't a stable experiment. Many of the test subjects didn't hold out well against the injections. I saw grown men rip themselves apart when the dosage proved incompatible. Others were compatible but not up to snuff. Those were the ones Balaur liked to pit against each other in a cage for sport."

He swiped the thread from his trouser leg and it wafted in the air, suspended for a moment like a curled snake before floating to the ground. "He looked for a specific kind of subject to condition. True soldiers. I still didn't quite meet his standards, but he was more than happy to continue running tests on me in preparation for his true Riser to come along."

A blast of wind spiraled flurries into their protected pocket. Jack dusted the cold bits from his face and leaned closer to the fire, ready to tend the fragile flames should another gust threaten them.

"Did he mention anything about the Order? Any clues that might lead us to this 'Silver One' who masterminds the group?"

"No. Balaur was very careful in his wording when he spoke to us, and the men he tasked to guard us day and night weren't allowed to speak at all. In fact, they'd had their tongues removed to prevent the possibility of letting loose a secret."

Philip watched an icy pellet melt on his exposed knee, apparently unconcerned with it freezing his flesh. "If anything was said around me, it's gone from memory. Between the delirium, starvation, and drugging, I barely remembered I was human."

"This pompous Order and its tedious titles." Jack's wife stirred next to him and cracked open one green eye. "Order of the Rising Moon. Risers. Silver One. Balaur Tsar. I'll be surprised if they don't wear capes and fake fangs to further worship their esteemed founder, Drăculea himself."

Relief shot through Jack. "I know you've returned to me when you start throwing in foreign words." He brushed the tangled hair from her cheek as she struggled to sit. She squeezed her eyes shut and pressed a hand to her head. He gently pushed her back down and pulled his coat over her shoulders as a shiver passed through her body. "No need for moving around. Rest."

Grunting in discomfort, she shifted to fluff the pine needles beneath her and saw the embroidered eye of a red dragon.

Jack smoothed the rumpled banner he'd spread over the needles to prevent them from poking her in the face. "Found it hanging in what I assume was once the great hall of this hellhole. I thought it fitting I should rest my warrioress upon it to claim victory over the spoils of battle."

"Very Charlemagne of you. How long have I been out?" She blinked up at him. Dilated round as an owl's, her pupils were at least tracking him in awareness.

"A few hours. It spared you the pain when I wrapped your ribs, but you need a doctor." He gently stroked her cheek and tried to keep his worry in check. "You lost a great deal of blood, love."

"And you?" She reached out, stopping short of his bashed nose, which he'd had to snap back in place. Dried blood still caked the front of his shirt.

He caught her hand and pressed a kiss to her bruised knuckles. "I'll survive until morning when we can leave this cursed place."

They were a great deal worse off than either was letting on and they both knew it, but such lies were often a comfort when attempting to restore each other's sanity after balancing on the literal precipice of death mere hours before.

As her attention moved to Philip, the pain scrunching her face softened to concern. "Philip. How are you?"

He sat quietly watching them as more snowflakes landed unheeded on his skin. "Well enough."

"Don't lie to me. I know you better than that."

"We killed a madman. Everything else will sort itself out." Voice ragged as a rusted blade, he settled his eyes on Jack. "In time, all wrongs will be righted."

"What do you mean?"

Philip jerked to his feet. "I'll get more firewood."

"But we have plenty. Philip—" He strode off and her voice fell on the swirls of snow in his wake. The concern that had softened her face moments before creased with added worry.

"I fear a part of him may remain in that dungeon forever. It was the same when we were booted from the orphanage. We were free, but the place always kept a hold on him. He's still that same little boy fighting to be seen."

Jack stared after his friend wanting nothing more than to follow him into the darkness and emerge together on the other side. "All we can do is be patient and wait for him to come around."

"Were you able to speak with him about what happened?"

"Some." Words and truths had been spoken, but not enough to assuage the guilt still roiling within him. It, too, was a wound that would require the healing power of time. One that may require a knife to slice it open again and again until the festering was completely drained.

Tugging him closer to rest her head on his thigh, Ivy pulled his coat up to her chin. "What's our next course of action?"

"Getting you to a hospital. Oh, I found your hairpin." He patted his pocket. Safer to keep it stored away rather than jab her in the head with it.

"Good. Dolly would have my ears if I lost it. She said a woman should never be without a pretty to deliver death." She attempted to smother a yawn. "A bit of rest and I'll be quite all right come morn—"

"You will not be engaging in any fisticuffs until those ribs heal. Now close your eyes and try to sleep."

Two gimlet green eyes fixed on him. "Only if you tell me the plan. After we've crossed *hospital* off the checklist, of course."

Stubborn as always. He wouldn't change that about her for anything in the world. "We'll need to regroup. Procure what details we can from Philip about anything he may have learned. Consult maps. Source new weapons. Dig through history books for any mention of the Order of the Rising Moon—which I'll leave to you."

He traced a thread of reddish gold hair from her temple to where it curled around her ear, provoking a delicate shiver from his patient.

"Wire Talon for funds since we're down to our last kopeck. Scour the black market for news. Secure a lead. Track down the Silver One and exterminate the entire organization before it obliterates the world."

"Oh good. Here I thought assassinating an ancient underground cult was going to be terribly difficult." She smiled sleepily up at him. Warrioress. And all his.

"There's one more thing you should know." Bending down, he brushed a kiss to her lips. "I love you entirely."

I have a rendezvous with Death . . .
It may be he shall take my hand
And lead me into his dark land
And close my eyes and quench my breath—
It may be I shall pass him still.
I have a rendezvous with Death.

—ALAN SEEGER

RENDEZVOUS

A LONE FIGURE PICKS HER WAY DOWN THE ICE-CRUSTED BANKS OF THE Arges River. Her sodden skirts drag behind her, thick with mud and slush and plastered with dead leaves. She gives no notice to the deaths of season she carries, for the earth is hers as she is the earth's.

Numbing cold reaches for her, biting her toes and fingers and nose until her determined expression is nearly frozen in place. She pulls her thick shawl tighter over her head and leaves the unraveling ends to trail behind her hunched shoulders.

She was born to this place, bred in these mountains and vales, hardened against its winter storms, and bled through with its legend of old. Some may claim she was part of the gnarled root of lore, a branch once thought precluded from growing again. And they would be right.

Far on the cliff behind her stands Poenari Castle. Stones of ruin and history where greatness once ruled. Her fingers clutch at the wool scarf beneath her thick chin. Greatness will rule this place again. It is destiny.

Sheets of ice slide over the river, crashing into one another at the steep bends as the water surges along the valley floor. She treads carefully across the pebbles and icy chunks flung up from the watery depths. Snow is falling thicker, turning the light blue and freezing her sparse lashes together as her eyes water from the stinging cold.

That is when she sees it.

She takes a step, then another, always moving beyond her last step until it is the next and the next after that. Never enough.

The body is washed up along the bank, its heavy boots dragging in the water's current that seeks to carry the form farther down.

It is a man. *Her* man. Blood is frozen dark on his pale skin.

She kneels next to the man and presses her cheek flat to his chest. His wet robes sting against her skin as ice crystals claw over the shredded fur and torn cuffs. Lifting her head, she brushes the tangled hair from his face and presses a kiss to each socket, one whole and one empty.

The Fates did not gift her faithfulness with his survival. It is no matter. She will carry on without him.

Pebbles crunch under faltering footsteps. It is a weak footstep. Lacking in faith yet petulant with need.

"Silver One."

She turns and slaps his face. Once. Twice. A third time to leave a red hand imprint on his thin cheek. He does not fight back. The fight has been taken from him. Except for this one need. This one craving in his blood.

He was not strong enough to be her Riser, but this craving is the reason he is the only survivor. He is the bait.

He is what draws her true prize near. That is the only reason she allows him to live.

"Where is he?"

The boy's eyes turn upward to the cliff. Orange glows faintly against the fortress's walls where her prize sits. The one destined to be her true Riser. A warrior. A leader. She has witnessed his fights, his strength, and his determination. He is everything worthy of a Riser.

She imagines his eyes in the firelight. Startlingly blue as they were by a fireplace at Dobryzov Castle. The same blue eyes that hovered over a fired pistol that took her lover's eye. Her scream had rung throughout the castle as the man turned and fled with that woman. And now, her lover's final act has been to deliver the man back to her as requested.

Defiance was the last thing she saw in the man's blue eyes. She will no doubt see it again this night. Quite possibly one of the last emotions she will permit him to feel.

"Bring him to me."

Obedience stiffens the boy's shoulders, yet greed flattens his mouth. "Do you have it as promised, Silver One?"

She pushes away the shawl as frizzy brown hair scratches the sides of her long face. A creature creeping out from under its moldering mushroom. The flat lips beneath her colorless eyes crack open in cruel glee as she pulls the filled syringe from the folds of her cloak and hands it to him.

"Bring me my Riser."

To be continued . . .

JACK AND IVY'S STORY CONTINUES IN

TO FREE THE STARS

Coming August 2023

AUTHOR'S NOTE

THIS STORY BEGAN AFTER WATCHING TOO MANY HOURS OF THE CAPTAIN America Marvel movies, when suddenly the question popped unbidden into my head, *What would happen if the Winter Soldier fell in love?* I pushed it aside. *Pfft.* The Winter Soldier—the most deadly assassin imaginable—does not under any circumstances fall in love. Yet that tiny voice in my head refused to stay quiet. *But he could fall in love. With the right girl.*

Finally I gave in. There is no point in arguing with the relentless muse when she's got your imagination by the tail. I stewed on it for months, telling myself there was no way I could pull off a story like that, trying to imagine what kind of woman would spark a coldhearted assassin's internal flame of passion. After several more stints of Marvel movie viewing—for research purposes, not just to watch Sebastian Stan strut with his metal arm, I assure you—I finally cobbled together an idea of secret societies, assassin bootcamp, ancient occults, vampires, and one heaping dose of romance. Indiana Jones meets the Avengers.

Taking this Frankenstein of an idea to my editor, she didn't miss a beat—perhaps she'd grown accustomed to my crazy ideas by then—and quickly suggested I root it in historical fact, which turned out not to be so difficult after all. Truth is indeed stranger than fiction.

Secret Societies

Secret societies have existed for centuries. Many are well known, such as the Freemasons, the Illuminati, and the Skull and Bones Society. There are no doubt countless other orders that shall never reveal their names as they seek to fly by unnoticed. Such as Talon, which came to be by accident as my husband and I were strolling along Embassy Row in Washington, DC, where I heard bagpipe music blasting from a magnificent old building with great columns and stone steps.

Once known as Millionaire's Row for all the rich swells who built their grand homes along Massachusetts Avenue, the buildings became more of a burden to upkeep after World War II, so many of them were sold in the 1950s to become offices for foreign ambassadors and diplomats. Today a brass plaque stands outside to declare that the onetime home of an heiress is now the Cosmos Club, a private club for those distinguished in science, literature, and the arts whose members include three presidents, Nobel Prize winners, Pulitzer Prize winners, and recipients of the Presidential Medal of Freedom. The agents of Talon certainly aren't literary award winners, but the building's location was prime for secrets while affecting a genteel facade, so I housed a clandestine agency within its venerated walls.

The founding of Talon was based on the true-to-life spy ring of General Washington, known as the Culper Ring during the American Revolution and run by Benjamin Tallmadge. After the war, France plunged into its own revolution and expected the allegiance it had given America to be returned in its hour of need. At the time, however, the newly created government of the United States of America felt that the fledgling country was far too fragile and bankrupt to offer assistance for another country's conflict. Knowing how deeply this saddened the newly minted President Washington, I created a paramilitary group that could be sent out on secret missions anywhere in the world where help was needed as they followed the creed:

Seek and ye shall find. Find and ye shall protect. Living by this, Talon agents would strive to ensure that good would outweigh evil regardless of country boundaries or politics.

The Order of the Rising Moon is an amalgamation of the Hermetic Order of the Golden Dawn, Order of the Dragon from which Vlad II Dracul took his name, and the Dacian culture that lived near the Carpathian Mountains in present-day Romania and believed in a special relationship between humans and wolves. (They may have had rituals to turn themselves wolflike—more on that later.) Wanting to set the Order of the Rising Moon in Romania as a nod to the Romanian actor Sebastian Stan, who plays the Winter Soldier, I incorporated fact and myth about its most famous resident, Vlad III, son of Dracul. Vlad the Impaler was a prince and later ruler of Wallachia (a region of present-day Romania) in the fifteenth century. His legacy is one of controversy with a cruel reputation for impaling his victims on pikes being at odds with him driving the invaders from his homeland, which venerated him as a national hero. These days he is best known for being the inspiration being Bram Stoker's vampiric Count Dracula.

Locations

As *The Brilliance of Stars* globe-trots around on adventures, I took advantage of the many historical and near mythical locations in eastern Europe. Folklore of an Ice Queen truly seeps around the frozen edges of Lake Baikal, and while Swallow's Nest does perch on a cliff in Crimea and was once home to the court doctor to the Russian tsar, there is no evidence that a madman built a cannon in the subterranean rock.

Bran Castle is located in the Transylvanian region of Romania and is most popularly known as Dracula's castle. However, as Ivy pointed out, this is merely tourist lore. The original wooden castle that occupied the site was built in 1212, and the stone one present today was built a century later. Standing as a fortress against the Ottoman Empire and other invaders over the centuries, the castle became a royal residence in 1920 and soon the favorite home of Queen Marie of Romania, but it was seized by the communist regime in 1948. After a period of legal proceedings, Bran Castle was returned to the heirs of the Habsburg family, who opened the doors to the public as the first private museum in the country. Most historians agree that Vlad the Impaler, the inspiration behind Dracula, never set foot in Bran Castle, and the two only became linked to market tourism.

Poenari Castle is the true link to Vlad the Impaler. In the fifteenth century he realized the potential for a defensive fortress dominating a steep precipice of rock and built the structure using slave labor from his conquered enemies. It was used for many years after his death only to be abandoned to ruin by the seventeenth century. In 1913 an earthquake brought down additional parts of the castle, which crashed into the river far below. After two more earthquakes, a few walls and towers are all that remain of the mighty citadel that once was.

In later chapters you may have noticed that I use the location markers of Transylvania and Wallachia instead of Romania. At the time of the Great War the country we know as Romania was divided into several principalities with a great chunk belonging to Austria-Hungary. Not until after the war did this land became united into Romania.

Risers

Needing some kind of super-soldier serum to turn unwilling victims into mindless killers, I searched drug-induced experiments and came across Project Artichoke, a CIA mind-control project that researched interrogation methods in 1951. The primary goal was to determine if a person could be involuntarily tasked to perform an act of attempted assassination. Hypnosis, forced morphine addiction and withdrawal, LSD, and amnesia were also studied in correlation. A memo dated 1952 asked, "Can we get control of an individual to the point where he will do our bidding against his will and even against fundamental laws of nature, such as self-preservation?"[1] Subjects who left the project were afflicted with amnesia and faulty memories. The writer Richard Condon later went on to draw inspiration for his novel *The Manchurian Candidate*.

Around the same time the Soviet Union used a drug known as Haldol as a form of punishment. The drug was injected to cause dependency, then withdrawn for interrogation. If the subject complied with questioning, the drug would be reintroduced to relieve the excruciating symptoms of withdrawal.

While these experiments came many decades after the time in which *The Brilliance of Stars* is set, I thought they fit in well with the other advanced technologies used by Talon and seemed like plausible methods for those daring (or mad) enough to push the boundaries.

I am a history lover by nature, and nothing excites me more than discovering little-known moments from the past and bringing them to light for modern audiences to ooh and aah over. While an entire story may not be rooted in historical fact, I strive to include tidbits of truth—like the invention of mascara and the discovery of ancient languages that spark the imagination—but at the end of the day, I write fiction. Fiction in which I hope readers can lose themselves and enjoy a fantastical adventure filled with romance and daring. And hey, if you pick up bits of history along the way, even better.

---

1. Weinstein, H. *Psychiatry and the CIA: Victims of Mind Control*. Washington, D.C.: American Psychiatric Press, 1990.

ACKNOWLEDGMENTS

SOME STORIES ARE EASIER THAN OTHERS. THE IDEAS COME AND THE writer simply puts fingers to keyboard, and the words flow out like inspired water. Other ideas are like a two-year-old's tantrum in the middle of the grocery story. This particular story started out as the first, but quickly plunged into the second because of a thing called COVID. That's right. This is my COVID book. All writers have one at this point, where the inspiration and imagination well shriveled up and dried out. Many of us felt hopeless, depressed, and that each word was like pulling out a cankerous tooth. Writing was a slog, but somehow the idea that had sparked from watching too many Marvel movies finally pulled itself together to form a story. How, you may ask? Because I had an awesome team of supporters who carried me and Buck Winter to the finish line.

Jocelyn, thank you for not laughing your head off when I pitched this idea to you over breakfast at ALA. You may have brought me back down to earth by shrinking my blotted trilogy into a much more manageable duology, but you were the one to believe in Buck Winter first. Laura, thank you for jumping onto this train midway through with such enthusiasm and fresh ideas. I'm so delighted to be working with you. Jodi, you've been with me for this whole ride and have managed to keep this harebrained story from jumping the tracks, which it tried to do repeatedly, while keeping me giggling about our mutual appreciation for *Vampire Diaries*. Team Klaus!

Kerri, Margaret, Amanda, cover designers, sales, and the rest of my wonderful team at Thomas Nelson, thank you so much for all of your hard work and for believing in this story and setting it up for success. You work so hard on my behalf, and I can't tell you how much I appreciate it!

To my agent, Linda, thank you for your bottomless enthusiasm and encouragement. Rachel, Aimie, and Kim, you ladies are simply the best. Your constant uplifting and cheering made me feel like I may not be the worst writer in the entire world. Bryan and Miss S, this story was a monster undertaking, and there were many times I just didn't feel up to the challenge, but you kept me going by allowing me to lock myself in the basement last summer to simply put words on paper and hope they made sense, and never rolling your eyes when I wanted to watch *Captain America: The Winter Soldier* again and again. Love you both to the end of the line.

Lastly, this book would not have been imagined without Sebastian Stan aka Buck Winter/Bucky Barnes/Winter Soldier. His portrayal of a sweetheart turned cold assassin turned man trying to scrape his life back together was simply masterful.

DISCUSSION QUESTIONS

Includes Spoilers!

1. Joining Talon was a huge risk and leap of faith for Philip and Ivy after years of relying only on each other. Would you dare to join a secret agency like they did, or would you feel safer keeping to a life that is predictable?

2. Ivy, Philip, and Jack have unique differences while also sharing similarities. How has joining Talon allowed them each to flourish?

3. One of the major themes in *The Brilliance of Stars* is belonging and finding a home. What does this look like for each of the characters? Do they discover what they are looking for by the end of the story, and if not, what prevents them?

4. Ivy wrestles with the moral ethics of becoming an assassin. While she values human life, it is also her duty, and that of all Talon agents, to snuff out evil in order to preserve good. Do you agree with this mission? Do you think the ends justify the means?

5. Jack is a natural leader. Easygoing yet quick to assess a chaotic situation and wrestle it under control. How do his

code of ethics and backstory lend credit to his leadership talents, and in what ways do they cripple his abilities?

6. Jack was put in an incredibly difficult position at Lake Baikal when he was forced to choose between saving his wife or his best friend, both highly trained professionals. Did he make the right choice? Why or why not? How might the story have changed if he had chosen differently?

7. After Jack chose to save Ivy and lost Philip to Balaur Tsar, guilt weighed on him. Did Jack deserve the guilt or was he too much of a martyr?

8. *The Brilliance of Stars* is set during a time that was very much a man's world. Jack and Ivy fit into the traditional roles of their era but also managed to forge a balance of power and mutual respect. How is Ivy able to break the restraints placed on women in her time and explore her own power and skills?

9. With World War I, or the Great War, as the backdrop of the novel, *The Brilliance of Stars* takes the opportunity to juxtapose real-life evil with fictional evil. How do historical events influence the main characters' decisions and beliefs in their struggle against such evil?

10. As with the *Avengers* movies, which inspired this novel, there are many twists and turns in *The Brilliance of Stars*. Do you anticipate where the next half of Jack and Ivy's story will lead?

ABOUT THE AUTHOR

Photo by Bryan Ciesielski

BESTSELLING AUTHOR WITH A PASSION FOR HEART-STOPPING ADVENTURE and sweeping love stories, J'nell Ciesielski weaves fresh takes into romances of times gone by. When not creating dashing heroes and daring heroines, she can be found dreaming of Scotland, indulging in chocolate of any kind, or watching old black-and-white movies. She is a Florida native who now lives in Virginia with her husband, daughter, and lazy beagle.

★★★

jnellciesielski.com
Instagram: @jnellciesielski
Pinterest: @jnellciesielski